RELICS OF POWER BOOK 2

THE
PERILOUS
SEA

EMMA L. ADAMS

PROLOGUE

Naxel Daimos threw the Relic into the ocean, where it vanished beneath the glittering waves.

Useless, he thought, as the strong current caught the stone and tugged it outwards into the icy sea. The Power within the stone had been sealed away elsewhere, so the Relic had been nothing but a dead weight in his pocket throughout the three days of his voyage across the ocean. Yet its absence brought an immediate pang of regret. All the blood he'd fed to the deity had been for naught. *What a waste.*

He'd been sure that giving Orzen a human form would enable him to track down the young Astera boy with ease, but he hadn't counted on his target finding allies in the mountainous region of Zeuten, nor his new companions doing the impossible and imprisoning the deity he'd sent to destroy them.

Regrets aside, Orzen had already given Daimos everything that he'd desired most in the world, and now that he held the staff of Astiva, he had no need of the other Relic

1

any longer. While the staff's former wielder remained inconveniently beyond reach, Daimos doubted he would be content to remain in hiding forever. Daimos knew the embers of vengeance burned within his chest, and he'd come in search of retribution soon enough.

As for Daimos? He had another purpose in the cold and unappealing nation in which Arien Astera had sought refuge. The chill of the mountain air fought the ocean breeze for dominance, and even the furs he'd purchased from the market at the docks didn't entirely keep out the cold. As he'd lived his entire life in the warmth of the Aestinian continent, Daimos wasn't used to such temperatures, and he inwardly resolved to spend as little time as possible on land.

Wrapped in his furs like everyone else in the port of the small market town, he drew no unwelcome attention while he waited on one of the short wooden piers that jutted from the gravelly shore. The visibly foreign vessel in which he'd arrived drew some attention, but since he'd concealed Astiva's staff inside his thick cloak, there was nothing in his current appearance to connect Daimos with the large, proud vessel and its well-dressed crew. He'd had no trouble finding allies; few in Aestin would dare to risk the wrath of the eldest child of Gaiva, who'd once served the most powerful family in the nation. On these unfamiliar shores, however, he would have to proceed with a little more caution.

The thornlike marks on the backs of his hands prickled his skin under his thick gloves for a brief instant, a warning. He lifted his gaze to the overcast sky, from which a grey shimmer resolved into two figures that swooped downwards and landed near the pier on which he waited. While they moved as if borne on wings, their billowing silvery cloaks folded against their sides when their feet touched the ground. *Interesting.* The Changers might have proven rather insignificant allies in his attempt to corner his enemy, but their abilities were not in doubt. He could still use them.

The two figures—a man and a woman—lowered their hoods and surveyed their surroundings. The man's scars and thinning hair suggested he'd seen many battles in his time, while the woman's darker complexion suggested ancestry from Aestin, despite her current position serving the Crown of Zeuten. Their gazes lingered on the market stalls selling furs and weapons, produce and the narrow wooden boats that seemed common in the region. When the pair began to approach the market, Daimos strode out to meet them. "Good. You received the note to meet me here as planned."

The two spun around, taking in his foreign appearance with raised eyebrows. His furs showed nothing of his current status, and he kept the staff hidden from sight, preferring to keep that particular object of curiosity out of their conversation. Detailing how he'd obtained it would bring about complications that might sour their alliance before it got off the ground. Talk of murder was not always a solid foundation for forging a bond of trust, and his true identity was irrelevant to the message he intended to convey.

"What is this?" asked the man. "We received a communication from the Crown of Zeuten ordering us to meet with an ambassador for the Crown Prince here in Carthen, but you... you are no ambassador."

"I certainly am," Daimos told them. "A new one. A recent development, if you will."

For all their talents, he feared them not at all. His staff's capabilities made the magic within their cloaks seem insignificant.

"And just what does that mean?" the man demanded, his tawny skin reddening.

Daimos kept his expression calm. The temptation to reveal his staff and silence their contempt arose, but he quashed it at once. He'd come here to leave a very deliberate trail, one that didn't involve showy displays of power. "It means that I am the current ambassador between the Crown of Zeuten and the nation of Aestin, and I am here on a diplomatic mission. The letter told you as much, did it not?"

"The Crown sent an emissary from *Aestin* to inform us of the deaths of our leaders?" The man exchanged incredulous looks with the cloaked woman at his side. "I find that hard to believe."

"I believe the Crown Prince himself already sent a letter conveying the tragic news, did he not?" Daimos queried. "Our meeting is for another purpose. The letter itself should have told you what that was."

They exchanged glances again, this time with less outright hostility present. They couldn't deny that they'd received this news, though the Crown Prince had not, in fact, written such a letter at all.

The woman addressed him first. "Tell us the purpose of your visit, and we will believe you are who you claim."

That was easy enough. "I intend to convey the news of a certain series of events in your nation that occurred while you were on your own mission in the Isles of Itzar.

While you know that the Masters were slaughtered by an unknown enemy, the Crown Prince thought it would not be prudent to put certain details in a letter that might fall into the wrong hands."

"So he sent *you?*" The man gave him a considering look. "How do I know you didn't intercept the letter yourself?"

Daimos ought to have known that presenting himself as someone from a rival nation would incite distrust. He might have used an emissary, but despite his new allies, he trusted nobody with this particular mission but himself.

"Zeuten came under attack from a dangerous foe," he told them. "The people responsible for defeating that enemy were the Sentinels, in alliance with a man called Arien Astera. You might have heard the name."

"Astera." The man's gaze sharpened. "The Invoker? There's another one of you here in Zeuten?"

No doubt he meant an Aestinian and not an Invoker, since while Daimos was both, he kept proof of the latter hidden behind the gloves that covered the marks on his hands. "That is correct. I believe he's lying low, but word of his achievements will spread fast. I wanted to ensure the news reached you before you stumbled upon rumours that distorted the facts."

As it happened, his own allies had started those rumours, both here and in Saudenne. He hadn't set foot in the Zeutenian capital himself, since Aestinian travellers were more common in the capital than in this small port town and there was a chance that he might have been recognised, but it didn't matter what form the rumours took. The more outrageous, the better.

At his words, the cloaked strangers murmured

between themselves. He let them, content to leave them to use the information he'd given in any way they saw fit. If they chose to disbelieve him and go to learn the truth for themselves, then so be it. His job here was done, and the trap he'd laid ought to have found its target by now.

In the meantime, he had another three days' voyage to return to his home country. That would give the rumours time to spread, to lure Arien Astera out of hiding and send him to seek out his target.

This time, the young Astera boy would perish. Daimos would make sure of it.

*Z*elle Carnelian entered the Sentinels' cave and walked over to the large, polished rock that lay in the centre. Stalagmites protruded from the ground, and stalactites jutted from the ceiling like fangs, while the rock itself exuded an aura of coldness that penetrated her skin beneath her thick fur-lined coat.

The staff in her hand spoke, its voice echoing in her mind. *You're stalling again.*

Zelle frowned at the staff's knotted dark wood. "That's because I'm trying to decide what to ask. I'd like a straight answer this time."

Though that might be hoping for too much. The Sentinels' cave's function was ostensibly to offer guidance, but the large rock before her contained a piece of the consciousness of the same deity that dwelled inside the staff in her hand, and from the nameless Shaper, straight answers were hard to come by.

Zelle's ancestors had been the first people to settle in Zeuten's mountains, yet even they hadn't known that one of the original three Great Powers had been imprisoned here. Imprisoned, the Shaper had claimed, by none other than Her fellow deities themselves. Due to the Shaper's reticence to share any more information on the subject, the details remained unknown to Zelle, but she was due to leave with Rien for the capital of Saudenne later today. She'd hoped the Shaper might offer her a little advice before she ventured away from the mountains for the first time in weeks.

"Am I making the right decision in leaving Tavine?" She extended a hand to touch the smooth surface of the rock.

At once, the cave faded from her vision, to be replaced by a large chamber with indistinct features. She had the vague impression of swooping arches overhead and flagstones beneath her feet, all wreathed in white mist. The outline of a human figure appeared etched against the mist, and as she walked closer, the person became more distinct until she recognised her own face looking back at her from a reflective surface.

Zelle studied her face as though it might turn into someone else's if she looked hard enough. The red tints to Zelle's brown hair were the only splashes of colour against her surroundings, while her pale face was set into a stern expression. In her hand, the wooden form of the staff glowed faintly with bluish light.

"This is new."

Her reflection's mouth moved as she spoke, her words echoing in the empty chamber. Whether her surroundings were conjured up from the depths of her own mind or some creation of the Shaper's, she had absolutely no idea, but the Sentinels' cave had never shown her this before.

Zelle lowered her gaze to the staff. "Are you going to answer my question?"

If you expect me to make your decision for you, you're going to be waiting a long time.

She couldn't tell if the voice came from the misty chamber or from the staff, but it sounded the same regardless. "No need for the attitude. You asked me to help deal with your wayward fellow deities, but it's been weeks since I bound Orzen. I need to get home to my aunt's shop. Someone in my family has to earn a living, after all."

Then do as you like. You've already made your mind up, haven't you?

Zelle supposed she had, but a knot of worry remained in her chest at the prospect of leaving her family behind.

"Even if I didn't have to get back to the shop, Rien and I need to find out what's happening in Aestin," she said. "I always intended to help him with that, but I'd rather know if I'm making a mistake in going home before I'm out of reach of the cave."

It depends if you're planning on accompanying him back to Aestin, I imagine.

"What?" She blinked. "No, I'm not going to Aestin. I'd have to be out of my mind to set foot near the place. So would Rien, come to that."

The two had discussed the matter and decided remaining in Saudenne would be a wiser choice. While word from the capital was that the seas had calmed in recent days, no longer torn apart by storms that prevented anyone from leaving Zeuten's shores, that didn't make a trip to Aestin any less treacherous.

The storms, after all, had been sent by Naxel Daimos, a rival of Rien's family, who'd stolen his Relic and almost killed him before he'd fled over the ocean to Zeuten. Not one to let his target escape, Daimos had gone as far as to gift the deity known as Orzen with a humanlike form and sent him to slaughter Rien in person. While Zelle had bound Orzen to a new Relic and sealed it away in the mountains, Daimos himself was no doubt waiting for his target to return to Aestin so he could finish the job.

Isn't that what he desires the most? the staff asked. *To get back to his family's house and reclaim his original Relic?*

"I doubt it'll be that easy," said Zelle. "Daimos holds Astiva's Relic now. He won't give it up without a fight, especially as he no longer has Orzen doing his bidding. Besides, we don't know how he was able to convince Orzen to obey him in the first place. Rien says Daimos's family was outcast with no Relics at their disposal. How'd he walk out of exile with a Relic powerful enough to oust the entire Astera family?"

A question you should certainly try to learn the answer to, but not here. I might have reams of knowledge far beyond your own limitations, but I am confined to these mountains. I cannot see what is happening in Aestin—or in the realm of the Powers.

Her brow furrowed. "You knew Orzen, though."

I know of him. As I know of many other descendants of Gaiva. There are rather a lot of them.

The Shaper's evasive tone made Zelle's hackles rise. Yes, Gaiva, the creator goddess and sibling of the name-less Shaper, was the only one of the three Great Powers who'd had children, grandchildren, and countless generations afterwards. Zelle didn't need the Shaper to tell her *that*, but there'd been other information which might have been handy for past Sentinels to know. For instance, the existence of hidden Relics that her ancestors had brought here when they'd first settled in the mountains.

Still, that wasn't relevant to the question she'd asked, so Zelle pushed her irritation aside and drew in a breath. "You asked me to close the doors between the two realms. Does that request contradict my plans to go to Saudenne and learn the latest news from Aestin? Simply a yes or no would do."

You can start by demonstrating some patience. You forget I've been buried in these mountains for longer than humans have existed on this continent.

"I'm aware of that," Zelle told the voice. "However, we humans have a shorter lifespan than you do. I know you can't see what's happening outside of the mountains, but you must know if leaving Tavine is a wise course of action. We've been at a standstill for days, and we need a clear goal."

There's only one certain way to prevent another door between the realms from opening, and it isn't something you're ready for yet. Until then, yes, gathering information will suffice.

"What…" She trailed off. "You mean find Daimos."

And kill him.

Unease slid down her spine. She'd never met Daimos, but he'd killed Rien's family and left him for dead after claiming his Relic. Zelle herself had, until a few weeks ago, never wielded any magic in her twenty-two years of life, with her sister Aurel inheriting the family's gift instead. The staff had landed in her hands by mere chance, and regardless of its considerable powers, a nagging voice in the back of her mind whispered that she was the wrong choice for the job.

On the other hand, Rien had had access to magic his entire life and had still been stripped of his connection to Astiva at Daimos's hands. When she'd first met him, he'd been as powerless as she, and it wasn't until he'd claimed a new Relic within these very mountains that he'd begun to gain back what he'd lost. He had a lot of preparation to do before he was ready to confront Daimos, though he reacted with tight-lipped annoyance to any insinuation that he was in any way struggling to adjust to his new Relic.

Aloud, she said, "So you're saying I should keep an eye on Daimos's movements, but I can't hunt him down myself."

You're welcome to try, but I gather you would prefer to stay in one piece.

"Hilarious," she said. "Does he even know I exist?"

He knows Arien Astera has allies. Perhaps he suspects the Sentinels' involvement in Orzen's defeat too.

"But not mine." Zelle didn't register to Daimos as a threat, which was frankly a relief. She had enough responsibilities to handle without incurring the wrath of a vengeful Invoker.

Not yet, warned the voice. *Be ready for when he does learn of the power you wield.*

"You mean the power *you* wield." Zelle was simply the instrument, the conduit. She was under no illusions that her bond with the Shaper was anything like Rien's connection with his own deity, based on a mutual under-standing and shared goals.

The staff hadn't even been Zelle's to begin with, and

the notion of having to choose between leaving it behind in Tavine or else leaving Grandma Carnelian without the means of defending herself against another attack was one of the reasons she was apprehensive at best about leaving for Saudenne. With or without the staff.

The voice didn't answer. Instead, the vision released its grip on her, to be replaced by the cool interior of the cave and the gleaming black rock beneath her palm. Zelle transferred the staff to her other hand, stretching out her cramped fingers, and turned away from the rock, facing the daylight.

When she left the cave, she found Rien standing with his back to her, a staff of crimson wood in his left hand. Thorn-covered vines rippled up its length and over the back of his hands, and the veins appeared to glow beneath his skin, resembling the vines which wrapped around the staff in his hand.

When she drew nearer to him, the thorny vines lashed towards her, striking the path at her feet. Zelle took a step back, alarmed. "Powers above, can't you at least try to check there's nobody behind you before you start throwing thorns everywhere?"

"It was an accident." Rien lowered the staff. "What did the Sentinels' cave tell you?"

"It rightly berated me for indecisiveness and then told me I'm not ready to face... him." She didn't mention Daimos's name, never quite sure what reaction it would draw from Rien.

He might not yet be prepared to see Daimos again himself, but he'd changed significantly from the ragged man she'd met in a storm near the Sanctum a few weeks prior. He wore his long, dark hair loose, flowing past his shoulders in the style she'd been told was popular among Aestinian nobility. His grey eyes had lost their vacant expression, while his white shirt collar stood out crisply against his brown skin. It didn't hurt that his fine coat and boots were the best that money could buy in a remote region like this, either. Zelle knew he didn't like that Aurel had bought them for him, but he'd hadn't had a single coin on him when she'd met him in the mountains, so he'd had no choice but to rely on her family's charity.

"You knew it wasn't likely that the cave would be able to give you any useful advice," Rien remarked as they began to walk downhill towards the village of Tavine.

"I hoped it might give me some direction, at the very least," she said. "Leaving Tavine might cause more problems than it solves, and it doesn't feel right to turn my back on the Sentinels."

"If you're concerned for your family, then you have a good reason to stay here, don't you?"

They'd already had that argument at least twice, and it always ended the same way. Grandma and Aurel didn't need Zelle to stay, and frankly, she wasn't sure how much longer the money they'd stockpiled would last. Their family's once substantial fortune now consisted of a large number of worthless objects scavenged from the mountains, which Zelle sold in her late aunt's shop. Before the staff had landed in her possession, that had been her life.

"I'm also concerned that we'll run out of money," she said. "Aurel charges a pittance for Readings and believes every sob story her clients tell her, but the lifestyle she keeps isn't cheap."

Her sister's penchant for buying expensive gifts and wearing lavish jewellery as well as spending her free hours at the tavern was even more of an annoyance when she had to live in the same house as her. Zelle was looking forwards to an end to *that,* if nothing else.

"Doesn't the Crown Prince owe you a payment for defending Zeuten from Orzen?" asked Rien. "If the Invokers of Aestin performed such an act of service to the nation, they would be handsomely rewarded."

Zelle gave a faint snort of laughter. "No. It's not as if there's a precedent for these incidents, and I'm pretty sure the last useful thing a Sentinel did for the Crown was when my great-great-great grandfather helped create the Royal Road from the mountains to Saudenne. I think the King at the time gave him a medal, but no cash payment."

"That seems rather unfair."

"We aren't a rich nation." The vast majority of Zeutenians were farmers or craftspeople. Her family was one of the few who'd even *met* the Crown Prince, and that didn't mean he had any intention of rewarding them for their trouble. Neither did his father, though the ancient monarch had been on his deathbed for close to three years now, and his son had all but taken over from him as the public face of the royal family.

Zelle and Rien reached the foot of the mountain path and began to walk along the dirt track that wound through the thick pine forest surrounding the village. She'd been meaning to bring up the question of what he intended to do for work while they were in Saudenne, but he was never happy whenever anyone reminded him that he was in a foreign country, cut off from his former resources. He disliked being dependent upon Grandma and Aurel's hospitality, and she was certain he'd react the same to any setbacks he encountered in Saudenne.

When they neared the Reader's house, she knew this would be her last chance to talk to him alone before they left, so she gave him a sideways look. "Do you want me to find you lodgings when we arrive in Saudenne? I can't promise staying above the shop will be comfortable."

He didn't meet her eyes. "I've endured worse."

Of that she had little doubt. "Ah, you don't have to assist me in the shop itself if you don't want to. It's a decent source of gossip, but most of the idle chatter I hear might not be relevant to your goals. If it was, I might have heard of the happenings in Aestin sooner."

His grip tightened on his staff. "You wouldn't have, but I have little doubt news will have spread by now. People talk."

If he was right, there was a chance he might be recognised in Saudenne himself. Another reason staying here would be better for his need to keep a low profile, but she knew his home nation weighed heavily on his mind, even more so than his financial state.

She fell silent as they reached the Reader's house. Separated from the rest of the village by a wide fence surrounded by trees, the wood-frame house sat between two large oaks and behind a gate, which Rien opened. Zelle walked in behind him and unlocked the front door.

Inside, Aurel and Grandma sat in armchairs in the living room, surrounded by cabinets containing the array of curiosities that generations of her family had acquired over the centuries. These ranged from crockery to tools, and even the occasional piece of fossilised animal dung. Her family members had a long history of hoarding fragments of the original settlements their ancestors had established, but most of it was hardly worth keeping, let alone selling.

Aurel lifted her auburn head. "There you are. I was beginning to think I'd need to tell the carriage driver he needn't have bothered leaving the Royal Road."

"The carriage isn't already here, is it?" asked Zelle.

"Yes," Grandma said to her. "Which you'd know if you hadn't gone wandering off."

You're one to talk. Grandma didn't usually live at this address any more than Zelle did, but while she'd claimed she'd stayed to make sure no more deities came to meddle with the Reader, she spent most of her time meandering on long walks in the forest instead. Zelle had to admit she wouldn't miss having to drag the old Sentinel back to the Reader's house at least once a day, but that didn't make her feel any less like she was being kicked out.

"I'll get my things, then." She made for the stairs to the guest room to collect her pack, in which she'd put her new clothes and a few pieces of ancient pottery and tools to sell in the shop. After lifting the pack, she headed downstairs to join the others.

"Thank you," Rien was saying to Aurel, "for allowing me to stay in your house for these past weeks."

"The pleasure was all mine." Aurel lounged in an armchair, sipping from a glass of wine, while a faint thump drew Zelle's eyes to the tall, lanky figure in the corner. Zelle frequently forgot that a former Changer lived here, too, since Evita was generally unobtrusive regardless of whether she was wearing the silvery cloak with the power to render her invisible. Except when she occasionally knocked things over in the cabinets while dusting, that is. Why Aurel had hired her, Zelle had no idea, unless she'd genuinely wanted a new servant to replace the ones who'd quit after being subjected to the impossibility of cleaning up after the Reader. That, or she'd felt sorry for the girl, who'd been as penniless as Rien when they'd met.

"Aurel," Zelle addressed her sister, doing her best to ignore the flirtatious note that had entered her tone when she'd spoken to Rien. "You'll make sure Grandma doesn't take any more unnecessary excursions into the mountains, won't you?"

Aurel rolled her eyes. "You think I can stop her from doing whatever she likes?"

"I'd find it easier to relax back in Saudenne if I didn't think there might be a repeat of the incident when Grandma walked into the realm of the *Powers*."

Aurel openly laughed. "If you think I can stop the Powers from hauling her away if they want to, then you're mistaken. Oh, don't look at me like that, Zelle. That was a joke. Lighten up."

Zelle raised a brow at her sister's derisive tone. "You're drunk."

Intoxicated or not, her sister hadn't used that arrogant tone with her since they'd been teenagers. While she'd matured over the past few years, Aurel had been reverting to her old habits lately, like drinking expensive wine during the day instead of coming up with reasonable ways for her family to earn a living. Irritated, Zelle sought out her grandmother, who'd ducked into the Reading Room.

"Grandma, are you sure I can take the staff with me? If you need it—"

"Oh, go ahead." Grandma gave her an impatient wave.

"Frankly, it'll be a nice break from having that voice muttering in my ear all the time."

"If you're certain." When her grandmother didn't offer her another word of encouragement, she added, "I'll see you soon."

Rien cleared his throat. "Thank you for your hospitality, Sentinel Verica Carnelian. It will be repaid once I have claimed my family's estate."

Assuming you don't end up buried there. Zelle suppressed the comment and headed through the living room, waving at the others as she did so. "See you soon, Aurel. Bye, Evita."

The former assassin startled to hear her own name, and she gave Zelle a jerky wave before turning back to dusting the cabinet. Meanwhile, Zelle led Rien outside, feeling rather put out.

Rien turned to her when she closed the door behind them. "Is something going on with your sister?"

"She's jealous," she told him in an undertone. "She's been the Sentinel's successor since we were children, and now she thinks I've taken some of that away from her."

"You haven't taken anything away from her, though," said Rien. "The staff…"

"The staff is Grandma's, I know." She walked with him to the gate and into the village, where dirt roads ran between the simple wood-frame houses. She'd packed enough supplies for a couple of days, though the journey wouldn't take longer than half a day unless they ran into trouble on the road. "Aurel was mostly raised by our grandmother, and you've seen what she's like."

Upon leaving the village, they followed another dirt track through the woods towards the carriage's location.

It was a miracle her grandmother had been able to arrange transport for them at all, since Tavine was a small village whose only feature of note was the Reader's house. If not for a former King's liking for skiing in the mountains, there would be no major roads in the region at all. Fallen branches littered the path, while rustling sounded in the trees. Zelle glanced around, lifting the staff, until she recognised the large reptilian creature crouched in the bushes, watching them.

"That's Evita's dragonet," she said. "I think he came to say goodbye to us."

Rien gave a nod to the dragonet, while Zelle lifted her hand in farewell as they made their way towards the carriage waiting to take them to Saudenne.

2

The journey to Saudenne began with an uncomfortable stretch of bumping along dirt tracks through the woods before they reached the Royal Road, a major trade route leading directly to the capital. Tavine was around the same distance from Saudenne as her grandmother's home in Randel, on the opposite side of the Range, but the Royal Road cut the duration of their journey by a third. Zelle had no complaints about reducing the amount of time they spent on the road, especially with her companion's current taciturn mood.

Rien sat in silence, his hands clasped on his staff, while Zelle found herself unconsciously mimicking his pose. When they hit a particularly abrupt bump in the road, she tightened her grip to avoid the staff clattering out of her hands. She'd grown more cautious ever since she'd discovered the identity of the being whose magic resided within its knotted wood, although she had no doubt that like Rien's, the staff was stronger than it appeared.

She was pretty sure that Rien's staff didn't make sarcastic comments at him the way hers did, of course. Stretching her neck, she peered over the side of the carriage, glad of the roof arching over their heads to keep them from being showered with raindrops or struck by low-hanging branches.

"How do you get around in Aestin?" she asked Rien. "I'm guessing you have no need for carriages with roofs, considering your warmer climate. I imagine your roads are better maintained too. This one is only in good shape because one of our Kings had it built especially so he could go skiing in the lower parts of the Range in the winter."

"With the aid of your ancestors, you said."

"Occasionally, one of us did something useful." She wondered what the staff had thought of being pressured into using its magic to clear a swathe of trees out of the way for the Crown.

It was the most excitement I'd seen in years, the staff told her.

Rien gave no signs he'd heard the staff's comment, but it typically spoke to Zelle alone aside from her grandmother. "Our roads are well-maintained," he acknowledged, "but our country has been occupied for many centuries longer than yours has. I'm surprised Zeuten wasn't settled sooner, in all honesty. Aestin used to have colonies all over the world at one time, but they never came here until a thousand years ago."

"Might have something to do with all the wild magic in the mountains and forests." Her gaze dropped to the staff. "Magic has been here longer than any humans have, anyway."

The Shaper had been imprisoned in the Range since before Aestin's first empire had ever been heard of, as far as she knew. Rien glanced at the carriage driver, who sat in front of them, as if wondering if they should be discussing the subject with a potential eavesdropper nearby.

"True." Rien lowered his voice. "Aestin has places of wild magic, too, but largely cut off by mountains. That's where Daimos and his family were banished to when the families kicked them out. We little expected their return."

Zelle braced herself against the staff when they hit another bump in the road. "What exactly did they do to get themselves banished?"

"They tried to overthrow the Emperor," he said. "Collectively, the other families overpowered them. Or rather, my father and his allies did. My brother was a small child at the time, and I wasn't born yet. Daimos and I had never met before he confronted my family."

And now he carries your staff. She didn't voice that thought aloud. The loss was still raw for him, after all. "So Daimos was left without any access to magic when he was banished."

"Yes, but he found himself a Relic somewhere," Rien murmured. "Incidentally, that is what gave me the idea of seeking out my own."

"Your father once came to Zeuten himself, too," she remarked. "I hoped my grandmother might have told me more about their meeting."

"It was a long time ago," Rien said. "I know my family did maintain contact with some of the Sentinels in the past, but I never had the impression that your grandmother kept up their correspondence."

"Grandma doesn't really have friends." That was one trait Zelle had inherited, to her chagrin, but after spending so much time alone, she just plain didn't *know* how to connect with other people. All her attention had been focused on helping in her aunt's shop, nursing her through her sickness, and then keeping the shop running after her death. The little free time she had, she'd spent visiting her grandmother in the mountains. "Besides, it's been years since any overseas ambassadors have visited the Sentinels. Even the Crown Prince tends to forget we exist."

She vaguely recalled attending an important function as a young child, when her family had known that either her or Aurel would be chosen as the next Sentinel, but not who it would be. As a result, they'd both been forced into their nicest clothes and had been dragged in front of a parade of strangers. At the time, they'd both felt equally out of place and had sought solidarity in climbing a nearby tree and poking fun at the guests from a distance, but Zelle's memory of that day was so distant that it might have belonged to someone else.

"I believe this is the longest stretch I've ever gone in my life *without* an endless series of ceremonies and meetings with ambassadors and diplomats," Rien commented. "Aestin's nobles are known for their commitment to making everything into an unnecessary show."

He fell into silence, no doubt reminded of something in his past. Ever since he'd regained his memories, it was almost impossible to get through a conversation with him without bumping into at least one unpleasant recollection —an inevitability, really, considering he'd lost everything shortly before his arrival in Zeuten, and his struggle to best Orzen had rubbed salt into those raw wounds. Zelle tried to think of a reply that wouldn't hit the wrong note. She'd lost most of her family, too, but she hadn't been close to anyone except for her aunt, and Aunt Adaine's death had been the result of an illness that had stolen her strength, so Zelle's grief at losing her was tinged with relief that her suffering was over. She'd lost other relatives to accidents, an alarming number of which had occurred in the mountains, but none of them had been murdered. Certainly not recently, anyway.

Daimos might have been justified in his anger against the other Invoker families, but that in no way validated his decision to slaughter the entire Astera family, including those who hadn't been involved in his banishment. The fact that he'd sent Orzen over the ocean and let him murder innocent humans with impunity was further proof that the man was depraved—and dangerous.

Zelle sought a change of subject, if an equally unappealing one to Rien. "Have you need of any money to start off with in Zeuten? You told me your belongings were destroyed along with your house, and access to your money cut off too. I'd be happy to help you out, if it's not too much of a blow to your pride."

He replied in clipped tones. "I will make do."

Zelle frowned at his dismissive words, but she'd spoken a touch too bluntly herself. In any case, he didn't elaborate on his actual plans for their arrival in Saudenne, nor did he engage her in conversation again for the duration of the journey.

Several hours later, the carriage rolled into the sprawling capital, which covered a large section of Zeuten's southern coastline. Even here, the Range shadowed the domed shape of the palace at the city's highest point. The entire city stood on a hill, at the very bottom of which lay the docks, and it was near there that the carriage rattled to a halt outside the market.

Zelle and Rien disembarked with their luggage, while Zelle tossed a spare coin to the carriage driver. The briny scent of the sea wafted in along with the smell of baked goods from the market earlier that day, while other aromas drifted over from the shops in the neighbouring streets. If Zelle closed her eyes, she'd be able to find her way home by scent alone, and she knew this neighbourhood as well as any of the mountain trails.

"We're not far," she told Rien, stretching her cramped legs before picking up her pack again. A cold breeze brought a chill to her skin, a reminder of the closeness of the mountains they'd left behind. Only the very edge of the peaks was visible from this close to the sea. While the closest part of the Range was rumoured to be the location of the Changers' base, she hadn't seen any signs of the assassins since the survivors from their ranks had fled certain death at the hands of the deity who'd hired them. Except for Evita, who'd opted to work as Aurel's new servant instead of returning to their base. With the way Aurel had been acting earlier, staying with the assassins might have been a better fate, but she didn't blame the girl for wanting to turn her back on the people who'd turned out to be working for her family's killer.

Zelle and Rien approached the seafront. A glittering blanket of blueness dotted with ships and boats stretched as far as the eye could see, while the familiar streets bore no sign of the events of several weeks ago. She'd heard the havoc Orzen had wreaked on the local inns while he'd been walking anonymously in the form of a human child, yet the city remained the same to her eyes, as if she'd never left at all.

Not for the first time, Zelle had to give herself a stern reminder that Orzen was gone; she'd bound his power into a Relic and tossed it into the Sanctum herself. If the mountains had bound the nameless Shaper for centuries, they could hold Orzen, and it was highly unlikely that the childlike form he'd adopted would be waiting for her in the shop. She had more reason to be worried that thieves had ransacked the place during her absence, and the odds of burglars finding anything worth stealing on the dusty shelves were laughable.

Her first thought upon setting eyes on the shop was how small it looked compared to the Reader's house, crammed in a row of similar stone houses and with red paint flaking from the wooden door. Zelle rummaged underneath the doormat for her spare key and unlocked the door to reveal dusty shelves and worn floorboards.

"Welcome to my home," she said to Rien. "It's not much, I know."

A single room occupied each floor, resulting in quarters far more cramped than even the smallest guest room at the Reader's house, but at least they were hers alone. Until her aunt's death, the two of them had shared the upstairs quarters—along with Aurel, before she'd been chosen as the Sentinel's successor. She and Zelle had lived here together from their mother's death up until the day when Grandma had taken Aurel on as her apprentice and swept her away to live in the Reader's house.

Zelle ought to be glad to return to some familiarity, but the knot in her chest at the sight of the shop was diffi-

EMMA L. ADAMS

cult to ignore. Each step stirred a cloud of dust from the worn floorboards.

"It's certainly…" Rien paused for an instant as though gathering his words. "Neat."

Meaning: half the shelves were empty. "I know it needs dusting. Not a surprise, considering how long I've been gone. I'll do that tonight."

Rien said nothing, and Zelle glanced sideways at him. "Rien, whereabouts do you want to stay? I can offer you a couple of inn recommendations, but frankly, I'm not sure if that ghastly creature left any of them unscathed. I assume you don't want to sleep on the shop floor."

He cleared his throat. "There's no need. I intend to travel to Aestin overnight."

"You intend to travel… *where?*" Questions spilled into her mind, tumbling over one another like coins from a slit purse.

He didn't quite meet her eyes. "I can't stay away from my home forever. I'm needed there."

"You're aware that there's a murderer waiting for your return so he can finish you off, aren't you?" Zelle hadn't acknowledged the fact aloud in some time, not wanting to put Rien on the defensive, but perhaps she ought to have reminded him sooner. "Have you forgotten that the last time you crossed the ocean, you ended up shipwrecked on Zeuten's coast, without any of your belongings and on the brink of death?"

His hand clenched on the staff, and Zelle regretted her blunt words despite her roiling emotions. "No, I haven't, despite someone's best efforts."

By 'someone', he meant the nameless Shaper. Another a sore subject, as he'd temporarily lost his memories upon

28

his arrival in Zeuten due to the Shaper's desire to prevent Aestin's troubles from reaching the mountains. The Shaper's hopes had been in vain, of course, but while Rien hadn't made a direct reference to the matter for a while, he clearly hadn't forgotten.

"I didn't intend that to happen, Rien," she said softly. "You don't have to leave now."

"I do," he said. "There's nothing for me in Saudenne, and waiting for rumours doesn't suit me. I want to see what's happening in Aestin with my own eyes."

She hardly heard the last part, her mind snagging on the word *nothing*. As if everything she'd offered him had been meaningless. Thoughts tangled in her mind, and she spoke the most mundane of them. "I thought you didn't have any money."

"I found a captain willing to wait for payment until I return to Aestin," he explained. "I sent word via a courier in Tavine to find someone willing to agree to my offer. This is the earliest day they had available."

"You made your arrangements days ago, and you decided not to tell anyone until now?" Zelle asked, unable to believe he'd had the nerve to lie to the Sentinel while living under her roof. "Why?"

"Because I assumed you'd try to talk me out of it, and I didn't wish to make our last few days together uncomfortable for both of us."

"Or you were a coward."

She knew the word would hurt him, but she could hardly believe he'd lied to her face as well as her family, who'd offered him shelter when nobody else had. After everything they'd been through, she'd assumed he held them in higher regard.

When he didn't reply, she gave him a pointed stare. "Good luck, then."

The merest flicker of guilt shone in his eyes before he turned to leave. "I wish you the best, Zelle."

He left, the door swinging shut behind him. Heading back to Aestin, and potentially to his death.

He has a new Relic now, the staff told her. *He'll be fine.*

She released a frustrated breath. "I hope you're right, because there's nothing I can do to help him now."

A voice that didn't belong to the staff lurked in the back of her mind, whispering that it wasn't too late to go after him.

And do what? Get herself killed, too? Rien had made it quite clear that he didn't want her company. She was the one who'd ignored the obvious signs of his desire to leave, unwilling to break the newfound trust that had formed between them, when even the Sentinels' cave had dropped obvious hints of his intention to return home. She wouldn't stand in his way, regardless of how much his words had stung. She was perfectly capable of gathering information on the situation in Aestin without his help.

Zelle opened her pack and began unloading the trinkets she'd brought to sell, arranging them on the shelves despite her tiredness from the long day on the road. Perhaps if she tired herself to the point of exhaustion, she'd be able to sleep without dwelling on Rien's departure. However unappealing it might seem, she needed to rise early tomorrow to open the shop and to get back to some semblance of her old routine again. Unlike Rien, she had no stores of riches or servants waiting to help her achieve her goals. All she had was the staff and her own two hands, and she knew better than to allow herself to wonder if leaving her family had been a mistake after all.

I made my choice, she told herself firmly. *Right or wrong, I'll see it through, and I'll do so by myself.*

————

Rien watched the shoreline fade into the distance from the deck of the ship, trying to ignore the guilt stabbing at his chest. He'd deceived Zelle, though not with any malicious intent, and while he'd known he'd have to leave her behind when he left for Aestin, he might have handled the situation better. He would never have asked her to abandon her family to travel into certain danger alongside him, yet that was no excuse for the way he'd treated her, and that knowledge lay heavily upon his shoulders while the sun painted orange stripes across the blue expanse of the ocean and the city of Saudenne vanished from sight.

He was no stranger to regret. On his journey here, he'd survived drowning by bargaining for his life with a deity who lived within a Relic he'd taken from his brother's corpse. Sooner or later, the deity in question might expect him to return that favour, but when he'd claimed his new Relic, Zierne had offered to help protect him from the consequences. His new deity could not, however, heal the damage he'd done to his friendship with Zelle, and after days of being surrounded by people, he felt the absence keenly.

As they began to pick up speed, he turned his gaze in the opposite direction, watching the waves skim against the side of the ship. He couldn't yet see the coast of Aestin, but with the rate at which the horizon was swallowing the sun, it'd be dark long before it came into view. Soon, he'd retire to the cabin he'd rented, and by morning, they'd arrive in Tauvice, the capital of Aestin and his family's home.

He'd never been away from the city for so long before, and the knowledge of what awaited him momentarily overtook the regret at leaving Zelle behind. It was too late to give his family the burials they deserved, but he should at least see if any of their possessions could be retrieved from the wreckage of their estate. It was unlikely that he'd be able to unearth the records of his ancestors' correspondence with the Sentinels, though, and he wished he'd asked his father for details of his knowledge of the lost Relics in the mountains while he'd had the chance. He'd little expected that he'd ever have reason to visit Zeuten himself, much less claim one of those Relics in place of his own.

Despite his efforts to stem the regret welling within him, it continued to seep through his bones. He owed the Sentinels, including Zelle, his life, and it was he who had brought misfortune on their heads to begin with. He couldn't even blame the choice to flee to Zeuten on his missing memories, since at the time, he'd known exactly what he was doing. His certainty that he'd had no choice but to seek out the Sentinels didn't erase the consequences of his choice, though his father had been clear that was the last possible option if ever his family had been threatened.

He hadn't even told Zelle the details of his father's instructions, but truth be told, he'd forgotten most of them. While he'd hoped Zelle's grandmother would have more recollection of her own meeting with his father many years prior, she'd declined to discuss the subject with Rien. Of course, it'd been at least two decades since she and Volcan Astera had seen one another, and his family hadn't held a formal meeting with the Sentinels in years. He'd only known of their correspondence because he'd seen the letters his father had carefully stored in his office, but it had been years since he'd read them in full.

The salty air stung his eyes, but he didn't blink. He fixed his gaze on the horizon as the ship sailed towards Aestin—and towards home.

3

Evita swept another cloud of dust from one of the cabinet shelves, her eyes watering and her cloth encrusted with grime. She'd never seen so many oddities in one place, from cracked pottery to strange tools and broken weaponry which, according to Zelle, had belonged to the original settlers in Zeuten who'd gone on to become the first Sentinels.

At first, Evita had wondered if the Reader ran some kind of museum, before it'd occurred to her that if she did, more people would have come to visit the house. Instead, she'd begun to suspect that both Aurel and her grandmother liked collecting these artefacts for nothing more than sentimental value, the same way her father had collected seashells and pretty rocks from the beach.

The memory brought a familiar ache to her chest, and she scrubbed harder in the hopes of driving the gloomy thoughts from her head. After Zelle and Rien's departure the previous day, she'd become acutely aware of how her position here depended on Aurel's tolerance for a stranger living in the house, and Zelle's sister was rather unpredictable, to say the least. She'd hardly said two words to Evita all day.

As if she'd sensed the direction of Evita's thoughts, Aurel came sauntering in her direction, dressed in an embroidered blue coat with gold brocade. She always dressed impeccably, and put together with her broad, tall frame and confident stance, it made for an intimidating picture. Evita found her shoulders tensing automatically. The Reader had done little for the past day except go on periodic visits to the tavern and argue with her grandmother, and she'd begun to assume Aurel had outright forgotten she was here.

"Is there something I can help you with?" Evita asked warily.

"I have good news," Aurel informed her. "You can have one of the guest rooms now that Rien and Zelle have gone. You don't have to sleep downstairs anymore."

Whatever Evita had expected, it wasn't an offer of a room. "Won't they be coming back?"

"Zelle might come and visit at some point, but not for a while, I imagine," said Aurel. "As for Rien, he's wanted to go back to Aestin from the start."

"To kill the man who murdered his family." Would he take the risk? Evita had been under the impression that Zelle and Rien intended to stay in Saudenne for a while, though she hadn't been privy to most of their discussions.

"I expect so," Aurel said. "He told me that he wants to see if there's anything left of his family's estate before hunting down Daimos, but it wouldn't surprise me if the scumbag was waiting to ambush him when he gets home."

While Evita and Rien came from very different backgrounds, she, too, had seen her family's home razed to the ground at the hands of the same deity who'd helped kill Rien's family. She didn't blame him for wanting to go back to Aestin to hunt down the person responsible for unleashing the deity known as Orzen in the world. Evita's own revenge plan had ended with Orzen's defeat, which had left her at a loose end. She might have gone back to join the Changers, but the idea had lost its appeal after they'd tried to have her killed. Besides, they'd suffered a major shock to their reputation as elite assassins who protected Zeuten from external threats when they hadn't been able to do anything to prevent Orzen's rampage.

Grandma Carnelian entered the house, clutching a package from the market in one hand and using the other to close the door behind her. Her gaze found Aurel, then Evita. "You're still here?"

"Yes." Evita's back straightened. "I'm happy to stay as long as the Reader requires my services."

Grandma Carnelian made no secret of her disdain for Evita's presence in the Reader's house, but it was Aurel who had control over her fate, not her. From what she'd heard, the old Sentinel usually lived in another village on the other side of the mountains, but after her disappearance a few weeks ago, her grandchildren had insisted she ought to stay here instead. Given that Zelle claimed her grandmother had been held captive in the realm of the Powers—and Evita had seen as much for herself—it was no wonder she and Aurel had watched the old Sentinel like a pair of mountain eagles.

Whatever had transpired between Grandma Carnelian and the deities, the old woman flat-out refused to share the details with anyone, including her own family. It shouldn't be any of Evita's business, but she would have liked to know if she ought to worry about more deities potentially appearing on the doorstep. While working for the Reader was more likely to make her a target for the deities than any alternative, her survival odds had been much lower when she'd trained with the Changers, and at least she had a roof over her head now.

Grandma Carnelian hobbled to an armchair and sat down, not taking her eyes off Evita. "I heard at the market that your people are back in the village."

Evita's heart missed a beat. "You mean the Changers?"

"Who else?"

She frowned. "They're not my people. I quit."

"Do *they* know that?"

"I assume they guessed when I stabbed the deity who was giving them orders."

Aurel snorted. "Yeah, you'd think that would give them a clue."

"Don't give me cheek, Aurel," said Grandma Carnelian. "The Senior Changers have been out of the country on a secret mission for months."

"That's news to me," said Aurel. "It explains why they let that Orzen storm through their ranks, though, if most of their best assassins were out of the country."

"I did wonder where the Senior Changers were," Evita supplied. "The Masters didn't like to share much about secret missions with the novices, though."

"I expect not," said Grandma Carnelian. "I don't doubt the Senior Changers returned to Zeuten as soon as they heard the news of the masters' unfortunate deaths."

The Senior Changers. Since Evita had been at the very bottom of the Changers' ranks, she'd known nothing of the elite assassins' whereabouts or the mission they'd been taking part in, but it explained why Master Amery had sent a team of novices to hunt down Arien Astera. Not that that had been Master Amery's primary motive in picking *her* for the job. No, he'd wanted to send someone who wouldn't be missed.

The joke was on him, though. She'd lived, while he'd perished at Orzen's hands.

"Whereabouts did you see them?" she asked, wondering if she ought to check up on the dragonet to make sure he hadn't run into the Changers on the road.

"I didn't see them, but I heard several of the villagers mention they saw them flying above the forest while I was buying supplies," answered Grandma Carnelian.

That means they're close. "If they want to talk to me, I expect they'll get in touch."

She picked up the cloth again, but Aurel shook her head. "Leave it. I don't mind the dust. It gives the artefacts more character."

Evita dropped the cloth and reached for a broom instead. "What else do you need me to do?"

"Nothing," said Aurel. "Take the rest of the day off. I'm going to the tavern, and I'd rather my artefacts stayed intact while I'm gone."

Evita left the broom leaning against the side of the cabinet. "All right. Er, thank you."

She wasn't sure that the Reader had meant to do her a favour, but she *was* glad of the chance to visit Chirp rather than embarking on a futile quest to remove endless layers of dust from the cabinets.

Grandma Carnelian gave Evita a disparaging look as she went to pick up her shoes, which she ignored. After

Master Amery, the old Sentinel wasn't nearly as intimidating to her. After pulling on her silvery cloak—she preferred to wear her Changer's gear whenever she went outside—and her new fur-lined boots, she bade farewell to the Sentinel and left the house.

Evita closed the door behind her and headed for the nearest route into the woods. In recent weeks, she'd done her best to memorise the various paths from the village to the forest, though the woods seemed designed to confuse anyone who might stumble into their midst.

When the last stone building had disappeared among the trees, she heard the crunch of branches trodden under large feet, and the dragonet emerged from the bushes. Chirp made the noise that had earned him his name and lowered his head, and she ran a hand over the hard scales, a smile tugging her lips upward. The creature had grown dramatically in the short time they'd known one another, and his head now reached her shoulders, enabling her to meet his eyes without crouching.

"How're you getting on?" she asked. "I know I haven't been around much lately, but I've been busy cleaning the Reader's house. It's a big job."

The dragonet made a snorting noise, perhaps because he'd seen the inside of the Reader's house with his own eyes.

"I know the house is a complete mess, but that's why she needs me."

Chirp snorted again.

"Don't judge me," she said. "I lost my home and everything I owned, so I have to save up everything the Reader can pay me. She's been generous so far, but she's not rich."

Given the contents of her house, finding out the state

of the Sentinel's finances had surprised Evita, but from what Zelle had told her, most of the junk in the Reader's house wasn't worth much money. If she'd wanted, Evita might have left for Saudenne with Rien and Zelle instead, but it wasn't as if she'd had a job waiting for her in the city, and she didn't want to throw away the Reader's generous offer. For now, staying in Tavine was her best option, so she finished petting Chirp and reached into her pocket for a bag of dried meat she'd bought from the market with the little coin she'd earned so far.

Holding up a piece of meat with one hand, she pointed into the trees with the other. "Fly to that tree and back."

She always started their training sessions with the same simple exercise, but he obeyed with enthusiasm, and she tossed the scrap of meat into his mouth when he reached her side again. As Evita had had no experience of dragonets before she'd met Chirp, she'd initially been unsure about treating him as she would a pet. He was more intelligent than a wolf or a wildcat, but he responded in a similar manner when praised or offered treats, and he returned her affections readily.

Evita pulled out a second piece of meat. "Now fly in a circle."

Chirp let out a chittering noise and then obeyed. She might not understand his speech the way he did her own, but they'd established a mutual trust after she'd saved him from being devoured by a wyrm during her first and only trial as a novice Changer. He'd saved her life in turn several times, and while she hadn't expected him to stay in the area after the danger had passed, he'd been waiting in the forest for her every time she'd left the Reader's house.

Chirp landed, devoured the meat, and gave her a familiar hopeful look. Her stomach swooped downward. She knew what that look meant, and sure enough, the dragonet lifted its claws in an imitation of the motion he made when he picked her up to fly with her over the mountains.

"Ah—not now. Maybe later."

His head drooped, but he lowered his claws. Guilt gnawed at her. She knew that the dragonet enjoyed her company, but while he was clearly ready to fly together without the added danger of the Changers and Orzen, that didn't mean *she* was. Since his wingspan rivalled a mountain eagle's, she might have been able to sit on his back instead of being carried, but that wasn't enough to make Evita keen to take to the skies again.

The dragonet stiffened, his head sweeping around as movement stirred in the undergrowth. Then several individuals emerged from the bushes, their silvery cloaks rendering them difficult to see, aside from their faces.

Changers.

Evita recognised Vekka first. The burly Changer stood at the forefront of their group next to his heavyset friend, Izaura. Near the back, Evita spotted Ruben, one of the few Changers who'd ever treated her kindly, but the others looked upon her with wariness or open hostility. She hadn't known they'd survived to return to their base, but they looked in better shape than the last time she'd seen them, haunted and on the run from the deity who'd taken over their ranks.

"I thought we'd find you in here," said Vekka.

"What do you want?" She addressed the question to their group. They couldn't possibly all be here to see *her*, could they? She would have assumed they'd have more pressing concerns, like whoever would take the place of their dead Masters.

"The Senior Changers want to speak to you," Izaura informed her. "You're to come with us."

"You expect me to believe that?" asked Evita. "If I follow you into the woods, how do I know you won't stab me the instant my back is turned?"

"I'm not going to stab you." Vekka's gaze went to the dragonet when Chirp made a displeased grunt. "The Senior Changers are back in Zeuten, and they're interested in meeting the Changer who witnessed the downfall of the Masters."

"I didn't see the downfall of anyone except for the deity who *murdered* the Masters," she corrected. "Do the Senior Changers know that Master Amery was tricked into doing his bidding?"

"You can't say that," hissed one of Vekka's companions. "Master Amery was our superior. He should be honoured."

"He *did* die at the hands of the deity, though." Evita eyed Ruben, hoping he or one of the others would back her up. "He also sent us to kill an innocent man and capture the Sentinel, against the will of the Crown."

"The Crown hasn't made a statement yet." Izaura's face flushed at the implication that their entire group had betrayed their country, intentionally or not. "We don't yet know what the Crown Prince thinks of all this, but I bet he'll want to hear the story too."

"I'm not the only witness," Evita pointed out. "Besides, I'm not beholden to the Changers anymore."

"Really?" Vekka arched a brow. "Isn't your family dead? Who're you working for now?"

She lifted her chin. "The Reader."

Izaura gave her a sceptical look. "What use does the Reader have for the likes of you?"

"I'm her, uh, assistant." That sounded a little more impressive than 'cleaner' or 'servant'. "She'll be angry if you're planning to have me killed. Besides, I don't have time to leave the village and trek all the way to your base."

"You don't have to." Ruben finally spoke up. "The Senior Changers are staying here in Tavine."

Really? "Where are they staying?"

"Above the tavern," he replied.

"What about you, then?" Evita tilted her head at Vekka. "Did they make you camp in the forest?"

"What's it to you?" Vekka said defensively.

"Just wondered if they were treating you any better than that deity did." She found herself unable to resist needling him.

"If you speak to *them* like that, they might stab you in the back themselves," growled Vekka.

"If they want to risk angering the Reader." In truth, she had no intention of starting another fight with the Changers, but Vekka had been a thorn in her shoe from the moment they'd met. "I'll see what they have to say, then."

Hadn't Aurel told her she was going to the tavern herself? If Evita met the Senior Changers in broad daylight with other people around, they'd be less likely to harm her, especially with the Reader watching them. Besides, Evita was curious to hear what the Senior Changers had been doing while an enraged deity had run

43

amok throughout Zeuten instead of saving their own Masters from certain death.

"I'll let them know." Vekka swaggered through the trees towards the village, followed by his cloaked friends.

The dragonet hissed at the Changers' backs.

"I know. I don't like them either." Evita lowered her voice. "But I want to know how much the Senior Changers know of the deity's influence over Master Amery and the others. It wouldn't surprise me if the other Changers hid the truth from their superiors, and if they did, I think I ought to set the record straight."

So it doesn't happen again, she added silently.

Orzen might be imprisoned inside a Relic that Zelle had secured somewhere in the mountains, but it would take a long while for Evita to stop waking from sleep in a cold sweat, convinced she felt the chilling presence of one of Orzen's magical constructs in the room.

In her old life, her fellow villagers had uttered prayers to the creator goddess Gaiva for clear skies and good fortune, and had conducted rites to Mevicen, deity of the ocean, when the fish were in short supply or stormy seas battered the coasts. Yet none of them would ever have conceived of a deity walking among humans and slaughtering them all, and Evita had to admit that her primary motive in staying in the Reader's house was that the Sentinels were among the few people for whom the odds of surviving another deity's appearance were higher than zero. Even the Masters of the Changers hadn't been able to match that claim.

Evita bade farewell to Chirp and followed the Changers' progress towards the village, tensing when a figure stepped onto the path behind her.

"Relax, it's just me," said Ruben. "Are you all right?"

Her mouth parted, her mind trying to discern any hidden meanings in his words. She'd told him that she wasn't interested in him romantically on at least one occasion, but she wasn't sure he'd been entirely convinced at her efforts to repel his advances. His tone signalled simple concern, though, so she nodded. "Yes, but I'm a little confused as to why the Senior Changers came all the way here just to see me."

"They're here to speak to everyone who witnessed the recent events," said Ruben. "Not just you, though you had a more close-up view than most."

"Not as much as Zelle and Rien, but they just left the village," she responded.

"Who?" asked Ruben.

Right—he and the other Changers wouldn't have had the chance to talk to her companions. "Zelle is the Reader's sister and the one who saved our lives up on the mountain. Rien—Arien—is the man we were sent to kill."

"Oh, the Aestinian magician," said Ruben. "He didn't turn out to be working against the Crown, right?"

"Of course not," she said firmly. "He made an enemy of someone back in Aestin who sent that deity to hire the Changers."

That was the simplest way to explain a complex situation, but it must have been alarming for the Changers who'd found themselves caught in a war between a foreign magician and a furious deity who'd killed the Masters when they'd failed to fulfil his desires. She even found a little pity for Vekka and Izaura, though that faded when they beckoned impatiently to Evita from the other side of the gate.

"The Senior Changers are expecting you," Vekka called to her. "No dawdling."

"They aren't my bosses anymore," Evita returned. "It's my decision to speak to them."

Vekka scoffed. "You have their property, in case you've forgotten."

He meant the cloak. She *had* forgotten that the Changers might want it back, though it'd been Master Amery who'd given it to her for her first and only mission. "They never asked for it back the last time we spoke."

Evita had no intention of parting ways with her most valued possession; the cloak had saved her life on more than one occasion, and if the Senior Changers wanted it back, then she'd have no option but to walk away without telling them a thing. Hoping speaking to them wouldn't anger the Sentinel or her granddaughter, she approached the squat stone tavern and pushed the worn door inward.

Inside, the pleasant smell of roasting meat mingled with the scent of woodsmoke. Wooden beams supported a low ceiling, and carved tables filled the floor space. Aurel didn't appear to be there, but a man and a woman wearing the silver-and-blue cloaks of the Senior Changers sat at a table in the corner. The man's thick brows more than made up for his thinning hair, and his tawny skin was marked with faded scars. The woman's severe expression dimmed her otherwise handsome features, while her complexion was dark enough that Evita assumed some of her family must have been from Aestin.

"Evita Govind." The man beckoned to her with a hand. "I've been interested to meet you for some time."

Evita didn't move. "Who are you, exactly?"

"Verne," he said. "Senior Changer. This is Briony, my partner. We recently returned from a mission in the Isles of Itzar to find news of the deaths of a number of our fellow Changers and some rather... outlandish tales, passed on by someone purporting to be an ambassador."

"We came here to learn the truth," put in the woman, leaning forwards in her seat. "And we hear you played a large part in those events before turning your back on the Changers."

There was a notably accusatory note to her tone which Evita didn't like in the slightest.

"Not exactly." Admittedly, she'd played a larger role than most of the villagers had, including the Reader—but it was Zelle who'd been responsible for ridding them of Orzen. The Senior Changers hadn't done a thing. "Why didn't you come back when the Masters were slaughtered?"

"We were beyond reach of any communication." Defensiveness underlined Verne's tone. "We did not receive any contact from Zeuten until long after the tragic events occurred, and it's for that reason that we would be grateful to hear your account."

While she perched on the edge of a seat opposite the two Senior Changers, Evita gathered her story, which she'd told in various forms over the last few weeks. "I'd just completed my first trial as a Changer when Master Amery chose me to take part in an important mission. I was to come to Tavine, to the Reader's house, and ask her to find the location of Arien Astera, who was marked for death."

She looked between the two Senior Changers to see

what they thought of that, but neither spoke a word. Telling them about the staff or the Sentinels' cave was out of the question. Who knew what Aurel or her grandmother would do to her if she shared their deepest secrets?

"And?" Briony prompted.

"I went looking for her," Evita went on, "and on the way, I ran into the person who originally hired the Changers to find him. He'd already found Arien Astera himself, and he wasn't… human."

She faltered on the last word. The tale sounded outlandish to her own ears despite her all-too-vivid memories of the events, which was, no doubt, why the Senior Changers wanted her to confirm the rumours they'd heard.

"Go on," Verne said impatiently.

"Ah." She scrambled to recollect her thoughts. "He didn't succeed in killing Arien Astera, but he *did* kill Master Amery. He told me himself. When I learned he had the Changers under his command, I decided to ask for the Reader's help." She sucked in a breath, debating whether to mention the Sentinel's apparent kidnapping at the Changers' hands, too, and decided against it. Instead, she briefly summed up the battle without mentioning her own role. Her account was as ridden with holes as a pair of old socks, but it would do.

"The individual who hired the Changers was known as Orzen, correct?" asked Briony.

Evita flinched at the name. "Yes. He was sent across the ocean to murder Arien Astera."

"But he was unsuccessful," Verne concluded. "How curious. I have a number of questions that I am sure only the Reader can answer, but I would dearly like to know if it was her who defeated the deity."

Evita's words caught in her throat. Quite apart from risking the Reader's wrath by exposing the Sentinels' secrets, she would also prefer not to bring the wrath of the nameless Shaper on her head. "I didn't see."

They wouldn't be able to dispute her claim. Evita had been hidden beneath her cloak of Changing while Zelle had performed the binding spell on Orzen, and while Evita had contributed in part by giving Zelle the token Zelle had used to create Orzen's new Relic, she hadn't been the one who'd bound him.

"Pity," said Verne. "Defeating a Power is a feat that even most wielders of Relics would struggle to achieve, yet nobody on this continent owns such an item except for the Sentinels. Is that right?"

His intense stare made Evita uncomfortable. "I assume it is, but I would never have known the Powers themselves might be able to walk among us."

"We live in unusual times, no doubt," said Briony. "Nevertheless, these events are greatly concerning for the safety and security of Zeuten as a whole. Where is Arien Astera now?"

"Gone," she said. "He's on his way home to Aestin, I expect. Was that all you wanted to ask me?"

The two exchanged glances, and then Briony looked directly at her.

"We would like to make you an offer," she said. "That is, an offer of employment among our senior ranks."

4

___

As Rien had predicted, the ship reached Tauvice's shore not long after he'd risen at dawn. He hadn't slept well, jolting awake in his cabin bed every time the ship rocked against a wave, but a sense of purpose energised him when he watched the familiar port of the capital city from the deck, and the warm air of his home country washed over him.

Carrying his pack in one hand, he disembarked. As he thanked the captain, the tongue of Aestin felt almost foreign in his mouth, whether due to his length of time away or because it was the first time he'd spoken the language since before he'd lost his memories. Around him, a dozen dialects mingled in the air, while the smell of freshly caught seafood brought back memories of fishing with his father off this very coast. The air was humid, a contrast to the perpetual chill of the Range, which prompted him to remove his heavy coat.

Rien chose a route home which took him around the market rather than through it. He wasn't yet ready to walk on the cobbled streets that had led him to his family's estate too late to save their lives from Daimos's massacre. All the same, the memories grew more prominent the closer he drew to his home, until he fancied that he could smell the smoke and hear the screams beyond the chatter of the market. He walked swiftly, hands clenched on his new staff, until he came to the wide cobbled street leading up to the Astera family's estate.

The road had been cleared of debris, but the gate was a twisted mess, while pieces of shattered stone barred the way to the front entrance. This time he did smell the smoke, the lingering traces that clung to the air like thick mud. Gritting his teeth, he picked his way through the piles of stone in an attempt to find a clear route into the house.

"What in Gaiva's name are you doing, boy?" asked a voice.

He spun on his heel, raising his staff. A man of around sixty or so with skin that resembled crumpled brown paper raised his hands slowly. When he spotted Rien's staff, his eyes widened, and then he lowered his head in a gesture of respect. "Master Astera."

"Linas?" Shocked, Rien let his guard drop. "You're alive?"

"So are you," the old man observed. "You've been gone an awfully long time, boy."

"Not my intention." Bitterness choked his throat in addition to the dust and smoke. "The house... did anyone make it out?"

"Most of the servants escaped," said the old man. "Or hid. No doubt they wished they could have done more... as do I."

Daimos's target had been the Astera family, and he'd left none of them alive save for Rien himself. The knowledge clamped a vice over his lungs, and his eyes burned when the old man rested a hand on Rien's shoulder. Linas had been a good friend of Volcan Astera, and they'd stayed close long after he'd retired as the groundskeeper at their estate, but he wouldn't have been able to do anything to stop Daimos's rampage. He had no magic of his own, after all.

Rien lifted his head. "The bodies?"

"In the crypt," he said. "I would not have had them touched without your permission, Arien."

"Thank you." His words were soft, laced with relief. Most Aestinians burned their dead, but the Invoker families held the less common practise of interring the bones of their deceased in their private mausoleums. Thanks to an unfortunate spate of grave robbing some centuries prior, each prominent family's crypt was located in a secure part of the imperial district, barred from access to anyone but a select few. It did not sound as though Daimos had managed to breach those boundaries, and it came as a small measure of comfort to know that at least his family's killer had left the dead untouched.

Speaking of whom… "Where is Daimos? Is he still in the city?"

Linas shook his head. "No, and good riddance, frankly."

"Then where is he?" asked Rien.

"As far away as possible, I hope," he responded. "After he grew bored with wreaking devastation on the city, he got himself a ship and crew and set sail. That's the last I heard of him."

Strange. Rien had thought Daimos's aim was to enact revenge on all the leading families in Aestin, or at least take the Asteras' place in the hierarchy among the prominent Invoker families. Perhaps he'd decided politics was not for him. Admittedly, Daimos had taken the Relic of Astiva by force and slaughtered its original wielders, which wouldn't win him any favour with the Emperor, so it wasn't entirely a surprise that he'd left the city. Had he left the country altogether, though? For what purpose?

Rien would have to think further on the matter, but if Daimos wasn't in the city, he'd need to use the opportunity wisely. Starting with some loose ends he'd been waiting to tie up. "I'll go to the mausoleum."

"Of course," said the old man. "Do you want company?"

Rien was silent for a moment, the dust stinging his eyes. "I would like that very much, yes."

———

The two of them opted to walk to the crypt rather than taking a carriage, since Rien would have preferred not to alert anyone else to his return. The smell of burning faded eventually as they drew farther from the ruins of the estate, and while he'd have to return later to see if anything might be salvaged from the house, he was grateful for the reprieve.

The Astera family's crypt was located near the imperial palace, surrounded by a high fence of interlocking metal rings. Daimos had left the imperial district alone despite the carnage he'd wreaked on the coast, but the Invokers had been his targets, not the Emperor. Perhaps that accounted for the relative calm he'd observed since his arrival, as if life remained unchanged for the majority of the city's people.

If the Emperor had died and not the head of the Astera family, the public would be in mourning for months, a fact that some outside of Aestin might find strange, given that the Invokers held far more political power than the Emperor did. Despite the thousand years that had passed since the major Invoker families had brought Aestin's monarchy to a violent end, they retained a certain level of notoriety in the eyes of the common people. Many respected and feared the Invokers in equal measure yet saw the Emperor's lack of magical talent as a sign that he was as an ordinary man like them.

This had never made much sense to Rien, who felt little connection to his ancestors' decision to protest the harsh restrictions placed upon Invokers at the time by storming the imperial palace and executing the royal family before installing an Emperor of their own choosing—but his country's future might easily have taken a very different turn if someone like Naxel Daimos had taken power.

In any case, it was his family's more recent history that surrounded him as he undid the bolts on the gate and walked up to the door of the Astera family's mausoleum. The exterior was decorated with elaborate stone carvings of ravens and other birds—Astiva was said to have an affinity with avian creatures—and twin thorn-covered staffs stood on either side of the stone doors.

The staff in his own hands appeared to grow heavier as he operated the lever that caused the stone doors to swing open, and guilt clenched inside him at the reminder of how he'd failed his deity as well as his family. His hands fumbled as he lit a candle to light the way past the rows of stone coffins on either side of the wide room, and the sight of remnants of old offerings to Astiva littering the stone flagstones made him want to retreat again.

Could he even call himself the head of the Astera family now that Astiva no longer bowed to him? That was a question he couldn't answer yet, but he found himself fighting the urge to turn tail and leave the dead to their rest.

Coward. The word echoed in the back of his mind, goading him to walk on. His steps echoed on stone until he halted before a row of open coffins that hadn't been here during his previous visit. The bodies inside each were preserved carefully, dressed in their finest, as though waiting for him to return.

Something cracked inside his chest, and when Linas's footsteps closed in behind him, he didn't turn around.

"You didn't have to do this," he murmured to Linas. "You didn't know I would come back, did you?"

"I had faith that you would," Linas responded. "It didn't seem right to leave them to rot, after everything Volcan did for me."

Rien bowed his head over his father's calm face. The absence of the staff that ought to lie at his side snagged him like a thorny branch. His family should have been buried with their Relics, but Daimos had taken that option away. Just one more act that Rien would make him pay for when next they met.

For now, he sank down to the floor and wept for all that he'd lost.

———

Upon leaving the crypt, Rien returned to the Astera family's estate without sending word to the Emperor. Not out of shame, but necessity. The Emperor was not known for being quick to get to the point, and the weeks Rien had spent in Zeuten had driven home how much of his former life had been occupied by rituals and ceremonies. Whether Daimos had left the nation or not, Rien had little time for either.

"What do you wish to do?" asked Linas. "All the valuables that could be salvaged from the estate were brought to the crypt. There's unlikely to be anything of value left in the house."

"I have reason to believe there was certain information in my father's correspondence that might be of use."

"Information?" he echoed. "Pertaining to what, precisely?"

In answer, Rien raised the staff, revealing the thorn-covered vines twisting up and down its length. "Pertaining to this."

"That's a new Relic." Linas spoke in a hushed voice. "I thought... but I didn't want to assume anything. After As..."

He trailed off, unwilling to say the name of the old god in front of Rien, and for that, Rien was grateful.

"I obtained this Relic during my time in Zeuten," Rien told him. "However, I would like to know how much contact my ancestors had with Zeuten's Sentinels, since it was they who helped me obtain this staff."

"Oh?" Linas blinked in surprise. "I suppose... no, that's your business, not mine. As for your father's correspondence, I'm afraid it's unlikely to have survived the fire."

I thought not. "I would like to look, just in case. How is the Emperor, do you know?"

"He is well, last I heard," said Linas. "He and his advisors requested extra security after the events of a few weeks ago, and the Trevains were happy to step in."

"The Trevains did *what?*" Rien had the sudden urge to turn towards the imperial palace himself. "They offered to protect the Emperor?"

"Why not?" Linas asked. "Imagine what a disaster it would be if Daimos were to target the Emperor."

"The other families are an even likelier target." Rien found his temper rising. "The Trevains were selling Relics to ordinary folk at the market the last I saw of them. They're tricksters."

"I meant no disrespect."

"No, I... I'm sorry." He pressed a hand to his forehead. "Thinking of that time is difficult for me. If I hadn't been at the market that day, my family might still be alive."

His father had sent him to look for his brother, true, but if Rien had been at the house before Daimos had shown up...

He would have killed you either way, a voice whispered at the back of his mind. And if the Trevains had gained the Emperor's favour in his absence and taken his father's place in influencing imperial decisions, then there was nothing Rien could do to intervene.

Linas gave him a sympathetic look. "We cannot change the past, Arien. Not even the Relics can grant anyone that power."

He inclined his head in agreement. He'd been given a

second chance at life—more than once—and he intended to use it.

The faint smell of burning returned as they approached the estate, Rien climbing over the ruined gate to find a way into the house. Crumbled stone covered the old bloodstains, but Rien's stomach lurched when he recognised the spot where Daimos had nearly ended his life.

Rien glanced over his shoulder at Linas. "Would you prefer to stay outside?"

"My lungs can't handle the dust, I'm afraid." The old man's eyes were watering. "I would very much like to help you, however. Is there anything you wish for me to do for you?"

"If you have an idea of where Daimos obtained the means of destroying my family, I would appreciate it if you were to let me know," he responded. "He held a Relic of some kind, and not one he acquired in Aestin."

"Ah, I would if I knew," he said. "Frankly, I thought the Daimos family all died in exile and disgrace."

"So did I." He vaguely recalled his father mentioning the Daimos family while he'd been explaining why the Invoker families had been reduced from four to three, but he'd given no details of his own involvement, and Rien hadn't questioned him on the matter.

Another regret to add to the list.

With a farewell gesture towards the old man, Rien stepped over the rubble and crossed the cracked flagstones, a detached part of him wondering if the dried bloodstains he came across were his father's or his own.

While the front of the house had been reduced to rubble, he found that the back had been mostly spared, as had the door to the east wing. The exterior was relatively intact, but the fire had left the rooms as little more than gutted ruins. Anything made of wood or paper had stood no chance, but he hoped—perhaps foolishly—that some of the records might have survived.

He pushed the door inwards and walked in, his eyes screwed up against the lingering stench of burning. His feet trod a familiar path to his father's study, and he found the door unlocked.

Turning the handle inward, he found himself greeted with a scorched ruin that was somehow even worse than he'd expected. Imagining what Zelle might have said at the sight of the charred books brought another stab of guilt to his chest, and he coughed uncontrollably at the burning smell rolling off the shelves. The flames had scorched his father's desk and the papers within it to cinders, and he wouldn't have known he was in the right room if he didn't recognise the skeletal outline of his father's favourite reading chair among the ruins.

A faint noise came from behind him. When he rotated on his heel, he saw a pair of eyes watching from the other side of the cracked window.

As he ran for the door, the staff reacted before his conscious thoughts caught up with him. Thorny vines shot from its end, wrapping around the target and lifting him off the ground. Rien halted on the doorstep while the man—no, it was only a boy—coughed and cried out, arms flailing as the vines held him captive in the air. He recognised him now as one of his family's former household staff.

A jolt of horror hit him. "Wait, stop!"

For a long, painful moment, the vines remained locked

around their target. Then they released him, dropping the boy into a heap on the ruined flagstones. He was bleeding, but alive. Thank Gaiva. Thank—

Astiva.

The name burned hot on his tongue, and he choked back bile. He'd almost killed the boy—or to be precise, *Zierne* had almost killed him.

5

E vita looked between the two Senior Changers, half expecting one of them to take back their offer. If she didn't know better, she'd say they were lying outright. Or joking. None of the Changers she'd met so far had demonstrated any sense of humour to speak of, but why would they offer her employment after her involvement in the catastrophe that had seen to the deaths of their superiors? It made no sense.

"Why?" she asked. "Why do you want me to work for you? I left the Changers. I just told you so."

"An understandable decision on your part, given the circumstances," said Briony, "but you have skills which would be valuable among the ranks of the Senior Changers."

Skills? She'd barely passed one test before her ill-fated mission, and it generally took years to reach the senior level. Besides, she hadn't been close to the top of her novice class, and Master Amery had gone as far as to send her to her death to get rid of her. One would have thought that would be reason enough for them to think twice before making her an offer—and for her to think twice before accepting it.

"I appreciate the offer," she began, "but no, thanks."

"Excuse me?" said Briony. "We are offering you a great honour."

"I already have a job," Evita told them. "I don't need to work for the Changers any longer."

Verne shifted in his seat. "What could possibly be more important than helping to protect your country?"

Evita's mouth opened and closed. She'd never joined the Changers out of a firm desire to protect the Crown, but she'd prefer not to admit so to two Senior Changers' faces. Neither did she want to bring the Reader to their attention, since there was no telling how Aurel would react if Evita told the Senior Changers about her new employment. She'd told Vekka and the others, of course, but she'd little expected to be offered a chance to rejoin their ranks.

Even if she hadn't had her new position to consider, the Senior Changers' offer reminded her in an uncomfortable manner of how Master Amery had hoped giving her an important mission would get her out of his line of sight... even if she died in the process. The Senior Changers might not be taking orders from Orzen, but they had a good reason to want Evita somewhere she couldn't spread unfortunate rumours. Who was to say what they'd do to her once they'd lured her away from Tavine?

"I'm a cleaner," she told them. "Cleanliness is very important to the protection of the nation, you see."

"A cleaner?" Briony sounded incredulous. "*That* is what you chose to do when you left the Changers?"

Thankfully for Evita, the door swung open and none other than Aurel herself entered the tavern. "There you are, Evita."

"And who might you be?" asked Verne.

"Aurel Carnelian." She snapped her fingers at the bewildered tavern owner. "I'd like a mug of your strongest ale, please. And another for my assistant."

"Assistant?" Briony's gaze flickered between Evita and Aurel. "You said you were a cleaner."

Verne stared at Aurel, comprehension dawning on his face. "You're the Reader. The Sentinel's successor."

"I'm also Evita's employer," said Aurel. "I'd rather you didn't steal her away."

Evita closed her mouth before her staring gave away her surprise at Aurel's declaration. "Yes. I work for the Reader now. I'm her…"

"Cleaner, allegedly," Briony ventured.

"I promoted her to my assistant." Aurel thrust a mug of ale into the hands of a stupefied Evita and drank deeply from her own.

"Yes," agreed Evita. "Like I said, I'm protecting the country… from dust."

Aurel gave a snort of laughter and choked on her ale. Coughing, she gestured to the two Changers. "Who exactly are you, anyway?"

"I am Briony, and this is Verne," said the woman. "We're Senior Changers, in the employ of the Crown."

Aurel wiped froth from her chin with the back of her hand. "Have you spoken to the Crown Prince lately?"

"As a matter of fact, we have." Verne eyed Aurel with a mixture of disdain and wariness. "A letter from him reached us in the far north, where we'd been assigned to an important mission, and informed us of the tragic loss of our leaders."

"What mission would that be?" Aurel drained her mug and set it down on their table.

"That's classified," said Briony. "Since your, ah, assistant turned down our offer of employment, then she will not be coming back with us, I take it?"

"No, I'll be taking her back with me. Right, Evita?"

When Aurel caught her shoulder, Evita left her full ale mug on the nearest table and gladly hurried out of the tavern.

Aurel closed the door behind them, a grin on her face. "Pathetic, aren't they? No wonder the Changers are dying out."

"I was trying to avoid mentioning your name," said Evita apologetically. "In case they came to hassle you next."

"You thought they might do me harm?" Aurel laughed. "You're adorable, you know that? *I'm protecting the country from dust.*"

Evita's face flushed. "I'm not a good liar. Anyway, I've seen enough weird shit lately to assume at least some of it has a basis in truth. Most of what I heard about the Changers turned out to be true, like their magical abilities."

"Whatever magic they have, they're irrelevant." Aurel gave the tavern door a withering look. "That's why they're desperate."

Evita's brows shot up. "Desperate enough to recruit me?"

Aurel seemed to realise the implied insult in her words. "Desperate enough to recruit someone who already quit."

Evita wasn't fooled. "You can admit I'm not a good Changer."

"You didn't join that long ago, didn't you?" Aurel side-stepped the question. "You weren't fully trained."

"I passed *one* trial," she corrected. "Before Master Amery sent me to my death. Anyway, it's not my skills they're interested in. I think they have another motive."

"Like what?"

"I don't know," she said. "Last time they made me an offer, it turned out to be a ruse set up by that god."

"I wonder what their secret mission was about?" Aurel pondered. "Must have been important, if they waited until now to return."

"They mentioned they were in the remote Isles of Itzar, but they didn't give any more details." They hadn't mentioned whether they'd run into any more deities who'd begun walking among humans, but the Powers were hardly the only possible threats to the Crown.

Aurel led the way back to the Reader's house, where Grandma Carnelian glowered across the room at them when they walked in.

"What trouble have you managed to get yourself into this time?" she asked Evita.

"Nothing," said Evita, mildly annoyed at the accusatory note to the Sentinels' tone. "The Senior Changers wanted to invite me to join them, but I turned them down."

"Did they now?" she said. "I wondered how long it would be before they came sniffing around here."

Aurel sauntered through the room, her eyes shimmering with the hint of intoxication. "They're snooping around asking everyone about the battle a few weeks ago."

The accusatory hint to Grandma Carnelian's voice intensified. "What did you tell them?"

"I gave them the basics, nothing more," said Evita. "I think they already knew most of what I told them, but I didn't give away anything about the staff—or Zelle."

"Good," said the old Sentinel. "What did they know of Orzen?"

The name brought a chill to Evita's skin, an unwelcome reminder of how he continued to haunt her nightmares. "They knew he was giving the Changers orders and that he was unsuccessful at his goals, but not how his defeat came about. I pretended I didn't see any of it myself."

"Wise decision," said the Sentinel. "You'll live longer."

"Might they come here next, though?" asked Evita. "There are gaps in my story and in the Changers' too. They don't know how deeply you were involved, for instance, or that you spent time… *there.*"

Namely, in the realm of the Powers. Grandma Carnelian didn't seem afraid of the deities despite her recent experiences, but she'd neglected to assuage anyone's curiosity as to how she'd survived several days in their company.

Grandma Carnelian gave an approving grunt. "That's easier for all of us."

"They might find out, though," added Evita. "If they learn that you were briefly captured by the Changers, they might want to know the details. Did the, ah, the deities tell you anything?"

"You *won't* live much longer if you keep asking questions like that," the Sentinel growled.

Evita knew she ought to drop the subject, but her curiosity rushed in like a wave breaking on the shore. "You'd tell us if another deity planned to do what—Orzen did, wouldn't you?"

Aurel grinned. "She has a point there, Grandma. You'd tell us if another Power gets the sudden urge to escape their realm, right?"

"Oh, plenty *want* to," she said. "I'd direct your worries towards those that actually have the means of gaining access to our realm instead."

Aurel's grin faded. "Who else does?"

"I have absolutely no idea," said the Sentinel. "Orzen was the first to be called into this realm because someone found his Relic and performed a ritual to enable him to take on a human form."

"Then it depends which Relic is found next," Aurel concluded. "Right?"

"And by whom." The Sentinel made shooing motions. "Quit badgering me, and go and do something useful, both of you."

Evita went to pick up her cleaning materials despite Aurel's orders to take the rest of the day off, her mind churning with thoughts. Did Grandma Carnelian truly know nothing of what the deities might be planning? She'd previously mentioned that they were like humans in many ways, but if they all turned out to be as bloodthirsty as Orzen, the human realm might find itself in a world of trouble.

———

Zelle faced the customer across the desk, trying to resist the urge to politely tell him to leave. He'd been asking probing questions about her wares, one after another, and while she usually had a tale prepared for each of the objects she'd brought back from the mountains, she hadn't the energy for it today.

"This is cracked," he informed her, indicating a piece of crockery. "What use is this?"

"It's a genuine artefact from the time of Zeuten's first settlers," she told him. "You'd be hard-pressed to find one in better shape."

"You can't eat out of this." He put the bowl back on the shelf with more force than was necessary, causing its neighbours to rattle.

"Then might I suggest you try visiting a shop which sells crockery rather than antiques?" she said in biting tones. "The Crown Prince himself has plenty of our discoveries on display at his palace, and he has had no complaints."

She wasn't lying. Most of her customers were happy to fork out a small fortune for any remnant of the Zeuten's first inhabitants, but her patience for dealing with the public had somewhat withered after she'd been away from her job for the longest stretch of time since before her aunt's death. She was grateful to have customers at all, of course, but that didn't change her annoyance at the ones who insisted on wasting her time before leaving without buying anything. The staff might call her wares *junk*, but she needed the money and so did her family.

Whatever promises Rien might have made to repay her for the trouble he'd caused, he'd departed without a coin to his name. If he got himself killed back in Aestin, then she could say goodbye to ever seeing if he intended to keep his word. Not that the money was what mattered the most to her. Absently, she glanced at the staff, which stood propped up against the back of the desk, and wondered if she should grab it and run for the mountains before she lost her temper and caused her unwanted customer to tell everyone on the seafront to avoid her shop. Her dwindling business didn't need to suffer any further setbacks.

The man's staring at me, the staff told her. *I don't like it.*

She glanced up. Sure enough, the customer's gaze lingered on the knotted wooden edge visible behind the desk. "What is that?"

"Oh, nothing," she answered. "It's not for sale."

"Looks like a genuine Relic to me," said the man. "Why… those markings…"

He reached out to pick up the staff, and Zelle instinctively pushed it out of sight behind the desk. "It's my grandmother's walking stick. I doubt the Sentinel will be thrilled if I sell her property while she's away."

"I didn't know the Sentinel was in Saudenne." The man backed up a step. "Is it true that she was responsible for the storms that wrecked the coast a few weeks ago?"

"No, of course not. Who told you that?"

The man shook his head. "If there's magic involved, I want no part in it myself."

He left the shop, closing the door behind him. Zelle rubbed her temples, torn between exasperation and relief.

"You're welcome," she muttered to the staff.

For what?

"I could have let him buy you," she said. "Or any of my other customers, come to that. I might have spun a tale about finding you in the ruins of a thousand-year-old settlers' camp and given you to the person who offered the best price."

They can't afford me.

"Ha." She shook her head at the staff, wishing she'd put it in the back room and out of sight. In truth, though, she'd kept the staff close as a reminder that until recently, there'd been more to her existence than running her aunt's old shop. Granted, it also brought a reminder of what she'd left behind, and she found herself spending the long stretches of time between customers pondering on what Aurel, Grandma, and Evita might be doing, back at the Reader's house. Or Rien, back in his home country— but thinking of him darkened her mood even further.

If you're going to be like this for the foreseeable future, I'm going into hibernation.

"Stop reading my thoughts." She rubbed her eyes. "If I'm not interesting enough for you, then I *will* sell you to the next person to take a fancy to you."

If you want to give up, then go ahead.

"Give up on what?" Closing the doors between the human world and the realm of the Powers? She'd been wasting her time in Tavine, and the staff had all but encouraged her to return to Saudenne instead. Of course, she'd hoped Rien would be around to help her gather information, and the long hours she worked in the shop had given her limited time to ask for news on Aestin so far. Her customers were often travellers, but none had come from Aestin in the past few days. Perhaps travel between the two nations had yet to pick up again after the events of a few weeks ago.

The staff gave no answer, so Zelle returned to work.

Her current irritation with customers aside, she had little to complain about. A view of the sea greeted her each morning, the smell of baked bread drifted from the neighbouring shop, and she could take a walk in the fresh ocean air whenever she liked.

Undoubtedly, she'd miss the mountains for a while, but the lonely ache in her chest would fade in time. It had to.

———

A crash woke Zelle in the middle of the night, with the disorientating effect of someone tipping a bucket of ice-cold water over her head. She bolted upright, squinting around the dark room.

Someone's breaking in, the staff informed her.

Leaping out of bed, she grabbed the staff in one hand and ran for the stairs. In the shop, two broad strangers and a lot of broken glass greeted her.

The intruders barrelled towards her. Zelle swung the staff as she might at a magical construct, but the solid thud as the wood connected with the man's temple jarred her arms so sharply that she nearly dropped it. The man collapsed with an *oof* of surprise, while his companion bore down on her.

Zelle raised the staff, dealing a wallop to his chin that sent him sprawling on top of his companion. Breathing hard, she squinted at the two strangers. The lack of light hid their features, though a groan told her one of them was still conscious.

Zelle raised the staff again. "Who are you? What do you want with me?"

Watch it, the staff groused. *Be gentle with me.*

Zelle ignored the staff's complaints; it was sturdily made and incapable of feeling pain besides. She gave each of the men a prod, and one of them groaned.

"You sell... antiques," he growled in accented Zeutenian.

"You wanted to rob me?"

Ordinary, mundane robbers. She almost laughed at the sheer banality of the concept. Most of her shop's stock wasn't worth much unless one knew who would give the best price for each piece, but these two had evidently heard of her return to the city and had assumed she had something worth stealing. Which she didn't—with one obvious exception.

Zelle gripped the staff with both hands. "What exactly were you looking for in here?"

The man groaned and muttered a few unintelligible words. She couldn't tell what language he was speaking, but a flicker of unease stirred within her. They couldn't possibly have come for the staff, could they? The customer earlier had recognised it as a Relic, though, and if word had spread that she was carrying the Sentinel's staff... well, she was lucky these two had carried no magical weapons of their own.

More to the point, if the wrong people found out that the Sentinel no longer carried her staff, Grandma might find herself targeted next. Aurel, too.

Had Zelle made a mistake in bringing it here at all?

6

R ien stared in horror at the boy, who lay in a bloody heap on the flagstones. The thorns had left shallow wounds up and down his arms, but it could easily have been much worse. His eyes latched onto Rien, wide and terrified.

"I'm sorry," Rien said. "I thought I was being attacked. What are you doing in here?"

"I worked as a servant for the—the Astera family." The boy pushed to his feet with trembling hands and shrank away, plainly afraid of him. Rien couldn't say he blamed him in the slightest, given how close he'd come to bringing about his death.

Rien did his best to keep his tone gentle. "You... you escaped the fire, didn't you?"

The boy continued to retreat, his eyes on the staff in Rien's hands and the thorny vines wrapping around its hilt. Rien debated convincing him to answer some questions, but the poor child wouldn't know a thing about

Daimos or his Relic, let alone his family's correspondence with the Sentinels.

Rien indicated the door with his free hand. "Go on, you can leave if you want to."

The boy didn't need any encouragement to bolt. Rien himself remained still for a moment, watching him leave.

"What *was* that, Zierne?" he murmured to the staff. "Didn't you at least check your target was a genuine threat before lashing out?"

That had never happened with Astiva, though as the staff's wielder, the responsibility fell on Rien as much as it did on Zierne. In the past, he'd always prided himself on impeccable control. Not out of personal pride, but because it was necessary for the families to maintain their reputation as being fair and just. If he went around stabbing anyone who disrespected him, he'd taint their image in the eyes of the public.

Now, though? He had no family reputation to taint and nothing to keep him in check except for his own conscience. As for Zierne? Any hope Rien might have had of finding clues about how his Relic had come to be in the mountains had burned along with the house.

I shouldn't have come here.

The thought drifted through his mind, but he shook it off. He'd needed to pay his respects to his family, and it'd been worth checking if anything in his father's study had survived. He'd learned a few useful pieces of information, such as the Trevains' apparent new cosiness with the Emperor, which he never would have learned if he'd stayed out of the country.

But he hadn't found Daimos. If Rien's enemy had left the city as soon as he'd finished his killing spree, then where had he gone? All the main Invoker families lived here in Tauvice, while the other provinces of Aestin didn't strike Rien as likely targets for someone who seemed to be out for revenge and nothing else. Linas had mentioned Daimos might have taken a ship elsewhere, but he couldn't picture Daimos stalking around the Eastern Isles, either.

Unless... wait. Daimos had known Rien had left the country. He'd also likely found out that Orzen had met his defeat in Zeuten, since he'd been carrying Orzen's original Relic himself. He couldn't be in *Zeuten*, could he?

Rien had harboured the assumption that word would reach him immediately if his enemy was present in Zeuten, but there'd been no news on Daimos whatsoever since the battle. Yet he had no information pointing to where his enemy might have gone.

Rien's steps angled towards the docks. The market's chatter drifted on the breeze, while he soon found himself at the seafront again. He was following a hunch, he knew, but when he spotted the owner of the vessel on which he'd travelled home, he made his way over to him. The grizzled sailor's weather-beaten brown skin was marked with old scars, and his hat sat at an angle on his head.

"Back again?" A touch of wariness entered the old sailor's voice. He suspected Rien's real identity, even if he hadn't told him outright. "Have you brought my payment?"

Rien reached into his pocket for the coins he'd gathered from the secure store hidden in his family's crypt. He had yet to visit a bank, but this would suffice to pay for his passage. Placing the coins in the man's hand, he asked,

"Have you seen a man near the docks recently who carried a staff like mine? An Invoker?"

"A…" The man eyed the staff, pocketing the coin. "Not if I value my life, I haven't."

That means yes. "I have no intention of harming you. I just want to know if you've seen a man carrying an Invoker's staff anywhere near the docks and if he boarded a ship bound elsewhere."

"Those are two very different questions," he said. "You want to know if I saw such a man, or you want to know if he left the city?"

"Both," said Rien. "Would it help if I were to offer you a substantial payment for that information?"

"It's not the payment that concerns me."

Of course it isn't. Even if this man hadn't been in Aestin during the slaughter of the Astera family and the carnage he'd wreaked on the coast, he'd have heard the stories as soon as his ship docked.

"Would it assuage your fears if I informed you that I am the sole target of the man in question?" he asked. "I intend to prevent him from causing any harm to others once I find his location, and I will not breathe a word of your involvement to another person."

The man gave a relieved nod. "That does help."

"I'll give you the payment once you tell me when you last saw Naxel Daimos, and where he was headed," Rien told him.

The captain drew in a shuddering breath. "A man who matches your description hired a private vessel to transport himself away from Aestin, less than a week past. I wouldn't forget his likeness."

Few would, but where in the world had he been

headed to? Not to Zeuten, surely, because they would have found out within days. Daimos would have been quick to realise that Rien wasn't in Saudenne and would have gone straight to the mountains. To Zelle's family. Unless he'd docked elsewhere… but why?

If he *was* in Zeuten, then Rien had left at the worst possible time. He tried to keep his expression blank as he handed over the payment. "Keep the rest. I would like to book passage back to Zeuten on the next available ship."

The captain's brows shot up. "So soon after your arrival here? Not that it's my business, mind. I'll be leaving again this evening, if that would suffice."

"That will do." Whatever Daimos might be planning, Rien intended to reach him first.

In the meantime, he had a few hours to visit a bank and sort out his family's affairs and then buy some supplies. If nothing else, he wouldn't be dependent on the charity of others when he went back to Zeuten.

As for whether Zelle would forgive him… that remained to be seen.

———

Zelle had no choice but to leave the two men lying on the shop floor while she went to flag down a night patrol, since she could hardly single-handedly drag them both with her. She'd bound their wrists with some rope she'd found in the back room before opening the door, shivering as the cold night air ruffled her nightclothes. She'd have preferred to put on a coat before stepping outside, but the night patrol would already have reason to be suspicious that she'd knocked out two large men without suffering so much as a scratch. If she looked too polished and put together, they might start speculating on how she'd achieved such a feat, and whether there'd been magical involvement. Especially if that trouble-making customer had told *them* about the Sentinel's Relic.

The sun was close to rising, judging by the greyish light spilling over the rooftops, and Zelle wrapped her nightgown tightly around herself as she veered towards the bobbing light of a lantern at the street's end.

"Hey!" she called, cringing inwardly at the way her voice echoed down the street. "Night patrol! I've caught a pair of robbers."

The night patrol consisted of three men who looked half-asleep, dressed in uniforms with a lot of shiny buttons. The one who held the lantern swung its light in her direction and squinted at Zelle. "Robbers?"

"This way." She beckoned them towards her shop, feeling more and more foolish with each moment. It didn't help that she still held onto the staff, but she hadn't been sure if her attackers had had company waiting outside.

Zelle pushed the shop door inwards to allow them to enter, bringing with them the strong whiff of ale that suggested they'd taken a detour to a tavern in the middle of their patrol. The broken glass littering the floor would need to be dealt with at some point, but it was the two men lying in front of the counter that drew the patrol's attention.

"Would you look at that." One of the men poked the fallen would-be robbers with a foot. "Who tied them up?"

"I did."

The officer who'd been carrying the lantern studied her through bloodshot eyes. "Resourceful, aren't you?"

His companion lifted his head from examining the two intruders. "That one's dead."

Zelle's throat went dry. "He is?"

"Dead as dust."

Zelle's thoughts whirled, but she didn't need to think of an excuse for her actions. It was plain that she'd acted in self-defence, in which case the law would be on her side. What worried her was the possibility of word spreading about the weapon she'd used to defend herself with.

"They came to steal from my shop," she told the officers. "I heard glass breaking and ran downstairs. I don't think they expected me to fight back when they tried to grab me, and I suppose he must have hit his head. It was so dark that I couldn't see what was going on."

The leading officer crouched down beside the bodies. "They aren't from here."

"No... they had some kind of strange accent," Zelle recalled. "Not Aestinian."

"Powers, no," said the officer. "They're from Itzar, I'm sure. Imagine that."

"Itzar?" she echoed. "Why did they come this far south?"

"I'm not the person to ask." He rose to his feet. "You two, take 'em away. As for you, Miss..."

"Zelle," she said, half wishing she'd simply disposed of the bodies herself by pushing them into the sea or hiding them in an alleyway. "I need to clean up my shop."

"You can clean and talk at the same time, can't you?" He watched his fellow officers pick up and carry the two limp bodies out of the shop, while Zelle wondered what had driven two men from the most remote region of the world to visit her shop with the intention of stealing from her.

She barely knew anything about Itzar at all, except that Zeuten's closest neighbours lived on a set of islands off the western coast of the least inhabitable part of the Range, which even those brave enough to traverse the mountains generally avoided. It had been near Itzar that her father had drowned, which wasn't an uncommon occurrence in the dangerous seas surrounding the islands. While it wasn't unheard of for the occasional boat from Itzar to visit Zeuten's capital, she'd never heard of them being interested in the Sentinels before.

They were after the staff, she thought. *Why would someone from Itzar come all this way to steal from the Sentinel?*

You're convinced I was the target? The staff's derisive tone made her frown. She had nothing else that they might consider valuable—which the staff knew as well as she did.

I'd be more flattered if I had better competition, came the staff's response to her thoughts.

Zelle scowled then realised the officer expected her to offer him a seat. Hoping he hadn't seen any signs of her silent conversation with the staff, she pulled out a wooden chair from behind the counter and tried to ignore the baffled manner in which he scanned the shelves while she pulled out a broom to sweep up the glass from the broken window.

He shone his lantern over a shelf of worn metal tools. "What's all this?"

"Antiques," she told him. "I sell trinkets gathered from the mountains."

"That's what the thieves were after?" His incredulous tone made Zelle feel oddly defensive. "They didn't hurt you?"

She shook her head. "Never had the chance to. I heard the noise of them breaking in, and I ran downstairs and took them by surprise."

"Looked like they were hit with a blunt instrument to me," said the officer. "What'd you use, that stick?"

Oh, Powers. She'd known she should have put the staff away, but the habit of holding onto it had become ingrained in the past weeks. "It's my grandmother's."

The officer squinted at her face. "You're the Sentinel's granddaughter, aren't you? That's no regular walking stick."

At least it didn't have any obvious outwards signs that it contained the power of the nameless Shaper, but the last thing Zelle needed was the officers to strong-arm her into handing over her most valuable possession.

"I am," she admitted. "And this staff is my grandmother's property. I can't hand it over as evidence. She wouldn't be pleased."

He rose to his feet. "Why do you have your grandmother's staff? She isn't staying in the city, is she?"

Zelle hadn't hesitated to lie to that customer earlier, but lying to an officer of the night patrol was another matter altogether. "No, but she loaned me the staff temporarily. Given that I don't have any other means of defending myself, it's a good thing she did."

"This puts us in a sticky situation, Zelle," he said. "See, a man is dead."

"I didn't intend to kill anyone." Her head spun, and a sense of unreality washed over her. "He would have killed me, though. You aren't going to lock me up, are you?"

Self-defence wasn't a hanging offence, but if Zelle ended up being locked in a jail cell, who knew what would happen to the staff? Besides, she needed to ensure the same attackers hadn't targeted her grandmother, too.

"No, of course not." The officer studied her face. "I'm curious as to why a foreigner would come all this way to steal from you, but for now, I'll have to ask you to sign some paperwork if you want to keep that…"

"Staff," she finished. "Thank you."

Powers above. She hadn't even considered that she might have to answer to the authorities for using the staff to defend herself, but to their eyes, those men had been simple robbers.

To Zelle, though, they might have been something else entirely.

Someone wants the staff. And if they intended to target her family as well, Zelle needed to warn them.

———

Evita lay awake in the darkness. This was her first night sleeping in the Reader's guest room, and the bed was bigger than any she'd slept in in her life, but she tossed and turned so much that she found herself hanging off the edge whenever she came close to dozing off.

The third time she nearly fell out of bed, the distinct creak of a floorboard sounded below. Evita groped around in the darkness and grabbed the fluid form of the Changer's cloak, flinging it over her head so it rendered her unseen. Then she trod downstairs, doing her best to make as little noise as possible.

Ambushing someone in the darkness while barefoot and wearing nightclothes wasn't ideal, but she hadn't yet heard any movement from the Sentinel or the Reader's bedrooms, and waking them might alert the intruder.

Or rather, intruders. Two shadowy figures loomed over her when she entered the living room, both male and heavily muscled.

"Who's there?" one of them asked, in thickly accented Zeutenian.

Evita held her breath, thinking hard. Taking on two men at once would require luck as well as the element of surprise, but they both appeared to be human. They wouldn't have been able to get into the house if they'd been anything more. The man squinting at her couldn't see through her cloak, but he must have heard her footsteps, however quiet they might have been.

"I know you're there." The second man spoke in the same accent as the first. "I can sense you, whatever magic you've cloaked yourself in."

He might not be able to see her, but if he knew she'd used magic, then he must have some ability of his own. She'd stand no chance of bringing them down alone. She needed the Reader's help.

Drawing in a quick breath, she spoke in a loud voice. "Get out."

Both men looked directly at her hiding spot. One grabbed at her, but she dodged to the side. The second gave a lunge, and she tackled the man around the middle. The two of them collided with a hard surface, and several crashes followed as the cabinet knocked into its neighbours, spilling their contents onto the hard floor.

"Hey!" shouted Aurel's voice.

The Reader came crashing into the room, wielding a sword that Evita could only assume she'd taken from one of the cabinets, unless she'd slept with it in her room. The men both turned towards her, giving Evita the chance to scramble to her feet.

"Are you the Reader?" growled the man on the right, who was slightly larger than his companion.

"I'm the one who should be asking questions. What are you doing in my house?" Aurel brandished the sword at them. "Go on, start talking."

"We want the Reader." The man raised a hand, and a chill raced through the room. Brightness swirled around his palm like the light of a candle, coalescing into a mass of solid whiteness that he flung at Aurel.

Aurel held up her sword to deflect the projectile, which slammed into the side of the blade, breaking apart like shattering ice. In fact, it *was* ice, but instead of falling to the floor, the broken shards melted before Evita's eyes, sliding up the surface of the blade as though they possessed a will of their own.

Aurel's eyes bulged, and when she tried to lift the blade, it remained rigid. The sword had frozen solid in Aurel's grip, its hilt fusing to her hand.

Evita's heart leapt into her throat. *What kind of magic is that?* Did they have a Relic?

"What in Gaiva's name *was* that?" Aurel said through chattering teeth. "What do you want with me?"

A series of loud thuds echoed from the stairs. A moment later, Grandma Carnelian came into view, a lit candle in her hand illuminating her incandescent expression. "Who are you people?"

Without waiting for an answer, Grandma Carnelian flung the candle at the men. The flame struck one of the intruders, who batted it aside with a growl. Unfortunately for all of them, the candle landed face down on a wooden table, which promptly caught fire. Flames leapt up, greedily spreading, while the second man grabbed Aurel's sword and wrenched it out of her grip. She cursed between her teeth, but her hand remained locked in place, frozen by the strange magic the man had used.

A quiver of dread travelled through Evita. None of them had any Relics with which to defend themselves because Zelle had taken the staff with her when she'd left for Saudenne. Aurel's magic wasn't designed for combat, while Evita had nothing but her cloak. In desperation, Evita ran forwards and grabbed for Aurel's dropped sword, but searing pain burned her hands, forcing her to let go. One of the men seized Aurel and slung her over his shoulder. She screamed and kicked at him, but he held her tightly.

"Hey!" Evita lost her head and grabbed a porcelain bowl from the nearest cabinet, flinging it at the man. He yelled aloud when it shattered against his thigh, but he didn't relinquish his grip on Aurel. The second man, meanwhile, turned towards the spot where Evita stood next to the cabinet, whiteness coalescing around his hands.

Evita dove to the side when he flung a shard of ice at her, and the cabinet's glass front shattered. Grandma Carnelian advanced on both men with a cry of fury, but the next bolt of whiteness hit her in the chest and sent her staggering back.

Evita ran to the old woman's side as the two men carried the struggling Aurel out into the night. Her shrieks echoed through the open door, while the old Sentinel collapsed against the armchair.

Fading screams rang from the garden, while flickering flames continued to devour the remains of the wooden table. Panic seized her for an instant, until the old woman gave her a sharp prod in the leg. "Put that out."

"With what?" Evita ran around the dark room and grabbed the damp cloth she'd been using to clean the cabinets, tossing it over the flames. They fizzled but didn't go out. With a curse, she yanked one of the decorative throws from the back of an armchair and flung it over the table.

"Not the embroidery… foolish girl." The old Sentinel coughed, sagging backwards. Evita glimpsed a dark patch where the icicle had struck her in the chest, but the stain appeared to be water, not blood. Nothing in Evita's training with the Changers had prepared her for this.

Wringing her hands, she looked around the room. "What should I do?"

"Light a fire." The old woman coughed again. "Need… warmth."

That she could do. Evita hurried over to the fireplace and nearly set the place ablaze again while trying to light a fire with shaking hands. Once flames filled the grate, she surveyed the sorry state of the room, from the broken crockery to the shattered cabinet. She'd probably caused enough damage to the Reader's house that it would cost the entirety of the wages she'd earned so far to repair it all.

She's gone. Those two strangers had taken the Reader with them, and Evita could no longer hear her indignant screams. She ran to the door anyway and closed it before the draught put the fire out again.

"Gaiva's tits," she muttered to herself.

At least the fire did its job, reviving the Sentinel enough for her to lift her head and peer at Evita. "Where's Aurel?"

"I'm sorry," whispered Evita. "She's gone. They took her."

7

The instant she escaped the officers' questioning, Zelle went to arrange transport to Tavine again. That proved considerably more difficult than dealing with the night patrol, and she had to invoke her grandmother's name *and* promise a substantial bonus to her driver to convince him to take her all the way to the top of the Royal Road. He very nearly threw the money back in her face when she requested that he wait an hour before returning to Saudenne, in case Zelle wanted to take the same carriage back to her shop if it turned out her family was perfectly safe.

"None of the lords give me this much trouble," he grumbled, pocketing the coin she'd given him. "Even the bloody Crown Prince. What's this trip for?"

"An emergency family visit." One that might not be necessary, but if the staff had been the target, the attackers might have gone after her grandmother first and then come to her shop when they'd found no signs of the staff in the Reader's house. Without the staff, Zelle would have been ill-equipped to fend off the attackers herself, but they might have left her alone if she didn't have what they were looking for.

It was clear to Zelle that she should never have left the Reader's house at all, but how was she to know an attack would come this quickly? The staff itself had offered no opinion on her plan, so she took that as a sign that she hadn't made the wrong choice. With her pack ready, she climbed into the carriage and began her second long journey of the week.

The Royal Road was mercifully quiet at this hour of the morning, and she found herself nodding off as they rattled along, waking only to take brief sips from her waterskin and nibble on a lump of fresh bread she'd bought from the bakery before departing. As the weather was clear, they made good time, and she startled awake when the carriage halted. From the position of the sun, it was close to midday.

"I'm not going any deeper into these woods," growled the driver. "Come on, get out."

Zelle grabbed her pack and handed a pouch of coins to the driver as she hopped out of the carriage. "Thank you. I'll return within the hour to let you know if I need passage back to Saudenne today."

"If I get eaten by a wild beast, your coin won't be much comfort to me," he said to her retreating back, and one of the horses whinnied as if in agreement.

I like him, the staff said, inexplicably.

"You would," she muttered. "If the Sentinels hadn't decided to build their settlements in such remote locations, there wouldn't be any need for this nonsense... what is that?"

A rustling noise shook the leaves in front of her. Then a reptilian head poked out of the bushes, and she relaxed. The dragonet was the size of a horse now, if not bigger, and it struck Zelle that she could probably comfortably fit on his back at this point. If he would let her, which was debatable. He seemed to obey Evita alone, for the most part.

"Hello, there," she said. "Nice to see you again."

The dragonet chirped a greeting, but it surprised her when he accompanied her through the winding paths of the woodland, padding at her side as he usually did with Evita. *Did something happen to Evita?* She didn't understand Chirp's speech, but when she asked the question aloud, the dragonet simply motioned with his wing for her to follow him.

They skirted the village's fence on their way to the Reader's house, at which point the dragonet slunk back into the bushes, leaving Zelle alone. Heart in her throat, she made for the door.

After nobody answered her first knock, she unlocked the Reader's house with shaking hands. *I was right—but I'm too late.*

In the living room, Evita stood amid a pile of broken ornaments in front of a shattered cabinet, while her grandmother sprawled in an armchair in front of a half-empty fire grate. Aurel was nowhere to be seen.

"What's going on in here?" Zelle closed the door behind her.

Evita jumped, dropping the brush she'd been using to sweep up the broken glass. "Ah, you're back. Thank all the Powers. We were attacked."

Grandma didn't stir. Alarm flickered through Zelle. "Is she hurt? Does she need a healer?"

"No!" said Grandma, loudly enough to make Evita jump again. "I'm absolutely fine. You, however, are late."

"I got here as soon as I could." Zelle hastened to close the door behind her. "Where is Aurel?"

"They took Aurel," said Evita. "They used magic…"

"*Magic?*" Zelle repeated. "Who were they, exactly?"

"Strangers," replied Evita. "They weren't from here."

"Not Itzar, by any chance?"

"Yes, I believe so." Grandma lifted her head to peer at Zelle. "Why, did you have a run-in with them, too?"

"Two of them broke into my shop last night," she explained. "I handed them over to the night patrol, but I worried they might have come after you as well. Neither of them used magic, though."

"What did they want with you?" asked Evita. "Did they say?"

"They wanted to steal from me, apparently," Zelle told her. "I assumed they wanted the staff, since it's the only valuable thing I have."

"Then why would they take Aurel?" Evita's eyes rounded. "They said they wanted the Reader before they took her…"

"She was their target. The ones who came to the shop must have thought I was her." Why would they take her sister? "She's the next Sentinel… but why her and not Grandma?"

She wished she'd asked more questions of the two who'd attacked her in the shop. Or the survivor, anyway, though he might not be keen to talk after she'd accidentally killed his companion.

"I'd wager you're right." Grandma gave a cough. "Nasty attack they hit me with, too."

"Attack?" Zelle moved closer, her heart in her throat.

"They were throwing—icicles, they looked like." Evita faltered. "They froze Aurel's sword to her hands, and the Sentinel—she's freezing cold."

There was no blood; the strangers hadn't dealt any visible wounds to any of them, but to a woman of Grandma's age, a mere chill could be deadly. Zelle backed towards the door. "I'm going to get help."

"If you want to do something useful, I'd start with finding your sister," Grandma said. "Don't worry about me."

"We don't know where they took her," Evita cut in. "They might've gone anywhere."

"I'll talk to the tavern owner," offered Zelle. "I can guarantee someone in there will have seen the strangers. And they might be able to offer me some medicine which will prevent you from dying of a chill in your own house, Grandma."

Grandma scowled. "I'm not going to die, but if there are more of those foreigners at the tavern, I won't have you getting yourself injured again."

"I'm not the one who got injured," Zelle pointed out. "I'll be back soon."

With the staff in hand, she left her grandmother by the fireplace and left the Reader's house.

Evita caught up to her at the gate. "The Changers are staying at the tavern. The Senior ones, I mean."

Zelle frowned. "The Changers? Since when?"

"They arrived shortly after you left," Evita said in apologetic tones. "The Senior Changers were on a mission outside of Zeuten while all this business with Orzen happened, so they came here to find out who killed the Masters. They also tried to recruit me to join them."

"They wanted you back?" That made no sense. Evita had left the Changers, and besides, Zelle would have assumed those who'd survived Orzen's slaughter would want to put the entire matter behind them. "I wonder if they know about our strange new friends?"

Zelle pushed open the door to the tavern. The owner, Marita, waved her over with her usual friendly smile, recognising her as Aurel's sister. Marita wore an apron over her ample frame and had her grey hair tied back behind her ears. "Zelle, I thought you went back to Saudenne."

"Change of plans." Zelle closed the door behind her. "Are the Senior Changers still in town?"

"Verne and Briony?" added Evita.

"Ah, no, they left last night," said Marita. "Paid their bills and returned to the mountains, I believe. Why anyone would want to go up there at night is beyond me, but that's the Changers for you."

"They left?" Zelle couldn't keep the surprise out of her voice. From Evita's words, it sounded like they were staying for a while, but they might have left after she'd refused their offer.

"They did," said Marita. "They paid in full and left their rooms spotless, so I can't really complain. Can't say I'll miss them, though. Makes folks uneasy, those assassins do."

"Did you see a group of strangers in town, too?" asked Zelle. "Foreigners, I mean? From Itzar?"

"From *where*?" asked Marita. "The Isles?"

"Yes," ventured Evita. "Two of them broke into the Reader's house early this morning."

"Powers above," said Marita. "Is the Reader all right?"

"She's fine," Zelle said smoothly, not wanting word to spread of Aurel's disappearance, "but I came home to make sure everything was in order. Are you sure you've seen nobody who matches that description?"

"No foreigners here," she said. "Those Changers were the only noteworthy visitors I've had for a while. City folk aren't keen to travel here these days, and I can't say I blame them."

Then the strangers must have camped out in the woods, or perhaps travelled using the mountain paths. The odds of them crossing paths with the Changers were high, especially if they'd left the village mere hours apart.

"Did the Changers mention where they were going?" asked Evita.

"No, but I assumed they were heading back to their base," said Marita. "Didn't you turn their offer down?"

"Yes," said Evita. "I wondered if they might have seen the people who attacked us, but if they didn't stay here, then I guess not."

"No, and I'm glad they didn't," said Marita. "No injuries, were there?"

"My grandmother," said Zelle. "She was knocked down when chasing off the intruders, and I think she's caught a chill. I don't suppose you have anything that might help with that?"

"That I can do," said Marita. "Back in a moment."

While she was gone, Zelle dug out her coin purse. "I don't know if any medicine will help, but it's worth a try."

"She's better than she was earlier," Evita told her. "I don't think the attacker was aiming to kill."

"They took Aurel." She fell silent when Marita returned and handed over the payment for the medicine before leaving the tavern.

The intruders, it seemed, had come and gone in the night like ghosts, leaving no traces behind. The ones who'd attacked Zelle hadn't used magic, but she'd struck before they'd had the chance to demonstrate any abilities they might have had. She hadn't known Itzar even *had* Relics.

Evita cleared her throat. "Maybe they camped out in the woods. The strangers, I mean. But I'd have thought the Changers would have seen them."

"So would I," said Zelle. "You said the Senior Changers were away on a mission, right? Do you think *they* might have been in Itzar?"

"No idea," Evita answered. "I don't know anything of Itzar myself."

"You aren't the only one." Zelle retraced her steps towards the Reader's house. "The Changers are probably halfway across the mountains by now. As for the strangers, they either took the same route or went through the woods. I suppose that with the magic they have, they wouldn't need to worry about predators."

"I guess not," Evita acknowledged. "Some of the Changers were camping out in the woods, too. The Senior Changers rented rooms at the tavern, but I think they made the novices sleep outside."

"That's nice of them," Zelle commented.

"It's pretty normal for the Changers," said Evita. "The Senior Changers might be able to fly, but the novices can't, so they must be walking on foot. I might be able to catch up with them."

"Are you sure?"

Evita nodded. "One of them might have seen the attackers."

"All right," said Zelle. "I'll meet you back at the house. Oh, and I should probably tell the carriage driver that I won't be needing transport again today after all."

———

The head officer of Saudenne's night patrol closed the door to the jail, a frown tugging at his mouth. He'd rarely had such a strange night in all his time in charge of this precinct of Saudenne's law enforcement, starting with the young woman who'd called on his night patrol to help her deal with a break-in. Not such an unusual occurrence, except for the fact that the two men were strangers from outside the country, and their victim was none other than the granddaughter of the Sentinel herself.

An officer of the law had no time for superstitious nonsense, but the Sentinel lay at the centre of some alarming rumours that had reached the city in recent weeks. Furthermore, the woman had killed one of the would-be robbers herself, and while murder in self-defence was legal in the eyes of the Crown, the weapon she'd used to commit the deed had been no ordinary artefact.

This was nothing like the spate of brutal deaths at the city's inns that had racked Zeuten's capital a few weeks ago, nor the fanciful tales of a ghostly boy who may have been linked to those deaths, but it gave him the same sense of unease. The young woman had left town the instant she'd been freed from her questioning, leaving him with a dead man, a belligerent prisoner who refused to speak to anyone, and a lot of questions.

So far, nobody had been able to get a word out of the second would-be thief. It'd occurred to the officer that the man might be in shock over the death of his companion, but his well-honed instincts told him the stranger was more than he appeared to be. He intended to ask a few pointed questions at the docks about any strange arrivals in the city before he returned to question him again.

As he finished locking up, footsteps sounded from behind him. A man and a woman approached him, both broad and muscular, and with the same white hair and pale features as the men his night patrol had brought in. Identical tattoos marked the right-hand side of their faces, curving in the shape of anchors.

"We're looking for a friend of ours," the woman said, in accented Zeutenian. "I believe he's in custody here."

"Ah, yes," he said. "I'm afraid your friend has been implicated in a robbery, but he refuses to say a word in his own defence. He didn't give a name, either. Can you tell me?"

Neither of them answered. An inexplicable chill raced down his spine at the crystalline anger forming on both their faces.

"Where is she?" the woman asked, in a low voice. "Where is the one who murdered our companion?"

"Who?" he echoed. "If you mean the woman who reported the break-in, she isn't around, but that's neither here nor there. Your friend broke the law and will be punished accordingly."

"You don't want to make an enemy of us," said the man. "Get out of the way."

The stranger raised a hand, and a whirling light spun around his palm. Something sharp and cold struck the officer on the side of the head, then his world went dark.

———

Evita walked out of the village, her gaze skimming across the bushes in the hopes of finding a trace of the strangers who'd taken Aurel. Or the Changers. Either would do, but if she'd learned anything about Aurel in the past few weeks, she'd doubtless scream until her voice ran out. Instead, not a sound disturbed the forest save for the rustle of branches and a chirping noise when the dragonet emerged from a bush.

"There you are." Evita beckoned to Chirp, who ambled over to her, rubbing against her side like a cat. "Have you seen the Changers? Vekka and the others?"

The dragonet chittered, beckoning with his tail. Evita walked alongside him until he came to a halt next to the remains of a camp. This must be where the Changers had stayed, but they were no longer here.

"Did they go back to the base?"

Chirp lifted his head, as if to indicate the mountains beyond the woods.

"I think we're in trouble," she murmured. "Two strangers captured Aurel and took her away. I hoped the Changers might have seen where they went, but I guess they already left."

The dragonet's head drooped sadly. Evita studied the camp for a moment, thinking hard. The strangers couldn't

98

have gone much farther, surely, not without transportation. If they hadn't stayed at the tavern, they must have made other arrangements. Perhaps they'd had horses waiting for them in the woods, but if they'd used one of the paths, they'd have left footprints.

Then again, they'd had magic at their disposal. For all she knew, they could fly, like the Senior Changers. Speaking of which, while she was sure the novices would have been forced to follow on foot, she didn't relish the idea of spending the day lost in the woods.

Perhaps the time had come to face her fears.

Evita's gaze went to Chirp's wings, and she reached out a tentative hand. "I don't suppose you've missed flying?"

8

_____

hy did I think this was a good idea again?

Evita's stomach swooped as she dangled above the forest, Chirp's claws gripping the back of her cloak. She hadn't been brave enough to climb onto his back, and while this was a precarious way to fly, she trusted the dragonet's claws rather more than she trusted her own ability to keep her head this high up in the air.

At least Chirp seemed to be enjoying himself now that she'd finally granted his wish and agreed to fly together again. The dragonet's body vibrated like a cat purring, and she imagined his joy at feeling the wind stretching out his wings after the cramped paths of the forest to take her attention off her own significantly lower enthusiasm. The dense trees below prevented her from seeing the full extent of the long drop back to earth, at least, but if the strange intruders were anywhere in the forest, she hadn't a hope of spotting them from up here. The Changers would likely have taken the mountain path back home, though, and they'd have long since left the forest behind them.

"That way." She pointed to the sloping path leading from Tavine up the mountainside. "If they left at night, I can't see them going far without making camp."

They veered closer to the Range, Evita's nerves jangling like a bag of coins, until she spotted several bedraggled figures traipsing along a path.

Urging Chirp to fly lower, Evita caught up to their group from behind. When the dragonet released her and then took flight in a beat of wings, she yanked her hood down. "Surprise."

Vekka yelped and spun around, grabbing for his bow. "*You*. What are you doing?"

"Looking for you," she replied.

The other Changers blinked at Evita in confusion. Some half-heartedly picked up their weapons as though wondering if she'd come to rob them.

"You want to join us again?" asked Izaura. "You're too late. The Senior Changers already flew back to the base."

Evita arched a brow. "They're making you follow on foot?"

"It's good training." Vekka scowled at her. "What do you want with us?"

"Did the Senior Changers tell you anything about their mission in the north?" she asked the group.

"You climbed all the way up here just to ask us that?" asked Izaura.

"Strangers from Itzar attacked the Sentinel last night," Evita told them. "Since the Senior Changers mentioned they were on a mission outside the country, I wondered if they might have run into them."

And where they took Aurel, she added silently. Despite knowing there was little she could have done, she felt partly responsible for the Reader's capture.

"They didn't tell us much, either," said Ruben. "But— well, I heard them talking in the forest. They were meeting someone called the Blessed on behalf of the Crown before they got a letter from the Crown Prince telling them to come home to Zeuten."

"Blessed?" she echoed. "Was that their name, or—?"

"Quiet, Ruben," Vekka snapped. "She's not one of us, in case you've forgotten."

"I'm still on your side," Evita said. "Unless you're working for a deranged deity again, of course."

Ruben gave an uncertain laugh at her comment, but the others were not as amused.

"Think you're being funny, do you?" Vekka asked.

"No," she retaliated. "The people who attacked the Reader had powerful magic. They froze a sword into solid ice in her hands."

The colour drained from Vekka's face. "Piss off. You're lying."

"I wouldn't have followed you up here if it wasn't urgent." Her gaze travelled over the Changers, whose expressions primarily showed confusion, before focusing on Ruben again. "Ignore Vekka. What else did they say?"

"Not much," he mumbled. "Said something about the ambassador not being trustworthy, but I've no idea who they were talking about."

"Ambassador for what?"

"The Crown, dimwit, who else?" Vekka interjected. "That's none of our business, besides."

Evita scowled at him. "Are you sure you haven't seen

any strangers on the road? I'm doing you a favour, but it's not my problem if they sneak up on you and freeze your balls off from behind."

"We haven't seen any foreigners," said Izaura. "Haven't seen anyone at all, in fact."

"And the Senior Changers?" Evita queried.

"They'll be back at the base by now," Vekka said. "And so will we, within a day."

Thought so. She debated telling them the strangers had captured Aurel, but it wouldn't do for word to spread of the Reader's absence. "All right."

"Hang on," Ruben said. "Are you really leaving?"

"Of course," Evita answered. "I don't know why the Senior Changers wanted me back, but I've been used as bait for a god once before. I won't let it happen again."

I might have phrased that more tactfully. Her mouth had spoken without consulting her brain first, and the result was an array of shocked stares from the other Changers.

Vekka spluttered in outrage. "The Senior Changers aren't going to use you as bait, but I'll tell them you said that."

Evita was already walking away. "I told you, I'm not a Changer any longer."

———

Evita returned to the house within the hour, dishevelled and shaking like a startled horse.

"There you are." Zelle opened the door to let her enter and then closed it behind her. "Grandma's sleeping over there, since she refuses to let me move her away from the fire. How did you get on with the Changers?"

Frankly, she'd begun to worry the former assassin had taken off altogether. Evita didn't have any reason to come back, after all, now her employer had disappeared, and she looked as though she'd been through quite the ordeal.

"I had to fly to catch up to them."

Ah. She must have asked the dragonet to help, and while the beast was stronger than he looked, Evita's fear of heights had only worsened following her experiences in the mountains. "You did find them, though?"

"They hadn't got very far, so I caught them up on the mountain path," she said. "They said the Senior Changers had packed up and left them behind, and that they didn't give any details of their mission. They also haven't seen any foreigners."

"That's inconvenient," said Zelle. "Did they have nothing useful to say at all?"

"One of them said the Changers were in Itzar meeting with someone called the Blessed, but they got called back by the Crown Prince." Evita's teeth worried at her lower lip. "I didn't tell them about Aurel, though."

"Why not?" She wasn't sure if she was asking out of curiosity or simply because it felt like the right question to ask.

"I don't know," Evita answered after a moment's pause. "She's still my employer, even if I didn't do much cleaning."

"The living room has never looked better." Or it hadn't, before the scuffle with the intruders the previous night had broken several cabinets and reduced a priceless table to ashes. It was the absence of the Reader that made the house look different to Zelle's eyes.

"I don't know if you meant that as a compliment or not, but thanks," said Evita.

An unexpected twinge of pity struck Zelle. Evita must feel even more out of place here than she did.

"I'm going to visit the Sentinels' cave," she told Evita. "Want to come?"

Evita gave her a doubtful look, but a snore from the old Sentinel seemed to make up her mind for her. "All right."

They left the Reader's house and followed the dirt track leading uphill to the cave. The staff remained taciturn throughout their journey, and while the Sentinels' cave hadn't been much help during her last visit, she needed guidance before pursuing the strangers. Unless their stealth rivalled the Changers', it seemed unlikely that nobody had spotted the new arrivals when they'd left the area, but she knew so little of Itzar that they might have any number of unknown abilities.

Evita and Zelle reached the cave by mid-afternoon. Upon entering, Evita hung back, letting Zelle take the lead towards the gleaming rock in the centre. With the staff in one hand, Zelle extended her free hand to touch the rock's smooth surface.

"Who were the people who took Aurel, and where did they take her?" she asked of the Sentinels' cave.

Evita stepped up to her side, hesitantly brushing the rock with her knuckles. "Where is Aurel?"

At once, fog filled Zelle's vision, masking Evita from sight, and she found herself floating amid the white-grey haze. The voice of the nameless Shaper spoke, loud and clear. *You know who the attackers were. Strangers from Itzar. I think it's safe to assume that's where they took her, too.*

"Why would they capture Aurel?"

You're asking me for more than I can possibly know. I see and hear what you do, no more, and they did not tell you the details of their mission.

"The ones who took Aurel used magic," she said. "You can see into Evita's thoughts, can't you? She said the strangers threw icicles at them and froze the sword in Aurel's hand."

The only ones who possess magic in the Isles are the Blessed.

"The… Blessed?" she echoed, recalling that Evita had used the same word when she'd mentioned who the Senior Changers had met with. "Who are they?"

The Blessed use a magic only practised in the far north, said the voice. *Even the Sentinel knows little about them.*

"Which deity do they serve, then?"

The deity they serve is unique to the Isles of Itzar. To learn more, you must look for yourself.

"That's just bloody perfect, that is." She ought to have known she wouldn't be able to turn her back on Tavine for long before more unknown Powers had begun causing mischief among humans. "Why would they take Aurel? If they wanted her to Read for them, they could have just asked her."

Your guess is as good as mine.

"Where are they, then?" she asked of the disembodied voice. "Can you track them?"

It's not within my power to do so. The larger part of my consciousness is imprisoned in the mountain, and I can see nothing of the outside world except through the eyes of the person who holds the staff.

"You must have some idea how they evaded attention. How do the people from Itzar typically travel?"

By air or sea. A map might have told you as much.

"Very funny. How—?"

An image appeared in her mind's eye of a tremendous eagle soaring over the open sea. Even from a distance, it looked even larger than the dragonet had grown in recent weeks—and a distinctly human figure sat upon its back.

"Powers above," Zelle murmured. "How are we supposed to follow them? We only have one flying beast, and he only obeys someone who's afraid of heights."

The kidnappers might have already reached their home, for all she knew. The dragonet could only carry one person at a time, and while Zelle would have gladly offered to go alone, she couldn't rely upon Chirp to obey her like he did Evita. Which left one option... the sea.

The vision released her, and she pried her cold hand away from the rock. Evita looked up at her, a flash of fear in her eyes.

"What did you see?" Zelle asked her.

"Mountains," Evita answered. "Islands. It was freezing cold."

"You never showed me that." She addressed the rock and the staff at the same time. "Honestly. Let's go back, then."

They left the cave behind, beginning their descent down the mountain path. Evita waited a few moments before speaking again. "I assume the cave showed me Aurel's general location, but I didn't see her."

"I know how they got away so fast, though," Zelle said. "Massive birds. Eagles of some sort."

"Gaiva's tits," Evita swore. "No wonder they didn't need to camp in the forest. They might already have reached Itzar by morning."

"Exactly." Zelle stomped down the path, her temper spiking. "They practise a kind of magic unique to the islands and follow some deity the staff won't give me the details on. I'll see if Grandma knows anything more."

Their return journey passed in silence. Back at the Reader's house, Grandma sat up in front of the fire, looking positively relaxed.

"I thought you left," she remarked to Zelle. "To find your sister."

"Unless you have a boat I can borrow, then you'll have to be patient." Zelle closed the front door behind her. "The carriage already left, so I'm not sure I can even get us back to Saudenne tomorrow."

"The carriage didn't leave," Grandma told her. "I guarantee that poor driver had no desire to make the same trip twice in a day, so he'll have booked a room at the tavern for the night."

"You can't possibly know that if you haven't been out." Grandma's intuition was usually on the mark, but even a considerable payment wouldn't be enough to make up for the inconvenience of travelling to the most remote inhabited area in Zeuten. "Anyway, I hope you're fine with us leaving you alone up here."

"Obviously," said Grandma. "It's Aurel who's at risk."

"What—you don't think they'd have hurt her?" Evita's face went chalk white. "In the cave, I saw the islands they took her to. It'll take at least a day or two for us to reach her, even if we leave right now."

Grandma gave Zelle a sharp look. "Then you can't delay any longer."

"We don't even know *where* in Itzar they took her." Zelle recognised the flash of fear in her grandmother's eyes, but it would do no good to rush into this rescue and end up in even more trouble than they already were. "The Sentinels' cave told me that they flew across the ocean on giant birds. We haven't a hope of matching that speed. Besides, they needed her for a reason. They wouldn't do her any harm."

I hope, she added silently.

"She's no use to them without her Book of Reading," said Grandma.

Right—the thieves had only taken Aurel, not her Relic. Zelle hurried into the Reading Room to retrieve the leather-bound book, whose pages appeared blank, the way they always did when held by anyone other than the book's owner. She tucked it underneath her arm and returned to the living room.

Her gaze fell on the ruined cabinet, where a sword lay covered in what looked like ice crystals. "Is that one of their weapons?"

"No, it's Aurel's," said Evita. "The attackers used magic and froze the sword to her hand."

"The ice hasn't melted yet." Zelle's gaze travelled over to her grandmother. "Would that be enough for you to use your Reading ability on?"

Grandma made a derisive noise. "You want me to use my power on a few pieces of ice?"

"Why not?" asked Zelle. "I've seen you and Aurel use your Reading abilities on fragments of pottery before. This is hardly any different."

Zelle carried the sword across to Grandma and carefully laid it on the rug in front of the fire. Even the flames didn't melt the ice. When Grandma didn't move, Zelle gave the sword a prod with the end of the staff.

At once, the staff turned cold in her grip, almost causing her to let go. The chill was painful enough to burn, and she stifled a gasp.

The Shaper's voice echoed in her mind. *I was right. It is the Blessed.*

"The Blessed?" she said aloud.

Grandma's gaze sharpened. "Them?"

"You know of them." Zelle laid down the staff, her fingers throbbing with cold. "They're like the Sentinels? Or Invokers?"

"In a way," Grandma replied. "The Blessed are said never to leave their home."

"Clearly, they're getting adventurous." Wincing, Zelle extended her cold hand over the fireplace in an attempt to get some sensation back into her fingers. "And they need Aurel for some reason. Which deity do they serve?"

"That, I don't know," said Grandma. "There are said to be many Relics lost in the seas of Itzar. Perhaps the events that occurred in the mountains caused them to stir to the surface."

That made sense. Zelle didn't believe for an instant that the strangers' appearance was a coincidence, not so soon after Orzen's rampage. The Shaper had warned her that the other deities would wake, their Relics landing in human hands… but she'd little expected an attack to target her sister and not herself.

Evita made a choked noise from the corner. "I—the Senior Changers were meeting with the Blessed. The novices told me, but… I never guessed they were the ones who took Aurel."

"I forgot." It'd slipped her mind, in the aftermath of

everything else the cave had shown her. "Weren't they in the Isles on behalf of the Crown?"

The Crown Prince would never have ordered them to capture anyone, surely, but they'd thought he was the one commanding the Changers when it had turned out to be Orzen at the helm instead. A chill rose to her limbs, and the others didn't speak a word for a long moment.

"It's not impossible that a deity has led them astray," she murmured to the fireplace. "But... if these Blessed have power of their own, why would they need to capture the Reader?"

"You'll have to ask them yourself," Grandma replied.

"You still think it's a good idea to walk into a potential trap?" What choice did they have, though? Aurel had no means of escaping them on her own. "Even if I leave at dawn tomorrow, the carriage driver might not agree to take me back to the capital."

Grandma bared her teeth in a grin. "Tell him the Sentinel demands it."

———

In the end, there was no need to resort to threats. The carriage driver had intended to return to Saudenne the following morning anyway, and Grandma insisted on handing Zelle a pouch of extra coins to give him to thank him for the inconvenience. That didn't stop him from muttering about nobles and their unnecessary holidays throughout the journey, but Zelle considered that a small drawback.

Evita waved to Chirp as the carriage rattled along the dirt track through the forest, leaving Tavine behind. "Ah—

I hope he understands where we're going. I'm not sure if he's going to follow us."

Zelle arched a brow. "Might be hard when we're on the boat."

"He can fly."

Zelle decided not to argue the point. Evita would be disappointed to lose her companion, but it had come as a surprise to all of them that he'd remained in the forest long after the threat from Orzen had passed. If he followed them to the Isles, too, at least they'd have another ally.

Worry for the Sentinel's health in her absence lurked in the back of her mind, but she pushed it aside. She'd ignored Grandma's objections and told Marita at the tavern to regularly check up on her grandmother to make sure her condition didn't worsen. It wasn't a perfect solution, but they couldn't take the injured Sentinel with them, and Grandma flat-out refused to stay put until Zelle went after Aurel. Leaving Evita to take care of her wasn't fair either, since the former Changer wasn't an experienced healer and she technically worked for Aurel, not Grandma. Besides, Evita had made it clear that she wanted to help Zelle find the Reader—and in the process, find out what the Senior Changers had been doing in the Isles.

And so here they were, their packs laden with every item of warm clothing Zelle had been able to find in the Reader's house. She'd also packed the Book of Reading, on the off chance that Aurel needed it when they reached their destination, and a rolled-up map of the Isles she'd found in the back of the Reading Room.

While they rattled along the dirt track, Zelle unfurled

the map that showed the Isles' location. Itzar lay to the west of Zeuten's coast, so far north that no markers of human habitation lay on the mainland nearby. Instead, a cluster of islands gathered amid a frigid ocean marked with ominous-looking drawings of beasts. Zelle sincerely hoped they were some embellishments on behalf of the map's artist and nothing more, though it was no wonder the Senior Changers had taken weeks to receive the news of their superiors' demise.

Before they worried about what they might find in the Isles, though, they had to find a boat willing to take them there. Zelle rolled up the map again and did her best to focus on the next step of their journey and not her sister's unknown fate.

Evita had never been in a carriage before, but it wasn't long before the scenery grew repetitive enough that she stopped eagerly craning her neck to look and instead fell asleep, leaving Zelle to brood alone until she, too, found herself lulled to sleep by the rocking motion of the carriage.

They reached Saudenne by early afternoon. Once the carriage rattled to a halt, Zelle hopped out, followed by Evita. There were no signs of the dragonet nearby, but he'd have a hard time hiding in the city if he'd followed them at all. After retrieving their packs and paying the driver, Zelle led the way to the seafront, where vessels of all sizes were docked, their sails waving in the breeze and their hulls bobbing on the gentle waves.

"How do we know which boat might be willing to take us that far north?" asked Evita. "Do we just walk up and ask them?"

"If either of us was Rien, that idea might work." A hint

of bitterness crept into her voice. "Grandma's influence only goes so far."

"Where'd he go, anyway?" asked Evita. "Isn't he staying in Saudenne?"

"He went home to Aestin, of course—without telling me beforehand, I might add."

"He didn't, did he?" Evita winced. "I thought—Aurel seemed to know he was going straight home as soon as he reached Saudenne."

"Did she?" The news hit less hard than it would have if she didn't have more important matters on her mind. "He told her? No, I suppose she guessed. She saw the obvious where I didn't."

Evita said nothing, shifting uncomfortably from one foot to the other.

"It's done now." Zelle pushed down the wave of bitter regret that rose within her. "I assume he promised to pay the captain of the ship who took him home handsomely as soon as he had access to his family's vast fortunes again, but we don't have that kind of coin, so we'll have to do this the hard way."

"Or we can ask him." Evita pointed across the dock, and Zelle frowned. Then her gaze locked on a figure standing near a large vessel, and her heart leapt in her chest. *Rien.* What had brought him away from Aestin so soon after his return? Nothing good, she assumed, and he'd already betrayed her trust. She couldn't rely on him to help them gain passage to Itzar.

Zelle averted her gaze, but Rien had already seen her, too.

9

R ien couldn't take his eyes off the improbable sight of Zelle and Evita standing on the seafront as though hoping to find a vessel to carry them across the ocean. As little sense as that made, some of the worry that had nagged at him since his arrival in the city faded a little. The previous day, he'd disembarked in Saudenne and had made straight for Zelle's shop with the intention of offering an apology. Instead, he'd found the window boarded up and the owner absent.

The sight had prompted him to ask for directions to the local enforcement office in case she'd been inside the shop when the window had been broken, only to be told that the head officer was on temporary leave and that their office was closed. He'd suspected foul play, but nobody he'd questioned had given any hints of Daimos's presence in the city. Nor could he be certain that his foe had been responsible for the state of Zelle's shop. He'd hoped she'd returned to visit her grandmother instead, and that seemed to be true, given the large pack she carried and the travelling cloak she wore. Not to mention Evita's presence at her side. Why had she brought the former Changer to Saudenne?

Rien approached them, his hand raised in greeting, but Zelle strode straight past him, a determined set to her jaw. Rien watched in mild bewilderment as she spoke to the captain of the northbound vessel who he'd questioned beforehand about possible sightings of Daimos—not mentioning his adversary by name, of course—and asked about its upcoming voyage.

What in the name of the Powers did she need a *boat* for? Unable to restrain his curiosity, he changed directions and caught up to Zelle at the pier's end. Evita caught his eye and gave a guilty-looking shrug, but Zelle seemed more intent on questioning the captain. The man's steel-grey hair straggled around his ears, and his pockmarked face bore a deep tan from decades spent on the deck of a boat.

"Look, we don't send ships to Itzar," he told Zelle. "Few do, on account of how most of them don't come back."

"There's got to be an option, surely," said Zelle. "What about traders? Don't they come here from Itzar?"

"Rarely," he answered. "Most of us won't risk our vessels disappearing among those wretched islands."

Why was Zelle trying to get to Itzar of all places? Even Aestin's most adventurous merchants never traded there, and it didn't sound like the people of Saudenne did, either. Before he could concoct a plan, the captain caught his eye, and he found himself striding forward.

"I can help," Rien offered. "Whatever it costs, I can pay."

Zelle whirled on him with anger in her gaze. "No, thank you. We can handle this ourselves."

"I don't care about the payment," said the captain. "Nobody in their right mind would ever agree to take you to the Isles of Itzar for any price. You haven't a hope of finding a boat here in Saudenne that'll dare take the risk."

"Then where is the farthest town you're willing to sail to?" Rien asked. "Carthen, right?"

"Stay out of this," Zelle muttered out of the corner of her mouth. To the captain, she added, "There are two of us, not three, and I'll pay myself."

The captain cleared his throat. "Whatever your squabbles are, it doesn't matter a thing to me. Carthen is our northernmost stop, yes, and you *might* find a local willing to take you to the Isles from there. That said, there's no guarantee. You may end up being swindled instead, or else meet an unfortunate end in those frozen waters."

"But it's an option?" asked Evita. "We need to get to the Isles, by any means possible."

"Then welcome aboard." His tone was a mixture of friendly and bemused. "You've got an hour to prepare before we leave. That sound agreeable?"

Zelle hefted her pack in one hand. "Yes, it does. Thank you."

Rien might have offered to carry her pack, but she swept away down the pier before he could speak a word. Evita struggled along behind her and then shot Rien a look of gratitude when he helped her carry her own pack onto the vessel. It was a pleasant enough ship, much more so than the withering look on Zelle's face when she caught sight of him behind her.

"I told you, we don't need your company or your charity," she whispered. "If you're looking to do me a favour, then you can start by getting back on land before I push you into the ocean."

"She probably will, too." Evita wore a slightly apologetic look on her face. "Why're you so keen to get up north, anyway?"

"I could ask you the same question." He studied Zelle's tense posture. "Why are you going to Itzar? What happened?"

Zelle worked her jaw. "Strangers from the north captured my sister."

Rien's mouth parted. "Aurel? Why would they take her?"

"We're not too certain, but I'm sure things will become clearer when we reach Itzar." Zelle spoke in strained but polite tones. "Thank you for your generosity, but I'm sure you have pressing matters to deal with in Saudenne."

"I came back to apologise to you," he said. "When I was in Aestin, I found out that Daimos hired a private vessel and set sail. I thought he might have come back here to Zeuten."

"I bloody hope not," said Zelle. "That murderer is the last person we need to see."

"Maybe…" He paused. "Maybe he went north, too. The Isles have a rather unsavoury reputation."

"I worked that much out for myself, thanks," said Zelle. "I can tell you I've heard no mention whatsoever of Daimos. Why would you think he's involved with the strangers who took Aurel?"

"Because Daimos has his own reasons to target the Reader, if he suspects that the Sentinels were involved in defeating Orzen," said Rien. "Daimos isn't in Aestin, I'm sure. He must be elsewhere."

Zelle pinched the bridge of her nose. "I have to find my sister. If you want to pursue your own grudges, that's your prerogative."

"This isn't about my grudges," he said. "I'm offering to pay for you to travel to the Isles. It's the least I can do."

"If it means that much to you, then you can come," Zelle relented. "You can't buy back my trust, though. You took off without a care in the world and only came crawling back here when you realised that you'd missed the chance to take your revenge after all."

"That isn't..." He trailed off as the captain came into view with an expectant look on his face. When Zelle raised no more objections, Rien paid for all three of them in full.

Zelle, it seemed, would be slow to forgive him. In truth, he didn't quite know why he'd offered to travel with her and Evita, since there was no proof that Daimos had been anywhere near Itzar *or* Carthen.

Yet if Rien had stayed at the Reader's house, then Aurel might not have been taken. That was a truth he couldn't let rest easily upon his conscience. Besides, if the deities were stirring in the far north, then the odds of Daimos taking an interest were higher than not.

If his enemy wasn't in Aestin *or* Zeuten, then there were few other options. Itzar was not one that had crossed Rien's mind, but the remote area of the Range had contained hidden Relics that even Zelle's family had been unaware of. Who was to say Itzar didn't contain similar secrets, too?

———

Fog drifted around the vessel as it pulled out of the port. From her vantage point on the deck, Zelle watched Saudenne disappear into the distance to avoid looking at Rien. In the background, she could hear Evita telling him about Aurel's capture and their fight with the strangers, which was a relief, because Zelle had no intention of wasting time explaining everything to him herself. Not when he'd probably leave them behind in Carthen and go in search of his enemy instead.

She wouldn't let herself be taken in this time.

It'd take them a few hours to climb the coast of Zeuten to Carthen, a port town which sat in the shadow of the farthest reaches of the Range. No humans inhabited the frozen wastelands at the very north of Zeuten, yet the islands off the west coast had somehow maintained a small population despite their inhospitable terrain. The peoples of Itzar had always remained something of a mystery. Unlike Aestin, they didn't have a strong trading relationship with... well, anyone. Zeuten and Aestin had maintained a close alliance ever since the first settlers had departed Aestin to settle in the formerly uninhabited continent in the northwest, but Itzar had even managed to stay out of the old Aestinian Empire's conquering endeavours, which had swept up virtually every other inhabited island within reach.

As the temperature notably dropped the farther north they went, Zelle suspected she knew why Aestin might have given this area a miss. With every passing moment, Rien grew more visibly uncomfortable, burying his hands in his pockets and pacing the length of the deck. He'd never quite acclimated to Zeuten's damp, chilly climate, and he was the only one of the three who wasn't dressed in furs for the cold weather. That was his problem, not hers, and Zelle had no doubt it'd grow even colder once they reached the Isles.

Finding a local to take them to the Isles would be another challenge, but that could wait until they arrived in Carthen. She'd rather jump into the sea than admit she wouldn't have thought of travelling there if Rien hadn't suggested it, but he was more well-travelled than she was. And rich. She couldn't believe he'd gone as far as to pay for their passage just to prove a point, but whatever guilt she felt over continuing to snub him, she had a good reason to be angry with him despite his generosity.

You're being tedious, the staff told her.

"He's the one who owes me an apology," she muttered back. "He only came back because he wants to use us to give him a ride to Itzar."

I think we both know that's nonsense. He wants to help you find your sister.

"Out of guilt," she clarified. "That doesn't erase how he misled me and left me behind to pursue his own need for revenge. He'll probably take off again at the first opportunity."

Regardless of what you believe, it'll be a lot easier for all of us if you forgive him.

Forgiving him would be easier than trusting him to help her find Aurel. For a while, she studied the curve of the Range on their right, while nothing lay on their other sides except for an endless expanse of blue. Had she ever been this far from home before? She hadn't measured the distance, but she suspected that she'd surpassed her prior record some time ago. Zeuten might be familiar to her, but she'd never seen it from this angle, and she'd never felt quite so adrift. In a literal sense.

Perhaps Rien had felt the same upon his own return to Aestin. Powers above, maybe she ought to repair things between them, if just to make the coming days more pleasant.

When Rien walked up to her side, she didn't turn away this time. "Yes?"

"Zelle, I must offer my apologies for deceiving you before I left you in Saudenne."

"I understand why you did it." She kept her tone calm. "How was Aestin?"

His gaze lowered to the waves breaking across the ship's hull. "Different in some ways, and yet the same as I remember."

A reminder hit her that while vengeance had been on his mind, he'd also wanted to go and settle his family's affairs and to clean up some of the mess Daimos had left behind. She knew he didn't like to discuss his family, so she simply nodded in reply. "I could describe my return home to Saudenne in the same terms."

He glanced at her, and she detected some relief in his expression, as though he was glad that she wasn't arguing with him any longer. His long hair blew in the salt-tinged breeze, while his well-made clothes must have been scavenged from his family's house, because she didn't recognise them from the packages Aurel had bought in Tavine. His long, midnight-blue, buttoned coat and buckled boots might not have been appropriate for the weather, but he certainly was striking in his Aestinian noble garb. She realised she'd been staring and averted her gaze to the sea instead.

Sometime later, the ship docked in the harbour of Carthen among an array of other vessels ranging from large ships to simple wooden rowing boats. The port town consisted mostly of buildings made of a hard, grey stone, and at the seafront, a market had been set up in which stalls decorated in colourful banners sold freshly caught fish and other produce as well as furs and weapons.

Zelle disembarked with the others and was immediately swept up in the crowd of fur-clad traders and travellers. She managed to snag the arm of a passing trader, asking if he knew if anyone was going to the Isles, only to be met with a shake of the head and a mutter about absurd questions. The next person they asked gave the same response, which suggested most people didn't willingly discuss the Isles of Itzar even this far north.

When she found a quiet spot amid the chaos, Zelle saw Rien buying some furs from a trader, negotiating in fluent Zeutenian, and felt a spasm of jealousy towards him for being so comfortable in a foreign town. She hadn't even left the country yet and already apprehension rattled her at the sheer number of strangers around her, departing and boarding ships with an aura of purposefulness.

Evita, wrapped in her own furs, shuffled closer to Zelle. "That man over there? He's staring at us."

She followed Evita's gaze, feeling an uncomfortable sinking sensation in her chest when it became clear the man in question had the same pale hair and features as the strangers who'd attacked her shop. He was older, in his forties, and unquestionably staring directly at the pair of them.

"We probably look like clueless tourists," she muttered back. "Come on, we need to figure out a plan. Who else here looks like they might be travelling to Itzar?"

"How about them?" Evita indicated a burly group of men dressed in furs and with the same white hair and pale complexions. A fair number of people around the town had the same look, but most were buying and selling things.

Her heart gave a jolt when she realised the man who'd been staring at them was approaching at a fast pace. Then Evita gasped, and Zelle's gaze followed hers to another group of three muscular men, who were restraining a large reptilian creature in a tangle of ropes.

They'd caught the dragonet.

10

E vita stared in horror as the three large men restrained Chirp beneath their large rope net. The dragonet's teeth snapped, his wings beating, unable to escape the tangle of ropes. Zelle hissed out a warning, but Evita was already striding over to their group.

"Hey!" she shouted. "Give him back. He's mine."

The men exchanged a few words in what she assumed was their own language. Her heart plummeted when one of them laughed loudly, as though she'd told a hilarious joke, and then returned to restraining their quarry.

The older man who'd been watching them earlier continued to approach, halting next to Zelle. "You need help?"

Evita doubted the newcomer could take on the other three in a fight—he was lean and ropy where the others were large and muscular beneath their furs—but she was desperate enough to try anything at this point. "What are they doing with the dragonet?"

"The... dragonet?" he said. "Selling it, I expect. You can get a nice price for a creature like that."

"They can't do that," she protested. "He's mine."

"You want to sell the creature yourself?"

"No!" Evita bristled. "We're travelling together."

Zelle's lips pressed together. "We're not looking to sell anything, but we *would* like to arrange to travel to Itzar, if you know anyone who might be willing to make us an offer."

He lifted one pale brow. "You want to go to the Isles?"

"Yes, we do," said Zelle. "I understand that this is the most likely place to hire a ship to take us north."

"Ship?" he echoed. "No ship would survive those waters. You'll have to hire a rowing boat instead. How many of you are there?"

"Two." Zelle paused. "Three, possibly. I have to confirm with our companion."

"Then I might see you there." He indicated a small rowing boat docked off the pier. "However, I have no room for passengers."

"That's promising," Zelle whispered as the man returned to his boat. "If the seas up north are as rough as they sound, I'd be surprised if that flimsy thing got there in one piece."

Evita, however, had eyes only for Chirp. The three burly men had managed to subdue him and were now attempting to drag the dragonet into their boat. She advanced forwards, while she heard Zelle groan behind her.

"Give him back," Evita said to the three men. "He's not for sale."

More laughter ensued. Then one of them growled, in accented Zeutenian, "He is now."

"That isn't funny," she snapped. "He doesn't belong to you."

The speaker gave an amused look at his companions and then approached her. Each of the men was twice her size, and they carried sharp-looking knives made of what appeared to be bone, not metal. "Want to negotiate?" he growled.

"You're outnumbered, girl," added one of the others.

"No, she isn't." Zelle stepped up to her side.

The men's gazes fell on Zelle... or more specifically, the staff in her hand. They exchanged a few words which were lost on Evita, but their voices lost their menacing undertone and instead sounded worried. *They're afraid of the staff.*

Evita lifted her chin. "We're powerful Invokers. You know what those are, don't you?"

Zelle shot her a warning look, but the men reacted to her words by taking hurried steps backwards, murmuring to one another in their own language. Then to Evita's astonishment, they returned to their net, releasing the dragonet's head and then his wings. Evita stared at them, heart thumping, while Zelle hissed in her ear, "What was that?"

"The staff," she said out of the corner of her mouth. "I think they're frightened of it."

As for how they'd known it for a Relic, that would be a question for later. Once the net was loose enough, Chirp wriggled free of the ropes and sprang over to Evita, wrapping himself around her waist. Evita petted his head, relief spreading through her.

EMMA L. ADAMS

Behind her, Zelle cleared her throat. "You should probably move."

When she lifted her head, she found that everyone on the seafront within sight was staring at the pair of them. Evita gave the dragonet a final stroke behind the ears and whispered, "Can you hide somewhere until we leave? Don't let anyone grab you again."

Chirp took flight in a beat of his wings, while Zelle rolled her eyes. "Evita, *why* did you bring that creature with you?"

"I didn't. He followed me."

Zelle swore. "He had the sense not to show his face in the market at Saudenne, didn't he? Otherwise, the exact same thing would have happened. Traders of rare animals wouldn't be able to resist snagging him."

"He's not an animal." Evita knew better than to argue the point, but she couldn't bring herself to feel anything other than relief at Chirp for being at her side. "Why did they fear the staff, do you know? Have they seen it before?"

"If you want to ask them *that,* then feel free to risk them seeing through your ruse."

The men had returned to their boat, however, and were engaged in an intense whispered discussion, shooting wary looks in Zelle's direction. If their group hadn't drawn attention before, they definitely had now.

———

Rien was repacking his new furs when he saw the commotion break out between Evita, Zelle, and the three men from Itzar. He missed the words they exchanged, but when the dragonet safely returned to his companion, he returned to the traders he'd been talking to. So far, nobody had been particularly surprised to see an Aestinian like him walking around the markets, but that might change when they got to Itzar, and people had a tendency to gossip. If word reached Itzar that a foreigner, a dragonet, and two Zeutenians—one of whom carried a magical staff—were travelling together, they might as well have sent Aurel's kidnappers a letter informing them of their imminent arrival.

"So you're saying we have to hire a boat of our own?" he asked one of the two fur-clad men. "We've never been to the Isles before, so ideally, we also need a guide."

"You'll have to find someone when you're there," answered the man, who sported a thick white beard to match his bushy eyebrows. "You might get lucky. We don't get many tourists."

That, Rien could believe. He anticipated they'd have some difficulties with communication, too. He spoke fluent Zeutenian and had a rudimentary grasp on the languages of the Eastern Isles, but he had no knowledge whatsoever of the Itzar tongue. He doubted the others did either. "We'll handle that later. Who should I ask?"

The trader pointed across to the end of the pier, where several white-haired individuals gathered around a series of long wooden boats laden with cargo. "Some of those traders might have enough space for a passenger or two."

"Thank you."

Turning his back on the two traders, Rien made his way over to Zelle and Evita. The dragonet, it seemed, had had the sense to hide elsewhere.

"I'm told those people might be willing to allow us to

travel on their boats, for a fee," he told them, indicating the pier's end.

The boats were long but narrow, not as tough-looking as some seafaring vessels, but they were sturdy and well-made, so he'd have to trust the rowers knew what they were doing.

"So you're definitely coming?" Zelle asked.

He inclined his head. "Yes, I am. Would you have a problem with that?"

Zelle's lips compressed. "No, but I'm not certain what you're searching for is in the Isles."

"Perhaps not, but it's where I've chosen to go," he said. "I'll speak to the traders myself."

He approached the group of fur-clad men and asked if they minded taking the three of them to Itzar for a prearranged fee. The men readily agreed, but their boats were laden with cargo and there was only room for one extra person on each boat.

When he told them this, Evita nodded. "I should probably take the dragonet with me to make sure nothing happens to him."

Zelle's jaw twitched. "Haven't you learned your lesson already?"

"I can't exactly leave him behind at this point, can I?" Evita pointed out. "Look, I'm sorry. I didn't know he'd follow me here and cause this much fuss. Anyway, we might need his help."

She wasn't wrong. Evita would be the first to admit she was at a disadvantage compared to him and Zelle, as the only one of their group who didn't have magic of her own.

"She's right," said Rien. "There's no telling what we'll

end up facing in the north."

Zelle blew out a breath. "Fine, but don't let him get caught again."

Evita gave a grateful nod and sprang over to the nearest boat, which rocked a little when she climbed into it. Rien pulled his new fur coat into place before lifting his pack into his own vessel. His hands were already numbing in the chill breeze that blew in off the sea, colder than any he'd experienced before—with the possible exception of the magical storm which had assailed him on his arrival in the Range. When he climbed into the boat himself, it rocked slightly, water sloshing over the edges. He suppressed the unpleasant memory of being shipwrecked on Zeuten's coast, with difficulty.

You volunteered for this, he told himself. Besides, while Daimos might be waiting on the other side of the ocean, he didn't know that Rien had suspected he might be in the Isles. Rien had seen no signs of magical interference on his journeys between Zeuten and Aestin, either, but the boat felt rather precarious. He'd been kayaking on the river with his father as a child, but that was considerably different. Warmer, for one, and not in the open sea.

"How long will you be staying in the Isles?" asked the blond-haired man at the front of his boat.

"I don't know," Rien answered. "Not more than a few days."

"We'll need to return home at once when we've finished dealing with our business," Zelle put in from the neighbouring boat. "Will it be easy to find transport back to Carthen?"

"If you're lucky," returned the man. "If you're going to

be staying in Dacher, you'll have an easier time of it. Is that where you're going?"

"We aren't certain yet," said Zelle.

"You'd better make up your mind by nightfall," he said. "You'd freeze to death if you spent the night out in the open."

He had a point. The Isles were spread across a vast region, but the majority were sparsely populated, and their boat was heading to a village called Dacher, at the tip of one of the southern isles and where the largest portion of the population lived. The odds of Aurel being held captive in the most accessible place in the Isles were not high, Rien had to admit.

"We'll make arrangements when we arrive," he told the man.

Reservations aside, a group of magic-wielding and violent kidnappers ought to be noticeable enough that someone would have seen them. He'd ask around when they arrived.

The man shoved a pair of oars into his hands. "You'll need to row."

He glanced sideways at Zelle, who raised her brows at him as though to remind him he'd chosen to come with them, which was true. Zelle's manner remained frosty, but she hadn't thrown him in the sea yet at least.

What a fine voyage this would be.

———

Aurel woke with a start. She didn't remember falling asleep, but then again, her memories of the past day or two were as hazy as the blindfold stretched across her eyes. Shortly after her captors had dragged her from her house into the forest, they'd bound her hands behind her back and covered her eyes before bundling her into a thick furred coat. Thanks to the blindfold, she couldn't recall any details of her journey other than a frantic cycle of failed attempts to escape. Those attempts had ceased when her captors had dragged her out of the forest and hauled her onto the back of some animal or other. She'd assumed it was a horse until one of them growled, "Don't try to escape, or it'll be an unpleasant fall."

When she'd felt the ground drop away beneath them, Aurel had experienced an abrupt and unwelcome understanding of why Evita feared flying so badly. She clung grimly with both hands to her steed—which turned out to have feathers and not fur, prompting the assumption that it was some species of large bird—and held on for dear life.

Eventually, she fell into a dreamlike state. The flight went on for some indeterminate length of time, in which her world consisted of nothing but freezing wind that made her glad of the furs that they'd wrapped her in, and the sinking sensation of travelling farther than she'd ever been before.

Eventually, her journey had ended when they'd bumped back onto solid ground, and she'd found herself being roughly dragged off the creature's back. More voices had exchanged words she didn't understand, and when she'd complained loudly of thirst, one of the men had dribbled water into her mouth. This unexpected generosity had come to an end when she'd demanded to know where he and his friends had brought her. Upon receiving a non-answer, she spat and kicked at the man, and in return, he'd upended the waterskin on her head. Drenched and indignant, she made several unsuccessful attempts to undo her bonds while they argued and shouted over her in their own language.

In the end, their voices had faded, and she'd fallen into an exhausted sleep.

Now, Aurel found herself sitting up against a hard, rocky surface. She sincerely hoped that it meant she hadn't left the Range, because her knowledge of geography elsewhere was patchy to say the least. If they'd taken her to some uninhabited wasteland in the north, for instance, she'd be easy prey for any predator that might spy her sitting alone and vulnerable. At least, she assumed she was alone, because she could no longer hear her captors' voices.

Aurel stretched out her cramped legs and did her best to take stock of her surroundings. The ground felt solid enough, as did the cliff at her back, while the wind was frigid but not as strong as the upper reaches of the Range. They'd bound her hands and not her feet, so she leaned on the cliff to push herself into a standing position and then shuffled along the rock face one step at a time. Her captors hadn't left anything nearby with which she might free herself, and she had no possessions of her own save for the nightclothes she wore underneath the furs they'd bundled her in. They'd even left her Book of Reading behind, and frankly, she had no idea why she'd been captured if not for her magical abilities.

Finding a sharp section of the rocky cliff, she rubbed her bound wrists against the edge until she worked enough of the knot away to free herself from the bindings. From there, her hands scrabbled to remove the blindfold. When the cloth came free, her breath rushed out, fogging the air in front of her.

She wasn't in the Range. In fact, no mountains at all were within sight. Instead, a rocky stretch of land surrounded her, dotted with a few straggly trees and large stones. Beyond, she looked out across an expanse of blue sea in all directions. Her captors were nowhere to be seen, and neither was anyone else. They'd left her on an island with no means of escape.

"Oh, Powers," she said.

11

*Z*elle rowed. And rowed. Her arms were getting tired, but she'd have preferred not to admit so in front of Rien, so she suffered in silence. In the boat next to hers, Rien made easy conversation with the man steering, seemingly unbothered by the exertion of rowing for hours on end. In his new fur-lined coat, he already looked as though he belonged here.

From what Zelle heard of their conversation, he hadn't told the man what their actual purpose in the Isles was, and in truth, Zelle wasn't entirely sure if it was wise to admit they were involved with anything related to magic. After those men had reacted to her staff with fear earlier, she suspected that the regular folk of Itzar had similar views on magic to the majority of Zeutenians and would prefer to stay out of such matters. While the Sentinels and the Changers were widely enough known to be the source of gossip, she'd heard no similar rumours from Itzar so far, and it was hard to know if the unsavoury reputation circling the Isles had its origins in some unknown magic or simply its inhospitable location. Both were equally likely. So far, she'd seen no signs of any magic among the traders; their boat's cargo consisted mostly of furs and barrels of what she assumed must be food or wine.

The sea grew choppier as they rowed, and Zelle's arms protested at the strain. It was her first time rowing a boat in the open sea, and it felt a little precarious to say the least, like drifting on a narrow strip of wood within the vast expanse of blue. The people of Itzar had been using these boats to travel between their islands for centuries, she knew, but her body tensed at every shudder that rocked the boat, and a shiver of unease travelled up her spine when she realised that she'd lost sight of Zeuten altogether in the surrounding fog.

"How far are we from the shore?" she asked the man in the front of the boat.

"A while," came his terse answer. "When you see land, we're there."

That was instructive, she thought. The staff remained notably quiet from where it stood upright, wedged between her knees, but she didn't need to add to the conspicuous impression their group had made by having a discussion with a piece of wood in front of eyewitnesses. While she was glad the men had agreed to help them reach the Isles, she found herself wishing the dragonet could have carried all three of them instead.

Then again, the beast might have ended up flying in circles, given the fog. She could just about make out the outline of Evita's boat slightly ahead of hers and Rien's on her right, but how the men steering knew where they were going, she could only guess. Habit and practise, she assumed. It wasn't long before curiosity outweighed her caution, and she shifted in her seat and cleared her throat. "I have a question, if that's all right. Do many people in Itzar use magic?"

"Magic?" grunted the man.

"Yes," she said. "With Relics, you know?"

Out of the corner of her eye, she saw Rien glancing in their direction, but he didn't make a comment.

"Not Relics," he responded. "Most of us have more sense than to anger those who serve Gaiva."

"Gaiva?" Zelle frowned. "Who serves Gaiva, exactly?"

"The Blessed, of course."

The Blessed. She glanced down at the staff, but it didn't offer any input. Both Grandma and the staff had referred to the Blessed, but not which deity they worshipped. *Gaiva.* The creator goddess didn't *have* Relics—did She?

"Who are they?" she asked.

"Who...?" He trailed off with a disbelieving cough. "You don't know who the Blessed are?"

"We aren't familiar with the customs of the Isles," she replied. "Our trip was arranged in a hurry."

To say the least. While it might not be wise to admit to her ignorance, she wanted to get as much information from him as possible before they reached the shore. They'd drawn unwanted attention already, and when they were on the Isles proper, she couldn't guarantee they wouldn't run into a scam not unlike the ones that wily merchants in Saudenne unleashed on clueless travellers.

Incidentally, when she'd first met Rien, she'd assumed he'd been the victim of a similar scam himself, since he'd arrived penniless and with a nonsensical tale of a missing Relic in the mountains. While his stories hadn't turned out to be nonsense after all, she'd turned many would-be adventurers away from the mountain paths and had encountered both deceivers and victims alike as potential customers in her shop. She and her aunt hadn't set out to scam people, but it would have been all too easy to sell them junk and claim it was magical. She knew an easy mark when she saw one, and she had no doubt the folk of Itzar would view her and the others in the same way. Given the urgency of their search for her sister, they'd need to be careful.

The man was silent for a long moment. "In Zeutenian, it is difficult to find the words. The Blessed are revered, chosen by the goddess Herself. It is an honour to be granted an audience with them."

"Oh." That might explain why the Crown had allegedly sent the Senior Changers to meet with them. She lifted her head, her back cramping from her hunched position. "Is it likely that we will be allowed to speak to them?"

"With that staff of yours?" he said. "Perhaps, yes."

So he'd guessed the staff's true nature, even if he hadn't asked any direct questions. Frankly, she hadn't the faintest clue how much the Itzar folk knew of Zeutenian magic. For all she knew, as little as she knew of their own. "What kind of magic do the Blessed use, exactly? Gaiva doesn't have Relics..."

"Not Relics, no," he said. "No, they guard a fragment of Her divine Power. It is our most beloved treasure."

Zelle's mouth parted. A fragment of the creator goddess herself? Did one exist? Before, she might have said no, but a fragment of the nameless Shaper rested within her staff. Who was to say the same couldn't be true of Gaiva, too?

She leaned forward, ready to ask more questions, and

the boat rocked unsteadily beneath them. The man swore softly in his own language, and Zelle's gaze followed his to the north of their boat.

The surface of the water had begun to swirl in faint circles. Zelle's blood turned to ice as an image entered her mind of a deadly whirlpool, as described by Rien, which had swept up everything in its path and dashed his ship to pieces on the shores of Zeuten's coast. A boat the size of theirs wouldn't stand a chance. They'd all be pulverised.

The other two men had spotted the danger, and they called out to one another across the water in their own language.

"Can we avoid that whirlpool?" Zelle half directed her question towards the staff.

"It's no whirlpool," came the response from the man in front.

Then a large tentacle shot out of the water, aiming straight at Evita's boat.

———

Evita jerked back in alarm as a towering tentacle rose from the sea next to her boat, bringing a wave of icy water over the side. "What *is* that?"

The man in front of her muttered a curse in his own language instead of replying, while a second tentacle joined the first. Evita fumbled in her pocket and pulled out her knife, but her weapon felt laughably flimsy in comparison to the sheer size of those tentacles. They must have been easily twice or three times the height of a person and thicker than their boat.

The man steering her boat displayed no fear, however.

Keeping a grip on the oar with one hand, he reached for a knife at his waist made of what looked like sharpened bone. Her throat went dry as she realised the two other men had drawn similar weapons, as if they planned to *fight* that thing. Its tentacles looked as tough as leather, and given the swirling water, the rest of the creature's body must have been *beneath* their boats.

All notions of jumping into the water and swimming for her life vanished in a flash.

Rien, however, stood up in his boat and raised his staff. Zelle, her eyes wide and her face pale, did likewise.

The man in front of her shouted something at the creature, waving his knife. The boat jerked to the side, closer to the tentacle, and he brought his hand down in a slashing motion. The knife snagged on hard scales but drew a stream of bright-red blood to the surface. The tentacle reared back and hit the surface of the water hard enough to drench them both. Evita spat out a mouthful of salt water, gasping for breath, and her heart gave a lurch when she saw that several more tentacles had risen from the water to circle the other two boats, bringing swirling eddies to the surface of the water.

Zelle and Rien both wielded their staffs, hitting out at any tentacles that came near them, but it was impossible for them to reach any farther without falling into the water. At least six tentacles waved above the water's surface, and given the way they were spaced out, she had the sinking suspicion that the creature was big enough to cover the entire area beneath both their boats.

What kind of monstrosity is this?

A tentacle reached for Evita, who swiped with her knife. She might as well have fought with a toothpick, for the knife made no impact on the tough, leathery surface. The tentacle smacked into her wrist, freeing the knife from her grip and sending it plummeting into the depths of the abyss.

"Gaiva's tits," she said.

A screeching cry echoed overhead, and she raised her head. As the tentacle reached for Evita again, Chirp flew downwards and dug in his claws and teeth. The tentacle flopped from side to side, narrowly avoiding swatting Evita out of her boat, and droplets of crimson spattered the water.

The beast shook the dragonet loose, but the winged reptile flew too high for the tentacles to grab it in retaliation. While Zelle and Rien fought the best they could and the islanders' knives had dealt several deep blows, it was Chirp who did the most damage. Once again, he dove and swiped, until every one of the beast's tentacles had left the others alone in favour of trying to knock the dragonet out of the air.

Chirp moved too fast, though. He dove and swiped, dove and swiped, and each round riled up the beast more until Evita glimpsed the terrifying sight of its gigantic maw beneath the water's surface, almost wide enough to swallow their boat whole.

"It's coming to the surface!" she yelled.

The islanders exchanged more shouts, but Rien struck first. Leaning over the side of his boat, he shouted, "Zierne!"

At once, a torrent of thorny vines shot out of the staff, wrapping around the nearest tentacles and piercing them all over. The water's surface roiled, pitching their boats sideways.

"You're going to knock us all into the sea!" Zelle yelped, her sodden hair plastered to her face and her hands gripping the edge of her boat. Evita, in a similar position, watched the dragonet take another dive at the beast, whose toothy maw was close enough to snap at the edge of their boats.

Releasing the tentacles, Rien's thorns dove straight into the mouth of the beast, plunging below the water. A horrible screeching noise echoed from below, and a wave of salty water washed over Evita's head. She scrambled to grab the boat's sides but found nothing beneath her hands but icy water. She kicked frantically, but she'd never swum in this deep water before, and the cold turned her legs into dead weights. Her fur coat weighed her down, and the cloak of Changing she'd worn underneath didn't help in the slightest. Some use it'd be if she drowned.

Sharp claws dug into her shoulders, and then Chirp lifted her out of the water and high up into the air. Her breath escaped in a wheezing cough, her vision blurry and her mouth full of the taste of salt. The sea monster's discordant shrieks continued to echo while she flailed in the air, blinking hard until the fog cleared enough for her to see the water below. For once, it wasn't the distance back to earth that she feared the most. If the others had perished, she didn't know what she'd do.

Her heart lifted when she saw Rien's boat, upright amid the churning mass of tentacles and water darkened with the creature's blood. Zelle's had survived, too, but Evita's own vessel hadn't been so lucky. The man who'd been steering clung to the upside-down wreckage of his boat, waving furiously at his companions.

"I'm sorry!" she yelled at him, but she must have been

too high up for him to hear a word she said. The other men moved in to rescue their friend, while she released an exhale of relief. They'd survived... and Powers above, she'd never been gladder that she hadn't sent Chirp away.

The dragonet didn't relinquish his grip on her as they flew onwards into the fog.

12

R ien watched as the thorny vines returned to the water's surface, leaving a trail of crimson in their wake before wrapping around the staff again. The beast's last flailing tentacles stilled, lying in the water like collapsed pillars, and he shuddered inwardly at the sight of its maw gaping open to reveal several rows of sharp teeth. They'd had a narrow escape.

He had to admit, he hadn't expected the result to be quite so destructive, which might have been foolish of him, given Zierne's apparent propensity for overreacting to the slightest threat. Unlike the situation with the servant boy, the deity's response in this situation was entirely justified, but the man steering his boat didn't offer him a word of thanks, instead picking up his oar again and beginning to row through the wreckage.

That was when Rien spotted a pair of flailing hands in the water. One of the islanders had fallen into the sea when the beast had tipped over Evita's boat, but it seemed the dragonet had carried her out of range. He'd thought that dragonet was more trouble than it was worth, but now the beast had saved Evita's life. As he watched, the pair of them disappeared into the fog, towards... was that land ahead of them?

He sincerely hoped it was, because all of them were soaked to the skin and would catch their deaths of cold if they didn't reach warmth and shelter soon. When he looked at the other boat, he saw that Zelle's lips were blue, her hair plastered to her face and her grip on her staff taut. She'd been hard-pressed to use her staff to fight off a beast that was no construct of magic but made of flesh and blood, and even he'd had considerable difficulty despite his staff's longer reach.

And to think that they hadn't even reached the islands yet.

The man in front of Rien pulled his shivering companion into their boat, shaking his head at the discarded cargo floating in the water. The dishevelled, soaking-wet islander moved into the back of the boat, meeting Rien's eyes with an expression of distrust. "Be careful with that power you wield, boy. It outsteps you."

Rien hadn't the faintest idea what he meant by that, but he did his best to be polite. "I did what was necessary to save our lives. Are we almost at the Isles yet?"

"Not far," the man steering the boat said curtly.

Rien picked up his oar again, and they moved forward. When their boat caught up to Zelle's, she leaned over to whisper to him, "I can't imagine why people rarely travel to the Isles."

"I can guess why their boats tend to come back in pieces," he murmured back.

Thankfully, before long they came within view of a

shore that filled his peripheral vision. Rocky cliffs climbed in layers, dotted with stone buildings. More long boats in the same style as their own littered the beach that ran along the front of the island. From what he could tell, the village wasn't large enough to contain more than a few hundred inhabitants, but if this was Dacher, their destination, it was bigger than any other settlement in the Isles.

Their boats came to a halt near a short pier, at which point their companions all but threw his and Zelle's packs onto the shore and climbed out. Evita hadn't been so lucky, since her possessions had sunk with the other boat.

"Thank you." Rien dug into his pack for the coins he'd obtained from the market after convincing the trader he'd bought his furs from to give him change in the Itzar's large silver coins instead of Zeutenian currency. "We appreciate your help reaching the islands in one piece."

"I fear I may live to regret that choice," responded the trader. "Go in peace, visitors."

Zelle glanced over her shoulder at the islanders from her position beside Rien. "I think it's safe to say they have no intention of helping us get home when this is over."

"We don't even know how long we'll be staying here," he reminded her. "Best not to think of the return trip yet."

They were already attracting stares from the few locals milling around the pier. Rien's crimson staff was distinctive, as was his Aestinian colouring, while the dragonet was bound to have drawn attention as well.

Zelle's eyes narrowed, her breath puffing out. He probably hadn't helped her mood by mentioning the uncertainty of their trip's length, even if it was true. "We'd better find somewhere to warm up," she said. "Where in

Gaiva's name is Evita? The dragonet can't have got lost in the fog, surely."

He didn't see any signs of the former Changer on the seafront, though the sky was already growing dark, not helped by the low-level fog surrounding the island. Aurel was nowhere to be seen either, and her bright hair was distinctive enough that she'd stand out in a crowd. Especially in a place like this, where everyone either had salt-white or nut-brown hair. His gaze swept across the boats bobbing in the shallows, and a familiar lanky figure snagged his attention.

Evita waved at them, and behind her stood the man who'd accosted them at Carthen. As they approached her, Evita bounded over to meet them. "I talked to that man over there. He's willing to give us a tour."

"Is he, now?" Rien studied the man, who was in the process of unloading packages from his boat. He must have been lucky enough to escape the trouble they'd faced during their own journey, because his boat remained as sturdy as ever.

As if sensing them watching him, the man left his packages in a neat stack and faced Zelle and the others. "Good, you did make it to the other side."

"Despite the ocean's best efforts," said Zelle. "And you are...?"

"Name's Gatt," he replied. "Some call me Gatt the Lucky. I have to be, to make supply trips across these waters. Some call this the Perilous Sea, and they aren't wrong."

"You saw that beast?" asked Rien. "Do similar incidents happen often?"

"Not typically to folk like you." Gatt's gaze lingered on

the staff in Rien's hand. "They don't like magic, those sea monsters don't."

Rien and Zelle exchanged perplexed looks. If the beasts usually left Invokers alone, then why had it singled them out?

"Is that why our guides reacted the way they did?" he asked. "They were fine with us paying for our passage across the ocean, before…"

"Before you used magic?" said the man. "Yes, I expect they're the sort who respect the gods but prefer for them not to get that close."

"That makes no sense," said Zelle.

"I think it does," said Rien, having known a great number of people who placed the Invokers in high regard but who would have fled in terror if they met old Volcan Astera in person. The thought brought a familiar ache to his chest, but a disconnected one, outweighed by the current practical issues they had to deal with. "If you can recommend somewhere we can stay for the night, we'd be most grateful."

"And a warm meal, too," added Zelle. "Our friend needs to get inside before she catches her death of cold."

"The inn at the top of the hill would suit your needs," he responded. "Come, I'll take you there."

He did so, leading them up a narrow road between the stone houses. The settlement, he would guess, was slightly smaller than Tavine, and the inn sat near its topmost point, which afforded a picturesque view of the rest of the village. Long wooden boats filled the waters around the island, bobbing in the waves. Rien supposed most people must get around the Isles on the water, which struck him as a risky endeavour, unless that sea monster's appearance was a rare accident. Or perhaps it only targeted outsiders. Granted, a beast of that size would be hard-pressed to navigate the narrower passages between this island and its neighbours, but unless they obtained a new boat, so would they.

Rien thanked their guide when he left them at the doors of the inn, at which point he and Zelle had a brief argument over who would pay for their rooms. It must be a matter of pride for her as much as it was for him, but since Rien was the only one of the three who carried the right currency, the others agreed to let him handle the payment.

They were given a single room between the three of them, and they removed their sodden coats before leaving them in front of the fireplace. A cheery maid offered to draw baths for anyone who wanted one, and Rien and Zelle agreed to let Evita go first, as she'd been shivering violently since she'd fallen into the icy water. The two of them waited in chairs near the fireplace, a strained silence spreading between them. Rien supposed he ought to get used to those silences for the duration of their visit, unless he found a way to convince Zelle that he'd come here to help and not simply as another step of his quest for revenge on Daimos.

Zelle herself sat for only a moment before she went to speak to the inn's owner. He warmed his hands in front of the fire while he waited for her to return, which she did in due course.

"They're preparing a warm meal for us as we speak," she said.

"Good." His insides felt hollow with hunger, now that the shock of the clash with the sea monster had begun to wear off. "I didn't anticipate we'd have this long a journey."

"I can only assume that the people who brought Aurel here flew *over* the giant sea monsters." Zelle shook her head. "That's what I get for not listening to the stories. I know better than to leave everything to chance."

"Did the owner mention seeing Aurel?" he queried. "Should we ask?"

"I'm not certain she's been in Dacher at all," Zelle admitted. "The owner hasn't seen her, but he told me that he'd ask if any of the locals have spotted a redheaded woman from Zeuten. I imagine they'd remember if they had."

"True," Rien acknowledged. "If they haven't, she must be on another island, which means we'll need transportation."

Her brow pinched. "Powers above, I can't believe I'm thinking of getting into a boat again after that."

"I know." His hand strayed unconsciously to the staff leaning against the side of his chair. "The people of Itzar must manage fine."

"From what I've seen, they're more scared of us than they are of giant sea monsters." Zelle gave a short laugh. "Not all of them, of course, but I didn't tell the owners about…" She trailed off, but he didn't miss the way her hand lingered on the rim of her own staff.

"I know." He leaned forwards in his seat, gripped by the need to improve her mood but quite unsure of how to go about it. "If you ask me, I should have demanded a partial refund on our journey. Not informing your passengers of potential hazards in the waters is hardly ethical."

She gave a faint smile, suggesting her anger towards him had cooled a little after all. Good. They would need that trust if they wanted to survive.

"How many of those silver coins do you have?" she asked. "The last thing we need to do is overspend and end up stranded, and I'm not convinced that anyone here is willing to accept payment in Zeutenian coin."

"I have enough," he said. "The boat trip here wasn't expensive, and I asked for change in Itzar's currency at Carthen."

"I wish I'd thought to do the same," she said. "I don't suppose you know any of their language?"

"No," he replied. "My family, and Aestin in general, has never had a closely established relationship with the Isles. They're too far away to have been invaded or conquered."

"I'm guessing the sea monsters are a deterrent." She rolled her eyes. "This is my payback for being annoyed at the tourists who keep getting themselves lost in the mountains back in Zeuten, I can tell. Except we at least dressed appropriately for the weather."

"Yes, we did," said Rien. "I'd say our first order of business tomorrow will be to obtain our own boats and ask our guide to take us to see the... what did he call them, the Blessed?"

Zelle's gaze drifted to the fireplace. "I'm not so sure they accept visitors. I also get the impression they rarely leave their own island, so it's anyone's guess as to whether they'll have seen Aurel or not."

"No, but they're supposedly allied with *Gaiva*." He spoke in a hushed voice in case anyone was listening in. "I'd like to know if it's true, wouldn't you?"

"I would," she relented. "I'd also be very curious to learn why those men feared my staff so much."

"What does the staff have to say about all this?"

"Nothing," she said. "It's been quiet since we got here."

That didn't strike him as a good sign, though when he studied her profile, she didn't quite meet his eyes. Was she telling the truth? He wouldn't blame her for hiding things from him at this point, but if they wanted to navigate this unfamiliar land, they needed to trust one another.

———

Evita shivered, perched on an uncomfortable wooden seat at their table in the corner of the tavern. She'd taken a hot bath and changed from her soaked furs into some spare clothes Zelle had loaned her, but the cold sea air swept in through every crack in the walls and waged a constant battle with the fire roaring on the opposite side of the room. They'd dined on roasted fish and root vegetables, but even the warm food couldn't quell the chill growing inside her.

Zelle and Rien had settled into the inn's cosy atmosphere right away, and they were currently introducing some of the locals to a card game Evita was unfamiliar with. She was too distracted by her concern for Chirp, who'd been forced to sleep outside in the cold—and, gnawing at the back of her mind, the worry that she'd made a mistake in coming here at all.

It was all very well trying to make up for not being able to prevent Aurel's capture, but she had been the sole participant in the rescue mission without any magical talent to speak of, and she'd had nothing to contribute to their fight with the sea monster except for the dragonet and a slightly damp Changer's cloak. If they found worse awaited them deeper in the Isles, she'd be hard-pressed to help without being a burden.

Evita glanced up when someone said her name, finding Zelle peering at her face. "Are you all right?"

She shrugged. "Just tired. Might be getting a cold."

"Have another warm drink," said Zelle. "Anyway, we found out some useful information from the locals, concerning the Blessed."

"Who, exactly, are they?" she queried. "Aside from important enough to meet with the Senior Changers?"

"I think they're Itzar's equivalent to the Invoker families," Zelle explained, "but they're treated more like advisors than rulers. Anyway, everyone respects them and won't hear a word against them for fear of angering the gods. Specifically, Gaiva. I'm not yet sure if the people who took Aurel are connected to them, but so far, it's our only lead."

Evita turned this information over in her mind. "Do people often ask them for advice, or are they as remote as the Crown Prince is?"

"Most ordinary people keep their heads down and don't bother anyone with a connection to the deities at all. Sensible of them," she added wryly. "Anyway, if anyone knows where Aurel is, it'll be them, and I think they'll be intrigued enough to hear us out once they learn why we're here. Want to head to see them tomorrow?"

"I suppose," said Evita, thinking of the way those men had reacted when she'd claimed to be an Invoker. The Blessed, no doubt, would not be fooled if she tried the same with them. "Unless they're only willing to speak to, you know, Sentinels. And magicians. Whatever they call them here."

"I don't think they'd have a problem with you accompanying me to see them," Zelle told her. "It's up to you, but we can use all the allies we can get. Including the dragonet, if he's around."

Evita fidgeted in her seat, certain that Zelle had read more from her expression than she'd wanted to let on. "He is, I think."

"Also..." She glanced behind her at Rien, who was comfortably discussing the card game with the locals. "We can't count on Rien's money lasting throughout our trip, and it turns out it's damned difficult to exchange currency out here in the Isles. Rien had the bright idea of gambling with the locals for some of their own currency as well as information. They got the hang of the rules of Relics and Ruins pretty quickly, and I bet you can do the same. What do you think?"

Evita eyed the cards scattered on the pockmarked wooden table. "I've never gambled before."

"It's easy enough when you know the rules." Zelle beckoned to her. "Here, I'll teach you."

She gave Evita a brief explanation of each of the cards, which prompted a vague childhood memory of playing cards with her fellow villagers years ago. The locals had wasted no time in coming over to their table for a chance at winning the newcomers' coin, and when Evita offered to join in the next game, a large man with a shaved head pointed to her across the table and said a few words she didn't understand.

"I'm sorry, I don't speak the Itzar language," she told him.

Another pale-haired man joined their group, who she recognised as their aspiring guide, Gatt. "He's asking if you're willing to bet your cloak on the next game."

Oh, Powers. Evita had stripped off her furs to dry them out, but she'd kept her Changer's cloak on out of habit. However much they might need the money, she'd rather not risk parting with it in a game of cards.

"No," she said firmly. "That's off the table."

The men exchanged more words, which Gatt translated for her. "He said he's seen those cloaks before."

Her heart missed a beat. "You've seen the Changers?"

Had they stayed here while they'd been visiting the Blessed? There were few other places of accommodation in the region, so it was possible that they had.

"He said he'll tell you more if you win the next game," Gatt added.

Evita nodded. "All right, but I won't gamble with the cloak."

"If you lose, then tell me where you got it," said the man in a strong accent. "Deal?"

Zelle shot her a warning look, but Evita had no coin to gamble with, so she reached for the cards. "Deal."

The game was relatively straightforward, consisting of assembling a winning hand before one's opponent. Generally, they each kept drawing and discarding one card per turn, but on her second turn, Evita lucked out and drew one of the three Great Power cards—Invicten, deity of illusion—which granted her the ability to select one new card of her choice from the deck. That gave her a winning hand, which the others greeted with incredulity until she revealed her cards to the table.

"There." She found herself suppressing a grin as she

faced the man who'd made the offer to her. "Can you tell me when and where you saw the Changers? People wearing these cloaks?"

Gatt wore a slight smile when he leaned in to hear the man's words and then translated for her. "He says the cloaked ones came here to the Isles to speak to the Blessed."

That much she already knew. "About what?"

"I don't expect anyone knows what they spoke of except for the Blessed themselves," he said. "For more information, you'll have to play another game."

Flush from her victory, Evita agreed. "Fine, I'll play again. If I win, tell me where you saw them and what they said."

Perhaps she could make something of this adventure after all.

13

A long time passed before Aurel's captors returned to find her. In truth, she was almost relieved to see them by that point, having wondered if they'd abandoned her to starve to death on this Powers-forsaken island. From her best guess, it'd been a day or more since her arrival, and they hadn't given her any food during that time. The only animals she'd seen were gulls wheeling in the sky, and the only plant life consisted of bare, straggly trees and strange grasses that might be poisonous to humans.

She'd paced the length of the island so many times that she'd lost count before they appeared like mirages on the surface of the water, steering their long wooden boats towards her. In addition to the two men who'd brought her here, she glimpsed two newcomers, one male and one female. They all wore similar furred coats and thick boots, and their light-coloured hair was tangled, as to be expected with the wind battering Aurel's face and seeking out every gap in her furs. They also carried weapons strapped to their belts which appeared to be made out of bone. Aurel fervently hoped the bone was animal, not human. One of the men caught her looking and bared his teeth in a grin. They were all powerfully built, and they had her outnumbered, but she refused to show any fear. Instead, Aurel bared her teeth right back at him.

Rather than addressing her, the strangers exchanged a few words with one another, and she began to wish she'd learned more of the language so that she'd have some warning if they were readying themselves to attack her. In the Itzar language, she knew 'hello', 'goodbye', and several words that weren't appropriate for polite company. Not that this situation qualified as such, since they'd *kidnapped* her. She didn't think they'd have brought her all this way if they planned to slaughter her, either, though at the moment, they were acting as though they'd forgotten she was even there.

Aurel cleared her throat loudly and addressed the newcomers in Zeutenian. "Aren't you going to introduce yourselves?"

The woman gave her a brief, dismissive glance. A tattoo of an anchor covered one of her cheeks, while her salt-white hair was tied back behind her ears. Her voice was heavily accented, but she responded in fluent Zeutenian. "She's younger than I expected."

"She has a name," Aurel retaliated. "You know, it's common courtesy where I come from to look at the person we're talking to when we introduce ourselves. I'm Aurel. And you are?"

Frostiness slid into the woman's eyes when she glared down at her. Too late, Aurel remembered the icy magic the two men had wielded against her, and she had no doubt that the others had the same abilities.

"My name is Del," she said grudgingly. "This is Toth, my brother."

She jerked her head at the man at her side, who had an identical tattoo on his face and several others visible on his neck above the collar of his furred coat.

Aurel's gaze flickered to the two muscular men who'd brought her here. They had similar salt-white hair to their new companions, but one was thicker and more scarred while the other was younger, around Zelle's age. When neither spoke, she said, "And what about these..." She then used one of the few words she knew in their language, which roughly translated as "herring-brains".

It was the politest insult she knew, but her words had quite the effect. The two men turned on her, furious expressions rippling across their faces.

"Careful what you say, girl," the younger man growled at her in Zeutenian. "You're a long way from home."

"Why'd you bring me to the arse-end of nowhere?" she responded. "What do you want with me?"

"We need your abilities," he replied. "You're the Reader, aren't you?"

"If I said no, would you return me to Zeuten unharmed?"

Toth gave an unfriendly laugh. "We already know you're the Reader. We need your help."

Aurel blinked at him. "You can't be serious."

If they needed the Reader, why in the name of the Powers had her captors left the Book of Reading behind? They ought to know she couldn't use her abilities effectively without it, and besides, it made no sense for them to have dragged her all the way here unless they planned to ensure that she would never return home. They intended her to meet her end here.

Aurel would not accept it.

Del beckoned to her. "You'll come with us."

"I don't think so." Aurel's hands clenched at her sides, but she was painfully aware of being outnumbered and unarmed, while the only way off the island was across the expanse of freezing ocean. She might stand a chance if she stole a boat and rowed her way to safety, but the last thing she needed was for another escape attempt to end with her hands bound and her eyes covered again.

"I wouldn't try to run, girl," said Toth. "You already know you're no match for us."

Her hands gleamed with blue-white light, confirming Aurel's suspicion that they all had the same kind of magic. Did they carry identical Relics? Maybe they'd split a single deity's power among them, like the Invoker families often did in Aestin, but Itzar was a literal world away from the type of magic she was familiar with.

Aurel might not be in a favourable position, but she was still alive. They *did* need her, and she could play along with them until she had an opportunity to get away.

With a casual shrug, she said, "Very impressive. Fine, by all means, take me with you to your home, wherever it is. Oh, and do you have anything to drink? I'm thirsty. Starving, too."

One of the men threw a waterskin at her, which she caught in both hands.

"There. No funny business." He added an epithet in the Itzar language that Aurel didn't understand, but she somehow doubted that it was a compliment.

———

Rien woke early. He'd let Zelle take the only bed in the room the three of them shared, but it wasn't the uncomfortable wooden floor beneath his bedding that had woken him. Or the cold, though a chilly breeze crept in through every crack in the walls. His gaze landed on the staff he'd laid carefully on the floor beside his makeshift bed. The crimson wood emitted a faint glow, and he wondered if it had somehow prodded him awake.

"What is it?" he whispered.

The staff made no response, but he didn't expect one. Zierne hadn't directly spoken to him since he'd removed his Relic from its original home in the mountains. Only Zelle seemed to be able to converse with her staff on a regular basis.

Rien hastened to dress himself in clean clothes and had a quick wash in the basin a servant had laid in the room's corner for that purpose. Zelle hadn't yet stirred, while Evita lay curled up in a pile of blankets next to the rather substantial winnings that she'd gathered yesterday. He was sure the girl had never gambled before in her life, but by the end of the night, he and Zelle had practically had to drag her away from the table before the locals started a fight. It was possible that their group hadn't made the best first impression, but it'd undoubtedly be easier for them to get around with some of the local currency in hand.

Careful not to wake the others, Rien headed downstairs. The tavern's owner wasn't yet up, he assumed, and darkness swathed the downstairs room now that the fire had burned down to embers. As quietly as possible, he made for the door and walked out into the crisp, cold morning air. Below the cliffs, he could see traders loading up their boats. They must have to cross the appropriately nicknamed Perilous Sea every time they wanted to fetch supplies from Zeuten. His respect for the people of Itzar grew. They made his ancestors' own voyages when they'd mapped out the world some several centuries prior seem tame by comparison.

Admittedly, he'd found the Aestinian Empire's history distasteful when his father had explained the costs other nations had paid for their expansionism, but Volcan had thought it necessary to teach his children a wide knowledge of their country's history, good and bad. Since Rien's grandmother—Volcan's mother—had been from the Eastern Isles herself, he'd paid close attention to her perspective on the old Empire, and Rien had been far more assiduous a pupil than his brother had been.

An echo of a familiar pain rose inside his chest, and he glanced down at the staff, which retained its faint glow. "What is it?"

No reply came. He looked out across the island, towards the fog-wreathed seas, and a bright glow on his left-hand side drew his attention. A wooden bridge he hadn't noticed before connected the settlement to a smaller island on his left, which seemed to be the location of the faint glow. Was that what the staff was reacting to? Might it be the people who'd taken Aurel?

Rien made his way down the narrow sloping paths, descending through the settlement until he reached the rickety bridge arching across the water. From there, he crossed over to the neighbouring island. It immediately became clear that this island, consisting of rocky bluffs and a few trees, was far smaller than its neighbour. There were no signs of any human habitation, and he thought he was alone on the island until he spotted someone standing at the top of a cliff at the northern point. While Rien couldn't see his face, a faint glow emanated from the figure. *Is that an Invoker?*

Careful not to slip on the uneven rocks, Rien climbed up the rise until the man tilted his head towards him. Up close, he saw no signs of the glow, and the man looked entirely ordinary, if rather out of place in the desolate landscape. He wore a long garment that resembled a nightshirt, with no apparent regard for the chill wind, and he was barefoot, for some inexplicable reason. His features were youthful yet indistinct, and he didn't look like a local, despite being as pale as one of them. His hair was as black as oil, his smile wolfish as he took in Rien's appearance.

"I know you." The man spoke in Aestinian, and the sound of his own language brought Rien to a bewildered halt. "Arien Astera."

A chill gripped him. "How do you know my name?"

The man tilted his head to one side. "You know the name Igon, yes?"

Igon. The name brought back the taste of salt water and the echo of a sharp pain in his chest—and a name etched into a medallion that had once belonged to his brother.

Igon was the deity whose name he'd cried out while his ship had been pulled into the path of a whirlpool, which had dragged him deep into the abyss. Looking at this man, this *deity*, momentarily brought back the sensation of salt water flooding his lungs and the cold press of death on his shoulders. He tightened his grip around the staff, forcing himself to focus on the present moment.

"You owe me a favour," said the deity. "For saving your life."

Rien's mouth parted in disbelief. "What? You can't be serious."

Igon laughed. "You may have destroyed the Relic from which you accessed a small portion of my power, but the debt remains."

A flash of annoyance tempered his growing fear, and Rien's eyes narrowed. "What kind of favour would you like in return, then? I have money."

"I do not desire human goods, mortal," he responded. "I require a sacrifice to maintain this form."

Like Orzen. The god had needed to regularly slaughter humans and use their blood to keep himself present in this realm, but Rien would never agree to such a thing. If he had to break his word and destroy the deity to keep him from murdering innocent people, then he would gladly do so.

"What kind of sacrifice are we talking about?" he asked.

"Magic," said Igon. "Relics, to be precise. I wish for you to find them for me, and if necessary, dispose of their wielders."

"I won't be your servant," he said. "You're going to have to ask for something else."

"It wasn't a request." A warning note entered Igon's voice. "I can make you regret refusing me, mortal. I can take away the life I gave back to you."

"Another Power serves me now." He lifted the staff.

"Zierne answers my call, and I will not wield his magic against others."

Igon gave another laugh. "Really, now? That seems to run counter to the temperament of *that* particular deity… but I suppose you know him best."

What is that supposed to mean? The deity was trying to unnerve him, and despite Rien's best efforts, he was succeeding.

Having had enough, he raised his staff. "I will fight you for it, then. If I win, you'll leave me alone. If I lose, I will keep my word and honour our bargain."

Igon reached out a hand, and the cliff gave a sudden lurch beneath Rien's feet. Without warning, he fell, scarcely able to utter a gasp of surprise before the ocean slammed into him like a heavy force, driving the breath from his lungs. Water filled his mouth, stung his eyes, overcame his senses.

Not this again. With a furious kick, he surfaced, spluttering, treading water, his heavy fur cloak weighing him down. Above, the image of the smiling deity standing atop the cliff wavered before his eyes.

"You shouldn't be able to do that." He clung to the staff with both hands, willing the deity to answer, but no thorns materialised. "*Zierne.* Take him down."

Zierne didn't respond. The staff remained floating in the water like a hunk of wood, no more.

Igon raised a hand, and the water surged over Rien's head, pushing him into the abyss. Despite the roaring in his ears, he heard the echo of Igon's voice, all around him and yet intimately close at the same time.

"You lose," whispered the deity. "You are mine now. You will obey."

I'll die first, he tried to say, but the water sealed his mouth, the air squeezed from his lungs. Fear cramped his heart, the terror of the emptiness creeping into the corners of his vision—and then the spell released him, allowing him to break the surface of the water.

"Pity," said the deity, watching him from the cliff above. "I expected more."

"Zierne." The word choked him, and yet even when he reached for the staff's floating edge, the deity did not respond to his command.

"Your deity knows that you owe me. He will not strike me down."

He promised to erase that debt. He'd made a bargain. Was it worth so little? Treading water, Rien grasped the edge of the staff and lifted it out of the water.

The sea tugged back, as though a pair of hands beneath the surface gripped the wooden edge and pulled it downwards. Rien held firm, but he found himself dragged along with the staff until his arm plunged below the surface, then his shoulder. He grabbed the staff with his other hand, too, but it was like fighting a relentless current. The deity was too strong. *How can he be a match for Zierne?*

Zierne, however, had made no move to resist him. Instead, the water closed over Rien's head, forcing him to choose between releasing his staff and taking a breath or remaining under the surface until he drowned.

No. He would not accept that choice. Gritting his teeth, he dug his fingers into the wooden edge of the staff and *pushed*, forcing it to the surface—only for an instant, before the sea took it back.

"A mortal's strength is no match for a deity's." The god

was taunting him, speaking as clearly as if he stood at Rien's side while he fought the ocean for dominance. "You know that. Give up, Arien Astera."

His vision began to blur again. In his mind's eye, his father and brother appeared, looking upon him in disappointment as his passing marked the end of the Astera family forever.

No, he cried out, silently. *Please. Stop.*

"Then agree to my bargain," whispered the god. "I have a simple request of you, and if you agree to serve me, there will be no need for anyone to die."

No need for anyone to die. *You claimed you wanted me to bring you Relics and destroy their wielders. You mean kill them for you.*

"Their wielders are your foes, Arien. Did you forget what brought you here?"

What did he mean? He couldn't possibly know about Rien's intention to seek out Daimos—unless the deity somehow knew of Aurel's kidnapping. If the latter, did he know whereabouts she was? Had he been involved himself?

"Your companions would not want you to needlessly die, Arien. Do not resist me."

His lungs screamed for air. His grip on the staff, long since numbed, broke, and yet the sea held him below the surface all the same. As consciousness began to fade, the deity's voice whispered in his ear, *I win.*

———

Zelle frowned at the inn's owner. "What do you mean, he's gone?"

"I heard him come downstairs a couple of hours ago," the grizzled man replied. "I assume he thought I was sleeping. Early riser, is he?"

"He's the restless sort," she acknowledged. "I suppose he didn't want to delay our trip."

Typical. It was just like Rien to take off without telling anyone where he was going. Maybe he'd found a lead on Daimos's location, but he was just as likely to have gone in pursuit of Aurel on an ill-conceived impulse.

"What trip would that be?" he queried.

"If we wanted to arrange transport to the island where the Blessed are located, how would we go about doing so?" she asked. "Are there boats available for travellers to hire?"

"Were you planning to go alone?" he said. "You'd be hard-pressed to navigate the way to the Isle of the Blessed without a guide."

"We have one," she said promptly. "A local volunteered to show us around, but we need the boats first."

"I'd be happy to make the arrangements for you," he replied. "Given your lucky friend's winnings last night, you won't have any trouble affording the cost, though you might have a little difficulty convincing one of those surly individuals to play as your tour guide after the trouncing you gave them."

Ah. Evita had made several of the locals rather angry last night with her odd streak of luck, but the money they'd obtained wouldn't need to be converted into the local currency before they used it to pay for what they needed. While her worry for Rien remained beneath the surface, she'd just have to hope he'd return by the time they were ready to leave.

Zelle and Evita ate a simple breakfast of fried herrings at the inn before the owner returned with the news that their boats were ready and waiting for them. They thanked the owner profusely and left the inn.

"You have your money, right?" she asked Evita.

Evita jangled her pockets in answer. "I need to buy new supplies to replace the ones that fell out of my boat."

"We can do that later," said Zelle. "We'll have time, depending on whether or not we can get any useful information from the Blessed."

"Like what they said to the Senior Changers," Evita said. "I know that isn't the most important part, but I can't help feeling there's a connection."

Zelle had thought the same herself, but all they'd learned from the men they'd gambled with the previous night was that the Senior Changers had stayed at the inn for a single night before journeying to see the Blessed. Whether they'd stayed with the Blessed themselves for the duration of their visit or elsewhere, they didn't know. When Evita had accepted that they wouldn't learn anything new, they'd returned to betting money instead of information.

"From what I gather, the Blessed live on another island to the far north of here," Zelle said. "They use some form of Gaiva's magic, allegedly, though I can't think how or why people who never leave their home might have kidnapped Aurel. Best not to accuse them of anything either way."

"I'll try to avoid it." Evita's expression brightened. "Look, there's our guide."

Zelle turned towards the pier, where Gatt stood waiting for them. He waved them both over.

"There you are," he said. "Do you still want me to show you the sights?"

"We'd like to travel to the home of the Blessed," Zelle responded.

"The Blessed don't typically meet with outsiders," he said. "That being said, you should have no trouble getting an audience with them, given your status."

Status? He must assume that being able to use magic afforded one the same prestige as the Invokers in Aestin, which wasn't the case in her own country. Admittedly, the Sentinels did hold favour with the Crown of Zeuten, but that didn't give them any particular level of authority, especially in a foreign country. It certainly wouldn't help their case if the locals decided they weren't welcome here after all or if the Blessed turned them away.

"We need to find our friend first," said Evita. "Have you seen him?"

"The Aestinian man?" he guessed. "No. He didn't take a boat, so he must be somewhere on this island."

"There are only so many places he might have gone." Zelle had seen no sign of him on their walk down from the inn. "Are you sure he didn't take a boat?"

"He might be over there." Gatt pointed across the narrow stretch of ocean on their left to a smaller island formed of rocky cliffs. "Maybe he went for a walk."

Zelle squinted through the fog, making out the outline of a narrow bridge connecting Dacher's island to its neighbour. "What's over there?"

"Nobody lives on that island," he said. "If your friend's the adventurous type, though, he might have been curious enough to have a look around."

As he spoke, there came a bright flash of light from that direction. *Rien.*

"Hang on." Zelle broke into a fast stride up the sloping street, her gaze on the bridge. "I'll be right back."

The wooden bridge turned out to be as rickety as the one the Sentinels had put in the mountains to deter visitors, but Zelle hardly noticed the way it shook under her feet. Evita hurried along behind her, swearing under her breath at each rocking motion, until they touched down on the other side.

At the island's north point, a steep cliff jutted over the water. On the edge stood a strange man, his back to them, and his hand stretched out in front of him. He made a gesture, and a second man emerged from the water, pulling himself onto the rocky bluffs.

Rien.

Something was wrong with him. His eyes were closed, water ran in rivulets down his face and into his long hair, and he seemed oblivious to her presence altogether.

"Rien!" she shouted, beginning to climb the cliff to reach him.

His companion glanced back at her with a wide smile. Then a squarish doorway opened in mid-air, and the stranger vanished within it, pulling Rien along with him.

Zelle scrambled across the rocks, but not fast enough to catch up before the doorway blinked out of existence.

---

14

*Z*elle had circled the island several times before she accepted Rien wasn't coming back, and neither was the person—*god*—who'd taken him. Evita waited beside the bridge, having suspected much sooner that the deity had no intention of returning his prisoner. Zelle kept muttering to her staff as she walked, but whatever the staff said in response didn't seem to improve her mood.

When Zelle stomped downhill towards the bridge, Evita said, "I'm sorry, but I don't think that god is going to bring him back."

"He might be anywhere," she murmured. "Not just in Itzar, either. I don't know how far those doorways can reach, but we've never seen proof they stay local. Powers above, what if the same deity took Aurel?"

"He might have." Evita had no idea how she was supposed to reassure her companion when she was equally out of her depth. "If we talk to the Blessed, they're the authorities on magic. They must know deities are wandering around the Isles, right?"

Zelle nodded. "Yes, you're right."

Evita led the way across the bridge and back to the guide, who patiently waited for them near the pier. She should have known her brief streak of luck wouldn't last. With Rien gone, they'd better hope the Blessed would listen to her and Zelle, because they now had one extra missing person to track down.

On the other side of the bridge, they found Gatt waiting next to the boats they'd rented using her winnings from last night. It was a miracle he hadn't run away instead, although thanks to the fog and the cliffs hiding most of the neighbouring island from sight, he might not have seen the deity or Rien disappear into the realm of the Powers.

Regardless, there was nothing left to do but speak to the Blessed and hope that they might be able to help. Assuming they hadn't been involved with Aurel's capture. Knowing that they'd spent the past few weeks meeting with the Senior Changers did not help Evita's apprehension in the slightest.

"Thanks for leading the way," Zelle said to their guide, climbing into one of the long boats. They were designed for up to two people, and Evita joined her by mutual assent, trying not to look at the spare boat they'd left behind and hoping the guide wouldn't ask too many questions about their missing friend.

They let Gatt take the lead and rowed their way around the island's eastern edge, passing underneath the bridge and farther north. A low-level fog hung in the air, though with daylight now streaming in between the clouds, they could see several other islands protruding from the water, a welcome change from the expanse of open sea that had surrounded them during their voyage to Dacher.

Thinking of their near-fatal journey over the Perilous Sea was not a wise idea, though the water between the islands was almost shallow enough for her to see the bottom, and the waves were much gentler than the ones out in the open sea. Nevertheless, she'd avoid considering their inevitable return trip until after they'd found Aurel.

They rowed past several more islands of varying sizes, some inhabited and some not. The ones with settlements built on them were often connected by bridges, while between others ran thin ribbons of water that their narrow boats could easily traverse. Finally, the looming shape of a giant rock sculpture met their vision, covering one island almost entirely and leaving only a narrow strip of beach in front.

"By the Powers," Evita murmured, realising that the sculpture resembled a human figure from the shoulders up, which had been carved out of the very rock itself. The figure was unmistakably female, with long, flowing hair, and two large birds perched on her shoulders. She had to be Gaiva, the creator goddess—and if the Blessed lived here, then they must live *inside* the rock sculpture itself.

Gatt bowed his head and muttered some inaudible words as he brought his boat to a halt in front of the statue. Zelle and Evita joined him, climbing out onto the beach. Nobody came to greet them, and she saw no obvious doors or entryways in the carved rock, nor did there seem to be any path to reach the rest of the island.

"They're inside, right?" asked Zelle. "How do we get in?"

"You have to be invited." Gatt remained in his little boat and seemed to have no intention of disembarking. In fairness, he'd volunteered to bring them here, not to come inside with them.

"Do they speak Zeutenian?" Zelle hefted the staff in one hand, looking uncertainly at the carved visage towering over them.

"I expect some of them do, yes," said Gatt. "Luck be with you."

Zelle approached the sculpture, tilting her head back as though to look into Gaiva's giant eyes. "Hello?"

After no response came, Zelle repeated a word of greeting that she must have heard from the Itzar locals. Then she cleared her throat. "Excuse me? I wish to speak with the Blessed. I am Zelle Carnelian, representing the Sentinels of Zeuten."

Zelle cast a glance at Evita, but she found herself reluctant to approach the statue herself. She was no Invoker or magician, and if not for the cloak on her back, she wouldn't qualify as magical at all. When Zelle gestured at her to move forward, however, she spoke up. "I'm Evita Govind. I… I work for the Sentinels of Zeuten."

True, in theory. She had an inkling it wouldn't be wise to mention her prior connection with the Changers in case they and the Blessed had parted on bad terms.

For a while, Evita wondered if nobody had heard them at all. Then there came a grinding noise from within the statue, and a piece of the rock slid aside to reveal an opening the height of a human. A woman walked out, wearing a long tunic-type garment of a floaty, moon-white material, and a flowery headdress sat atop her pale hair. Her face was weather-beaten, and Evita would estimate her age as fifty or older.

"I am Tamacha of the Blessed," she told them, in accented Zeutenian. "What brings you here, Sentinel of Zeuten?"

Ah. Do they think Zelle is the Sentinel?

"I'm not the Sentinel." Zelle must have come to the same conclusion. "I'm her granddaughter. I came because my sister, the Reader, was taken captive by some strange men from Itzar who attacked my grandmother using magic I haven't seen before. I hoped you might be able to give me some direction."

Tamacha's gaze travelled between them, lingering on the staff. Then she beckoned them to follow her into the opening in Gaiva's side. "You'd better come in, both of you."

———

Whatever Zelle had expected from the Blessed, her imagination had never conjured anything like this. A glittering tunnel extended ahead of them, its walls dotted with shards of clear white rock that reflected her own bewildered face back at her. The caves must have been chiselled out of the heart of the rock itself, a job easily as time-consuming as carving the exterior into Gaiva's likeness. While the tunnels put her in mind of the Sentinels' shortcuts through the Range, the Shaper's magic had been responsible for those, whereas this was surely the work of human hands.

The staff offered no commentary on their surroundings. The tunnel widened outward, revealing a number of openings to small caves. Tamacha beckoned them through one such opening into a cave in which several other individuals sat upon smooth rocks, all of them dressed in the same moon-white tunics. All except for one wore identical headdresses, and the exception was a young girl of around fifteen, whose tunic was blue instead of white. She also wore a necklace of seashells and had startlingly bright blue eyes. The girl gave Zelle a wide smile upon her entry, but the older men and women appeared much more interested in Zelle's staff, exchanging whispered words in their own language. They surely didn't know the nameless Shaper lived within it, but she wasn't certain how much information about the Sentinels of Zeuten had reached such a remote location.

The whispers petered out when Tamacha gestured to Zelle and Evita to sit on two of the large grey rocks littered throughout the room. Zelle picked out the one that looked the least uncomfortable and perched on the edge.

"Granddaughter of the Sentinel," Tamacha said, "you came here hoping to find your missing sibling, you said?"

"Yes." Zelle cleared her throat. "My sister was captured by two men who wielded strange magic, and I believe they came from Itzar. The Sentinel wasn't able to come here and search for her, so I travelled here in her place."

"You're certain these strangers brought her here?" asked Tamacha.

"Yes." Zelle pondered how to explain the advice she'd received from the Sentinels' cave and the staff without giving away the identity of the Great Power who lay buried in the mountains. While the Blessed lived in a cave decorated with Gaiva's visage, Zelle had yet to see proof of their own abilities. "I heard you serve Gaiva, and since the Sentinels have long held a strong affinity with the creator goddess, I hoped we might find common ground."

"I have heard the tale of the Sentinels' journey across the ocean to Zeuten a thousand years ago." Tamacha's expression relaxed minutely. "You are the guardians of Zeuten's magic, is that correct?"

"Yes," said Zelle. "We're peacekeepers, mostly, but we do have access to our own Relics. That's how we found out that the people who took Aurel brought her to the Isles of Itzar. Do you have Relics, too?"

"Only one." She pressed a hand reverently against the rock wall. "This is Gaiva."

Zelle's mouth parted. The *rock* was the Relic, or Itzar's equivalent thereof. "Can you use her—Gaiva's—magic, then?"

"Only in Her presence," said Tamacha. "And only for the initiated, those who are chosen by the goddess Herself. Lenza is our youngest, and she has been our only new recruit in recent years."

The girl gave a solemn nod, adjusting her seashell necklace. "Welcome," she whispered, shyly, in Zeutenian.

"So how...?" Evita began. "The people who took Aurel used magic. If this is the only magical source in the Isles and you can't use Gaiva's power outside of the cave, how can that be possible?"

Zelle tensed, concerned that they might take offence, but Tamacha's expression clouded with sadness. "A group of individuals have turned their backs on the Blessed. They stole from us, chipping away at pieces of Gaiva's Relic in the hopes of gaining power beyond what they already had access to, and in the process, they have committed a terrible crime against their deity. It should not surprise me that they have taken to kidnapping, too."

Zelle stared at her, as did Evita. The latter spoke first. "You mean—they defected from the Blessed, and they used Gaiva's magic to take Aurel?"

"What kind of magic did the kidnappers use?" asked Tamacha.

"They were able to wield... ice," recalled Zelle. "Evita saw them freeze a blade in Aurel's hand and hurl a shard of ice at my grandmother."

"I wish it were not true, but that was them," said Tamacha quietly. "The rogues who have the audacity to call themselves Gaiva's Blades stole the heart of our magic. The Relic is not meant to be removed from this cave, but none of us can challenge the traitors without leaving the cave ourselves. They mean to convince us all to betray our deity."

"Why would they have done so in the first place?" asked Evita.

"They acted in response to outside threats," said Tamacha. "Threats against the Isles and attacks on their fellow villagers. It's a situation I can sympathise with, but not enough to betray my deity."

Zelle's heart lurched. The defectors had taken pieces of the Relic in the hopes of standing up to other unnamed threats. Did that include the deity who had taken Rien? Her insides contracted with guilt, since she'd almost forgotten him in her absorption in the Blessed's words and the awe-inspiring knowledge that they were in the presence of a Relic of Gaiva Herself. Yet if the people who'd taken Aurel captive had been using pieces of

Gaiva's magic, then it didn't sound as if any of the other deities might be involved.

If Rien had been taken by someone else altogether, their quest to find them both had become a lot harder.

Evita leaned forward. "What do you mean by outside threats? Monsters? We were attacked by a sea monster on the way across the ocean."

"Worse than that," said Tamacha.

"Gods," Zelle murmured. "The Powers."

A ripple of distaste passed among the others. Tamacha said, "We would not give them the honour of that title."

"I think I know who you mean," said Zelle. "We came here with another friend of ours, but he was taken through—a doorway."

Tamacha's expression turned ashen. Several of the others uttered hushed, panicked words, while their discussion left Zelle and Evita awkwardly sitting there, waiting for them to return to speaking a language they understood. Regardless, it appeared that her fears were true, and Rien and Aurel weren't held by the same individuals or even in the same location. In fact, she had the distinct suspicion that Rien had been taken by one of the same deities the people who'd taken Aurel had betrayed their *own* deity to fight against.

Zelle glanced down, wishing she could communicate with the staff without words. Then she remembered she theoretically could, if the staff deigned to listen to her.

Can I trust them? she asked silently.

No more or less than you can trust your allies.

That was little help, though at least the staff was speaking to her again. She watched Tamacha for a moment, reasoning that she and the others had little

181

reason to deceive her and Evita. They hadn't manipulated them into coming here. Zelle and her allies had made that choice all on their own.

"That is terrible news." Tamacha returned to speaking Zeutenian. "Who is your companion, exactly? The one who was taken?"

"He's from Aestin," she said. "You'd call him a magician, I think, or an Invoker. He's not defenceless, but I don't understand why he was taken. Is that… common?"

"No, but it's not unheard of," said Tamacha. "There is nothing we can do for him, I'm afraid, not as long as we cannot leave this cave."

As she'd feared. "And… my sister?"

"We do not know the current location of the defectors," she said. "I wish I could be of more help. I can point you in the direction of an island where you might find out more, but I know you aren't familiar with the Isles. You have a guide, yes?"

"I also have a map." Zelle reached into her pack. "It might be easier if you marked it on here."

Tamacha extended a hand. "I would be glad to."

Zelle handed over the map, hoping it wasn't too many years out of date.

"Why now?" Evita whispered to Zelle. "Why would a deity show up here? This isn't Zeuten."

"Clearly, someone borrowed Orzen's idea," Zelle whispered in response. "It's hard to keep that kind of thing quiet, and it's not impossible that another deity decided to guide their own Relic into an unwitting human's hand. I wonder what this one requires to keep his human form? On second thoughts, maybe I don't want to know."

Evita paled. "You mean, like Orzen required blood."

"Precisely why I'd avoid thinking about it," advised Zelle.

Evita fidgeted. "The creature might have taken Rien anywhere."

"You're forgetting Rien has Zierne," said Zelle. "He can fight back. What I'd like to know is why he was taken in the first place."

From what she'd seen, he hadn't even fought back against the deity. Might the newcomer have been connected to Daimos? Had he somehow suppressed Rien's magic?

Evita cleared her throat. "I had another question, if that's all right. At the inn over in Dacher, I heard that several of Zeuten's Senior Changers came here to Itzar recently in order to speak to you. Is that true?"

Tamacha's hands stilled on the map she held. "Yes, it is true. You are familiar with the Changers?"

"We know of them." Evita, it seemed, did not want to reveal her own connection to the assassins, and it would create an unnecessary source of tension if they mentioned their involvement in the recent events in Zeuten. Best not to discuss their home country at all. "Ah, I was curious to know if they were here to discuss these... recent events."

Zelle expected Tamacha to reprimand the former assassin for asking nosy questions, but she simply shook her head. "No, they arrived here before the trouble started. When it did, we did our best to keep the truth of the Blades' betrayal from our visitors, but they might have begun to suspect something was amiss. They left rather abruptly."

I expect they did. The Senior Changers, though, seemed to have mostly remained ignorant of Aurel's captors.

From Evita's crestfallen expression, she'd hoped for more direction.

Tamacha returned Zelle's map and pointed to a spot somewhere east of their island. "This island has been the subject of many of the rumours that have reached us in recent days. You may have a look around, but please be careful."

"Thanks for your help," she replied. "Do let me know if there's anything I can offer in return."

She'd be more than happy to give the defectors a firm thwack with the end of her staff in exchange for capturing her sister and turning against their fellow Blessed, but hadn't the Shaper also told her to close the doors between this realm and the realm of the Powers?

Did you conspire to bring me here? she silently asked the staff.

No, I did not, came the staff's reply, sounding somewhat affronted. *Not every coincidence is the work of the deities, you know.*

15

R ien surfaced, gasping for breath. The white edges of the doorway faded, revealing a cliff beneath his feet several times higher than the one he'd been on prior to following the deity. The ground felt sturdy enough, but he'd have a hard time climbing down even if he hadn't already unequivocally lost his attempt to challenge the deity, who could now compel Rien to obey his every command.

Powers. Why had he been arrogant enough to make such a bold declaration to begin with? The deity had overpowered him with ease, and the sour taste of salt on his tongue was proof enough of his failures. He spun on his heel, his heart lurching when he found that Igon *and* the doorway had vanished, leaving him stranded on the high bluff. Grey clouds hung low over the harsh cliffs, mingling with the low-level fog that never seemed to end here in the Isles. Nothing at all like the tropical Eastern Isles near Aestin, although by this point, he had a fair idea of why his ancestors had never set foot here.

He'd never considered that there might be Relics buried in this rocky, desolate landscape. Yet where else had Igon materialised from? He lowered his gaze to the staff, wondering why Igon hadn't taken it away, but he'd already defeated the Power within it. Or rather, the Power in question hadn't even fought back.

"Why didn't you'd defend me, Zierne?" he asked. "Did you *want* us both to end up at Igon's mercy?"

Zierne made no reply, which made him feel more alone than it had the right to, given that the deity hadn't made a verbal response to him since he'd first claimed the Relic up on the mountain. Had Zierne retaliated against Rien's control to teach him a lesson, or had he simply been no match for Igon's strength? The former was more likely than Rien was inclined to admit. After all, he *did* owe Igon. While Zierne had once promised that he would help Rien find a way out of the bargains he'd made, they hadn't discussed strategies at any point.

He drew in a breath. "I'm sorry if I made any assumptions, Zierne, but I thought you let me remove your Relic from the mountain because you wanted us to work together. Not because you had a sudden desire to be exiled to the most remote part of the world."

Again, no response came. Annoyed, he held up the staff so that he could look directly at the crimson magic pulsing within it.

"If we're going to escape," he said, "then you're going to have to cooperate with me. Unless you truly want to murder other Invokers to give their Relics to that monster who captured us?"

Did Rien know Zierne at all, though? Astiva had adhered to a strong set of morals which closely aligned with the Invokers he served, and while he would have always protected the Asteras first and foremost, he remained respectful of the other Powers who served his fellow Invoker families. Yet Rien didn't know what Zierne thought of the other deities, and he'd never even considered that his views might diverge from those of his siblings. For all he knew, Zierne was as disdainful towards his fellow deities as Orzen had been. And, perhaps, towards Rien, too.

No. Zierne wouldn't have let Rien remove the Relic from the mountain if he intended to betray him. He'd yielded some control of his magic over to Rien when they'd made their bargain, after all, and he wouldn't settle for his wielder being ensnared in another bargain for the long term.

For now, Rien would just have to find a way to fulfil the terms of his agreement with Igon without letting the other deity force him to harm innocent people. Which started with him finding a way off this rock. If he dove into the sea, he might be able to swim to another island, but the idea of plummeting into that icy water again didn't appeal. The memory of the deity's power shoving his head under the surface was too raw, and besides, Igon might show up again at any moment.

Or perhaps he'd changed his mind and gone in pursuit of Rien's companions instead.

Rien moved to the cliff's edge, his heart hammering against his ribcage. A breeze kissed the back of his neck, and a voice whispered in his ear, "I hope you aren't thinking of running away."

He startled, covering the movement by swinging the staff—but the deity was no longer within reach. Inhumanly fast, the figure glided to Rien's other side, while Rien caught his balance at the cliff's edge.

He gave the deity as derisive a look as he could muster. "I wondered if you got bored with me and left me here. I have a number of other things I'd rather be doing than standing on this Powers-forsaken rock."

Igon chuckled. "I would never have taken you for a coward, though I shouldn't be surprised, considering your initial escape from Aestin."

White-hot rage burned through him. "I came here to kill Naxel Daimos, not dally with the likes of you."

"You came looking for Daimos *here*?" Igon laughed again. "Why would he come to this, as you called it, Powers-forsaken rock?"

He was still speaking Aestinian. It was generally believed that the Powers spoke all human languages, but Rien suspected that this one wanted to ensure that Rien understood every single one of his insults.

"I imagine Daimos desires a new Relic to replace the one he lost." Rien looked directly at the deity, doing his best to ignore the sinking sensation in his chest. "They seem to be in ample supply here."

Powers above. He'd guessed wrong about Daimos's involvement, and another deity entirely now held him captive.

"You know so very little, mortal," Igon said softly. "You didn't even bind Orzen to a new Relic yourself, did you? Your companion did."

Zelle. There was no way for him to know *how* Zelle had achieved such a feat, as no deities had been present except for Orzen, Zierne, and the nameless Shaper. Yet the fact that he knew at all was a bad sign.

"If you want to suffer the same fate, you're on the right path," Rien told him. "If Daimos didn't give you that human form, then who did? Your summoner seems to have abandoned you."

The deity tilted his head. "Orzen was desperate enough for freedom to ally with someone like Daimos, but I am not so pathetic as to require a *human* to provide for me. In any case, you owe me a debt, so you'll work for me until I am satisfied."

He arched a brow. "Why do you need me to find Relics for you? What makes you incapable of doing so yourself?"

"It is not *finding* the Relics I need you for, Arien," said Igon. "I want you to assist me with taking the power within those Relics for my own."

So that's how he's managing to stay in this realm. He's draining other Relics. The Invokers who'd captured Aurel had wielded Relics themselves, which presumably meant Igon wasn't allied with them. Perhaps Rien could use that to his advantage.

"Where is the nearest Invoker, then?" he asked. "The Relics have wielders, I assume?"

"Incorrect." Igon beckoned, and to Rien's own horror, he found his feet obeying even as he urged them not to. A doorway swallowed them an instant later.

This time, Rien and Igon landed on a beach. A bitterly cold breeze hit them, though the deity didn't react to the cold despite his thin clothing and bare feet, and the sand was dotted with pale rocks.

Igon gave him a sideways look. "The locals say there's power in the very rocks here in the Isles, and they aren't *entirely* wrong. Of course, the Blessed are too afraid to acknowledge it. Most of them are, anyway."

What does that mean? From what he and Zelle had learned so far, the Blessed were the only people here who wielded magic—but that didn't explain the Invokers who'd taken Aurel. He kept a tight grip on the staff as he crossed the sandy beach and prodded at the nearest rock. "Looks ordinary to me."

"Keep checking," Igon commanded. "When you find a Relic, bring it to me."

Rien studied the deity for a moment. He might look solid, but when he looked closer, Igon's feet hovered a short distance above the sand, a reminder that he wasn't entirely of this world. It struck Rien that despite his confident manner, the deity *did* need the power inside the Relics to keep himself alive. He also, for some reason, needed Rien's help to take that power.

"How would a Relic end up lost at sea?" he asked. "Did humans trap the deities' power inside the rocks and then lose them?"

"Bring one to me, and I might tell you." The god jabbed a finger across the sands. "I'll be waiting for you."

Rien half expected him to vanish again, but the deity remained on the shore while Rien scanned the beach. Frankly, he didn't know where Igon had brought him— they might have hopped halfway across the Isles for all he knew—but at least he was no longer stranded upon a cliff. None of the rocks stood out to him, but after several minutes, a faint crimson light drew his gaze.

The staff in his hand had begun to glow again, casting a stream of light across the sand. Frowning, Rien followed the path of light, which extended as he walked, directing him to the edge of the water, where the sea's gentle waves had deposited a bright shard of rock on the sand. The gleam emanating from the piece of rock put him in mind of the Sentinels' cave, and Rien had little doubt that it was indeed a Relic. One that had not yet been claimed.

When the waves retreated, he lifted the shard into the air with his free hand. Power hummed beneath its surface, not as potent as his own staff, but undeniably present. Igon approached, holding out a hand for the shard of rock. "Good. Give it to me."

Rien didn't move. "I thought you wanted its power, not the rock itself. How exactly do you want me to transfer its magic to you?"

Igon's mouth parted then he lifted his head. "Well... this is interesting."

"What?" An idea struck him. Igon himself must have his own Relic hidden somewhere on his person. If Rien managed to get his hands on it, he might have a chance of overpowering him.

Igon smiled at him. "We aren't alone here."

———

Zelle and Evita returned to Gatt and their boats, which floated gently against the shore of the island. Gatt looked up at them as they approached. "I take it your trip went as planned?"

"More or less," said Zelle, unfolding the map to show him the direction the Blessed had told them to go in. "If it's not too much trouble, would you be able to take us there?"

The colour drained from his face. "Merciful Powers. I'd take you anywhere else, but there... they say that place is terribly cursed."

Zelle had anticipated his reaction, after what the Blessed had told her. "That's fine. We can follow the map ourselves. Is there anything we ought to watch out for?"

He pointed at the narrow channels of water between the islands on the map. "Take the left turning around there to avoid some sharp rocks in the water. Otherwise, you should have no trouble reaching the island."

He didn't mention *leaving* the island, but Zelle might be reading too much into that omission. "Thanks for your help."

Sitting down in the boat, Zelle propped the map on her knees so that she could row and keep an eye on their destination at the same time. She had to lay down the staff at her side, though, which brought exactly the response she'd expected.

What do you think I am, a prop? the staff groused.

It's that or hold the map one-handed and accidentally steer the boat into a cliffside, she silently replied.

Evita picked up an oar. "So much for him giving us the tour."

"Can you imagine being an ordinary villager caught up in the deities' games?" she said to Evita. "I'm fairly sure the Blessed are the only ones out here with any magical abilities at all. Nobody else has any means of defending themselves against enemies who aren't human."

None that she'd seen so far, anyway.

"I *am* an ordinary villager caught up in the deities' games," was Evita's response. "But yes… I see your point."

They rowed on, following the map. As Gatt had told them, the currents between the islands in that region were more straightforward, and soon enough they came within sight of a small island which corresponded with the mark on the map. This area was uninhabited, as far as she could see. The Blessed had picked the most remote location possible for their base.

Zelle brought the boat to a halt on the beach—roughly, she'd be the first to admit—and clambered onto the shore, looking around for any signs of a disturbance. Perhaps a doorway like the one through which the deity had taken Rien, or another oddity like the rock carved to resemble Gaiva's face. Yet the beach was utterly bare.

Zelle turned back to the boat, and a screeching noise sounded from above her head. Two large tawny birds had appeared in the sky, heading in their direction. They reminded Zelle of the giant mountain eagles which lived near the Sentinels' base, except much larger, more than big enough to carry a person or two.

"I think," Zelle said, "we might have found Aurel's captors."

16

A urel and the others reached land sometime later, where her captors wasted no time in hauling her out of the boat onto the shore. The new island was as unremarkable as the one she'd left, with its sands dotted with pale rocks. She might have stopped to admire their crystalline sheen if she hadn't been occupied with more pressing matters.

Aurel yanked her arm out of Toth's grip. "I can walk by myself."

"We won't have you running off and getting yourself killed," said the younger of the two men who'd initially captured her, who she'd heard the others call Kolt.

"Where are we even going?" No obvious landmarks caught her attention. Her throat was parched, though she'd drunk all the water they'd given her, and her insides were tight with hunger. Worse than her discomfort was her bewilderment at their inexplicable behaviour. They didn't act like ordinary kidnappers in the slightest.

"This way." Del strode out across the sand. "There's a Relic here."

Whose Relic might that be? Since no answer was forthcoming, she followed the strangers across the beach and kept a close lookout for an escape route. She was reasonably sure she could outrun them if she really pushed herself, but the island was small enough that she wouldn't get far without requiring a boat to get away. The desolate landscape wasn't helped by the low-level fog snaking among the islands and around the pale beaches and grey clifftops.

Aurel came to a halt behind her companions, who'd returned to their native tongue and exchanged angry words with one another.

"Would one of you care to translate?" she asked.

"I sensed a Relic here." Toth swung his head to the left and the right, pale locks of hair sweeping around his face.

"Clearly, you were mistaken," Del replied. "There's no Relic."

"There *was*." Toth looked directly at Aurel. "Someone took our Relic."

"That's unfortunate," she said. "What do you expect me to do about that? I've been with you the whole time."

"I can sense someone else here," he went on. "Human."

"Human?" she echoed.

Zelle? She shook the thought away. There was no chance that her sister could possibly have made it all the way here, even if she'd somehow known whereabouts Aurel had been taken. Her captors had left no traces behind them, as far as she was aware.

Del's head snapped up. "There."

Aurel's gaze drifted over the beach, her heart jumping

in her chest. A figure stood near the water's edge—tall, broad-shouldered, and holding a crimson staff.

Rien?

Aurel gaped at him. The incongruity of the sight immobilised her, and it took a moment too long for her to realise he wasn't alone. A second man stood behind him, a stranger whose features were indistinct to her at this distance. All she could see was that he had dark hair and wore a shift-like garment that looked entirely unsuitable for the cold weather.

Aurel's four companions muttered to one another and then moved in unison, stalking towards Rien. She unfroze, panic rising as she realised what they were about to do.

"Wait!" She ran forwards at the same moment that Rien raised the staff.

Thorny vines shot from the end, aimed at her companions. Aurel leapt aside as the thorns whipped past her face, snagging her hair and her fur coat and forcing her to roll over on the sand to shake them free. Her captors shouted incomprehensible words at Rien, drawing bone-knives from their belts.

"Hey!" She was on her feet an instant later, running across the sand. How Rien had ended up all the way out here, she had no idea, but she wasn't about to let her captors poke holes in him or freeze him using their icy magic.

Vines shot from the staff in his hands, lashing two of her pursuers off their feet and wrapping around their ankles. Toth swore and kicked out, unable to free himself, but Kolt ignored the thorns digging into his legs and raised his hand, bright magic coalescing in his palm.

Aurel yelled a warning at Rien, who raised his staff. Kolt's magic formed a shard of ice that missed Rien's face by a hair's breadth, while Del and the older man whose name Aurel didn't yet know moved to help free their companions. They were outnumbered even if you counted Rien's unknown ally, who'd made no move against her kidnappers yet.

Kolt took aim again, and his second attack froze the staff in Rien's hands. Thorns formed at its end, only to freeze and shatter as the icy magic stiffened his fingers and barred the staff's magic from leaving his hand.

"What manner of Relics do you wield?" Rien demanded.

Aurel's heart sank. This was how her kidnappers had subdued Aurel herself, not to mention injuring her grandmother. They might need her help, but they'd destroy her allies without a moment's thought.

She refused to let them.

"Enough!" She strode out, placing herself in front of Rien. "If you want to get at him, you'll have to go through me."

Rien's companion laughed. He hadn't spoken yet, but his tone was as cold as the ice freezing Rien's hands when he addressed the four kidnappers. "What an interesting turn of events. Did your new pet turn out to be less loyal than you thought she would?"

"I'm nobody's pet," Aurel said loudly. "And I'm loyal to my allies, not these strangers."

Whoever the oddly dressed man was, he plainly knew her kidnappers, but there was no time for questions. Losing patience, Kolt fired off another attack. Rien leapt forward, the ice around the staff shattering as thorny vines extended towards the strangers once again. Aurel jumped aside, narrowly avoiding being hit. Rien really did need to work on controlling that Relic of his, but its viciousness was exactly what her captors deserved. Thorns carved sharp cuts into Toth's face before they shattered, and the warrior bellowed in rage.

Aurel's gaze snagged on a bone-knife one of the attackers must have dropped on the sand, and she trod in that direction, keeping one eye on the fight as she crouched down. All four of her captors' hands were aglow with white-blue energy. *They must have the same Relic. Or pieces of one.* Worse, they had Rien surrounded. Frozen thorns littered the sand like pieces of broken glass, and his teeth were bared in anger.

Aurel snatched up the knife and faced her captors, unsure who to target first, but instead of closing in on Rien, they turned their attention to the man behind him.

"Give us the Relic, Igon." Del addressed the stranger in Zeutenian. "You'll lose this fight."

Igon. His name echoed somewhere in the back of her mind, as if she'd heard it before, and when he moved forward, he hovered above the sand as though he didn't entirely belong to this world. He was a *deity*. What had Rien been doing with him?

Igon didn't seem concerned about the four angry strangers bearing down on him. He simply gave Del a smile. "How bold of you. I wonder what your companion thinks of all this?"

"Meaning me?" Aurel lifted her chin. "I think you're *all* full of shit."

"Aurel, get out of here," Rien warned.

"What?" How exactly did he expect her to do that?

Even if she'd been inclined to flee and abandon him to his fate, her captors would pursue her in an instant, while the deity might be able to walk on the water for all she knew. Orzen had. "I don't think so. Save your heroic impulses for Zelle, if you will."

Rien's jaw clenched, his gaze darting to the deity, but the four others seemed to have concluded that he and Igon were on the same side. Two of them continued to approach the deity, but the others veered towards Rien instead.

Vines caught them around the ankles and dragged them onto the sand. As they made to strike him in retaliation, Rien raised a hand. "Wait. I want to ask you a question."

"No time to talk, Arien." The deity spoke in an odd sing-song voice. "Fight them, or else I will have to take you elsewhere."

What? Since when did Rien take orders from deities, especially ones that weren't his own? Whoever this Igon was, he had no connection to the Power whose magic resided within Rien's staff, as far as she was aware.

Rien's eyes narrowed in anger, but the staff in his hand glowed, conjuring a fresh wave of vines. Thorns shot in all directions, including at Aurel herself, who dropped to the sand in a roll, thorns snagging her legs.

"Be more careful!" she yelled at Rien. *What is he doing? Did he and that deity make some kind of bargain?*

Her shout drew the kidnappers' attention, who spotted the knife in her hand. Del reached her first, spitting out a curse when Rien's thorns struck her across the back. The next vine narrowly missed Aurel's face, but it gave Del an opening to grab her arm and twist hard, forcing her to drop the knife.

"Damn you!" she spat, struggling to free herself.

The other three men closed in on Rien and the deity, hands aglow with bright, icy magic.

"Don't you *dare* kill him." She broke free from Del's grip, but the deity had already grabbed Rien from behind and tugged him backwards.

A doorway appeared behind the pair of them. Her captor's icy attack struck empty air, as both Rien and the deity vanished along with the doorway.

———

Two giant eagles descended upon Zelle and Evita with screeching cries, claws outstretched and beaks gaping wide. Zelle raised her staff like a shield, but Evita had only a short knife to defend herself with, and she simply didn't have the reach. The eagles swooped around the island in a circle, forcing them to crouch down to avoid being struck. They put Evita in mind of Master Amery's giant eagle, but even that bird hadn't been big enough to fit a human on its back.

"What do they want with us?" She raised her head, knife in hand, and watched the birds circle the island in a large sweep.

"Maybe it's their island." Zelle shook the staff. "Come on, nameless Shaper. I know you can do more to fight them off from the ground."

"We should go." Evita backed towards the boat. "If we paddle far enough, they might leave us alone."

"That's a terrible idea." Zelle tensed when the birds began to descend again, drawing closer.

"You said it might be their island, right?" It wasn't worth staying on land. Not only had they found no signs of Aurel *or* Rien, but they risked being impaled on those claws if they stayed here for much longer. "Come on."

She ran towards the boat, but one of the birds followed their path, letting out a loud screech. A second screech answered, this one lower pitched. Evita halted midrun, recalling the training exercises she'd practised with Chirp—but did she want him to risk his life on her behalf?

The eagles drew closer. Panic rose, and she whistled between her teeth. Zelle shot her an alarmed look, but almost at once, she glimpsed a familiar reptilian form appear in the distance. He'd been nearby all along, and the eagles stopped their chase when they realised they had company in the sky.

The dragonet caught them up in no time, and while Chirp was smaller than their attackers, he made up for his size by flying in circles around the eagles and dodging their claws. His own claw found its target, who trailed crimson droplets onto the sand, but their fight had barely begun when a bright flash came from somewhere nearby.

Both eagles changed direction midflight and took off in a heavy beat of wings. A final splash of blood landed on the beach, and then they were gone.

Zelle's baffled stare met Evita's. "What was that?"

"You think I know?" asked Evita. "Maybe they got bored of toying with us."

That bright light, though, signalled something magical.

Friendly or not, she didn't know, but she'd bet her hard-earned winnings on the latter.

"Those beasts belong to the people who took Aurel." Zelle ran towards the boat. "They brought her here. If they're going back to their owners, we might be able to track them down."

"And you think we're in with a fighting chance against them *and* their owners?" Nevertheless, Evita pushed the boat out into the sea again and climbed into it, hoping the birds wouldn't change their minds and attack them again while they were out in the open water. Granted, if they stayed on the island, they'd be even more obvious targets.

Picking up the oars, they rowed on, following the retreating shadows of the winged shapes in the sky. The narrow passages between islands were hard to navigate, but the boats seemed to have been built for that very purpose. Rather innovative on the part of the people of Itzar, she had to admit. Now if only they'd invented some means of flying that didn't involve murderous giant birds.

The dragonet remained visible overhead, following them in flight as though reluctant to leave them open to attack. The two eagles were difficult to see in the fog, and their path through the islands grew even more convoluted as they were forced to slow down to avoid crashing into rocks or ending up wedged between cliffs. Zelle made no audible complaint, but she must have been frustrated that they were losing their adversaries with each passing moment. Chirp couldn't carry them both at once even if he'd been willing to, though, and it was hard to see their reptilian companion in the thickening fog. The grey haze reminded her of the Range's highest peaks, but even the

Changers would have trouble finding their way around the Isles from the ground.

Abruptly, her oar bumped against something solid. Evita tried to lift it, but the oar caught on a hard edge. Zelle stopped rowing, too, eyeing the water below the boat. "I think we have company."

Evita's heart lurched. The water had begun to freeze beneath them, growing more and more solid, with their oars trapped beneath the surface. Evita let go of hers swiftly as a shadow fell overhead.

Two figures ascended the cliff that ran alongside them on their right-hand side, both male. One, she recognised from among the attackers who'd taken Aurel. The other met Zelle's gaze with an expression of recognition and outrage which made Evita suspect that he was the survivor of the two who'd attacked her own shop. Their hands glowed with blue-white light, while the water solidified beneath them.

"Gaiva's tits," Evita murmured. "We're in trouble."

17

R ien glared at the deity from their perch on the clifftop. "You might have killed her."

"Why would I have any regrets if I did?" Igon scoffed. "She's only a human, and she's allied herself with those mortals against you. She doesn't realise we are bound by an agreement."

"She's not allied with them," he snapped. "She's the Reader. The Sentinel's successor. If you're not familiar with who that is, the Sentinels are Zeuten's most powerful and revered magic users. Those Invokers captured her for their own purposes, but if you'd killed her yourself, you might well have started a war with the entirety of Zeuten as well as the Powers they serve."

The deity's expression turned calculating. "You might have mentioned that earlier."

"You didn't give me the chance to," he retaliated.

Igon smiled at him. "You are adept at bluffing, Arien Astera, but I doubt the entirety of Zeuten would come to the aid of a single human."

Unfortunately, he had a point. Aurel's individual life probably didn't mean *that* much in the grand scheme of things, not to the Powers, who were effectively immortal whether their magic was bound in Relics or not.

"What about two of the three Great Powers, then?" he went on. "The Sentinels serve Gaiva Herself as well as the nameless Shaper."

"The nameless Shaper has been buried for millennia," said the deity. "And Gaiva's scattered remains are what those humans used against you."

Rien momentarily forgot his anger. "You're lying. Those Invokers... they weren't using Gaiva's magic."

They couldn't have been. One of the original three Great Powers would never serve kidnapping bastards like them.

Igon laughed. "Relics bind us to this realm, and those who wield our Relics wield our power. Even Gaiva is not autonomous, and while those pious Blessed might have objected to their companions turning their backs and taking pieces of Her magic for their own, that doesn't mean their deity agrees."

His mouth hung open for a moment. Was Igon implying that the Invokers who'd attacked them had once been among the Blessed? It wasn't implausible, given that the Blessed were the only known Invokers in the Isles, but the question remained of why they'd travelled all the way to Zeuten and captured Aurel. Did they not already have enough magic at their command?

"Speechless, are you, Arien?" Igon goaded him.

"Don't call me that," he told the deity. "I notice *you* had considerable difficulty fighting back against them, since you left me to do all the work. What would you have done if they'd succeeded in stealing the Relic back?"

"Oh, I wouldn't have stayed for as long as I did if I hadn't been so very curious to know the connection between you and that Zeutenian they brought here."

"There's no connection," he ground out. "She's been kidnapped against her will. As have I."

"You agreed to this willingly, dear Arien."

Rien met Igon's eyes, pushing down his anger. The idea of slaughtering other Invokers had repelled him, but those strangers had captured Aurel. They deserved any harm that came to them, and if the kidnappers and the deity destroyed one another in the process, it would only benefit both him *and* Aurel.

On the other hand, those Invokers' magic had been strong enough to challenge even Zierne. No wonder, if it belonged to fragments of the creator goddess Herself. Even split between multiple wielders, Her power had been formidable. If not for his dire situation, he might have pondered on how the creator goddess's magic manifested in their hands. He hadn't ever associated Gaiva with coldness before, but it made sense that Her magic would adapt to the frigid landscape and the fierce Invokers who inhabited it.

"What do you want me to do now, then?" he asked of Igon. "I brought the Relic you requested."

"Yes, you did." The deity reached into a pocket and pulled out the gleaming shard of rock Rien had retrieved from the beach. "Now... you are to transfer its magic to me."

Rien looked sceptically at the rock. "You think I can manipulate a fragment of Gaiva Herself?"

"A fragment, Arien Astera," said the deity. "Nothing more."

Rien lifted the staff. Igon had put himself in a notably vulnerable position, which was a little difficult for him to ignore. "How exactly am I to transfer its power to you, then?"

"Like this." The deity retrieved another glittering stone from his pocket. Unlike the first, this stone was smooth-edged rather than jagged. Whole, not broken. This must be Igon's own Relic, the source of his power that anchored him to this realm.

If Rien used his own magic to destroy it, then the deity would vanish from this realm until someone summoned him back. Igon was willingly handing him the tools he'd need to free himself of their bargain.

He only had to wait patiently for the right moment.

Taking care to keep his expression blank, Rien extended his free hand, holding the staff in the other. "You still haven't told me how to move the power from one Relic into another."

Igon handed him the rock—not his own Relic, but the jagged shard which had washed up on the beach—which glowed faintly in his palm. The deity flashed him a smile, holding up his own Relic between his fingers. "Your own deity will know what to do."

Rien kept one eye on the gleaming stone in Igon's hand as he held up the shard of rock and the staff alongside one another.

Zierne, he thought. *If you want to be free of Igon, then I need your help to get that Relic.*

At first nothing happened. Then thorny vines began to twist around the staff. *Yes. Come on, Power. You obey me.*

One vine extended and wrapped around the shard of rock in his free hand, and then a second vine stretched in Igon's direction. Rien held his breath when the vine encased the smooth Relic in Igon's palm, and in the same moment, both stones began to glow simultaneously.

Light flickered up and down the vines in his hands, flickering from one Relic to another. Zierne hadn't listened to him, instead obeying Igon's orders.

Damn you, Zierne, I thought we had an agreement.

Zierne, it seemed, thought otherwise. The jagged rock grew less bright as the thorns tightened, while Igon's own Relic glowed more vibrant than ever. The glow outlined his humanlike form, which already appeared more solid to Rien's eyes.

Zierne. Desperate, Rien flung his entire will against the staff, jerking it backwards and *demanding* that the vines yank the deity's Relic from his hand.

Instead, the vines released both the Relic in Igon's hand and the useless one in Rien's. Panic and anger rose in equal measure, and he drew back and hurled the shard of rock at Igon's face. Surprise flickered in the deity's eyes an instant before he lowered his head to avoid being struck, while Rien lunged forward, his hand closing around the Relic in Igon's palm.

A sharp pain burned through his fingers, but he clenched his jaw and tugged the smooth stone loose.

Before the deity could do more than blink, he hurled himself over the cliff's edge and into the mist below.

For a terrifying heartbeat, he expected to slam into icy water. Instead, his booted feet stumbled against jagged rocks. Ignoring the twinge of pain that shot up his right leg, Rien launched into a sprint across the uneven terrain, keeping a firm grip on the smooth stone until the burning pain seared his palm.

"Zierne," he ground out. "You're either on my side or against me at this point. If I die, you'll be buried here."

He'd never had to threaten his deity before. It gave him no joy, but the staff began to glow faintly almost at once. Vines wrapped around both his wrists, shielding his palm against the pain of holding Igon's Relic.

The shadow of the deity appeared etched against the cliffs above him, and Rien did the only thing he could think of. He ran.

———

Zelle felt like a rat caught in a trap when she looked up at the two men who'd brought the boat to a standstill. The oars had frozen to the water, while ice surrounded the edges, pinning the wooden boat in place. They were well and truly stuck.

"Who are you?" she called to the new arrivals. "Are you the ones who betrayed your own deity?"

"We betrayed nobody," spat the man on the right, adding an unknown phrase in his own language that sounded harsh enough for her to guess the intent.

"According to the Blessed, you betrayed Gaiva Herself," she retaliated. "You also kidnapped my sister and attacked my grandmother. And *you*," she added to the second man, "tried to steal from my shop in the middle of the night. You're supposed to be in jail."

"You murdered my brother," he ground out.

An objection rose on her tongue—she hadn't intended to kill the man, but he'd been trying to take the staff, and the Powers only knew what he'd have done to her if she hadn't fought back. "Both of you attacked me first. Care to tell me what you did with Aurel?"

Aurel clearly wasn't with them, but she must be nearby, otherwise they wouldn't have left her unsupervised. No, there must be more than the two of them. She wished she'd asked the Blessed precisely how many of their number had gone rogue.

"We need your sister's help," said the first man. "You, however, are in our way."

Shards of ice shot from his palms. Zelle raised the staff over her head, and the ice slammed into the wood with such force that the entire boat trembled. They were nothing but targets down here. Whatever the risks, they needed to get out of the boat.

A shriek sounded when the dragonet flew overhead, seeing they were in trouble. The two men appeared unsurprised at his appearance, though, and aimed their next attacks at the sky. Evita shouted a warning, while Zelle rose and placed a careful foot onto the solid surface of the water. Land wasn't far off, but the ice was slippery, and the men both broke into laughter when she skidded onto her backside. The dragonet had retreated farther back, unable to get close enough to rescue her or Evita.

Scrambling to her feet, Zelle leaned on the staff while she made her way towards solid ground. One of the men took aim at her, forcing her to raise the staff to deflect his attack—and then her heart dropped like a stone when a crack appeared beneath her feet.

Zelle gave a final lunge for shore, but the crack widened, the ice splintering below her feet until she slid into the water's icy embrace.

Kicking hard to keep her head above the water, she held onto the staff, pushing it to the surface. The man whose brother she had killed took aim at her, his face twisting in concentration as he formed a shard of ice in each palm.

Holding her breath, she dove underwater to avoid his attack. Shards of ice pierced the surface above her head, and then to her horror, they spread across the water in a bright sheet, preventing her from surfacing again. She kicked frantically, hands locked around the staff, but the wood was rapidly turning into dead weight, and she could no longer see the land above her head.

Blackness encased her vision, and despite her frantic kicks, the world began to fade.

———

Evita watched in helpless dread as two shards of ice flew at Zelle, who dove under the water's surface to avoid being hit. Instead of sinking, however, the ice shattered on impact with the water—which began to freeze, solidifying the area above Zelle's position until she had no way to pull herself out.

I have to do something. The others barely spared Evita a glance, and while they shouted incomprehensible words at one another, she lifted the hood of her Changer's cloak over her head, hiding herself from sight.

She didn't expect it to work, but when the men turned back to the boat, one of them spoke in Zeutenian. "Where's the other?"

"Drowned, I assume," said his companion. "Good."

They turned and retreated along the clifftop, while

Evita moved as fast as she dared, leaning over the side of the boat. She couldn't see Zelle at first, but a faint blue glow shone underneath the sheet of ice. The staff floated loose in the water, freed from Zelle's grip, and bumped against the surface below the thin layer of ice.

Evita grabbed the nearest oar and slammed it into the ice above the staff, causing its end to pierce the surface. She then dropped the oar and snatched the protruding end of the staff, gritting her teeth against the cold shock against her fingers. Drawing the instrument out of the water, she raised the staff and brought it down on the ice sheet as hard as she could muster. Cracks spread across the surface, and she glimpsed Zelle's hair floating loose in the water beneath. She gave the staff another swing, and this time, the ice shattered enough to expose Zelle's head. She didn't surface, however, and alarm flickered through Evita. What if she was already too late?

Evita leaned out of the boat as far as she could without falling in herself and reached her arms below the surface. Her hands closed around the back of Zelle's fur coat, and she tugged hard until the other woman's head surfaced.

The hardest part was getting her back into the boat. Zelle's clothes were sodden and weighed her down, and if not for the ice pinning the boat in place, she might have overbalanced and fallen into the water herself. With a final heave, Zelle toppled into the boat, her face bluish with cold. She coughed uncontrollably, vomiting water, and fell unconscious almost at once.

Evita used the staff to shatter the ice pinning the boat's edges in place, her heart hammering in her ears. Picking up the oars, Evita began to row with numb hands, scattering the remaining shards of ice littering the surface and steering the boat out into the free-floating currents between the islands. At this point, the only people who might save Zelle from freezing to death were the Blessed, and so she fixed her gaze on the mist-cloaked shape of Gaiva's statue in the distance.

Evita pushed on with more strength than she'd thought she possessed, doing her best not to look at Zelle's unconscious form too often. A bluish glow drew her eyes to the staff, which lay at the bottom of the boat, and a similar glow swirled around Zelle's prone body. Might it be helping to keep her alive? Evita hadn't known the nameless Shaper held any influence here, but Zelle was dying, and if she perished, the staff would no longer have a wielder.

Whatever the case, Zelle was still breathing when they bumped against a narrow beach, and Evita looked up to see Gaiva's face looking down at them. Hopping out of the boat, she struggled to drag Zelle up the beach towards the cave entrance. Arms aching, she grabbed Zelle's staff and used it to knock on the wall of the rock.

"It's Zelle and Evita!" she gasped. "Please let us in. Gaiva's Blades attacked us, and Zelle's unconscious... I think she's dying."

The cave wall peeled back, exposing Tamacha's face. "Bring her in here. Immediately."

18

Warmth cocooned Zelle when she awoke. Since the last thing she'd been aware of was unbearable cold, that came as something of a surprise. Her second surprise arrived when she opened her eyes to find herself alone in a cave with smooth, glittering rock walls. Warmth filled the air around her, soothing the chill in her bones.

Then the memories trickled in. She'd fallen into the water, had been trapped beneath a sheet of suffocating ice, and should by rights be dead. Instead, she was not only breathing, but her clothes had dried, too. The staff snagged her gaze, propped against the rock wall, and she picked it up with shaking hands.

"Where are we?" she whispered.

Good, you're awake, said the staff. *I thought I was going to have to lie here all day and wait for you to recover.*

"How did I get here?" Even if the staff itself had somehow helped her survive, it was physically incapable of lifting her out of the water. "Evita?"

Your friend is with the others. She was in better shape than you were.

"Good." As she'd suspected, she was in the Blessed's caves, albeit not a section she'd been to before. The warmth was strange, though, and so was the odd shimmering light emanating from the walls. Almost like...

A gasp escaped as the truth dawned on her. "Gaiva."

Part of the creator goddess dwelt within the rock itself, according to the Blessed. Did that mean Gaiva had helped to save her life? Or had it all been the nameless Shaper's doing? She rose to her feet, taking the staff in her hand, and looked around at the shimmering walls of the cave. Her own reflection watched from several places where the rock had turned clear, reflective, and parts of it were uneven, as if an instrument had chipped away at them.

Hadn't Tamacha said that the defectors had stolen pieces of Gaiva's magic out of these very walls? If the deity could hear her right now, then it wouldn't be a good idea to anger Her, but if the creator goddess *was* present, was She also aware of the staff?

Had any of the original three Great Powers been in the same room as one another in the past thousand years or more?

No, said the staff. *I assumed I would never see my sister again.*

"So you *are* siblings," she murmured back. The stories and legends had never been completely clear on the matter.

In a manner of speaking.

YOU.

The voice hit Zelle like the crack of a whip, as sharp as

215

one of the thorny vines from the end of Rien's staff. Zelle froze for a moment then spun on her heel, looking for the source. The voice, however, came from the very walls themselves.

"I—I'm sorry," she said. "If I'm trespassing, I mean. I just woke up here."

You should not be here. You should be imprisoned in the darkness.

Her heart crept into her throat. The cave seemed to be yelling at the Shaper and not her, but that didn't make her less inclined to cringe and back away.

"The Shaper isn't here." Zelle's voice sounded small compared to the loud echo that had jolted the entire cave. "Part of the Shaper's power is inside this staff, but She is still imprisoned in the mountains. Was it you who trapped Her?"

You serve the nameless Shaper, mortal. That was a very unwise decision to make.

"It wasn't exactly a choice." Zelle's pulse fluttered, her instincts telling her to get out of this cave while she had the chance. The goddess was nothing like she'd expected. While the nameless Shaper's attitude had surprised her when she'd first spoken to Her directly, she'd grown used to the staff's sarcastic whisper in her ear. Gaiva was the opposite—loud, domineering, and angry. "Also, I don't serve anyone, including the Shaper."

Not that she could entirely claim the nameless Shaper served *her*, either, or not in the manner of a typical bond between a Relic and the person who owned it. The staff only contained a fragment of the Shaper's power, after all, and their alliance was tentative to say the least.

You're conflicted on the matter. Such uncertainty might get you killed.

"Someone did try to kill me." Two of Gaiva's own former supporters had, in fact. Gaiva must be aware of their actions, in some fashion, much like the disparate parts of the Shaper were aware of what happened to the others. Gaiva's dominant Relic was clearly here in this cave, but that didn't change Zelle's memories of the breath being driven from her lungs, of slowly drowning beneath a sheet of ice.

A gasp sounded from behind her, and she turned on her heel to see that the teenage Blessed, Lenza, had appeared in the cave's entryway. The girl's eyes were as wide as plates. "Ah... you're awake." Her Zeutenian was fractured, but Zelle understood the gist. "I feared the worst, but you're stronger than you seem."

Zelle didn't move. "Did you bring me here?"

"Your friend helped." Lenza beckoned, but Zelle hesitated. Gaiva had fallen silent, though, and she knew better than to start another conversation with both Her and the staff in front of a witness.

Leaving the cave, she let the girl lead her down the tunnel. Lenza wore an awed expression, and she kept glancing over her shoulder at Zelle.

"I've never spoken to Gaiva yet," Lenza admitted. "You were talking to Her, weren't you?"

"I wouldn't say we had a full conversation." That might have been too much for Zelle to handle, given the furious manner in which She had spoken to Her fellow Great Power.

Lenza's eyes rounded again. "That's more than me. I only got selected as an apprentice last summer, so I'm

217

new to the caves. I've never been into Gaiva's cave before. Has—"

She broke off when they reached the cave where she'd met Tamacha and her fellow Blessed, whose attention immediately turned towards them. Evita was also there, looking distinctly uncomfortable, while the others watched Zelle with a stillness that made her suspect that they had some idea of what had transpired within the cave.

"You spoke to the goddess," said Tamacha. "Didn't you?"

Zelle inclined her head. "Thank you for saving my life. I didn't know it was possible for Gaiva to... to speak directly to anyone."

Tamacha looked directly at her. "Not for outsiders, certainly. You are not merely the Sentinel's granddaughter, are you? That staff you carry is no ordinary Relic, either."

Did the Blessed have any idea of which deity's magic dwelled within the staff? If Gaiva spoke to *them,* then She might have already told them that part of the nameless Shaper had entered their caves. If so, then Zelle wouldn't have anything to lose by giving them more detail.

"It isn't," she acknowledged. "I hold a Relic of the nameless Shaper."

Lenza gasped aloud, while the others all looked at her with awe—and yes, fear.

Tamacha spoke first. "Gaiva told us that She sensed the nameless Shaper had become active in this realm again. She knew the Shaper had returned to consciousness, but not the specifics. Even She cannot see events that transpire so far away from Her Relic."

"She seemed... angry to find out I'd brought part of the Shaper into the cave." Zelle looked down at the staff, which remained silent. "I don't know the details of the history between the pair of them, but they've been separated for millennia and little expected to see one another again."

"I suspect not," Tamacha said. "I doubt the rogues who call themselves Gaiva's Blades knew the nature of your Relic when they tried to have you killed."

"No, they didn't," she said. "But they must have sensed the Shaper become active, too, right?"

Anger flashed in Tamacha's eyes. "No. They willingly cut themselves off from Gaiva's presence when they turned their backs on us."

Then why would they capture Aurel? To help them deal with the other deities menacing the Isles, she'd thought, but the defectors had no idea how close they'd come to drowning the wielder of the nameless Shaper and leaving the staff buried at sea.

"Imagine that," one of the other Blessed said softly. "The nameless Shaper has a Relic... and it is in the hands of a mortal. How did this come about?"

Zelle's spine prickled under their stares, a nagging doubt in the pit of her stomach warning her that if she gave too much away, she'd be putting herself in a vulnerable position. Given her near-drowning, they must know that holding the Shaper's Relic did not make her invincible.

"The Shaper's magic was needed to deal with a rogue deity who was released into this realm," she said carefully. "My grandmother was indisposed at the time, and so the staff fell into my hands instead. I was able to use it to defeat the deity in question, but I believe you may be having similar difficulties yourself."

Tamacha's brows rose. "You told us you came here to rescue your sister."

"I did," said Zelle. "I didn't know about the trouble you were having before I arrived, but I wonder if the defectors took Aurel because they assumed it was the Reader who defeated the last deity to walk in this realm. Not me."

It didn't explain where they might have heard of the events in the mountains, but something had drawn them to believe they'd find help in Zeuten. What other reason could there possibly be? Besides, if the defectors had assumed the Reader had been the one who'd defeated and bound Orzen, then it made perfect sense for them to bring her here so she could do the same to the deity who plagued them. Whether they knew of the Shaper's involvement or not didn't matter, because it wouldn't be long before they figured out that Aurel couldn't give them what they desired.

Yet there were too many other unanswered questions surrounding the situation. Was the deity who'd taken Rien the only one present in the Isles? If so, why had the defectors gone to the trouble of capturing Aurel if they held the power of Gaiva at their fingertips? Surely one lesser deity would be no match for the power of the creator goddess Herself.

"They knew nothing of whom they were dealing with." Tamacha nodded, an expression of satisfaction on her face. "We are blessed indeed that your friend was able to bring you here before you perished."

That's one way of putting it. Zelle cleared her throat. "I'll need to go after the defectors again if I want to find my sister. Is there anything you can do to help us?"

"The Relic you wield ought to more than suffice for the task," said Tamacha. "Certainly, the Shaper is more than a match for the mere slivers of Gaiva's Relic that the traitors wield."

"They nearly killed me." Zelle didn't like to admit to being beaten, but the Blessed must know how their defectors' ability to freeze the water was downright inconvenient when Zelle and Evita had to pursue them in a boat. "If Evita hadn't got me out of the water, I would have frozen to death or drowned. Is there another way to find their location that doesn't involve going in the open water?"

"With Gaiva's blessing, you live," Tamacha said. "Perhaps She watches over you still."

That doesn't help. The Blessed already said they couldn't leave the cave, and they *had* saved her life, so asking for more might be too much.

Zelle rose to her feet. "All right. We'll leave."

"What about the—deities?" asked Lenza, earning a few stern looks from the others. "You said they were walking in this realm, right? Have you seen one?"

A couple of the others whispered reprimands in their own language, but Zelle gave them an assessing look before speaking to the cave as a whole. "I saw a deity on the smaller island to the east of Dacher. He took a friend of ours."

The girl's eyes rounded. "Who?"

"Lenza," Tamacha said. "Enough questions. Leave the Sentinel alone."

"I'm not..." Zelle gave up on arguing that she wasn't

the Sentinel. It wasn't as if Grandma was around to explain, and if the Blessed didn't know the defectors' location, they'd never be able to track down a deity who could open doorways to travel wherever he liked. "We'll go. Thanks again for the help."

Tamacha rose to her feet, all too eager to guide them through the tunnel out of the caves until they emerged onto the rocky protrusion of the island.

"Good luck, Sentinel," she told Zelle, before withdrawing into the cave again.

As the rock wall slid back into place, Evita moved closer to Zelle. "Not much help, are they?"

"They did save my life," she said. "And so did you."

Evita gave an awkward shrug. "I think that staff of yours helped. It was glowing the whole time I was rowing."

"Was it?" Had the staff helped keep her alive? She'd think on that later. They needed to leave the island, preferably before she could think too hard about the unpleasantness of getting back into a boat after she'd come close to drowning.

It was a miracle that the boat had survived in one piece at all. The wooden edges were a little battered and salt water sloshed around their ankles when they climbed in, but it might have been much worse.

"They didn't know who you were." Evita picked up her oar again. "Those defectors, I mean. They didn't care who *I* was either. Tamacha was right—they weren't paying any attention to either of us."

"They mistook Aurel for me," said Zelle in a low voice. "I'm not sure they actually know the Shaper awakened, but they must have found out that someone bound a deity and assumed it was the Reader's doing. I can't think where they heard the news, but I suppose the traders might have picked up rumours in Carthen."

That would also account for the fear those men at the market had demonstrated upon seeing her staff. Rumours tended to take on a life of their own, and it wasn't surprising that the defectors had gone after the wrong target. In their place, she would have also assumed that Aurel was the person who'd defeated the deity, not Zelle.

"The defectors want her to *help* them?" asked Evita. "Wait, doesn't that mean we're fighting the same enemy? If the deity is the same as the one who captured Rien, then…"

"Then we are, if we forget that the defectors kidnapped Aurel, tried to kill my grandmother, and almost drowned me."

Picking up her oar, she began to row. Zelle gritted her teeth when they were swept out into the current between the islands, her eyes alert for any sign of the defectors. She watched the sky, too, but no giant eagles appeared, either.

"Wish we could fly," she murmured. "Do you think the dragonet might be able to track the rogues?"

"I don't know where he is," admitted Evita. "The eagles were heading north, I think. What's the plan?"

"If they attack us again, hide under that cloak of yours. I'll wave the staff and draw their attention, and then tell them I'm the one they were looking for when they took Aurel."

"And if that doesn't work?"

"Call the dragonet and ask him to drive them off?" Her mouth tugged in a grimace. "It's not much of a plan, but if we *are* fighting the same enemy, then they should want to keep me alive."

Don't count on it, was the staff's contribution.

"Oh, are you talking to me again?" Zelle muttered. "Not you, Evita. The staff has been rather uncommunicative since we arrived."

That is because I had no desire for a conversation with my sibling.

"You'd think at least one of you would be happy to see the other," she remarked. "Aurel and I might be at one another's throats on a regular basis, but I still worry about her."

Has she ever helped imprison you underneath a mountain range for thousands of years?

"Well... no."

Evita raised a hand. "Can you not do that when I'm trying to row? I keep thinking you're talking to someone else, and it's distracting me."

I am someone, said the staff.

Zelle ignored it.

They rowed for a while, past islands of stone cliffs and sparse trees, pale sand and low-hanging fog. When they veered past a particularly rocky island, Zelle brought the boat to an abrupt halt. A figure moved around the cliffs in front of them, and she couldn't tell if it was a friend or foe. "Tell me that isn't one of them."

Evita stood up in the front of the boat. "It's Rien."

Zelle squinted through the fog. "It isn't, is it?"

"Yes, and I think he's running away from someone." Evita picked up the pace, and Zelle began to row again, too. The figure grew larger and then came into focus, running over the uneven rocks as though pursued by an angry beast.

They rowed faster, catching up to Rien when he reached the island's edge. He stared down at them, breathless and wide-eyed. "Zelle? Evita?"

"That's us." Evita indicated the boat. "We might have room for one more, but there's not much space."

Relief swept over Zelle. "You got away from the deity?"

"Sort of." He clambered into the boat, which rocked alarmingly, and held onto the wooden side to steady it. "I don't suppose you know how to destroy this Relic?"

"What…" Zelle frowned when he held up a rounded stone that glowed faintly at the edges. "Why are you trying to destroy it?"

Rien lowered the stone. "Because its owner is currently chasing me in the hopes that I'll submit to his every command."

"Of course," said Zelle, with an eye-roll. "Come on, then. We'd better go."

19

I t wasn't the reunion he'd been hoping for, Rien had to admit, but the relief of escaping Igon outweighed the discomfort of steering a boat that was scarcely big enough for two people, let alone three. Luckily, the vessel moved smoothly between the islands regardless of its heavy cargo, while the others looked to be in better shape than he was. Zelle's windswept hair was stiff with salt water, and her furs were wrinkled as if they'd had at least one soaking and dried off, but she rowed steadily with the staff propped against her knees. At every turn, part of him expected Igon to appear from a doorway to take back the Relic, but the islands were a maze and the low-level fog covering this area made them difficult to spot.

Evita sat in front, but she kept sneaking glances at the smooth stone in his hand. "How in the name of the Powers did you get that Relic?"

"I stole it from its owner," he answered. "It was the only way to escape him."

Zelle adjusted her grip on the oars, steering them around a tight corner. "Why would he capture you to begin with?"

"Because I owed him a favour." Humiliation burned in his chest, though he refused to regret what he'd done to survive, and he could tell from Zelle's tense posture that she wanted an explanation. He briefly summed up their history together prior to Igon gaining a human form of his own, followed by his shameful defeat.

"I stole his Relic at the first opportunity and fled," he finished, "but I little expected to find you all the way out here."

"We came from the cave of the Blessed," Zelle told him. "Our second visit of the day. It's been a rather eventful morning."

Rien listened in awed silence while she told him of their first encounter with the Blessed, followed by their narrow escape from the two giant birds and then Zelle's near-drowning.

Her account of her plunge into the water drove the breath from his own lungs. He averted his gaze from her face, his chest tightening. He should have been there to help her, yet because of his foolish bargaining, he'd been at a deity's mercy instead.

"You..." He struggled to find the words. "You spoke to *Gaiva*? She saved your life?"

"A fragment of Her," said Zelle. "She dwells inside the rock where the Blessed make their home, like the main part of the Shaper that's buried deep in the mountains. Speaking of whom, they weren't exactly happy to see one another."

Rien turned this over in his mind as they wove their

way through the islands, the barren fog-wreathed rocks gradually turning into larger islands with small settlements built upon them.

Zelle rowed them around a corner, her gaze lingering on a small cluster of what appeared to be stone houses. "The defectors—Gaiva's Blades, they call themselves—captured Aurel because they believe the person who bound Orzen can do the same for the deities here in the Isles. Including the owner of that Relic you stole, I'm betting."

"They think Aurel bound Orzen?" Was that why they'd targeted the Reader? If so, then was Zelle capable of binding Igon and causing him to be stripped of his human form? Rien hated that he couldn't depend on his *own* deity to come to his defence, but as long as Igon's Relic was destroyed, the outcome would be the same. "Igon—that's the deity's name—maintains his human form by draining the power from other Relics, the same way that Orzen relied on blood."

Zelle's hands faltered on the oars. "He feeds on the magic of other deities?"

"Yes, from Relics that wash up on the beaches," he said. "Do the Blessed know of him?"

"They know, I think," Zelle said, "but they can't leave their cave without losing access to Gaiva's magic. The defectors wield separate fragments of Gaiva's power, but they betrayed their goddess in the process."

"Are you sure it counts as a betrayal?" he said. "Almost all our current Relics are fragments, aren't they?"

His own family had split Astiva's power between several Relics without any negative consequences, after all.

Zelle's brow wrinkled. "This is Gaiva we're talking about. I'm pretty sure the creator goddess doesn't want people chipping away at Her sacred rock. Besides, they kidnapped my sister."

"Fair point," he acknowledged. "I suppose if they don't leave the cave, Igon feels he has nothing to fear from them."

The defectors, though? Igon hadn't seemed to be afraid that they'd harm him, but he'd stayed out of the fight for the most part. Instead, he'd wanted the amusement of watching Rien forced to fight against Aurel... with his own deity at the helm.

Powers above. How in the world was he supposed to explain that to Zelle?

"What's he been doing with you, then?" Zelle asked him. "Looking for Relics, you said?"

Rien held onto the boat's edge as they steered around another corner, past a settlement a little smaller than Dacher. "We only found one, but we were interrupted by the defectors... and Aurel."

"You *saw* Aurel?" said Zelle. "Why didn't you say?"

"Because I don't know where she is now." True or not, it was a feeble argument, and he knew it. "Igon escaped through a doorway and dragged me along with him before I could see where they took her."

He summed up his encounter with Aurel and her captors, feeling once again the sting of shame that the deity had manipulated him into attacking her. Except Zierne was equally to blame, and considering Zierne had also got him caught by Igon in the first place, he was feeling slightly less than charitable towards his supposed benefactor.

Zelle frowned. "So Igon forced you to attack the people who took Aurel, but almost ended up being destroyed in the process?"

"He wouldn't have been destroyed unless they'd got hold of his Relic." He gripped the rounded stone. "He claimed he wanted to watch us fight. I believe it amused him."

Evita sat up straighter in the front of the boat. "We're almost back at Dacher. Look, there's the pier."

"Good." Zelle lifted the oars, relief evident in her voice. "I'm not sure this boat can take much more abuse. Rien..."

He found himself avoiding her eyes. "I can't stay in Dacher for long. If I don't destroy the Relic..."

Then Igon might come back for him again.

At the same time, they needed to rescue Aurel, and while her life hadn't looked to be in immediate danger from her captors, that might change when they realised that she wasn't the person whose help they needed to bind the deities. The problem was, Igon had been just as much of a threat to both her *and* her captors, and Zierne had been more than happy to act out his commands. No, the others would have to go to find her, not him. He couldn't risk his deity hindering their attempts to retrieve Zelle's sister.

"We'll figure that out later." Zelle steered their boat alongside the island, where stone buildings sat on jagged cliffs in layers up to the inn at the peak. "I'm going to talk to the staff and see if it has any suggestions as to how to rebind Igon or destroy his Relic."

"Since that's what the defectors wanted Aurel for," Evita added. "If we speak to them and explain that we have the same goal, then we might be able to come to an agreement. Wouldn't that be an easier option?"

"They tried to kill us both," Zelle reminded her. "Besides, do we really want them to know about the staff?"

No, we don't. While part of him thought Evita had a point, the idea of telling anyone else about the nameless Shaper's connection with Zelle was out of the question. Especially those rogue Invokers. For all they knew, they'd simply slaughter Aurel once they learned they had the wrong target and then take Zelle in her place.

Their boat reached the shore, where they found their guide waiting on the pier. When they emerged from the boat, Gatt looked them over, his gaze lingering on Rien. "Good, you found your friend."

"One of them." Zelle's tone was clipped, wary, as though she was carefully considering how much to tell him. Evita and Zelle had evidently trusted him to lead them to the Blessed, but Rien had the impression that he'd swiftly backed off when Zelle and Evita had wanted to probe further into the presence of the deities in the Isles.

Gatt's expression showed relief mingled with concern. "Ah... I am glad of it. The stories I've heard from that island are unpleasant enough that I questioned the wisdom of you travelling there. If anyone other than the Blessed had sent you there..."

"Does everyone here respect the Blessed's decisions?" asked Evita. "I heard there haven't been any new apprentices for a while."

"Absolutely," Gatt said solemnly. "The Blessed act on Gaiva's will, which is for the benefit of all of us."

"And the ones who call themselves Gaiva's Blades?" asked Zelle. "What about them?"

Fear flooded their guide's features. "You didn't meet *them*, did you?"

"We met their giant eagles," Zelle hedged. "They tried to chase us off the island. Is that a common occurrence?"

"No," he said. "Ordinarily, they leave the villagers alone, except for when they occasionally steal livestock. But lately, they've grown bolder, and they come near human settlements more often."

"What about their riders?" asked Evita. "We're hearing contradictory stories about them. The Blessed condemn the defectors, but aren't they the ones fighting off the deities running around the Isles?"

Gatt blanched, while Zelle shot her a warning look. "What Evita means to say is that we'd like to know if the rogues frequently come to the village or not."

"No, they do not," said Gatt. "The ones who call themselves Gaiva's Blades see themselves as Itzar's defenders, so they are no threat to us, but they wouldn't hesitate to attack anyone who they perceived to be a threat to the Isles."

Or kidnap someone to help them achieve their aims. Yet Rien couldn't concern himself with the defectors, not when Igon was searching for him as they spoke. He needed to figure out how to destroy the Relic first and foremost. Keeping it close at hand in a place of human habitation was a risky venture, while abandoning it wasn't an option either. Neither was telling the other villagers in case they retaliated against his allies as well as Rien himself.

"I'd believe they were Itzar's defenders if they didn't

attack the wrong people," Zelle said. "Anyway, let's get back to the inn. It's freezing out here."

He had the impression she was trying to get rid of their guide, but Gatt tailed them uphill and fell into step with Rien while he walked behind Zelle and Evita.

"We haven't spoken yet, but I heard your name," Gatt said to him. "You're Arien Astera, aren't you? I have heard stories about you."

He inclined his head. "What kind of stories would those be, exactly?"

Had he heard of Arien Astera the Invoker of Aestin or the wanderer who'd cheated death countless times and who wasn't sure he held a claim to the name Astera anymore?

"Stories of how you aided the Sentinels in their fight against a terrible foe," he said. "Have you come here to do the same?"

Uncomfortable, Rien averted his gaze, wondering if Gatt would say the same if he knew that Rien's will was bound to another deity. "No, I came here as a favour to Zelle. Where did you hear the news from Zeuten?"

"I travel back and forth between Carthen and here frequently," he said. "I hear rumours from travellers, and it wasn't hard to make the connection between the arrival of a noble like yourself and the stories of the events in Zeuten."

That was a simple enough explanation, but Rien didn't feel fully at ease with the knowledge that people in Itzar knew his name. He could only imagine what might happen when they realised that he was under the grip of one of the same deities who had driven some of Gaiva's followers to turn on their own goddess in their quest to defend Itzar.

Zelle reached the inn first, while Evita hovered by the door to wait for Rien. When they caught up, Evita's gaze went to Gatt. "I don't think we'll be needing a guide for the rest of the day."

"Nevertheless, I hope I can be of help." His attention lingered on Rien for a moment. "I can't help wondering if your presence here has stirred up certain forces that were already active in the region."

Caution warred with curiosity, and curiosity won. "Perhaps. Gaiva's Blades claim that they stand in opposition against the deities who threaten Itzar, and from what I have seen of the Isles so far, there are similarities with the events that occurred in Zeuten some weeks ago."

Gatt flinched. "That is what they claim. The Blessed disagree with their approach."

"I'm curious, though…" he began. "It's my understanding that the ritual to summon a deity into this realm needs to be performed by a person. That is, an Invoker or magician."

The colour drained from their guide's face. "That is out of my realm of understanding," he croaked. "I'm sorry… Evita, was it? What is your relationship to Zelle and Arien here?"

"Nothing," she said. "I work for the Sentinels."

That was the line she'd started using as a neat way to sidestep revealing her identity, but it also concealed the fact that she had no Relic. As the only one of the three of them without magic of her own, she must have felt even more out of her depth here than he and Zelle did.

Gatt, on the other hand, wore an expression that

suggested he wished he could step through a doorway and disappear to avoid prolonging their conversation. "It is a pleasure to meet you. Enjoy the rest of your day."

He retreated downhill, while Rien felt mildly guilty for driving him off with his questioning, even though he was genuinely curious to know if someone in the Isles had summoned Igon. He certainly hadn't been in possession of a human form when Rien had last encountered him, at any rate.

Evita gave a slight smile as she pushed open the door to the inn. The interior was as warm and cheery as ever, and he confirmed with the owner that they'd have a warm meal on the way to them soon.

"You didn't expect Gatt to actually know anything, did you?" asked Evita. "You just wanted to get rid of him."

"We can't trust anyone," he answered. "Besides, who *did* summon Igon, if not Gaiva's Blades or the Blessed?"

"I don't trust the Blessed," Evita said decisively. "I sat with them while Zelle was recovering from falling into the sea, and they're so... I don't know. They don't leave their cave. They don't fight. They let Gaiva's Blades run amok with their magic, capturing people, and they don't lift a finger in defence despite all the power inside their cave."

He studied her. "You suggested that we might be able to reason with the defectors."

"Zelle isn't a fan of the idea." She glanced towards the stairs. "I think she went to have a warm bath."

"I don't blame her," said Rien, who'd had quite the soaking himself. "Gaiva's magic does still seem to work for the defectors despite their disconnection from their deity."

To what extent did Gaiva have any control over the actions of Her wielders? Not enough to stop the actions of Her descendants, evidently, but there was a world of difference between Igon's murderousness and Zierne's refusal to obey his new owner.

As for Gaiva's Blades? He hadn't spoken to them outside of their fight, but he'd need to get rid of Igon before he could even think about reasoning with any of them.

Starting with disposing of the Relic. The others would be angry with him if he left so soon after their return, but he wouldn't put ordinary people in danger by staying in the village while the Relic was still intact.

No. At the first opportunity, he'd slip away, and he'd settle matters between himself and Igon alone.

———

Aurel's captors manhandled her over the beach and back towards their boats. To no one's surprise, Rien's attack had put them in an even sourer mood than before, despite the way they'd come out as the victors in the fight. Some of them sported shallow wounds where the thorns had cut their skin, but they'd escaped without serious injuries. *More's the pity*, Aurel thought.

"Hey!" she said indignantly. "If you want me to cooperate, then I'd appreciate if you stopped tossing me around like a sack of grain."

"Was that man a friend of yours?" Del asked her.

"Yes, but not his godly companion," said Aurel. "I have no idea who *he* was, but you can't attack him and expect him not to defend himself."

"That deity is called Igon," said Kolt. Despite his rough manner, he was the only person who'd asked if she was hurt after their disastrous fight on the beach. "A terrible scourge on the Isles and one of the reasons we brought you here. Yet you had the audacity to defend *him*."

Aurel blinked. "I don't know what Rien was doing, but he's an Invoker who also happens to be a friend of mine. Of course I defended him. Also, if you go around making enemies of everyone you run into, you shouldn't be surprised when people don't want to help you."

"You *will* help us." Toth's tone dared her to argue. "As the one who bound the other deity, Orzen, only you can rid us of the deadly menace of Igon and his fellow deities."

What?

Aurel looked between her captors, the truth dawning on her. They thought she'd bound Orzen herself. But she hadn't. Zelle had.

"You want me to... to bind Igon?" she said. "To get rid of his human form?"

"Yes," said Kolt. "We can temporarily drive the deity away with the aid of our own magic, but he keeps coming back. The only way to be rid of a deity is to bind their power into a Relic, the way you did to Orzen. We know you did."

Her heart raced. "Where did you hear that, exactly?"

"We are not so removed from the rest of the world that we are unaware of what occurs outside of the Isles," growled Toth. "When Igon began his attacks, we sought out every rumour, every story that pointed to the cause of his arrival here. Not all of those stories proved true, but every one of them pointed to Zeuten, to the Range, and to the home of the Sentinels. It wasn't hard to deduce fact from rumour."

Powers above. They'd almost guessed the truth, except with one obvious mistake. If she told them they'd captured the wrong person, then they'd go after her sister instead and leave Aurel herself to die. Who *was* Igon? He hadn't struck her as dangerous in the way Orzen had been, but the Blades had been willing to chase a rumour to Zeuten in order to be rid of him. He must have been holding back during the fight at the beach.

As for why Rien had been there, alongside a rogue deity… that remained a mystery. *He* hadn't summoned Igon, had he? No, that didn't sound right at all. Rien was fixated on his revenge on Daimos, but he already had his own deity at his command. He didn't need another.

Granted, that didn't explain why he'd come all the way up north to Itzar. Was Zelle here, too? If she was, and she found her way to her sister, how could Aurel hope to keep her from taking her place in captivity?

20

*Z*elle spied Rien leaving the inn when she glanced out of the upstairs window as she was changing into dry clothing. She was surprised he'd stayed long at all, but she swiftly pulled on her fur coat and boots before hurrying downstairs. After sprinting across the inn's lower floor, she caught up to Rien halfway down the slope leading away from the inn.

"Don't you even think about sneaking off again," she warned. "Don't you remember the last time you went off alone?"

"Igon is chasing me," he said in a low voice. "He can make doorways appear anywhere he likes, and there's no telling what he might do now I've escaped with his Relic. If he starts a massacre like Orzen did..."

"As far as we know, he never attacked anyone while he was on the island over there." Zelle pointed across the bridge above the stretch of sea. "Orzen killed because he needed blood to maintain a human form, but Igon doesn't. He needs magic, or Relics, and there aren't any here in Dacher."

"Except for ours?"

"He hasn't seen mine yet, has he?" Zelle reminded him. "It'll get dark soon. I don't know about you, but I don't want to navigate those currents at night. Besides, you forget that *I* have the means of binding Igon into a new Relic myself, if the staff cooperates."

Rien paused for a moment as though to consider her words. Then, with obvious reluctance, he walked back to the inn. Inside, Evita sat at the table where she'd held her lucky streak the previous night, though none of the locals had come here for their evening meals yet. Zelle and Rien joined her, and the warmth from the fire burning in the grate soothed the lingering chills in Zelle's limbs from the time she'd spent in the ocean.

Evita looked up at them. "So… what's the plan?"

"We need to find Aurel," said Zelle. "And bind Igon. Failing that, it's not out of our reach to set Gaiva's Blades and the deity against one another and rescue Aurel while they're distracted."

"Not if Igon tries to use me as his instrument again," Rien said firmly. "I won't be forced to attack Aurel—or you."

Zelle felt a flush rise to her cheeks which she couldn't entirely blame on the heat of the fire. "Fine, forget Igon. I'm the one the defectors want, not Aurel. I can offer myself in trade."

"They might kill you," Rien insisted.

"I don't think they will," Evita put in. "They needed her help badly enough to fly over to Zeuten to bring her here.

Besides, if they've been dealing with Igon for a while, then we might be able to learn from them."

"You think they'll want to have a friendly chat before they throw me into battle against the deity?" Zelle shook her head. "I doubt it."

"I don't like the idea that we have two separate enemies to contend with either," said Rien, "but the defectors have already proven that they don't value our lives. Look at what they did to the two of you already."

"They didn't know we might be able to help them," said Evita. "Besides, what if they figure out Zelle is the one who bound Orzen before we find Aurel?"

"They think I'm dead," Zelle reminded her. "At their own hands. Besides, if they do have useful information about the deities, Aurel can tell us after we rescue her."

"I think Igon is more likely to reach us before they do," Rien said. "The rogues can't use doorways to transport themselves around the Isles."

"They can fly, though," said Zelle. "Those birds of theirs are well-trained, and they might not even have a permanent base. Moving between the Isles would make it harder for the Blessed to track them."

"You're forgetting we can fly, too," said Evita. "Well, one of us can."

"The dragonet?" Zelle's brow furrowed. "Are you saying *you* want to fly after Aurel?"

"Why not?" Evita sat up straighter. "If I go alone and hide underneath the cloak, I'll be able to sneak up on them and find Aurel. From what Rien said, it doesn't sound as if they have her restrained or locked in a cage."

Rien's lips pressed together. "I thought we weren't going to split up."

"It's not ideal," Zelle acknowledged. "But Evita has a point. They aren't keeping Aurel as a regular kind of prisoner, not if they need her help. They probably don't know about the dragonet either. He did a good job of fighting off those giant eagles earlier."

Would the dragonet be willing to carry Evita around the Isles until they found Gaiva's Blades' hiding place? Given how well she'd trained him, it was certainly worth a try. While Zelle wanted to be the one to find her sister, she couldn't deny that she was the defectors' true target, and if she went to find her sister, she might find herself trapped alongside her.

Rien leaned forward. "If we try to find them from the water or land, they'll see us coming. From the air, on the other hand... if you're careful to hide yourself, Evita, then I agree. It's our best chance to surprise them."

"Assuming they can't see through the cloak," added Zelle.

"They can't," Evita said. "In the Reader's house, they sensed me using magic, but they couldn't find me until I made a sound. When I used the cloak to hide myself in the boat, they assumed I drowned."

"Good," said Zelle. "If you can find their location, Rien and I can wait at a strategic distance in case something goes wrong and you need backup."

That didn't take Igon into account, admittedly, but there was no telling when or where the deity might reappear next.

"Will this be before or after we confront Igon?" asked Rien, who'd evidently had the same thought as Zelle had. "He might take the opportunity to strike if he sees us wandering around looking for Aurel."

"Good point." Zelle drummed her fingers on the table. "You said he relies on drawing magic from other Relics into his own to maintain a human form? How long would it take for him to lose his human form if you kept hold of his Relic indefinitely?"

"I don't know," Rien replied, "but he drew in some of the power from the Relic I brought him before I was able to run away. I imagine it'll take a while for the effects to wear off, no matter the distance between his Relic and his human form."

Zelle drew in a breath. "If I consult the staff, I can find out how to permanently bind him back into his Relic. I might be able to repeat the spell I used last time, but we're a long way from the Sentinels' cave, and I'm not sure how large a role the magic in the Range played in binding Orzen. It might be possible to destroy the Relic instead, but not by any regular means."

Despite her confident words, worry gnawed at her insides. They weren't in the Sentinels' domain anymore, and even the nameless Shaper hadn't been able to prevent her from almost drowning.

They all fell silent when the owner walked over to their table, telling them their evening meal would be ready soon. As kind as he was, Zelle didn't want him to hear her consulting the staff, so she excused herself and went outside. The sky had begun to darken, aided by the fog creeping among the Isles. Like it or not, they'd have to stay here until morning and hope that Igon didn't track them down in the interim.

As she looked across the darkening waters, Rien approached her from behind. "Didn't you just lecture *me* about sneaking off alone?"

"I'm not sneaking off," she said. "I need to ask the staff how to destroy Igon's human form if I'm to stand the slightest chance of ridding you of that Relic you're carrying, and I'd rather not have witnesses."

"Is the staff being communicative, then?"

"Not particularly," she replied. "Gaiva wasn't happy to see the Shaper in Her domain, but I don't know if the feeling is mutual. Shaper, what do you think of our plan to bind Igon? Can you do that?"

I think you're a fool to carry that Relic around without a plan to deal with its owner.

"That's why I'm asking you," she muttered.

"What did the staff say to you?" asked Rien.

"It called me a fool for carrying the Relic around without a plan," she said. "I hardly think leaving it lying on a nearby island or throwing it into the sea are good options, either. It'd end up back in Igon's hands and would probably ensnare some other poor soul in the process."

Igon targeted your friend because he already owed him a favour, the staff retaliated. *Few others would be that foolish.*

"You really aren't helping, you know," she told it. "Igon is stealing magic from other Relics, too, including Gaiva's. Can you destroy his Relic or otherwise redo the binding and get rid of his human form?"

Silence, for a heartbeat. Then: *Let's see it.*

Zelle related the instruction to Rien, who pulled the rounded stone out of his pocket and held it up so she could see its carefully smoothed edges. It would be all too easy to misstep and call Igon here simply by speaking his name, but he might not be aware of the Relic's current location. Pity that he hadn't given any

244

hints as to who'd performed the summoning to begin with.

Zelle held out the staff, gingerly pressing the end against the stone in Rien's hand. "Can you bind Igon to this Relic? Or can you destroy it? Which would be the best option?"

No.

"What do you mean, no?"

Firstly, I cannot perform the binding without the deity's human form nearby. Secondly, this is not the only Relic of its kind.

She lowered the staff. "Rien, was there another Relic?"

"Igon has more than one?" His jaw slackened. "Not that I saw, but... Powers, no wonder he was confident enough to place it in my hands without fearing its destruction."

"Regardless, would the binding work on him?" she asked. "If we were to bring Igon's human form to you?"

I wouldn't guarantee it. He is strong.

"He can't be stronger than the nameless Shaper."

I am not all of the Shaper, and I am a long way from home.

Shivers raced along Zelle's arms. Rien saw her discomfort and inched closer to her, turning the Relic over in his hands. "It makes sense that there is more than one. I should have guessed from the way he casually handed it over to me."

She placed the staff's end on the ground again, trying not to let herself feel too defeated. "This must be why Gaiva's Blades have yet to thwart Igon. Destroying several Relics is harder than simply obtaining one."

"And Gaiva Herself?" Rien queried. "You spoke to Her directly, didn't you?"

"Yes, but She's as inscrutable as the Shaper, and She can't leave the cave. Neither can the Blessed." Zelle heaved a sigh. "I don't get the impression that She knows what all her missing parts are doing at any given time, either. I think we'll need to wait to see Igon face-to-face before being able to bind him, but he might not be so quick to come back for his Relic if he has more than one."

Unless he comes back for your friend instead, the staff helpfully told her.

Quiet, she replied silently.

"I hope you're right," said Rien. "You don't have complete control over the Shaper's magic, do you?"

"What does that matter?" Did he have to remind her of how out of her depth she was? "You don't have total control over Zierne either."

"Zierne is the reason he took me." Rien spoke so quietly she had to strain her ears to hear the words.

Startled, she turned towards him, but he ducked his head as if ashamed. "How is that possible?"

"When I agreed to fight Igon to earn my freedom from the bargain we made, I thought Zierne would be willing to fight on my side, and I paid dearly for that assumption." He lifted his chin, brow furrowing. "I confess I don't know what Zierne's intention was, unless he took issue with my claims of ownership over his Relic, and he decided not to fight back in order to teach me a lesson."

"To teach you what kind of lesson?" The words came out automatically, though she'd little expected him to admit to such a lapse in control over his Relic. "That if you don't show him the proper respect, he'll let you get captured?"

"I believe he intended to remind me he isn't Astiva." A

note of pain entered his voice, as though it still hurt him to think of his former deity. "Zierne's magic manifests in such a similar way to Astiva's that I sometimes forget his Relic was imprisoned in a mountain for a thousand years and didn't serve my family for generations."

He was telling the truth, Zelle was sure, and the admission doubtless hurt his pride. How to reassure him without saying the wrong thing? She didn't want to cause a rift between the two of them again, but neither could she afford to let Rien's doubts about Zierne derail their quest.

"It sounds like you already know what the issue is," she said carefully. "Perhaps you can talk to Zierne directly and explain your reasoning. He allowed you to claim his Relic, so he must believe you worthy of wielding his magic."

Rien looked startled. "It's not a question of worthiness but of compatibility. His magic often strikes before I intend, and in Aestin, his thorns attacked someone they shouldn't have."

But not Igon. She pondered this, swiftly concluding that this was far beyond the realm of her own understanding. Rien must know it, too, but he also must have had no opportunities to confide in anyone at home. Ought she be flattered that he'd chosen her, or put out at the notion that everyone seemed to want her to fix their problems? Even Gaiva's Blades did, although they didn't know it yet. Rien, though, asked for nothing but her attention, and it thawed the remainder of the barrier that had formed between them upon his abrupt departure.

"Regardless," she said, "you should speak to him

directly, if you can. I'm sure Zierne has no more desire to be held captive in the Isles than you yourself do."

"I wish I could be sure of what he wants." A note of doubt remained in his voice. "Back at home, I hoped to find more information on how Zierne's Relic came to be in the Range in my father's notes, but they were all destroyed."

Her mouth parted. "You mean your family's communication with the Sentinels?"

"Yes," he said. "I know it was unlikely that I'd find anything in the house's ruins, but there's much I never asked my father when he was alive."

At the stark pain buried in his voice, something clenched inside her in response. "I'm sorry I reprimanded you for going home. I would have done the same if I'd been in your place."

"I should have told you the truth from the start. You were right… I behaved in a cowardly manner." He drew in a breath. "Even Daimos himself wasn't there—and he's not here, either. That's what truly needles me. I let myself get taken in by Igon for no good reason at all."

"Did you truly think Daimos was here?" Despite her repeatedly telling herself that he'd come here in pursuit of his revenge and for no other reason, that notion had shattered upon the shock of his capture, as had her resolution to keep him at arm's length. "Rien, I don't think you came to Itzar for Daimos alone."

Rien's gaze slid past her, his face colouring. "What does it matter? I am Igon's to command, and everything I was taught about the deities' willingness to obey humans no longer applies. While Astiva might have been happy to do my bidding, most other deities would just as happily see me dead." *Even Zierne.* She heard the unspoken words at the end and understood, despite her mild exasperation at his insistence on bringing the topic back to his own supposed failings. Perhaps she ought to return to the subject of his intentions in coming to Itzar once they'd put this business with Igon behind them.

"No, I don't think that's true," Zelle said to him. "Besides, have you ever heard me agree with the staff?"

A slight smile touched his mouth. "No, but I can't hear your whispered conversations."

"Be glad you can't." Rien sharing his difficulty in understanding Zierne's intentions made her feel less self-conscious about not being able to make herself heard to the staff most of the time. "Rien, I can't pretend to under-stand what it's like being bound to a deity, but I don't think we're meant to fully comprehend them. If we did, then we wouldn't be…"

"Human?" A hint of doubt still underlaid his tone, but his mood had brightened a little. "Yes, I expect you're right, and I apologise for burdening you with my worries."

"It's no burden." She smiled back at him. "The deities don't listen, so we have to make do with one another."

His expression shifted, minutely, becoming more guarded. "I expect so. Ah… our meals are ready."

The inn's owner had come to call them into the warmth, true, but had she misspoken in some way? She wasn't quite sure how much help her advice had been either, but she'd assumed the evidence of common ground between them would help both with their current dilemma and in smoothing out the mistrust that had formed between them after Rien had left.

On the other hand, perhaps like Zelle, a part of him

suspected that building common ground upon the untrustworthiness of deities might prove deadly to both of them.

————

Evita went looking for Chirp at dawn, hoping he hadn't travelled too far away or been attacked by those giant eagles during the night. Luck was with her, though, and she didn't need to walk far before she spotted the dragonet's dark shape flitting across the sky. She could have sworn Chirp had grown even in the short time they'd been in the Isles together, and she'd be quite comfortable sitting on his back as one might ride a horse—if they never left the ground, that is.

Evita waved, and the dragonet flew down to perch at the edge of the island's highest rise. "It's good to see you. I never thanked you properly for fighting off those eagles earlier."

The dragonet chirped. He looked none the worse for wear from his scuffle with the eagles, and Evita ran a hand down his bumpy nose. "I need your help. Would you be able to carry me across the islands so we can look for Aurel's kidnappers from the sky?

The dragonet's claws gently touched the back of her cloak, but she shook her head. "Can I fly on your back?"

Chirp made a pleased noise and rested his clawed feet on the ground, while Evita assessed how to climb up. "Can you lower your head?"

The dragonet acquiesced, and Evita grabbed his scaly hide, clambering awkwardly up and falling into a sitting position in the joint between Chirp's neck and shoulders.

His back wasn't particularly comfortable, but this position felt less precarious than dangling from his claws.

Evita swept up her hood, covering her face, before leaning forwards over Chirp's neck. "Ah... can you fly slowly to start off with?"

The dragonet chirped. Then he gave one beat of his wings, and the cliffs fell away on either side of her. Evita's stomach plunged, and her hands dug into the scales on either side of Chirp's neck as they rode higher and higher.

While the low-hanging clouds and fog somewhat hampered her vision, the islands spreading across the sea held a kind of beauty that was more noticeable from this angle. They seemed to glitter underneath the waxing moon, as did the ocean's surface, and the unreal sight took her mind off the reality of the drop. When her fear began to return, she switched her focus to what she planned to do when—if—she found Aurel. The cloak hid her from sight but not the dragonet, but when she found Aurel, she'd be able to approach from the ground. Provided those birds didn't spot the dragonet first, of course.

Peering through the fog, she kept both eyes open for one of those giant birds. They ought to be a dead give-away of their owners' location, and they were enormous enough to put even Master Amery's eagle to shame.

Speaking of whom, she'd been so certain that the Blessed would point her to a clue as to whether there might be a link between the Senior Changers and the events in the Isles. Gaiva's own followers turning against Her was an anomaly that ought to have drawn notice, but the Blessed had claimed to have kept their betrayal a secret from their visitors. No surprise, though the Senior Changers must have been sworn to secrecy on the source of the Blessed's magic, too. They'd given no hints when she'd spoken to them, but Evita hadn't exactly been privy to their secret meetings, nor to the communication between the Senior Changers and the Crown Prince.

Regardless, Gaiva's Blades had certainly stepped on a few toes when they'd come to Zeuten for the purpose of kidnapping the Reader. It was probably too much to hope that the Senior Changers had heard of her capture and might be prepared to return to the Isles to help them, since they'd already left Tavine and had weeks of news to catch up on already. Would the Changers stand a chance against those giant eagles and their riders, even with their cloaks? She didn't know.

The dragonet came to an abrupt halt in the air, nearly sending her plummeting into the sea. Ahead of them, a doorway opened high above the ground, and a tall figure stepped out, looking directly at Evita as her cloak was nothing more than air. Barefoot and youthful in appearance, he spoke in Zeutenian when he addressed her.

"Interesting," said the deity. "Who might you be?"

21

E vita had already left the inn when Zelle rose the following morning. So had Rien, and for a moment she worried that he'd gone off alone again. Instead, however, she found him downstairs talking to the inn's owner. When the owner returned to the back room, Rien turned to her with a small smile that momentarily made her forget why she'd needed to speak to him. *Powers above, Zelle.* She couldn't afford to be distracted, but she couldn't resist taking a moment to savour the victory of getting him to listen to her for once.

While Evita might have found Aurel's location if she'd left early, Zelle and Rien needed to handle Igon themselves. The part they kept getting stuck on was how to draw the deity's attention, and when they rehashed their ideas over breakfast, it became clear that Rien had very different ideas about how to go about it than Zelle did.

"I'm not using you as bait," she told him firmly. "You won't be satisfied until you get to make a heroic sacrifice, will you?"

"That isn't it," he protested. "I'm the one he's hunting for. If he thinks I'm alone, he'll come for me, and then you'll be able to sneak up on him while I have him distracted."

"Assuming it's even possible to trap him," she added. "Which we can't guarantee, considering he can hop through a doorway at any time he likes."

Igon can only maintain his human form as long as he doesn't expend too much of his magic. The staff was being a little more communicative this morning, though not as much as Zelle would have liked. *I imagine it's harder for him to replenish his magic than it was for Orzen, who simply had to kill someone every time he was weakened.*

Zelle suppressed a shudder. "We can't know that for sure. If the Isles are full of buried Relics, then who knows how many he's already drained?"

Rien gave the staff a brief glance as though making sense of their seemingly one-sided conversation. "He specifically asked me to help transfer their power to him. I wonder if he's somehow unable to drain the Relics without the aid of an Invoker, unless he intended to use me as a compass of sorts instead."

"A compass?" she echoed.

"My staff pointed me towards the Relic on the beach," he explained. "Though... come to think of it, he was also keen for me to drive off Gaiva's Blades."

"You think?" Zelle studied the staff's knotted surface. "He wanted you to fight them on his behalf... which means he must fear them more than he admitted."

Exactly, the staff put in. *I would guess that the rogues are slowly wearing him down with each of their encounters. If you force him to use up all the power he's amassed in his Relics, then he'll be at your mercy.*

"I'm starting to think we should set up a fight between Igon and Gaiva's Blades," she murmured back. "Why did we throw out that idea before?"

"Because Igon might force me to fight on *his* side again," Rien said. "That's why I'm better off acting as bait."

"Not a chance," Zelle said. "Besides, I promised Evita that we'd meet her at the Isle of the Blessed if she hasn't found Aurel. I assume it was scarcely light when she left, but she hasn't returned."

She hadn't done anything foolish like try to *talk* to the defectors, had she? Zelle thought she'd convinced her to drop that notion, but Evita might have ended up backed into a corner if she or the dragonet had ended up getting caught. They and the defectors did share the same goal in opposing Igon, admittedly, but Zelle had almost died at their hands once already and she didn't trust them not to willingly sacrifice her or the others to achieve their goals.

No, their best bet was to set up a fight between them and Igon and smuggle Aurel out in the ensuing chaos. Then they'd make plans to deal with the survivors, if necessary.

"I'm sure she's fine," Rien reassured her. "She might be trying for a cautious approach. They can't see her, can they?"

"Igon can." At least, if he was anything like Orzen, he would be able to see right through her Changer's cloak.

"It's unlikely that Evita ran into Igon," Rien said. "Even if she did, she has the dragonet to help her get away."

"I hope you're right, and we'll keep the 'bait' plan as a last resort." Zelle pushed her plate away, already sick of the taste of herrings. "Let's see if she's waiting for us at the Isle of the Blessed."

After they'd wrapped up in their thickest layers, the two of them left the inn and began the steep climb down to the pier. There, they found Gatt, their guide from the previous day, loading up his own boat.

"Hello, there." He didn't sound quite as friendly as he had the last time they'd spoken. "Anything I can help you with?"

"We're going back to the Isle of the Blessed," said Zelle. "I think we remember the way, thank you."

"I have a question before we leave," Rien ventured. "Can you tell me which islands are inhabited and which aren't?"

"Any reason?" His brow crinkled. "You have your map, don't you?"

Zelle reached into her pocket for her now somewhat damp and crumpled map, while Gatt pointed to several islands surrounding Dacher. The majority of the settled areas were within the same region, clustered together, while those to the far north were smaller and mostly uninhabited—with the exception of the Blessed's home.

"Good luck," said Gatt. "If you're planning anything dangerous, then I wish you the blessing of Gaiva Herself."

"Thank you." Might he suspect that they planned to engender a brutal fight once they found a remote place where they wouldn't run the risk of human casualties? Whether he did or not, she accepted his blessing. After all, they'd need all the luck they could get.

———

Evita sat on the dragonet's back, facing the deity as he looked straight through her Changer's cloak. *Oh, Powers.*

"I'm nobody important," she told him. "I'm just going for a flight."

"I doubt you're unimportant," he said. "Why else would you be flying on such an intriguing beast, hidden from mortal eyes?"

Chirp growled at him, but the deity didn't even blink.

"Maybe I just like to travel alone." How had he even known she was here? Had he been watching the sky from one of the islands below? "Don't you have more important godly things to be getting on with?"

The deity made a forwards motion with his palm, and a blast of wind knocked the dragonet backwards. The beast reeled, while Evita leaned forwards and tightened her grip on his scales to keep from being swept away. "Gaiva's tits."

"I would be careful with your colloquialisms, considering whose mercy you now depend on," the deity said.

Anger spiked within her, hot and unexpected. While she knew little of this particular deity except that he'd manipulated Rien into making a bargain, she was utterly fed up with the gods toying with her.

"What do you want with me?" she demanded.

"Nothing," he answered. "You were in my way, and I was intrigued enough to speak to you."

"If I'm in your way, does that mean you're going to Dacher?" she asked. "Because I can't let you do that. There are humans down there who want nothing to do with the gods."

If Zelle and Rien's plan worked, Igon wouldn't harm a soul, but Evita wasn't supposed to run into him first. Even

EMMA L. ADAMS

if she and the dragonet flew out of his reach, he was too close to the village—and to Rien. She knew from her confrontation with Orzen that she wouldn't be able to do any physical damage to him regardless of whether he was in possession of his actual Relic or not, but she could at least divert his attention from the villagers.

"Is that what they told you?" He grinned. "Who exactly do you think enabled my return into this realm?"

Evita stared at him for an instant, her mind free-falling. Someone from the village had summoned Igon into this realm? Zelle and Rien had both agreed that it must have been a human who'd performed the ritual, but who among the villagers would have even *wanted* to summon a dangerous deity, much less had the magical skill and knowledge to do so?

Chirp released another growl, and Evita did her best to push Igon's revelation to the back of her mind. Whether he told the truth or not, this was her only chance to drive him away. He might be immortal and terrifying, but she'd suspected since Orzen that the gods weren't so different from humans in terms of their emotions and their desire for respect.

She leaned over Chirp's head and whispered an instruction in his ear, and the dragonet obligingly beat his wings.

"Don't mind me, then," she said breezily. "I'll be on my way."

As she'd hoped, Igon moved when she did, drifting in front of her. "Stop right there."

"Why?" As she spoke, the dragonet's flight veered around the deity, forcing him to move swiftly across the

258

air to keep up with them. "You already said you aren't interested in me. Go and talk to your master."

"I have no *master*." His anger vibrated in the air, prompting an aggrieved noise from Chirp, but she'd successfully drawn his attention away from the village.

Unfortunately, now the deity was following *her* instead, and while the dragonet picked up speed, the deity walked on the air as easily as walking on land.

"You will pay for your insolence," he told her.

"You aren't *my* master, either." She tried to squash her rising panic, not at all helped when Chirp's speed quickened yet again, the islands reeling beneath them.

A sudden blast of air struck her from behind and tore her grip free of the dragonet, sending her tumbling towards the waves. Evita's cloak billowed behind her in the air, and she heard Chirp's shriek as the wind dragged him away. *Oh, Powers.*

Her fall was slower than she'd expected, with far too much time to contemplate the drop. Her cloak spread outward, and through her blinding terror, she felt the stirring of the wind currents below the surface, and the image of the Changers swooping through the sky filled the part of her mind that wasn't blanked out with gruesome depictions of her impending death.

Fly, she thought in desperation, directing the command at the winglike folds of her cloak. *Fly. Help me.*

A gasp lodged in her throat as the air current swept her along with it, slowing her fall. Instead of plummeting, the cloak had spread outwards and seemed to be balancing her, somehow, in a manner similar to the dragonet's wings. Her downwards glide smoothed out enough for her to land on the nearest island, her feet touching gently down on the shore.

The cloak collapsed into billowing folds at her sides, while she sank against a rock, her body trembling. "What in the name of the Powers?"

Her command had *worked.* Had she somehow tapped into the same power the Senior Changers used to fly, or was some deity looking out for her, like Gaiva Herself? It was Gaiva whose magic lived on in the cloak, or so she'd been taught, but she couldn't have achieved the same level of control over her cloak as a Senior Changer, could she? It usually took years of training for a Changer to learn to fly, though now she thought back, most of the Changers who'd backed Orzen up in his fight against the Sentinels had been novices like her.

Whatever the cause, she was alive, and when she looked up, the deity was nowhere to be seen. Unfortunately, neither was anyone else, including Chirp. The wind must have blown him off course, like her, but there was still a danger that the deity would target the villagers now that his quarry had got away.

Evita raised her arms hopefully, but the cloak remained limp at her sides. The gale the deity had conjured had faded to a gentle breeze, and no matter how many times she flapped her arms, she remained stubbornly grounded. The cloak might have saved her life, but now the danger had passed, it had seemingly become dormant again.

It appeared that she'd have to wait for the dragonet's return after all.

22

Aurel tried to escape her captors twice in the night.

She'd bided her time all evening, after the warriors had finally dragged her to a halt on another of those ghastly islands. The only feature to distinguish this one from the others was the warren of caves someone had dug into the high cliffs, which her captors had made their home. Aurel assumed it wasn't a permanent habitation, based on the lack of any obvious markers or many personal belongings, but they seemed to know the caves well. No doubt they'd taken note of any potential escape routes.

Aurel estimated that her captors numbered more than ten but less than twenty, but their bulky fur coats and the way their voices echoed in the caves made them seem more numerous than they actually were. Their giant birds, meanwhile, circled above the island, occasionally diving into the sea to snatch up wriggling fish to devour. Her captors had started a large campfire in the middle of the cave and roasted their own fish on sticks, talking loudly in the Itzar language. It'd been Kolt who'd finally brought some food to Aurel in her corner of the cave, apparently out of pity. She'd accepted the meal in mute silence, suspecting that she'd have to wait for them to fall asleep before she could attempt to sneak away. Somewhat difficult, since at least two of them remained close to her at any given time.

Not a single one spoke to her, though, giving her no opportunity to attempt to explain that she couldn't give them what they wanted. Perhaps that was for the best, because when they inevitably realised they'd captured the wrong Carnelian sibling, they might throw her into the sea or otherwise dispose of her in some unpleasant manner. From the way they'd reacted towards Rien, they seemed to think of anyone who wasn't among their number as an enemy by default.

Time passed. Aurel waited until the fire burned down to embers and the guards' chatter fell silent. They'd bundled themselves in thick furs to sleep, and while she was evidently supposed to do the same, she lay wide awake.

When the last bit of noise petered out, Aurel rose to her feet, but she hadn't taken two steps before Del's eyes snapped open. "Where are you going?"

"Closer to the fire. I'm cold."

Del's brother, Toth, seized the back of Aurel's leg and yanked so hard that she overbalanced and fell onto her rear. "Then put another blanket on."

Aurel looked up at him. "You're a real bastard, you know that?"

"If you weren't our last hope to be rid of our enemy, I'd happily drown you with my own hands."

He cracked his knuckles menacingly, while Aurel scrambled back, her heart sinking in her chest. "Is that what you'll do if I fail?"

The question slipped out before she could think better of it, and Toth laughed, a low rumbling growl. "Worse, Reader. Much worse."

Great.

And so Aurel lay in a pile of furs and pretended to sleep until dawn painted grey streaks across the camp. Within a few short hours, her guards stirred and sat up, stretching, while a second group of guards strode over to join them. While they were engaged in bleary-eyed conversation, Aurel seized her chance to roll across the floor and scramble out of sight.

Cold, salt-tinged air greeted her as she left the cave. Holding her breath, she made her way to the nearest spear of sand, only to find that someone had moved the boats since her arrival. Even the giant birds were nowhere to be seen.

Footsteps came from behind her. "Going somewhere?"

Aurel spun around to find Del glowering at her, the anchor tattoo on her face stark against her pale skin and her hair dishevelled from sleep.

Aurel lifted her chin. "As a matter of fact, yes. What did you do with the boats?"

"Are you truly so eager to pit yourself against the deities?"

No. Not at all. On the other hand, if she didn't get away soon, she'd find out if Toth's threats had been serious or not. She'd almost rather face the wrath of an angry deity.

EMMA L. ADAMS

"Between that and death by drowning, I'll take my chances," she evaded. "Besides, the last time we came face-to-face with a deity, you didn't seem to need my help."

Del shouted a few words in the direction of the camp. Toth and another man came over to join her, at which point she switched to Zeutenian so that Aurel could understand. "Our guest seems very keen to confront Igon this morning."

Toth studied Aurel through narrowed eyes. "Would she rather we tied her up again? We did a kindness in setting her free."

Aurel snorted. "Yes, it was very kind of you to keep me imprisoned in your cave all night and demand that I solve all your problems. If this is how you treat all your guests, it's no wonder you don't have many visitors."

Toth pulled a length of rope from the pocket of his furs. "I think she needs to be taught a lesson."

Aurel took a step back. "Word of advice: you'd get on better if you *asked* for help before kidnapping people and threatening to drown them. Besides, I'm not—"

A loud screech interrupted her, and one of the giant eagles descended upon the beach. When it landed, a broad-shouldered man with salt-white hair slid off its back and ran towards her companions, who conversed in urgent voices. They also kept pointing at Aurel, which was alarming if nothing else.

"What is it?" asked Aurel. "What's going on?"

"It's your lucky day," said Del, switching back to Zeutenian. "It seems the deity is out hunting for Relics again. If you're as talented as you claim, you'll be able to bind him, and then we can be rid of you."

"Excuse me?" Aurel's heart began to beat faster. "You're

going to kill me even if I succeed?"

"Did we say that?" Del sounded affronted. "We are not so cruel as to keep you here indefinitely. You will do this task for us, and then you may return home."

"Home?" They had to be joking. Besides, the instant she went up against the deity, she'd be exposed as a fraud and potentially sentenced to death—or worse, they'd all be killed in the ensuing conflict.

"Do you truly assume that we keep you close at hand because we delight in your company?" Toth put in. "We had no choice but to bring you here, Reader. We know that you brought an end to Orzen's rampage, and if you fail to do the same for us, the consequences will fall on your own head one way or another."

"Are you selfish enough to let everyone in Itzar die?" Del put in. "To let the villages and towns of ordinary citizens be swept into the sea? Or will you only act against the deities to save your own nation?"

Powers above, they were serious. They genuinely thought she was their only hope to save the Isles from the deity's wrath. Del's words stung her a little, she wouldn't lie, but it wasn't selfishness that stayed her hand. It was the fact that she had no power over the gods to speak of and that she couldn't even use her Reading abilities without her Relic. She also didn't think Zelle had had the whole of Zeuten in mind when she'd stopped Orzen— she'd been trying to save her family's own necks, first and foremost. Evidently, that wasn't how her actions had looked to outsiders.

Del and Toth looked down at her, as did their companions, their expressions as cutting as the bone knives they kept in their belts. While she had no doubt that they told the truth, that didn't mean they'd spare her life when they figured out her unintended deception. How could she tell them she couldn't help them without putting herself or Zelle in danger?

"I…" Her throat went dry. "I'm not capable of what you think I am."

"That remains to be seen." Del snapped her fingers, and the giant bird shuffled over to them, leering down its cruel beak at Aurel. "Maybe if you're forced into combat with the deities, you'll remember your capabilities.

Aurel's pulse raced. "Look, if you really want me to get rid of these deities, then throwing me onto the battlefield won't achieve your goals. It'll just result in me ending up dead. You must know I can't use my magic without the right tools—which you forced me to leave at home."

"Is that true?" Kolt strode in to join the others, his salt-white hair tangled from sleep. She had to admit that he'd be quite attractive to her if he wasn't among the kidnappers debating sending her to her death.

"Might be." Del grunted. "Or she's lying."

"I'm not lying," said Aurel. "Besides, even if I *did* have my props, I can't perform a binding in the middle of a battle. It'd be like trying to recite poetry during a knife fight."

Her captors exchanged more words, while Aurel fervently hoped that the truth in her remarks got through to them. Of course, she hadn't yet admitted she didn't have the ability to bind the deity at all, but she didn't quite trust Toth not to follow through on his threats to drown her if she failed.

Kolt gave her an assessing look. "Then what circumstances would be right for you to perform a binding?"

"I can't. I don't have my Relic." When Toth cracked his knuckles, she suppressed a flinch. "You're asking me to do the impossible."

Zelle hadn't been able to bind Orzen until the collective strength of Rien's new deity and the nameless Shaper had managed to subdue him, and even Zelle might have difficulty with the task when she was away from the mountains and the source of the Shaper's power. The idea of them dragging her to Zeuten didn't appeal either, but there had to be another way.

Aurel shrank back when Toth reached out and grabbed her shoulders, lifting her clean off the ground. "Hey! Put me down. I told you, I can't do what you ask."

Kolt yelled something at Toth in their own language, but Toth ignored both his shouts and Aurel's struggles. He shoved her on top of the giant eagle's back and leapt on behind her. In one beat of feathery wings, they were in the air, the wind swallowing her scream.

Aurel could do nothing but hang on grimly as the eagle carried her towards her fate.

———

Rien sat in the back of the boat with Zelle in front of him while they rowed towards the home of the Blessed. Zelle seemed to know the route well already, not requiring a map to find their way among the various islands. Before long, his arms ached, but not in an unpleasant way. He'd grown somewhat used to not doing much physical labour in his time in Zeuten, and it was refreshing to have something purposeful to do.

As long as he didn't fall under Igon's spell again.

He rowed on, his eyes on the back of Zelle's head, and found himself glad they'd repaired the trust that had grown between them over the past few weeks. While he'd inevitably have to return to Aestin in the future and the question of where Daimos had truly gone lurked in the back of his mind, they had a shared goal. While that trust might evaporate when the deity showed up at their destination and tried to coerce Rien into helping him again, Zelle insisted the staff was prepared to help. Yet Rien's doubts remained, not helped by the staff's own lack of certainty on their ability to bind *or* destroy Igon.

After his conversation with Zelle the previous day, he'd come to realise that her desire to understand the staff's demands was not so different from his own thoughts about Zierne, in no way diminished by her comparative lack of experience. He admired her for that, yet he couldn't think of a way to tell her so which she wouldn't take as condescending or patronising. Regardless, she seemed more confident than he was about the approaching battle.

Frustratingly, Rien was certain that he was more than a match for Igon, but only if he managed to convince Zierne to cooperate with him. It didn't help that he couldn't quite recall the exact wording of the promise he'd made to Igon. He'd helped him take in the magic from the Relic he'd found on the beach, which theoretically counted as upholding his end of the bargain, but the deity might claim otherwise. Like Orzen, Igon was unpredictable, and Rien's conversation with Zelle had reminded him that not all deities were like the steady and predictable Astiva.

Instead, it might be easier if he was to treat Igon as he would any regular adversary.

"This way." Zelle pointed with the end of her oar, shaking him from his thoughts. "We need to turn right."

He hastened to help her turn the corner, and they rowed for a short distance farther before they bumped against the shore near the Blessed's cave. The huge carving of Gaiva's face towered overhead, Her eyes seeming to look down in judgement upon him.

As they made to leave the boat, the screech of a giant bird hit his ears like a thunderclap. Zelle tilted her head up, and the colour drained from her face. "Aurel."

He turned his gaze to the sky and spotted a group of large eagles soaring over the island. Several figures rode on their backs, and on the bird at the head of their group, a muscular man sat behind a white-faced and petrified Aurel.

He expected the birds to swoop down onto a nearby island, but instead, they carried on, soaring into the fog and out of sight.

"Evita can't have found them yet." Zelle picked up her oar and began to steer the boat away from the shore. "They have the sense not to attack the Blessed, at least."

"But once we're back in the boat, they might target us instead," he pointed out.

"That's a risk we'll have to take."

The birds far outpaced their boat, of course, but once they were moving with the currents, Rien and Zelle managed to keep the group of eagles within hearing range, if not within sight. It wasn't long before the birds descended upon another island, wreathed in so much fog that Rien couldn't make out much except for the outlines of a few rocks.

Zelle and Rien picked up the pace, rowing onward. They bumped up against a rock, and Zelle swore under her breath. A flash of light shone from amid the fog, indicating an opening doorway.

Igon was already here.

———

Evita's feet ached. She'd long since grown tired of pacing around the island, waiting for Chirp to find her, but the spear of sand was free of any other forms of entertainment, and the cloak seemed to have no intention of helping her to fly again.

She'd occupied her mind thinking of the reasons it might have helped her and always returned to the same points. She'd been in danger of imminent death, and despite her lack of training, she *had* spent a lot of time with the cloak compared to the average novice. Novices weren't usually allowed to carry their cloaks around for extended periods of time, but she and the cloak had travelled farther than even most Senior Changers did. Or it might have simply been her proximity to Gaiva, or to her Relic. If she was sensible, she'd regard it as a miracle that was unlikely to be repeated.

All she could do was wait for someone to find her. Evita's plan to find Aurel before the others did had long since collapsed, though it wouldn't have surprised her if Rien and Zelle had already left the inn to meet with her on the Isle of the Blessed. With a little luck, they might pass by her island. If not, swimming was an option, but the episode with the sea monster and Zelle's near-drowning had rather put her off the idea.

She'd also, worryingly, lost sight of the deity. Had he gone to the village or pursued the dragonet instead? Was that why he hadn't come back for her? She ought to have known better than to goad him while she was in a vulnerable position, but she'd been trying to divert attention from the villagers... though the deity had hinted that one of them had summoned him in the first place.

A winged shape passed overhead, and she raised her head, her heart lifting. "*There* you are."

Chirp descended onto the island, and Evita bounded over to meet him. She then gave him several affectionate strokes, while the dragonet prowled around her in obvious joy.

"Ready to go and find Aurel?" she asked. "Preferably without running into any gods this time around."

The dragonet chirped in agreement and allowed her to climb onto his back. While the sun had risen higher, the fog had also lifted enough to expose several distant islands she'd been unable to see before—and the unmistakeable outlines of a group of giant eagles descending upon them.

"Is Aurel over there?" She'd initially hoped to sneak up on the defectors' hiding place, but judging by the figures who sat upon the eagles' backs, some of them were already in the air. "We'll have a look, but please try not to let those birds spot you."

Evita pulled her hood up, hiding herself from sight, but Chirp was all too visible. He obeyed, crossing the sea in swift strokes of his wings, towards the island the birds circled.

One eagle had landed on the beach, and two figures leapt down from its back. The first was a large man, and the second—

Aurel.

23

A urel dug her heels into the sand and refused to budge, but her captor effortlessly dragged her across the beach no matter how much of a fuss she raised. A second eagle joined them on the ground, and Del leapt down to join them.

"Igon was here recently," she announced. "I sense him."

"I don't see anyone." Aurel snatched her arm out of Toth's grip. "I told you, I can't bind the deity. I need to be back at home, in Zeuten."

"A likely story," Toth said. "Don't worry. We'll make sure the deity doesn't kill you while you perform the binding."

"Did you intend that to sound so much like a threat?"

The answer was yes, apparently. Toth, Del, and another large man formed a circle around Aurel, seemingly more to prevent her from escaping than to protect her. As more eagles landed on the beach, their riders shouted orders at one another, which mostly flew over Aurel's head. At every attempt she made to leave, someone barred her path, and it wasn't until they all turned in the same direction that she spotted the brightening light at the far edge of the island.

A doorway to the realm of the Powers.

Some of the other defectors had already begun to approach the source of the brightness, their own hands aglow and ice forming above their palms.

"Are you out of your minds?" she demanded. "Stop. I can't do this. You're going to die. All of us are."

Ignoring her protests, Del caught her shoulder and dragged Aurel towards their target. The open doorway lay above the water, and the slim figure of the deity stood in front of the white patch against the air. He watched them, his brows arching at the number of individuals stalking towards him across the beach.

"Now this is an interesting turn of events." He stepped aside, revealing a boat that lay offshore, wedged between two rocks. "Do you know one another?"

Inside the boat sat Rien and Zelle.

———

Zelle half rose from her seat, her heart sinking when the boat bumped to a halt between two large rocks. The light shone above the water, forming the shape of a doorway, and then Igon stepped out. The deity was barefoot, hovering above the water and wearing an expression of polite curiosity while he studied their boat.

"Hello again," he said. "Zelle, is it? I've been curious to meet you."

"I can't say the feeling is mutual." She wished there was an easy way for her to climb out of the boat without risking another near-drowning. Behind him, eagles circled the beach, reminding her of the other danger they faced. The truth hit her in a sickening rush: Gaiva's Blades had brought her sister to fight the deity.

Noticing her attention slip, Igon turned around, watching the birds deposit their riders upon the beach.

"Now this is an interesting turn of events." He stepped aside. "Do you know one another?"

Despite herself, Zelle looked past the deity at the figures gathering on the sand. The defectors were advancing towards Igon as though preparing to attack him—except for one. Her sister.

Their gazes locked, but while Aurel's eyes widened, there was nowhere for her to run. She was surrounded on all sides by fierce-looking white-haired warriors with bone knives and hands aglow with magic. They displayed no fear at the sight of the deity, but he showed no apprehension at being outnumbered either. Instead, Igon smiled widely as though hiding a secret. And he was, in a way, if he'd worked out the mistake the defectors had made in capturing Aurel instead of Zelle.

Behind Zelle, Rien sat frozen in the boat as though unable to move. *Igon.* Anger cracked her fear like shattering ice. She'd told him she wouldn't let Igon take him again, and she refused to break her word.

As Zelle stood upright, raising the staff, another flash of white came from farther down the beach. Some of the defectors turned that way, shouting incomprehensible orders when they realised it was a *second* doorway—but the first was still open. Could Igon open more than one at a time?

The patch of shimmering whiteness hovered above the

beach before a tall figure stepped onto the sand. Dressed in a pale shift-like garment, he had a youngish face and glossy dark hair, and his pointed features were arranged in a grin exactly like Igon's. Zelle did a double take. *Are they identical twins?*

Zelle hardly had a moment to take in the implausible sight when a third doorway appeared at the island's other end, followed by a fourth and a fifth. Three more pairs of bare feet touched down on the sand. All identical.

All of them Igon.

"I think," Zelle whispered to Rien, "we might have solved the mystery of why the staff can't figure out how to bind him to a Relic."

If there were *five* of him, each with his own Relic, then even the staff would be hard-pressed to bind all of them at the same time. If it was possible at all. *Oh, Powers.*

The newcomers' arrival had taken the defectors by surprise, too, but the islanders recovered fast. The man who'd broken into Zelle's shop moved first, gripping a bone knife in his hand as he stalked towards one of the duplicates of Igon. Another islander conjured a handful of whirling silver-white light to his hand. The five deities, however, had surrounded everyone on the beach— including Aurel, who was trapped in the centre.

"I have to get her out of there." Zelle used the oar to push against the rock, but the wood cracked, the boat barely moving a fraction. Cursing, she dropped the oar and lifted the staff instead, giving the rock a firm shove in an attempt to free their boat. She ignored the staff's whispered objection. "Don't you dare complain. If we don't get out of here, we're *all* dead."

Rien rose to his feet, as if shaking off Igon's spell, and

raised his own staff. A torrent of thorny vines shot overhead towards the defectors and deities alike.

"Rien, can you even see who you're aiming at?" Zelle fell sideways with a curse as the boat came free, spinning in the water until it bumped against the shore of the beach.

Zelle climbed out first, staggering a little with dizziness, while Rien placed a hand on her arm, startling her. "I'll get your sister. You wait here by the boat."

"I don't think so." She could hardly see Aurel amid the confusion of the battle, where shards of ice shattered against the sand and gale-force winds rocked the battling deities and humans like ships in a storm. The five deities might have been outnumbered, but they moved much faster, dodging attacks by hopping through doorways and reappearing elsewhere.

The defectors had overlooked Zelle and Rien in favour of attacking the duplicates of Igon, which at least gave them one fewer problem to worry about, but the ruckus made it impossible to see her sister's location.

"You bloody fools!" Aurel's voice shouted from amid the clashing islanders and gods. "Now you've done it."

Zelle followed the sound of Aurel's voice. Three muscular defectors had her surrounded, their backs to Aurel as they fired off attacks at the oncoming deities. Zelle beckoned to her frantically, but Aurel shook her head, indicating the three warriors circling her.

Were they trying to *protect* her? They must have brought her to the battlefield themselves, but it seemed they had yet to figure out that Aurel wasn't the one they'd been looking for. Regardless, if they'd expected her to bind five copies of Igon at once, they might have been overestimating even the nameless Shaper.

Two of the copies of Igon each fired a quick blast of air that struck the beach hard enough to stir up clouds of sand. The warriors bellowed when the sand flew into their eyes, and the breeze intensified, creating a sandy whirlwind that forced them back.

When the dust cleared, the islanders' formation had broken apart. The defectors one-handedly rubbed their sore eyes as they took aim at the deities, their attacks colliding with nothing when the deities gleefully fled through doorways—but they'd left Aurel unguarded.

Zelle waved at her sister and mouthed, "Get over here!"

Aurel, who'd flung herself to the ground when the wall of sand had hit the islanders, lifted her head and then scrambled to her feet. Spotting her, two of the defectors shouted a warning, but at that moment, Rien sprinted into the midst of the battlefield, trailing crimson thorns in his wake. He raised his staff, targeting both defectors and deities alike, and that was all the distraction Aurel needed to sprint over to Zelle.

Zelle hurried up to meet her. "Are you all right?"

"I think so." Aurel cringed when a shard of ice broke against the sand nearby, missing its target when he leapt through a doorway.

"What are they doing?" Zelle held up an arm to shield her face from the clouds of sand. "Even Gaiva's power can't kill those deities. Or deity. Are they one individual or five separate ones?"

"You think I know?" Aurel stepped away from the whirling sand and ice, her face ashen. "They didn't tell *me* there'd be five of them when they brought me here. What *is* Rien playing at?"

"Oh, Powers." Zelle whirled around at the bright crimson glow from Rien's staff. "Of course he's joining the bloody fight. I thought he was just trying to give you an opening to run."

She couldn't tell who he was even attacking from this angle, but neither the deities nor the defectors had any reason to spare Rien's life. If they hadn't all been focused on one another instead of him, then he'd be in a world of trouble. As it was, she and Aurel were forced to throw themselves flat against the sand to avoid being hit by a stray attack.

"What're you even doing here?" Aurel gasped out.

"Looking for you," Zelle returned, crawling along the sand at her sister's side. "We have to go. The boat's over there on the beach, but Rien—"

"Zelle, why is your pocket glowing?"

She rolled onto her back, reaching into her pocket and feeling the smooth stone. *The Relic.* Inside her pocket, the Relic that Rien had given her to look after glowed brightly, as if drawn to the proximity of its owner.

"What in the Powers' names is that?"

"The deity's Relic." She needed to be close to the deity himself for the binding spell to work, assuming it was even possible to bind one deity and not the others. She might not have another chance, so she lifted the Relic in one hand and brushed the staff's end against it. "Bind him."

You might need to get closer.

"Closer?" She rolled onto her front to keep the Relic

from being swept out of her hands by the gust of air scudding across the sand. "Aurel—"

Put that Relic away, the staff commanded. *They're coming.*

"Shit." She lowered her hands when another blast of wind struck the sands, whipping around the island. At the edges, the waves pulled back, and when she risked a look over her shoulder, she saw that the boat had been dragged out to sea. "There goes our escape route."

Aurel pointed up at the sky. "Good job they showed up, then."

Zelle followed her gaze, her heart lifting when she caught sight of Evita and the dragonet flying towards the island.

24

R ien knew that involving himself in the battle wasn't wise, but once he'd diverted the defectors' attention away from Aurel, he found himself surrounded on all sides. Her kidnappers assumed that he was the enemy, while the deities didn't seem to care who they hit. The five copies of Igon were identical down to the last detail, and while they might be five separate deities, they might as easily be five parts of the same whole.

Around him, the defectors' hands glowed with blue-white light as they hurled icy blades at their enemies, while the deities vanished into doorways to dodge every attack. At this point, Rien couldn't even tell which deity was the one who'd originally ensnared him. He held the staff defensively to avoid being hit by any wayward attacks from either side. Gusts of wind battered the sand, and when he glanced over at the beach, he saw Zelle and Aurel retreating from the battlefield.

He called on his deity. "Zierne."

Thorny vines wrapped around the staff at his command, deflecting a blast of ice from the nearest defector. Ignoring the deities, the large man advanced on Rien instead, his hands aglow with blue-white light.

Another tremendous blast of wind swept across the battlefield. Rien braced himself against the staff, and when he glanced back at the beach, his heart dropped when he saw what was left of their battered boat propelled away from the shore by the turbulent waves.

Lifting the staff, he faced the oncoming defector. "Stop! We're fighting the same enemy."

He might as well not have spoken at all. White-blue light pulsed from the man's hands, turning into shards of ice, and the staff began to freeze in his grip.

Not again.

At that moment, a large shadow fell overhead. The dragonet swept into view, wings beating, Evita sitting on his back. As the defectors looked up at the newcomer, Rien took the opportunity to break the staff free from its icy trap and run down the beach towards Zelle and Aurel.

One of the copies of Igon appeared from a doorway in a flash, blocking Rien's path. "I wouldn't run from me. We still have a deal, human, and you owe me."

Zelle noticed, too. Taking a decisive step towards the deity, she lifted her hand and waved something bright and glittering in the air. *The Relic.*

"Hey!" she yelled. "Recognise this?"

To Rien's horror, the deity reached out a hand. "That is mine."

"Come and get it, then." Zelle broke into a sprint, but the deity moved faster, vanishing through the doorway and appearing in front of her in the blink of an eye.

"Zelle!" shouted Rien, running towards her.

The dragonet reached her first. His wings beat, stirring up a gust of wind that battered Igon from behind. It wasn't as strong as one of the deity's own attacks, but it gave Zelle an opening to raise her staff and strike him across the head.

The deity staggered across the stand, bleeding from his mouth, his eyes glittering with fury. "How dare you."

"How dare *you* target my companion." Zelle's mouth was an angry slash. "Rien doesn't owe you anything. He already brought you the Relic you asked him for. Leave him alone."

At the sight of Igon bleeding, a rush of bitter satisfaction flooded him, along with other emotions he hadn't the breath to consider at the present time. He raised his voice and called to the deity. "Exactly. Our bargain is over, Igon."

"You stole what is mine, and for that, your friend will pay."

Igon extended a hand towards Zelle, who raised the staff. "Touch me and you'll make an enemy of the Sentinels of Zeuten. If you don't want to share the fate Orzen did, then I'd suggest you leave my allies alone."

"It was *you*." Igon bared his teeth in a fearsome grin. "You're the one who bound Orzen."

———

The truth was out. Zelle watched Igon, silently urging Rien to get out of the way—but the fool insisted on standing at her side instead of saving himself. Too late, it hit her that the fight had stilled around her and everyone could hear them—from Igon's duplicates to the defectors. The other four Igons veered in her direction, while Zelle found herself abruptly regretting her moment of bravado.

Come on, staff, she thought. *Now would be a great time to demonstrate the power of the nameless Shaper.*

No reply came. Maybe she'd offended the staff when she'd used it as an oar earlier, and it'd decided to stage a mutiny against her in protest, but now was not the time for a temper tantrum. The five deities closed in around her, and a powerful breeze rose from behind them, whipping her hair back. Her hand tightened around the smooth Relic. The staff had claimed that destroying it wouldn't bring about Igon's end, but perhaps it would give him a sufficient shock to drive him and his duplicates away.

"Destroy the Relic," she growled under her breath.

Her fingers clenched around the stone, her ordinary human strength unable to break through. Out of the corner of her eye, she glimpsed Aurel and Rien backing away from the oncoming deities. The defectors simply watched, none of them raising a finger to help any of them.

"I said, *destroy it.*" Her words snapped out, and the staff ignited in response. A blue-white glow engulfed her hand before spreading up her arm. The deities reeled back, shock flittering across all five copies of Igon's face as the staff glowed, haloed in whiteness that made her screw up her eyes as if she'd looked directly at the sun.

The Relic shattered apart in Zelle's hand. Shards of broken stone tumbled onto the sand, their brightness fading to grey.

A cry of fury rose from all five deities at the same time,

but none of them appeared to have been physically harmed. The staff had been right—destroying one Relic wasn't enough—but she'd stunned Igon badly enough that all five copies of him reeled backwards. An instant later, five flashes of light dazzled her eyes when five doorways opened simultaneously, and every copy of Igon vanished within them.

The doorways winked out of existence as one, and a brief moment of silence followed before shouts filled the air. The defectors had scattered, some bleeding, others sporting broken bones. None had been killed as far as Zelle could see, but their furious tones and gestures towards the spot where the doorways had vanished suggested that they resented the deities for disappearing before they'd had the chance to finish their fight.

Zelle, meanwhile, turned towards Rien and Aurel. "We have to go."

They hadn't moved two paces before the defectors had them surrounded. One group of warriors attempted to herd Aurel and Zelle across the beach, while the others circled Rien, their hands alighting with magic. *Oh, Powers.* They thought he was working with Igon, and if she didn't intervene, they'd strike him down. Rien stood rigid, ice spreading across the staff in his grip.

"Leave him alone!" Zelle shouted.

The defectors ignored her, but they all ducked when the dragonet swooped low over the beach, his claws seizing the back of Rien's cloak and hauling him into the air.

Quick thinking on Evita's part—except Zelle and Aurel still had no way off the island. The defectors shouted orders to the sky, and some of their giant eagles peeled away from the group to chase the dragonet.

In the meantime, one of the defectors shoved her sister aside and reached for the staff.

"Hey, you can't take that." Zelle held it out of reach. "It's mine."

Aurel pushed at the muscular man, but he refused to budge. "What are you doing to my sister?"

The man looked down at her with contempt. "Leave us. We have no use for you any longer."

"I thought you needed my help," Aurel said, panic rising in her voice. "You captured me. You can't—"

"It was her we needed," growled the man. "Not you."

Oh, Powers. Zelle knew she'd given herself away during the clash with Igon, but she'd hoped the defectors would have had the sense to realise that their target had shown up willingly, and that no kidnapping was necessary.

"There's no need for this," Zelle protested. "Look, it's obvious that we have a common enemy. If you're willing to talk to us, we can work something out."

A loud screech came from above, and several of the giant eagles descended to land on the beach. Zelle could no longer see the dragonet in the sky, and she fervently hoped Evita and Rien had managed to escape their pursuers.

One of the eagles dove at Aurel, claws outstretched. Aurel recoiled in alarm as the birds drove her back along the beach, away from Zelle.

Then a pair of talons sank into the back of Zelle's fur coat, lifting her up into the sky.

25

"Put me down!" Rien said indignantly from where he dangled from the dragonet's claws.

"You're welcome," Evita called down at him. "You'd be a block of ice if I'd left you down there."

She'd been forced to leave Zelle and Aurel on the beach as it was, but Evita was more focused on not losing her balance than watching the chaos she'd left behind. Huge eagles swooped after them, driving the dragonet backwards and forcing him to fly at a lopsided angle that would have made her dizzy if she wasn't more concerned about being impaled on their sharp claws. Rien was in an even more vulnerable position, dangling from Chirp's grip, but he hardly seemed to notice the eagles. Instead, his attention was on the island they'd left behind.

"We have to get back there," said Rien. "Zelle and Aurel have no way off the island."

"Little difficult," Evita ground out. The giant eagles had them surrounded, and when Rien raised his staff, she added, "Don't you even think about using that thing in mid-air. You'll fall to your death."

Over on the island, meanwhile, the defectors had driven Zelle and Aurel apart, circling both of them.

"What are they doing?" Evita held onto Chirp's scaly neck as he flew higher, dodging the eagles' claws.

"They figured out they captured the wrong person," Rien said from below. "They're going to take Zelle instead."

"Hey!" Aurel yelled, loudly enough for them to hear from up in the air. "Give her back!"

An eagle descended upon Zelle, its claws digging into her back and lifting her off the sand. Rien shouted in anger, and a torrent of thorny vines shot from the end of his staff, lashing at the eagle that held Zelle.

Two more eagles flew to block his way, both with defectors sitting on their backs. The riders effortlessly held onto their steeds one-handedly, their other hands aglow with blue light.

Evita's grip on the dragonet's neck tensed. "Now you've done it."

Chirp veered to the side, and the two attacks narrowly missed Rien's dangling form. More eagles ascended behind them, the defectors riding the giant birds with practised ease while firing off magical attacks at them. Evita cursed Rien vehemently as they flew higher and higher to avoid being speared by icy blades.

"That's enough!" she yelled down at him. "Stop throwing vines around, or I swear I'll tell the dragonet to drop you in the ocean."

"You wouldn't dare." There was little heat in his voice, however, and a glance at the eagles confirmed that the one carrying Zelle had already vanished above the islands.

"I would." She leaned over the dragonet's head. "Fly towards the village. They won't dare start a fight where innocent people might get hit."

At least, she hoped not. The Isle of the Blessed was likely closer to their location, but the defectors had no love for their former companions, and they couldn't rely on Tamacha and the others to come to their defence.

The dragonet hadn't flown far to the south before the eagles gave up on chasing them, however. It seemed that their primary goal had been to drive the dragonet away before taking Zelle to their hiding place.

"Turn around," she whispered to Chirp. "Follow them... slowly."

"Not yet," Rien said from below. "Aurel's still on the island."

Oh, Powers, he was right. The defectors had left her behind, and frankly, she was lucky they hadn't killed her instead. "Can you fly down to her?"

The dragonet obeyed, bringing them down to land upon the now deserted island. Aurel stood alone on the sand, wearing an overlarge fur coat that her captors must have given her and an equally ill-fitting pair of fur-lined boots. She gave Evita and Rien a sheepish look when they landed next to her. "I don't suppose you've got room for one more person?"

———

The giant eagle carried Zelle for an indeterminate length of time. She'd seen the others attacking Evita, but as it took all her focus not to drop the staff, picking a fight at this height would only end in her premature death. With luck, the eagles would tire of chasing the others soon enough. After all, Zelle was their target. She always had been.

For that reason, the defectors ought to have been invested in keeping her alive, but Zelle preferred not to test their commitment by forcing the eagle to drop their quarry. Even the staff might not help her survive a fall from this height. Instead, she hung from the eagle's claws until they came to a halt on a beach in front of a set of jagged rocky cliffs. Several caves were visible underneath, but she couldn't see how far they extended from this angle.

The eagle set her down on her feet before releasing her, while its companions landed beside her on the sand, hemming her in. The eagles' riders leapt off their backs, while several others ran from the caves to join them. The islanders conversed in loud voices, occasionally pointing in Zelle's direction, while she stood with her hands clenched around the staff and waited for an opening to speak.

When none came, she cleared her throat and cut through their chatter. "I know these aren't ideal circum-stances for us to have met, but I believe we're facing a common enemy."

The man who'd attacked her shop gave her a glare then said something in the Itzar language to his compan-ions. At once, several pairs of hands seized the staff and tried to tug it out of Zelle's grip.

Zelle tugged back. "I told you, this is mine. I'm willing to have a discussion with you, despite the fact that you almost *drowned* me, but you're going to have to stop trying to steal my property."

"Is it true?" A woman, who had a tattoo shaped like an anchor on one cheek, addressed her first. "Are you the Sentinel?"

"No, that's my grandmother," she said. "I might add that some of you attacked her and left her for dead at the Reader's house in Zeuten, so believe me when I say I'd rather eat sand than negotiate with you. But I'm willing to overlook our unpleasant history if it means getting rid of that deity, Igon."

More words were exchanged, none of which Zelle understood. It sounded like an argument, which the man who'd attacked her at the shop cut short by grabbing the staff again and tugging hard. She hoped the staff might fight back by pinning itself to her hands or granting her superior strength, but it did nothing to prevent him from yanking it out of her grip. When she lunged after it, another warrior seized her arms behind her back, binding them roughly with rope before pushing her across the beach and into the cave under the cliff face.

The main cave was bigger than she'd first thought, with at least ten or fifteen rogues clustered around a fire pit and several smaller caves branching off the main one. In fact, it looked as though Gaiva's Blades had attempted to build their own version of the caves on the Isle of the Blessed, but they'd lacked the resources. Their home also didn't seem to be a permanent base, but that was to be expected. They'd turned their backs on their own deity, after all.

So much for negotiating with them.

Her captor shoved Zelle past the fire pit and down a

short passageway. He then pushed her roughly into one of the smaller caves and dragged a large rock into place, sealing the cave shut.

Zelle rose to her feet at once, but they'd tied the ropes around her wrists too tightly for her to free herself, and she wasn't strong enough to lift the boulder even if her hands were free. She fell back into a sitting position on the cave floor, cursing the Powers and her captors all at once.

The cave they'd sealed her in was even smaller than her quarters above the shop in Saudenne, and the only source of light came through a crack where the boulder met one side of the cave walls. When darkness fell, she wouldn't be able to see past her nose. Why had she thought the defectors might be willing to listen to reason? Admittedly, Evita had been more optimistic than she, but the defectors' fixation on defeating Igon had made her briefly hope they might be able to find common ground. Instead, they'd shut her away like a criminal.

The image of the intruders crumpling to the floor of her shop came to mind, and she grimaced. Maybe they did have a reason to treat her like a potential danger, given that she'd killed one of their companions. The furious way the second man from the shop had glowered at her made her certain he'd seen to her capture *and* the theft of the staff in retaliation, but how could she talk to the others when she was trapped like this?

Some time passed, though it was beyond her to tell how much, before the large rock shifted a little, and the face of the second man who'd broken into her shop glowered at her through the gap.

Zelle sat up against the wall, acutely aware of her

bound hands and the fact that the man had come to her alone. Did he plan to have her killed after all?

"I…" She swallowed hard. "I wish you'd told me the truth when you broke into my shop in the middle of the night. Your companion needn't have died."

"Don't you dare speak of him," he growled in Zeutenian. "You slew him without mercy."

"I was defending myself and my home," she said. "I had no other way to fend you off except the staff, and I had no reason to believe you didn't intend to have me killed. If you'd come to visit me during daylight hours and explained the situation, I might have been happy to come and help you."

"Forgive me if I do not believe you," he replied. "You deceived us into wasting our time with your sibling when you were the person we needed."

"I didn't deceive you." Powers above, she wished she had the staff in her hands. "I didn't *want* you to capture my sister any more than I wanted you to take the staff. Can't I talk to someone else? Someone who didn't try to rob me?"

He moved the rock a little more so that his large body barred her way out of the cave. "Some of them want to set you free, to listen to you. I disagree. You are a murderer, and your friend even fought on Igon's side."

"Which friend? Rien?" Oh, Powers. She had no explanation that this man would find reasonable, and Rien's entanglement with Igon was none of their business anyway. "He fought against you because you captured my sister. And now, me. I can guarantee you'd rather have him on your side than against you."

"I will not listen to any more of your lies."

"I'm not lying." Alarm spiked when he withdrew from sight. What would happen if the deity attacked the camp while she was trapped in here? Without the staff, she'd be helpless to defend herself, let alone anyone else. "Wait. I can help you."

"You *will* help us." His angry face reappeared for a brief moment. "But I will not allow the others to free someone who slaughtered one of our own."

And without another word, he shoved the rock back into place and left her in the dark.

26

E vita, Rien and Aurel stood on the beach, assessing their options. Chirp padded along the sand, but despite his recent growth spurt, Evita had her doubts that the dragonet could support all three of them at once.

"Can you find the missing boat?" she asked Chirp. "It's... where did it go, Aurel?"

"No clue." Aurel pointed vaguely across the waves lapping against the shore, calm where they'd been turbulent not so long ago. "Rien, did you see?"

"We need to get to Zelle," Rien insisted. "Aurel, where did they take her?"

"Back to their caves, I assume," she told him. "I can't say I'm sure of how to get there by boat, though. This place is a Powers-cursed maze if you don't have one of their massive birds."

"Why did you let them take her?" Rien's voice was quiet, but his grip on the staff was taut, and Evita sensed his temper rising.

295

"*Let* them?" Aurel echoed. "We were outnumbered by far. Besides, I notice *you* didn't do anything to help us."

"Don't argue," said Evita. "None of us could have stopped them from taking her. Not even Igon—all five of him—managed to kill any of those defectors."

Unfortunately, the reverse was also true. The battle-field was littered with spatters of blood and bits of frozen sand where the defectors' magic had struck, but no casualties had hit either side, with the possible exception of the Relic that Zelle had crushed in her hand with the staff's help. The shards had been lost somewhere amid the wreckage, but they'd retrieved one ally only to lose another one. Worse, Zelle was the only person who'd been able to put up a fight against Igon, and if he returned to attack the others while she was gone, Evita didn't like to think of the consequences.

Aurel's eyes narrowed. "Did any of *you* know he could split himself into five copies?"

"Of course we didn't," said Rien. "We thought there was only one."

Aurel focused on him. "What *were* you doing with him, anyway? It looked like you were fighting *for* him."

"Not intentionally." Rien lowered his gaze. "It's a long story."

"I think we have time," Evita said wryly. The dragonet had taken flight in search of the missing boat, but until then, they were stuck here. For Aurel's benefit, she added, "Igon tricked Rien into accepting a deal with him."

Rien lifted his head to glower at her. "That's not how it happened. Besides, he didn't mention that he shared his power between five Relics and had four copies of himself running around."

"Does that mean if we kill one, we kill them all?" Aurel asked.

Rien shook his head. "Not in my experience. The tradition among the Invokers of Aestin is to split their deity's magic between multiple Relics to ensure that if one Relic is taken, the deity's power remains within their family. Besides, Zelle destroyed one of Igon's Relics, but none of the copies of Igon disappeared."

Oh. It had slipped Evita's mind that Rien's own family had all met the same brutal fate at the hands of someone who wanted to possess the entirety of their magic, but Igon's Relics had no wielders. He'd been given a human form, like Orzen had.

"Bloody wonderful." Aurel sat down on the beach. "Those defectors still have Igon outnumbered, but that's no use as long as they keep fighting against us as well as the deities."

"I wish they understood we're on the same side," said Evita. "They took Zelle because they need her help to banish Igon, which is what she had every intention of doing anyway."

"They tried to drown her, too, didn't they?" Rien paced across the beach, his hands locked around his staff. "And now she's their prisoner. They don't care about her; they care about exploiting her connection with the nameless Shaper and the staff for their own purposes."

"They don't know about the Shaper, do they?" Guilt flickered across Aurel's features. "I never told them."

"No, but they saw her break that Relic," said Evita. "It was hard to miss."

"Yeah, there is that." Aurel's fingers absently carved furrows into the sand. "But unlike me, Zelle *can* bind Igon using her staff. They won't kill her, not if they want the staff to cooperate. Granted, it doesn't listen to Zelle most of the time anyway…"

Rien shot her a glare, while Evita racked her brain, unable to think of a single word to say that might improve the situation. Luckily for all of them, the sound of wings beating rose from nearby, and Chirp flew up to the shore, dragging a battered boat with a broken oar in his claws.

Aurel gave the boat a dubious look. "Are you sure three of us can get into that without it falling to pieces?"

"I'll fly on the dragonet, and you two can take the boat," Evita offered. "Only if you agree not to go chasing after Zelle, though."

"Agreed," said Aurel. "Stop looking at me like that, Rien. I barely escaped alive last time, and besides, I don't know how to find their caves from the water."

"I might be able to find them from the sky," admitted Evita, "but I'll have to be careful not to let those eagles spot me."

Rien eyed her. "Wasn't that what you intended to do earlier this morning?"

"Yes, before Igon tried to throw me into the sea." Heat crept up her neck at the memory of her failed mission. "I ended up stranded on an island and had to wait for Chirp to find his way back to me."

Aurel pushed to her feet. "Better than being tricked into doing the deity's biding, I suppose."

Rien's face reddened. "That won't happen again. I already found a Relic for him, which ought to count as maintaining my end of the bargain."

"A Relic?" Aurel echoed. "How'd he get a human body in the first place? Or five of them?"

Rien was silent for a moment. "Someone summoned him."

Evita's heart gave an uneasy flip. Igon himself had insinuated that someone among the villagers had been responsible, but he might easily have been lying. Besides, the summoner was the least of their problems. They needed to find Zelle before Igon did, but they were outnumbered. Unless...

"We can talk to the Blessed." The dragonet lowered his head next to Evita and made a chirping noise, and Evita stroked his nose. "They aren't on the same side as Igon *or* Gaiva's Blades. They don't seem to want to fight the deities, which is why the defectors left to begin with, but they won't want Zelle to remain their captive. They saved her life yesterday."

"They did?" Aurel pointed across the current of water in front of the island. "Wait. There's someone coming this way."

Sure enough, Gatt paddled into view in his boat. When he spotted them, he called, "Everything all right over there?"

"Not exactly." Rien strode to the edge of the island to wait for him to reach the shore. "Zelle was taken by the defectors."

Aurel turned to Evita with a questioning look on her face. "Do you know him?"

"He gave us a tour of the islands when most of the other locals wouldn't talk to us," explained Evita. "Mostly because a giant sea monster attacked us on the crossing from Zeuten."

Aurel's eyes widened. "A giant sea monster? Yeah, I can see why they wouldn't want to associate with you after that."

"It wasn't our fault," Evita protested. "I don't *think* it was, anyway?"

"How many times have you nearly died since you got here?" asked Aurel.

"A few."

Aurel's brow furrowed. "No offence intended, but what are you even doing here? You could have stayed at home. You don't have a stake in this."

A flush swept over Evita's cheeks. "I didn't have anywhere else to go. Besides, you're my employer, and Zelle couldn't find you alone."

That wasn't quite right either, but a combination of loyalty and curiosity had tangled together to draw her over the ocean, in addition to her deep-seated desire for adventure. And she couldn't deny this *had* been an adventure, even if she'd been terrified out of her mind for most of it.

Aurel blinked at her. "Wasn't Rien with her?"

"No…" From Zelle's reaction when they'd run into Rien at Saudenne's harbour, they hadn't parted on friendly terms, though Evita remained ignorant of the actual nature of their argument. Given the amount of time they'd spent talking outside the inn the previous night, she assumed they'd put the matter behind them. "Never mind why I came here. I'm staying because I want to help Zelle."

Gatt's boat bumped against the shore. He and Rien exchanged a few words before Rien returned to their side. "He doesn't know where they took Zelle, but he said the Blessed might be able to help. He also offered to loan us his boat, since ours is in a sorry state."

"Oh," said Evita. "There's no need for that… I don't want him to get stranded out here either."

"He said he won't have trouble." Rien indicated their guide, who'd climbed into their battered boat and picked up the cracked oar. "He knows the Isles well. Aurel, do you want to speak to the Blessed?"

"You're not going to chase after the defectors?" Something the older man had said must have convinced him it was worth asking the Blessed for help. Evita was less than convinced they'd be willing to fight their former allies, but it was better than running straight into another trap. "I'll lead the way."

Evita climbed onto the dragonet's back while Aurel and Rien approached the boat that Gatt had loaned them. He was a long way from home, and she wondered what had driven him to venture into this remote part of the Isles. He couldn't know he'd come close to interrupting the fight between the defectors and the deities, surely.

Rien climbed into the back of the boat behind Aurel. "I hope you remember the way, Evita, because Zelle had the only map."

"I remember." Despite the low-level fog and the sickening lurch as the island shrank beneath her and Chirp, she could see the direction they needed to follow. Less clear was the likely outcome of asking the Blessed to negotiate with those who'd betrayed their cause. Perhaps Zelle being taken would change their minds, since the Blessed knew she wielded the Relic of the nameless Shaper. They must know how dangerous it was for her staff to end up in the wrong hands, and how dire the consequences would be if she were to die.

Evita flew into the lead, keeping one eye on the small

boat weaving through the islands below. They hadn't got far, however, before the others' boat came to a halt. With a whispered instruction to the dragonet, she backtracked and flew low enough to hear Rien say to Aurel, "I think we hit a rock. There's a hole under my feet."

"Oh, Powers," said Aurel. "Right, keep rowing. We can still make it."

The boat rattled forward, but the faster it moved, the higher the water rose around its edges. Alarm flickered through Evita when she saw the water swirling over the sides of the boat, trapping Rien and Aurel.

Then a doorway opened in front of them, and Igon stepped out of it and smiled at Rien. "Have you changed your mind yet, Arien Astera?"

———

More time passed in frustrating silence as Zelle struggled to undo her bonds. Her captor had tied tight knots, and none had come to speak to her since the man whose companion she had killed. She'd have to wait for someone more reasonable to come along before she'd have a chance of getting through to them, but whatever they were doing with the staff, they hadn't come back to ask for her help yet.

The staff would never do as they asked, she knew, but that didn't mean she had it in herself to be patient until they reached the same conclusion. She leaned back, trying to work the ropes loose by rubbing the knot against the hard rock of the cave wall.

"Come on," she growled, half to herself.

A sudden jolt travelled through her limbs, and then the

rope fell to pieces on either side of her, her hands abruptly freed. As she blinked in disbelief, a bright glow shone from her pocket. "What the—?"

It couldn't be possible, but the glow could only have one cause. Holding her breath, she reached into the pocket of her furs and pulled out a shard of crystalline rock.

A piece of Igon's shattered Relic.

Igon's voice spoke in her mind, sharp and whispering. *I broke your bonds. Now, summon me, and I will get you out of that cave.*

"Nice try," she muttered to the Relic—or rather, Igon. "You shouldn't even be able to talk to me."

I helped you, and now you owe me.

"I didn't ask for your help." She stretched out her sore wrists. "I doubt you can move boulders, anyway."

You can either trust me, or you can stay in here indefinitely. They have the staff, and you need my help to get it back.

"Trust you?" She gave a short laugh. "Not likely. You aren't even here, besides. This Relic is a fragment. Scarcely that, given that I shattered you into pieces."

So is that staff of yours, he replied. *And that wasn't enough to destroy me.*

"Because destroying one of your Relics isn't enough." She'd worked that much out, but prying the other Relics from the hands of the identical copies of Igon would be much harder than obtaining the first one.

You understand, then. You should also know that I can see your surroundings, and I know these Isles well. I will find you in the end.

"There's not much to see." Yet her heart raced faster at his words. If he'd been able to see her journey to the defectors' caves, then he'd already know her location. She wasn't in a position to destroy his remaining Relics and bind him without the staff in her hands. "Why would you want to help me? You know what I did to Orzen, and you must know I have every intention of doing the same to you."

You know nothing of what you threaten me with, humans, whispered Igon. *Do you have any idea how long I have desired to see the realm of my kin again? For centuries, I was imprisoned in this realm, lost in the darkness, until my last Relic found its way into human hands.*

Zelle knew better than to fall for Igon's pitiful bid for sympathy after everything he'd already done. "You could have gone home when you were set free from your Relic. Instead, you decided to threaten the islanders."

Threaten? A bitter laugh sounded from the shard of rock. *It was they who set me free.*

Her heart missed a beat. "Who summoned you?"

She didn't expect an answer, but the deity spoke with barely restrained glee. *I believe you have met them.*

"What?" Was this some new trickery, or was the deity giving her a genuine clue about who'd freed him from his Relic and given him a human body? "It wasn't one of the defectors, was it?"

Surely not. They'd gone as far as to betray their own goddess to fight against Igon. They wouldn't have let the person who'd released him into the mortal realm join their ranks.

The Relic fell silent. A grating noise sounded, and within a few moments, the boulder shifted to the side, revealing the man who'd broken into her shop. He had company this time, a woman with an anchor tattoo on her right cheekbone and who wore her salt-white hair tied back with rope.

The woman's gaze went straight to Zelle's unbound hands—and then the glow emanating from her pocket. "What is that?"

Zelle weighed the odds, then pulled out the shard of rock. "It's a piece of a Relic. I broke it earlier, but apparently it wasn't enough to remove the deity's presence entirely."

Her eyes fell on the broken ropes. "You allied with *him?*"

"No," she said quickly. "He broke the ropes without my asking him to. He keeps trying to bargain with me, and he said he's coming here. You have to give me the staff back, or else I won't be able to help you fight him."

The woman reached for the shard of broken Relic, but Zelle backed farther into the cave, shaking her head. She didn't know what would happen if another person touched the shard of rock. Would the deity try to recruit them, too?

"Don't touch it." She held the piece of rock behind her back. "I don't know how it's still functioning after I broke the Relic, but it might be able to harm you."

The woman pinned Zelle against the wall with her forearm. As the shard of rock fell from Zelle's hand, the man reached out and snagged the piece of Igon's Relic from the ground.

"Gaiva is my goddess," he said. "Igon will not corrupt us."

"Stop!" She wrenched her hand free from the woman's grip, almost breaking her wrist in the process, but she was

EMMA L. ADAMS

too late. The glow around the piece of rock intensified, and the man let out a choked scream.

"What have you done?" the woman demanded.

Zelle fell back against the wall, rubbing her sore wrist. The man stood still for a moment before he flung the piece of broken Relic to the ground. With a trembling hand, he reached into the pocket of his fur coat and pulled out a second gleaming shard of rock. *His Relic.* Yet the shard's bright glow was dimming, while the piece of Igon's Relic glowed brightly at their feet.

He looked up at his companion, his expression taut with despair. "I can feel Gaiva's strength weakening."

"What?" Zelle looked between the Relics in dawning horror. Rien had mentioned helping Igon drain the power from a Relic he'd found on the beach, but Igon shouldn't have been able to drain a Relic that already had a wielder, let alone without his human form being present. Unless the mere act of the man touching Igon's Relic with his own hands had been enough for Igon to steal the strength of his deity.

It is. Thank you, human, Igon's voice whispered in her ear.

"You brought him here." The woman glared at Zelle. "You will die for this."

27

Rien looked up at Igon as the boat continued to fill with water, and a spasm of rage shook his whole body. "You again."

"Go away," Aurel said from in front of him. "We're busy here."

"*You* are nobody at all," said Igon. "Even the ones who call themselves Gaiva's Blades didn't want you, did they?"

Aurel's head snapped up. "Is that the best you can do? You're nothing but a fragment of a person. A pathetic one at that."

"Oh, but I'm not alone." Igon smiled, beckoning to Rien. "The two of us have a bargain, do we not?"

"Our bargain is ended," Rien ground out. "I gave you that Relic and ended our agreement."

Aurel scoffed. "Do you really need Rien to run errands for you, Igon? Or are you just fond of pushing people around?"

"Enough," Igon spat. "Arien Astera is mine to command."

Rien didn't move. "You have no power over me. How do I know I'm even talking to the same Igon I bargained with? You all look the same to me."

Irritation flickered through Igon's features. "We *are* the same. We are one, and we are never alone. Unlike you. You have nothing, not even that deity you think you command. He is no ally of yours."

Ignore him, Rien thought. Igon was trying to taunt him, nothing more, and he'd given away a little about his own motives. *We are never alone.* Had that been a condition of his summoning? If he'd wanted the company of other deities in this realm, then his only option might well have been to split himself into several bodies. "*Your* only true allies are your own shadows. You won't fool me again."

Igon's mouth twisted in anger, furthering Rien's certainty that he'd guessed the truth. "You may have found a new Relic to replace the one you lost, but no deity who bows to the will of a mortal is truly one of us. Zierne knows you're holding him back. He'll leave you, too, given the chance."

"You're wrong." Astiva might not have been his to command any longer, but that didn't mean he'd stand for him being insulted—nor Zierne, either. "About both of us."

"When we first met in the flesh, you showed yourself not to have changed at all since the day we met," said Igon. "I can see your desperation, Arien Astera. It's as stark as it was when you made that desperate bargain with me, begging for me to pull you from the depths of the ocean and give you a second chance at life. You're scared to die, yet you're even more frightened to see *him* again."

Did he mean Daimos? Or Astiva? Igon's words reached

deep within him to a place he hadn't looked at in a long time, but the water filling the boat around his feet reminded him of a far more immediate dilemma.

Raising the staff, he pointed it at Igon. "Get out of the way."

A glow ignited in Igon's eyes, and a sudden grin appeared on his mouth. "With every Relic I consume, I grow stronger... and someone has just generously gifted one to me."

"What does *that* mean?" Aurel demanded. "Gifted you with what?"

Instead of responding, Igon vanished through a doorway. He left behind a gust of wind that caused the boat to rock alarmingly, and Rien grabbed the edge to keep from falling in. A familiar spasm of panic rose at the sensation of the cold abyss beneath him, but Aurel's yelp when the boat rocked reminded her that he wasn't the only one who'd be in peril if they didn't get back on land.

"Rien!" Evita shrieked, leaning over the dragonet's side as they flew overhead. "Hang on—I can help."

At Evita's instructions, the dragonet grabbed the front of the boat in his claws before it could sink. Rien gripped the staff in one hand and hung on grimly until they reached a rocky formation jutting out of the water. He and Aurel clambered to safety onto the rocks before watching the remains of the boat vanish from sight.

Once again, they were stranded... but where had Igon gone? And just what had he meant when he'd claimed someone had gifted him a Relic?

———

The woman advanced on Zelle, who had nothing to defend herself with. Except the shard of rock that lay at her feet, which continued to glow as though the creature to whom it belonged was revelling in the power he'd stolen. Zelle hadn't known that simply touching the Relic would have such an effect, but the man had fallen to the ground in the cave's entryway, his own Relic's glow dimmed to grey.

Two more defectors moved in behind the woman, who stopped her advance to bark at them in their own language. When one of them reached down to pick up the glowing shard of Igon's Relic, Zelle stepped in. "Don't touch it! It'll do the same to you as it did to him."

Ignoring her warnings, one of them grabbed the shard of rock and left the cave. He hadn't taken two steps before he began to scream.

The two remaining islanders shouted at Zelle, who didn't need to be able to understand the Itzar language to know they were accusing her of somehow being responsible for draining the strength from their companions' Relics.

"It's him!" She jabbed a finger at the shard of Igon's Relic, which the second man had dropped when he'd fallen to his knees. "That Relic steals magic from anyone who touches it and gives that power back to Igon."

The woman with the anchor tattoo spoke in Zeutenian. "You're lying. Why would the deity steal our magic and not yours?"

Why indeed? The nameless Shaper must be immune to Igon's powers, but they seemed to think the trickery was Zelle's work and not the staff's. "The staff is different. Besides, I'm not holding it at the moment."

The notion of telling them the true nature of the staff's magic repelled her, but at this point, it might be the only way to keep herself alive. More shouts echoed from outside as the other islanders were drawn to the noise, until it seemed like half the camp surrounded her cave. The first man who'd lost his magic was on his feet, shouting along with the rest of them.

"I can't feel her any longer, Del," he sobbed in Zeutenian, addressing the woman. "Gaiva. She took Her from me."

Zelle tried to reach for the shard of Relic, but the crowd of defectors barred her way out of the cave. "Igon—the deity—he draws in the power of anyone who touches one of his Relics, and he might be using it to track your location right this instant. I need the staff."

"She might be correct," said a muscular man in halting Zeutenian. "Igon is getting stronger, and if she speaks true, then we cannot touch his Relic without losing our own link to Gaiva."

Was *that* what the Relic had done? Had it not simply drained the magic from their Relics, but also cut them off from their deity? She doubted her link with the nameless Shaper could be broken so easily, since the Relic hadn't drained *her* power...

Because it had nothing to take, she realised. She had no magical gift of her own without the staff, and that simple fact had likely spared her from suffering the same fate as the two stunned men who'd lost their magic *and* their bond with Gaiva in the same instant.

"Then why did she bring this Relic to our home?" The woman—Del—gave Zelle a contemptuous stare. "Did she and Igon intend to infiltrate our base?"

"You kidnapped me," Zelle retaliated. "And I didn't know Igon's Relic still had any power left inside it after I broke it into pieces. You saw me, didn't you?"

"Yes, we did," said an older man, elbowing his way through the crowd. Zelle's heart gave a jolt when she glimpsed the staff clenched in his hand. "It's curious that someone like you—not the Sentinel—was able to achieve such a feat."

"Like I said—" she had to raise her voice to be heard over the others' shouts "—I intend to rid the Isles of Igon's threat, but I've never fought a deity who can split himself into five parts before. I need access to all five of his Relics in order to bind or destroy him."

More voices shouted. The man holding the staff was shunted backwards, out of the cave, while the others closed in around her.

Then a new voice joined them, loud enough to mask them all, speaking in clear Zeutenian. "Thank you, Zelle Carnelian."

The light of a doorway shone from behind the enraged islanders. *Igon.* Zelle's blood iced over, dread pulsing under her skin. She'd seen his arrival coming, but not this soon.

The defectors backed away from her to face the new threat. Zelle wouldn't have a better chance to get the staff back for her own, so she pushed forwards and darted out of the cave, eyes open for the man holding the staff.

She didn't have to look far. The defectors had scattered, and she soon spotted her target. The older man's eyes flew wide as she ran at him, but he didn't fight back when she snatched the staff from his hands.

Searing cold burned her palms. Someone had used

their icy magic on the staff—perhaps experimenting to see if it would entice a reaction—but she held on, teeth clenched against the pain. A shout echoed across the beach, and she spun on her heel. Igon stood amid the defectors, crouching over one of the men who'd lost his magic. As she watched, Igon plucked the shard of rock from his hand. He gave them all another wide smile as he slipped it into a pocket. "Thank you for holding this for me."

The defectors advanced on Igon, shards of ice forming in their hands, but he vanished into a doorway in a blink. Icicles broke against the sand, prompting a flurry of defectors racing for the cave entrance to avoid being struck by their own attacks.

Zelle gripped the staff, the cold sensation fading as the ice melted, but the deity was no longer within sight. He'd gone… but a faint tremor underneath her feet warned her he hadn't left the island untouched.

Shouts rang out from farther down the beach. Zelle turned around and saw that the seas had swept in across the sands, lapping against the cliffs and causing the island to shrink at the edges.

Another tremor underfoot caused a thrill of dread to travel through her. Didn't Igon have some measure of control over the seas? If he did, then being trapped on an island might prove fatal for all of them. The shifting sands moved farther inland, pushed by the waves, while the rocks forming the caves continued to tremble. Several fragments of rock fell from the ceiling, prompting shouts from the islanders, but there was nowhere for them to run. If the waters reached them first, they might find themselves buried alive in their own caves, but if the alternative was to be swept out to sea, did they have any options?

"Help me," she whispered to the staff in her hand. "I'm sorry I let them take you, but we're in serious trouble if we don't find a way off this island."

The staff remained unresponsive. The reminder hit her that Igon hadn't been able to drain the staff's power because it wasn't linked to Zelle the way the others—the Blessed and Gaiva's Blades alike—held a direct connection to their deity. Rien, too, wore the godsmarks of both his current and former deities, but Zelle's allegiance with the Shaper had left no such marks on her skin.

If you want to form such an allegiance, there'll be no taking it back. The staff's voice spoke in her mind, cutting through the background noise of the panicking defectors and the tremors rocking the island.

"*Can* I do that?" she replied. "I thought—I didn't claim you, did I?"

Not in so many words. She'd allied with the staff, but that was a world away from the direct physical connection between Rien and his staff. He'd come close to death when his bond with his first deity had been severed, while the defectors had cried out in genuine pain when Igon had stolen their link to their deity.

Did she want that? To be bound to a Great Power in such a way was no choice to make lightly, yet each passing moment saw her forced back from the beach until she ducked under the trembling overhang of a cliff, surrounded by the waves lapping at the island's edges.

You decide.

"Tell me honestly if there's another way to survive this."

The islanders' boats were long gone; even their eagles would have nowhere to land. When a piece of rock the size of a boulder shattered amid the islanders, causing shards to slice into Zelle's legs through her thick furs, her resolve gave way to terror.

You know the answer, Zelle, but if you let me in, then you won't be able to undo that choice.

"I don't care." She squeezed her eyes shut against a shower of dust from the rock ceiling. "If I don't, I'm dead."

You might not like who you become.

Who she became? What would it mean to be truly bound to the Shaper? To channel the staff's magic through her own hands and to wield the terrifying strength of one of the three Great Powers, who had been feared enough to be imprisoned beneath a mountain for thousands of years?

Dust rained down. The sea closed in. Another shard of rock shattered at her feet.

"I bind myself to you, nameless Shaper." She gripped the staff with both hands. "Is that enough?"

As the staff began to glow, a rush of energy flooded her that made her eyes fly wide open. Lights spun up and down her arms in trails of swirling lines, radiating outwards from the staff and bathing the cave in the same vibrancy.

The tremors below their feet slowed, grinding to a halt, and she *felt* the Shaper's magic stilling the rocky walls and calming the churning seas. Bluish light shone from the staff, and Zelle's awareness expanded along with it. She sensed the strands of energy holding the island together, and a certainty hit her that it would be effortlessly easy to rip apart those strands with her bare hands, to unmake this island under the defectors' feet and bury them beneath the waves.

No, she told herself firmly—the staff's voice had quietened, but her own inner voice didn't quite sound the same as usual either. Nevertheless, it was Igon she needed to find. The defectors were no threat to the nameless Shaper, so she turned her back on them and raised a hand.

The seas receded, the waves peeling back and leaving the sands bare and glittering. As she ran out onto the beach, a grinding crash made her spin on her heel. The instant she'd left the cave, the tremors had begun anew, shaking the ground beneath the defectors' feet.

"Wait." She didn't know if she was addressing the staff or the new magic pouring through her own veins, but in any case, her words had no effect. Chunks of rock rained down in front of the cave entrance, forming a line of boulders that prevented anyone from following her.

Did I do that? Zelle glanced down at the staff, alarmed to see that the swirling lines on her wrists hadn't faded yet. Instead, they resembled the thornlike marks on Rien's own hands. Did that mean they were permanent? She hoped not, but now wasn't the time to worry about the long-term consequences of her choice. The tremors slowed, but the rocks kept shifting forwards until the entire cave entrance was hidden from sight.

"You trapped them in there, didn't you?" she asked the staff.

Yes, I did.

She was surprised at how much of a relief it was to hear the staff's voice, speaking as a separate entity to her. As badly as she'd needed the Shaper's help, she didn't want to think of the potential consequences to her own sanity if she and the nameless Shaper *did* join like a regular Relic and its wielder.

"Don't you think we might need the help later?" She indicated the rocks, behind which she could hear hoarse shouts from the islanders.

If you have the patience to waste more time trapped in a prison, then you're welcome to attempt to reason with them.

"No need for that tone." She didn't have time to deal with their reaction to her newfound bond with the staff, though, nor its magic rippling through her veins and urging her to reshape the very ground beneath her feet. "Is that you or me?"

Both. The connection between us has consolidated my own strength as well as yours.

Powers. She'd made the staff stronger, as much as the staff had done the same to her.

Don't get arrogant. You would be nothing without me.

Zelle snorted a little. "Nice to know some things haven't changed." She looked out to sea, trying to ignore the shouts rising from behind the pile of rocks concealing the cave entrance. "Let's find the others."

———

The dragonet released the boat after Rien and Aurel had climbed to safety on the small rocky outcropping. The outcropping wasn't big enough for her to land on, so Evita had to settle for perching on Chirp's back while Aurel lay on her side, coughing up water. Rien didn't look much better. The colour had drained from his face, and while she'd remained out of reach for most of their confrontation, she'd heard Igon's taunting comments about Rien's former deity.

Aurel coughed again, propping herself onto her elbow. "Powers, that was a close call. You know, I almost prefer being held captive to talking to that Igon. He likes the sound of his own voice entirely too much."

Rien pushed upright, an angry flush crossing his cheekbones. "Igon has no understanding of any of us, no matter what he might think."

"I hope so, considering he called me *nobody*," Aurel scoffed. "Where'd he disappear to?"

"Zelle." Rien rose to his feet, gripping his staff. "There's nobody else that could have drawn him away so swiftly."

"It might have escaped your attention, but he sank our boat," said Aurel. "We're not going anywhere until we fix it."

Evita thought she might be hoping for too much. The boat lay almost completely submerged under the water, leaving them suspended on the rocky island.

Rien eyed the spot where the boat had sunk. "I thought Gatt's boat would have been better made."

"Maybe he sabotaged us on purpose," said Aurel. "I don't know who he is, admittedly, but why'd he show up after the battle was already over? If he's an ordinary villager, you'd think he'd want to stay *away* from the warring deities."

Good question. Now Evita thought back, Igon had insinuated that his summoner had been among the villagers… but what use was that information now they were stranded again?

"I'll go and get help," she offered. "I'll find a boat that *doesn't* have holes in it."

"What the—?" Aurel grabbed the rocky floor as the island gave a sudden lurch as if pulled by an invisible force, the waters rising around its edges. Was Igon back already?

"What's going on?" Rien braced his hand on the staff to prevent himself from being tipped into the sea. "Is it him?"

While Evita's own feet weren't touching the ground, she was reminded vividly of the way the mountains of the Range had trembled when they'd been under attack, as if some great beast stirred beneath the surface. In fact, the surrounding islands were trembling in a similar manner, the waters rising and falling, an unseen current pushing the seas into a frenzy. A chill raised the hairs on her arms, while Aurel and Rien clung to the rocks below.

Then, just as abruptly as they'd begun, the tremors stopped. Evita craned her neck and glimpsed a silhouette of a person in a boat rowing in their direction. *Gatt?*

No... not him. A feminine figure steered, the boat effortlessly cutting through the waters that had until mere moments ago been threatening to sweep them into their midst. The others stared, too, as the boat rocked to a halt near their own island.

Rien spoke first. "Zelle?"

28

Z elle rowed, steering the small boat between the islands. Getting hold of a boat had proven tricky at first, since the deity's magic had swept all the boats on the defectors' island out to sea. The Shaper's magic continued to pulse through her veins, however, and when that occurred to her, she simply waved her staff and shifted the waters until a boat bumped ashore and she could climb into it.

The faintest tremor ran through the waters as she rowed, an echo of the power she'd unleashed in the cave. The staff, pinned between her knees, continued to glow, while the marks on her arms and wrists did likewise.

"Are these permanent?"

Would you rather be dead?

"No, but they're little conspicuous." Her voice shook, perhaps a delayed reaction to the shock of stilling an earthquake and moving the seas with her own hands. The marks on her skin were the least of her concerns, considering that her bond with the Shaper was permanent in a much deeper way than simple scars. She'd had no choice in the matter, but if someone stole the staff from her again, it might well cause her physical pain.

And if another person claimed it, as Daimos had done to Rien's first Relic?

She shook off the thought, concentrating instead on steering, though the currents did most of the work. Was that the staff's doing, too? It was hard to tell, but in any case, hardly any time seemed to have passed before she spotted the large reptilian form of the dragonet hovering above a small rocky island, where Aurel and Rien sat watching her approach. Both were soaked to the skin and shivering.

"Zelle!" Rien called. "You're alive."

"More or less." She rowed the rest of the way to the rocky island and brought the boat to a halt. "What are you doing sitting on a rock?"

"Our boat sank," Aurel explained. "That delightful deity showed up again."

"Igon." Zelle grimaced. "He's even stronger than he was before. Part of his Relic survived being broken, and he used it to find his way to the defectors' caves."

"So that's where he ran off to," said Rien. "How'd you get away?"

"Didn't you break that Relic into a million pieces?" Aurel interjected, her auburn hair plastered to her forehead.

"I did, but a piece of it somehow stayed conscious." Zelle buried her hands in her lap to avoid exposing the glowing marks on her arms and wrists. "It turns out that when someone else holds Igon's Relic in their hands, it somehow allows him to latch onto the power inside *their*

Relic and take it for himself. He drained two of the defectors' magic that way before taking back what was left of his Relic."

Rien's eyes rounded. "But *you* touched his Relic."

She gave a self-conscious shrug. "I'm not sure why it didn't affect me, but the staff is… different."

That was putting it mildly. Now she'd bound herself closer to the staff than any Sentinel had, had she unwittingly opened herself to the same risks?

Rien looked at her—*really* looked at her, as though he could see right through to the new marks on her arms. "How did you escape, Zelle? The islanders outnumbered you by far, and with Igon on top of that…"

She debated spinning a story about sneaking off in the midst of the battle, but what would be the point? Instead, Zelle pushed up her sleeves in answer.

Rien sucked in a breath. "Are those…"

"The Shaper and I had to join forces to escape." She pulled her sleeves down again, fighting a shiver. "Igon had already run, but he would have brought the whole place collapsing on top of us without my intervention."

"He ran?" Aurel's tone sounded far less surprised than Zelle had anticipated. "He wanted the Relic, then? Or what was left of it anyway."

"Yes, along with the power he stole from those defectors," she said. "Not that they didn't deserve it, but Igon… just *touching* his Relic completely severed their connection to Gaiva."

Rien looked down, his face ashen. "They did bring it on themselves by picking it up, didn't they?"

"Believe me, I tried to get through to them." Zelle released a weary sigh. "I left them stuck in their own caves, too, so I can't say they're thrilled with me. Which leaves us with a shortage of potential allies, to say the least."

"And boats," added Aurel. "Ours turned out to be a dud."

"Do you really think it might have been sabotaged?" Evita asked from her perch on the dragonet's back. At Zelle's questioning look, she added, "Gatt loaned them the boat. You'd think it'd be sturdy enough not to develop a hole within a few moments."

"That's how it sank?" Zelle looked between them. "I thought it was Igon."

"It was," said Rien. "Gatt saw the state of the boat we dragged away from the battlefield and loaned us his own. Out of kindness, I assumed."

"Or attempted murder," Aurel put in. "Not that I know anything about him, but the timing was suspicious."

"Exactly," agreed Evita.

Zelle frowned. "Now you mention it, Igon hinted that I'd already met his summoner. He can't have meant Gatt was the one who summoned him, can he? Gatt doesn't have magical abilities."

"Maybe he does," said Rien. "If someone from the village did the summoning, it would explain why Igon has left them alone so far."

True, but Gatt's avoidance of magic so far didn't make him likely to have enacted a ritual to enable a deity to take on human form... or rather, five of them.

Zelle cleared her throat. "Whoever it was, we have a major problem. If Igon can drain magic from anyone who holds a Relic, what happens if he gets into Gaiva's cave?"

At the mere thought, dread trickled through her. Igon

hadn't got close to the Blessed so far, but there was no telling whether he'd tried—and with the defectors currently trapped inside their own cave, nobody but the four of them would be able to stand against him.

Evita paled. "No, we don't want that. What's the plan? Do you want to warn the Blessed?"

"They might already know," said Zelle, "but I need to talk to them."

Or more specifically, she needed to talk to Gaiva. The deity must have an idea of how to stop Igon's rampage, surely, and Zelle couldn't risk turning her back on the Blessed, not when their magic was entirely dependent upon their cave staying intact.

"And the villagers?" Evita prompted. "Shouldn't someone warn them the summoner might be among them?"

"I don't see Igon going after them if he hasn't already," Rien said. "Most likely, he'll go back to torment those defectors."

And I left them trapped in a cave. Zelle swallowed down the brief taste of guilt. They'd given her few other options, and many of them would happily have killed her themselves. "I'm going to speak to the Blessed, but I can only take one person with me. Evita?"

"I think the dragonet can carry two of us," Evita said. "I'll head back to warn the villagers. Someone has to."

"Agreed," Aurel said, to her surprise. "I'll fly with you, Evita."

Rien began to climb down the rocky island. "I'll go in the boat with Zelle."

As Zelle had expected—and hoped. "Evita, stop at the inn when you reach the village," Zelle told her. "I left my pack in our room, and Aurel's Book of Reading is in there."

Aurel's brow crinkled. "You brought that with you?"

"You might need it."

Aurel looked away. "This isn't my battle. I know that much."

"It's everyone's battle," Zelle corrected. "Go and join Evita."

"Up here." Evita flew the dragonet lower, allowing Aurel to scramble across the rocks and climb onto his back. Chirp let out a disgruntled noise when she did so, but Evita soothed him by stroking the side of his head.

Zelle, meanwhile, waited for Rien to clamber into the boat behind her before picking up the oar again. "Let's go."

Rien leaned forward. "Are you sure you want me to come with you? Igon might be a threat to all of us, but he seems to be fixated on me."

Zelle tilted her head to study his worried frown, wondering what Igon had said to him during their last encounter. "He seems to be avoiding the Blessed for now. Besides, I trust you."

His brows lifted as though in surprise, though Zelle didn't think she'd said anything that revolutionary. In any case, it worked. Rien picked up his oar, while she found herself conscious of the way the swirling lines on her hands and wrists moved as they rowed onward.

"I'll have to be careful to wear long sleeves in future," she remarked. "Not difficult in Zeuten, I suppose. Small price to pay for the staff to listen to me, though there's no guarantee."

Rien was quiet for a long moment. "You won't always

know or agree with what the Shaper wants. You might be closer, but you're still two separate people. Don't forget that."

His words sounded as if they were addressed to himself as much as to her.

"You're right." She'd made her decision, after all, and now she'd have to live with the consequences. "I don't know what the Blessed will make of this, though."

As they neared the stone carving of Gaiva's head and shoulders, she saw Tamacha peering out of the cave.

"What's she doing?" Zelle sat up straighter in the boat. "They don't normally come outside."

"Maybe they're looking for the defectors," Rien suggested. "They might have heard the battle."

"Or they sensed what the Shaper did." Zelle brought the boat to a gentle halt at the shore, climbing out onto the sand.

When they reached the cliffs, Tamacha was already retreating into the cave. "Come in here, Zelle. Your friend will have to wait outside."

"What?" Zelle looked over her shoulder at Rien. They didn't know he'd been forced to work with Igon, did they? "He's with me."

"I am sorry, but this is not a good time for us to welcome strangers into our cave. He is more than welcome to stay on the beach."

Zelle blew out a breath. "All right… if that's fine with you, Rien?"

"Of course." His tone and expression were both neutral, and if Tamacha's words had stung, he gave no sign. "Go ahead."

"I'll be back soon," she promised, before following Tamacha into the heart of Gaiva's caves.

———

Rien watched Zelle disappear into the caves and tried to quell his misgivings at leaving her alone with the Blessed so soon after her narrow escape from Igon and the defectors. Harder to ignore was the knowledge that she'd joined forces with the nameless Shaper, so closely that a godsmark had formed on her skin, and while he firmly told himself that it was Zelle's decision, she was going to change as a result. Not through any fault of her own, but because it was impossible for a human to bond with a Relic and not be altered.

In a way, Igon had been right. Rien had, intentionally or not, expected Zierne to fill the void that Astiva had left behind without giving a thought to the deity's own wishes. He had no idea what Zierne desired, and he didn't even know what had led to him leaving his siblings for another continent all those centuries before. While his lack of access to information wasn't entirely his own fault, thanks to the destruction of his family's records, he'd still assumed that Zierne would always fall into line with his own demands, and his naivety had cost him dearly.

Maybe that was why Igon had been able to get his claws into him so easily. The thought shamed him, but it was his own pride that had been his downfall to begin with.

Feeling like a fool, he held up the staff in front of him and addressed it in a low voice. "Zierne, I apologise for not listening to you and for assuming you would behave in the same way as Astiva. It was wrong of me to make that assumption."

He felt rather like a chastised youth apologising for some misstep or other, but the staff began to glow faintly around the edges. Encouraged, he went on.

"I know we have differing goals," he murmured, "but I hope that we can work together to defeat Igon and escape the Isles."

The deity didn't reply, of course. Zierne was likely sceptical about Rien keeping his word, especially given how he'd done his best to dodge around Igon's attempts to get him to keep up his end of their bargain. Escaping Igon had been necessary for his own self-preservation as well as protecting his friends, but his actions had not been what he'd have called honourable in his old existence. That, of course, was before he'd had to choose between keeping his promise and living with himself afterwards. He was no longer the desperate person he'd been when he'd begged Igon to save him from drowning.

This time, Igon had needed him, too. He might have done his best to undermine Rien's confidence, but he and Aurel had shaken the deity during their last encounter, and he was certain that Igon's abilities depended upon a human handling his Relics. Perhaps that would give them a route to victory... if he could be certain that Zierne wouldn't turn on him again.

His grip on the staff tightened, thorny vines wrapping around his hands as his conviction grew stronger.

"If you promise not to hinder my attempts to defeat Igon, I will help you," he told Zierne. "Provided you do no harm to my allies or any innocents, I'll do my best not to go against your own desires. And… and if our alliance ultimately ends with us parting ways, so be it."

The notion was inconceivable, but it was the right thing to say. The godsmarks brightened on both his hands, and a whisper echoed in his mind. *Very well.*

29

E vita and Aurel sat on the dragonet's back. The two just about fit, if not comfortably, though it'd help if Evita would stop *wriggling*. The girl seemed distinctly ill at ease, though now Aurel thought about it, she was afraid of heights. It made no sense that she'd opted to bring the dragonet on this bizarre rescue mission anyway, but then again, nothing about this situation made sense. Aurel knew she'd been positively unpleasant to her sister the last time they'd seen one another, and yet Zelle had seemingly dragged both Rien and Evita halfway across the world to rescue her.

As they flew, Evita told Aurel the details of their journey to find her, starting from their arrival in Dacher and their first visit to the Blessed, followed by Rien's disappearance and their varied encounters with Igon. When she reached Zelle's near-drowning and her subsequent recovery in the cave of the creator goddess, Aurel was seized with a rush of panic that made her doubly impressed with Evita's ability to keep her balance despite her fear.

"Pity Gaiva can't come out of Her cave and knock Igon into the sea," she remarked.

"That would solve all our problems," Evita agreed. "As it is, it wouldn't surprise me if Igon wanted to get his hands on Her Relic himself, and it'd be just like the time Orzen tried to attack the Sentinels' cave."

Aurel grimaced. "Except Orzen couldn't drain the life out of any Relic he wanted."

"Exactly."

"How are we going to warn the villagers, then?" asked Aurel. "If they're completely unaware of the deities and magic in general, then we might want to break the news gently."

"Yes, but one of them summoned Igon to begin with," said Evita. "Specifically, Gatt. I think it was him, anyway. I also think he sabotaged the boat on purpose."

"Might be worth confronting him, then. Not that we need more enemies—" Aurel yelped when a giant eagle loomed ahead of them, and the dragonet halted so abruptly that both of them nearly fell into the sea. Aurel clung onto Evita, who plastered herself against the dragonet's neck and closed her eyes, whimpering.

The eagle, however, gave one half-hearted snap of its beak before flying past, joining two of its companions nearby.

"What was that?" Evita lifted her head. "Oh... they're looking for the defectors. I guess they still haven't found their way out of the cave Zelle shut them in."

"Hope not," said Aurel. "Pity they didn't finish each other off. Them and the deities, that is."

They flew onward, leaving the sparser islands behind and entering a region that seemed much more habitable. Clusters of stone houses were built on strips of land, most scarcely big enough to be called villages, and Aurel watched their inhabitants milling around as if entirely oblivious to the turbulence elsewhere in the Isles. White-haired locals gathered in gardens to gossip, fished from short piers, and carried barrels and containers across the bridges from one island to the next.

Evita straightened upright when the cliffs of a larger island came into view, upon which more stone buildings had been built in layers. "Chirp, land over there, not in the middle of the village."

The dragonet swooped towards a small rocky island next to the village, which he circled a few times instead of landing.

"Yes, I know Igon was here before, but he's not around," Evita murmured. "We're fine."

"Igon was here?" Aurel grabbed Chirp's sides as they landed on the rocks, while Evita gladly slid to the ground first. The island was small enough that the dragonet covered a fair proportion of its surface, while a narrow bridge connected the smaller island to its neighbour.

"This is where he captured Rien the first time around," Evita explained. "He dragged him through a doorway."

"In other words, nowhere is safe from him," Aurel concluded. "Including the village."

It might have been better if Rien had come in her place in case Igon was waiting in the village, but he'd had his own struggles against Igon's attempts to exert control over him. Zelle trusted him, but Aurel *didn't* trust the gods not to set them against one another.

Maybe even herself and her sister. Zelle had part of the nameless Shaper's magic running in her veins, and Aurel couldn't even begin to imagine how that would change her. How it had already changed her.

A chirp drew Aurel's attention to Evita and the dragonet. The girl stroked the reptile's head, and Aurel marvelled at the easy level of communication the pair of them had. She'd never seen anything like it before. They trusted one another, truly and completely.

As for Aurel herself? She'd pushed everyone away, yet they'd all come here to rescue her nevertheless.

A light shone somewhere, catching her gaze. Aurel clambered down, spotting a shard of glittering rock lying near the lapping waves at the island's edge. A Relic?

"Don't touch that!" Evita said from behind her. "That looks like one of Igon's Relics."

"I don't think it is." Aurel studied the gleaming piece of stone. "Would he leave it lying around?"

"As a trap? Yes, he absolutely would." Evita scrambled down the rocky cliffs. "I'll pick it up first, since it won't have any effect on me."

"It shouldn't work on me, either," Aurel pointed out. "If Zelle was fine, then I will be, too."

She was less certain than she'd like to admit, but even Igon wouldn't be arrogant enough to drop one of his Relics into the sea where anyone might pick it up.

"You can't know that," Evita protested. "Besides, if it isn't Igon's Relic, whose is it?"

"There are others," said Aurel. "There must be, if Igon gains strength from draining them. He can't be relying on the defectors, surely."

When Evita hesitated on the brink of picking up the

Relic, Aurel scooped it up herself. To her intense relief—not that she'd admit so aloud—nothing happened.

Evita peered at the jagged piece of rock. "No... that's too uneven to be one of Igon's Relics. The last one was perfectly smooth. Before Zelle broke it, anyway."

"Let's find out who it belongs to, then." Aurel pocketed the Relic and climbed up the cliffs again, heading for the rickety wooden bridge.

Once she reached the end, she waited for Evita to catch her up. The former Changer kept her gaze fixed straight ahead instead of looking down, and her hands were trembling when she reached the other side. "Where do you want to go first?"

"The inn, wherever that is," replied Aurel. "Zelle said my Book of Reading was in her room. I know it probably won't do us any good against Igon, but I might at least be able to figure out what this Relic is."

"Good idea." Evita led the way uphill to the topmost point of Dacher, which afforded a clear view of the surrounding isles. The settlement was smaller than her own village, at first glance, though it was hard to tell with the buildings layered into the cliffs the way they were.

Evita reached the door to a small but cosy-looking inn. "The inn's owner will have questions if I bring a stranger inside. I can sneak you in under the cloak..."

"No need." Aurel halted. "I'll wait outside. No sneaking necessary."

"All right." Evita darted into the inn, while Aurel stood on the clifftop, turning the Relic over in her hands. It didn't matter *that* much which deity it belonged to, but she wanted to do something useful, and in a fight between gods, her own options were limited.

Within moments, Evita reappeared and held out the Book of Reading. "Here you are."

"Thanks." Aurel took the leather-bound book from her, crouching down to lay it on the ground. "Not the best place to do this, but if the Relic turns out to be one of *his*, I can easily throw it into the sea."

Evita peered over her shoulder. "You can tell who owned the Relic?"

"I can Read where it came from and work the rest out from there." Aurel pulled the shard of rock out of her pocket, the other hand flipping open the book to reveal two of its many blank pages. Evita hovered anxiously at her side as she moved her hand over the piece of rock, which Aurel found rather distracting. She didn't usually need more than a few moments of contact to Read an object, but the pages remained stubbornly blank.

Then a tingle ran up her arm, followed by a flare of light that spread from her palm across the pages of the Book of Reading.

"Come on," she murmured. "Show me who you belong to."

Images flooded the page in front of her, visible to nobody but Aurel, each of them flitting past too quickly for her to make much sense of.

She was buried at the bottom of the ocean beneath layers of sand...

She was also inside a cave, surrounded by several figures dressed in white...

She lay on a beach, surrounded by rocks...

Shards of blue-white rock broke apart around her, and she was in a thousand pieces at once and somehow whole at the same time...

Aurel reeled, unable to stop the flood of images. She'd never used her power on a true Relic before, but this was nothing like any object she'd Read in the past. It was more like using her abilities on several objects at once, each with vastly different origins and locations. Only one image remained constant—the cave and the cloaked figures within.

Gaiva. This must be a piece of Gaiva's Relic—but how had it got into the water? Had it belonged to a defector who'd gone on to die, or had the large rock simply been chipped away by time? The power within the shard remained intact, despite the absence of a wielder, and Aurel idly wondered what might happen if someone without magic, like Evita, tried to claim it.

A shout jolted her back to the real world. She wrenched her gaze away from the pages when Evita pointed at the neighbouring island, her eyes wide.

Snatching the book in one hand, Aurel launched to her feet, seeing the bright flare of a doorway opening above the rocky shore.

Igon had found them.

———

Zelle walked through the tunnel, following Tamacha into the home of the Blessed. At least she hadn't seen any signs of Igon outside, but why had Tamacha been out on the beach? Had she and the others sensed what the Shaper had done? Or had Gaiva told them? Zelle tugged down her sleeves, and when she saw a faint glow rising to the surface of her hands, she buried them in her pockets to hide the new markings from sight.

Inside the main cave, the rest of the Blessed waited on their rocky seats, as though expecting her arrival. Only Lenza greeted her with a smile, while Tamacha took her own seat and faced Zelle, her expression taut. "What have you done?"

Part of Zelle had already expected the accusation to come, but that didn't stop her heart from sinking at the note of anger in Tamacha's voice.

"Gaiva's Blades captured me," she told them. "They then came under attack by Igon. I managed to escape, but I had to use the staff's magic in order to do so. That is... the Shaper's magic. I'm sorry if it had an effect on you here."

"Gaiva is very disturbed," Tamacha reprimanded her. "She stopped us from accessing Her cave altogether."

Zelle stared at her. "Really? I didn't mean for that to happen. I didn't know it was possible, in fact."

Tamacha's gaze clouded. "Gaiva's Blades committed a terrible crime in taking you captive. I greatly regret that we have allowed those who once existed among our number to harm a guest."

"They were desperate," Zelle found herself saying, though she wasn't feeling charitable towards the defectors in the slightest. "This situation could have been avoided, but instead of listening to me, they took the staff and tried to use it for themselves. Then Igon showed up."

"How did he find them?" asked Tamacha.

"It's a long story." She searched for an explanation that wouldn't paint Rien in an untrustworthy light, given that he was the one who'd stolen one of Igon's Relics to begin with. "I managed to get hold of Igon's Relic, and I hoped to use the staff to destroy it. I managed to shatter the Relic

337

into pieces, but part of it somehow survived, and I found the piece of broken Relic in my pocket when Gaiva's Blades took me captive. Not long after that, Igon himself showed up to reclaim it."

She told them of Igon draining the defectors' magic from their Relics, and by the time she reached her own escape using the Shaper's power, everyone in the room was staring at her, their expressions aghast.

"The defectors have done a terrible thing, and we will all pay the price for it," said Tamacha gravely. "I understand Gaiva's rage now. She knew that they took the staff of the nameless Shaper."

That didn't strike Zelle as quite accurate. Gaiva might have been angry at the defectors for stealing pieces of Her magic, but She hadn't sounded particularly pleased when Zelle had brought the staff into Her cave, either.

"The defectors are trapped inside their cave," she told them. "I didn't know what else to do, but I don't want to leave them in there indefinitely."

"Why not?" asked Tamacha. "They do not deserve to wield Gaiva's power. It would have been better for all of us if Igon had destroyed them all."

Zelle's mouth dropped open. "But—if he took their Relics, then he'd be even stronger than before. Each one he steals gives him strength."

"Then they are better left buried," said one of the Blessed, and several of their number nodded in agreement.

"They're trying to help the islanders," Zelle protested. "I'm not saying they made the right choices, but my allies and I are outnumbered. Would you not consider reconciling with one another, for the sake of the other islanders? Gaiva must agree with them on some level, if they're still able to use Her magic…"

"Absolutely not," Tamacha said firmly. "They betrayed us, spurned Gaiva, and would happily leave us all to die."

"What if Igon tries to take Gaiva's rock?" She braced herself for the Blessed to reprimand her for suggesting such a thing, but their faces showed more shock than anger. "He can drain the power from Relics, and there doesn't seem to be a limit. If he comes here, then what will you do?"

Gaiva's Blades might have turned on their fellow Blessed, but they remained loyal to Gaiva in their own way, regardless of whether or not Tamacha and the others agreed with them. But convincing the others of that fact might be an exercise in futility, and even if Zelle tried to make her own agreement with the defectors—well, she'd failed at that once already.

"They cannot take Gaiva's rock," said Tamacha. "Not as long as we remain here."

Zelle's throat went dry. She couldn't ask them to abandon their home, but if she and her allies tried to take Igon down alone, their next battle might end with one or more of them dead.

"Do you *all* have to stay here?" she asked. "If one of you left the cave to help us fight, it wouldn't enable Igon to get inside, would it?"

"We would lose our own link to Gaiva if we left," said Tamacha. "Unlike the traitors, we will not harm Gaiva's rock."

"I'll go," Lenza blurted. "I'll go with you, if you need my help."

"Absolutely not, Lenza," Tamacha said sternly. "You haven't the skills to fight against the gods."

"I don't have a full link with Gaiva either." Her eyes were wide. "My family is in Dacher. What if he goes there next?"

"He won't." The woman next to her gave the girl's shoulder a squeeze before saying something else in their own language. From the way some of the others eyed Zelle, she guessed it wasn't complimentary.

"I saw what Igon can do to a Relic," Zelle pressed. "I don't know who else to ask for help. Unless any of the villagers have a talent for magic—?"

"No," Tamacha cut in. "All villagers who are found to have a gift for magic are brought here to our island."

But they can use their magic independently if they take a separate Relic of their own, Zelle thought. If, in other words, they chipped part of Gaiva's rock away and claimed it. Not that the Blessed were willing to see that as a valid option... but did Gaiva necessarily agree?

"What would happen if an outsider came into the cave?" she asked. "Another Invoker or magic user? What if they tried to claim Her power?"

"The best case is that they would be overwhelmed and would perish in the process," answered Tamacha. "One individual could never handle the enormity of the creator goddess's power, but that deity... Igon... he is split into five parts. When one grows stronger, so do the others, and thus every Relic they steal gives equal power to all five of them. Perhaps that would be enough for them to steal the heart of Gaiva's magic. We could never take that risk."

"That's why I came here," said Zelle. "It's not possible for him to actually get into the cave, is it?"

"Not as long as we are here," said Tamacha. "The moment we leave, Gaiva becomes vulnerable. And so, by consequence, do all the islands of the region."

"All of them?" Zelle asked. "Including Dacher?"

"Every single one," said Tamacha. "Gaiva's magic sustains the entire region."

Powers above. That meant if she convinced any of them to leave the cave and help her, the village might end up doomed the instant Igon set his sights on Gaiva's rock. She could see no other way out of this. Convincing them to leave the cave had been a last-ditch option, but she was left with no choice but to leave them be.

Before she did so, Zelle had one pertinent question remaining. "Do you know who actually summoned Igon to begin with? For a deity to gain a human form, someone must have drawn him out of his Relic."

"We do not know who was responsible," said Tamacha. "However, we have little doubt that Gaiva Herself would strike them down without mercy."

"Did She tell you that?" Nobody answered, and Zelle's pulse began to race. "I think I should join my friends. Before I go, though… may I speak to Her? Gaiva?"

"We cannot leave this cave." Tamacha rose to her feet. "And, if we are to remain safe and to protect Gaiva's Relic, neither can you."

30

E vita watched in horror as Igon emerged from the doorway above the smaller island on the other side of the bridge. While Aurel had been staring at the open Book of Reading as though in a trance, she snapped out of it when Evita shouted a warning.

Jumping to her feet, Aurel tucked the book under her arm and hurried downhill towards the bridge. So did Evita. The dragonet had been on the island, and while he could easily have flown out of reach, the villagers didn't have that option.

Igon had already spotted them, and he waited at the other end of the bridge when Aurel reached the island. Evita followed more slowly, cringing when the rickety bridge shook under their combined footsteps, but keeping her attention on the deity didn't help her nerves, either.

Igon studied Aurel and Evita from his perch on the rocky bluff. "Your friend isn't with you?"

"Which friend?" asked Evita, not that it mattered. "Rien?"

"Whose Relic is this?" Aurel held up the glittering shard. "One of yours?"

Hadn't she seen the truth for herself when she'd Read the Relic's history? Evita would be the first to admit that she didn't understand how Aurel's ability worked, but she'd been staring into the Book of Reading's pages as if captivated by something unseen before the deity's appearance had diverted her attention.

"Nobody's," replied Igon. "Yet."

"Interesting," said Aurel. "I thought you were collecting every Relic you could get your hands on to drain their power."

"There's little power left in that fragment, but if you're offering…" He extended a hand, and Aurel held the shard of rock out of reach.

Alarm flared inside Evita's chest, while Igon's eyes narrowed at Aurel. "I wouldn't mock me, human. Give that to me."

"You didn't seem so keen on it a moment ago." Aurel casually tossed the shard of rock into the air and caught it in her palm again. "I might give it to you if you tell me what you're doing here. Visiting your summoner? What's your relationship with the villagers?"

"The villagers and I have an understanding between us," Igon growled. "They give us Relics. We keep them alive."

Evita's heart missed a beat. "You… you're working together?"

Igon's attention briefly lifted from Aurel to address Evita. "Yes, human. It's a wonder you've survived so long, if you are usually so slow to realise the obvious."

It's not just one of the villagers. It's all of them. Had they known what they were getting into? If even *Rien* had been taken in, maybe they hadn't, but Evita hadn't seen any signs of Igon's involvement in Dacher. Was he telling the truth?

"You're lying," said Aurel. "The villagers don't have magic. Where would they find Relics?"

"In the sea, of course," said Igon. "I lay buried at the bottom of the ocean myself for centuries, aside from the few Relics that found their way into human hands like Arien's family… but none of those Relics matter now I am free."

"You mean you have a human form," Evita guessed. "Or five of them. Do you ever get into fights with your copies?"

Aurel let out a snort of amusement, but Igon shot her a condescending look. "We are a unity. When one bleeds, so do the others. When one gains strength, we share it. And we will all share in the might of Gaiva's will once we take what is ours."

"What…" Evita's throat went dry. "What do you mean by that?"

She already knew the answer. He wanted to get into Gaiva's cave… which also happened to be where Zelle and Rien had gone.

"You're not strong enough." Aurel's voice carried less confidence than usual, as if she'd come to the same conclusion Evita had. "You might be able to pick up these small fragments, but you're too weak to claim *Her* Relic."

"I am strong enough." Fury radiated through his tone. "You will see when I take Gaiva's magic for my own."

"Then why are you standing on this rock instead?" Evita enquired.

"The Blessed refuse to leave their cave." Igon's lip curled with disdain. "There is only one way for us to lure them from their hiding place, and that means using the villagers who so kindly brought us into this realm."

"You're betraying them?" Aurel guessed. "That can't have been part of your agreement. If you ever made one, that is."

"If we've learned anything from humans, it's that you never keep your word," said Igon. "Besides, it's grown tiresome to wait for them to see sense, so I'll give them an incentive to come to me."

Evita glanced across the bridge at the village, and her heart plummeted. An ominous-looking cloud surrounded the island, masking the topmost layer of houses from view. Including the inn.

Aurel ran to the bridge, but Igon vanished through a doorway and reappeared in front of her in the time it took to blink.

"Oh, you aren't leaving this island," he told them. "Either of you."

———

Zelle stared into Tamacha's eyes, recognising the desperation within. She understood her reasoning, but it wasn't enough to sacrifice her own freedom. "I'm sorry, but I have to leave. There are people outside who need my help."

"No," said Tamacha. "The nameless Shaper has chosen you as a host for the same reason Gaiva chose us, and we cannot allow your death."

Dread bloomed inside her. The Blessed couldn't

believe that keeping her locked up in here would help the situation, could they? Especially if Igon came to seek out Gaiva and found Rien waiting outside. Abruptly, she wished she'd never asked him to come with her, but how could she warn him if Tamacha wouldn't let her leave without grievously insulting her hosts, or worse?

"The nameless Shaper and I have already spoken with one another," she told the Blessed. "We wish to fight. Both of us do."

"Gaiva is the foundation of life and of the Isles themselves," said Tamacha. "If Her power was taken away... it would be catastrophic for the whole of Itzar, if not the world. The Shaper must understand."

"Someone has to fight," Zelle said. "Gaiva's Blades... regardless of what you think of them, they're trying to protect the Isles. They'll be more than happy to fight Igon if I set them free. You don't have to leave the cave yourselves."

Her feelings towards the rest of the Blessed had soured somewhat, to say the least. Yes, she empathised with their position, but the fact remained that they'd stayed in hiding while Igon grew in strength. Meanwhile, Gaiva's Blades might have made plenty of questionable choices, but they'd at least tried to use their magic to stop Igon's threat, even if they'd resorted to kidnapping and threats to achieve their goals.

"They are not trying to protect anyone but themselves," said Tamacha. "We know our deity's will, and Gaiva's utmost desire is for us to protect Her Relic."

"Gaiva's magic created *all* life, didn't it?" If Gaiva was all that stood between Igon and the entirety of the Isles, there must be more the Blessed could do. "Everywhere, including Zeuten, Aestin, and the rest of Itzar. We can't leave the other islanders to die. I'm sure Gaiva wouldn't want that."

"You dishonour Her name," one of the other Blessed reprimanded her.

"Let her speak to the goddess," Lenza burst out. Zelle swung to face her in surprise, seeing tears glimmer in the teenager's eyes. "Give her that chance. Please show her."

Tamacha exhaled in a sigh. "You are young, Lenza. You don't understand what is at risk here. Nevertheless..."

When Tamacha beckoned Zelle to follow her out of the cave, she did so warily, feeling the others' glares on her back.

"We will find a room for you in our caves," Tamacha told her. "We haven't had guests in some time, but this won't be an unpleasant place for you to live."

"I..." Zelle trailed off, staring into Gaiva's cave. The walls appeared dark, not shimmering as they'd been beforehand, and no source of light disturbed the gloom. "What's happened in here?"

"The cave has been like this ever since this morning," said Tamacha quietly. "It started, I believe, during the conflict between the traitors and the deities. None of us has heard a word from Gaiva since."

"The goddess isn't speaking to you?" No wonder they'd given up hope. "It can't have helped that Gaiva's Blades lost their link to Her when Igon drained their Relics."

"The traitors stole from Gaiva in the first place." She turned away from the rock, and Zelle noticed that her hands were trembling. "They are the reason Gaiva is not responding to our pleas. She is grieving."

347

Oh, She's alert, the staff remarked. *She just doesn't want to deal with this nonsense.*

Zelle's hand jerked the staff into the air. *What?*

Tamacha looked between her and the staff. "What is it?"

"I'm asking the staff if it can reach Her," Zelle evaded. "That is, the nameless Shaper."

"Nobody can." Tamacha stepped entirely too close to the staff for Zelle's comfort. "It is futile, as I told you. There is nothing out there for you but death."

"No." Zelle refused to hide in a cave while her friends fought for their lives outside and the deities unleashed their wrath on innocent humans. While the Shaper doubtlessly cared little for human lives, the staff didn't want to be stuck inside the cave any more than she did. The Shaper's main form, after all, was imprisoned inside the Range, and She had sworn to help protect the Sentinels. Including Grandma and Aurel, both of whom had no access to the staff while Zelle remained trapped in this cave. "I will try to protect Gaiva's cave, but you aren't the only people who have need of my help."

Zelle turned her back on the Blessed and walked away, shoulders tensed in preparation for an attack—but none came. Instead, when she neared the tunnel leading outside, she found a shimmering barrier of ice blocking her path.

For a moment, she wondered if Gaiva Herself had barred her way out, but the glow from behind her signalled that Tamacha had called on her allies to assist. The Blessed were channelling Gaiva's strength through their own hands, but they hadn't consulted Gaiva Herself for permission.

Whatever Gaiva truly wanted didn't matter to them.

Zelle turned to face the Blessed who'd emerged to watch her, and when the swirling markings on her skin began to glow, she didn't bother to hide her hands. "I wouldn't try to keep me in here. You don't want to make an enemy of one of Gaiva's siblings, do you?"

"You do not speak for the Shaper," said Tamacha.

"No more than you speak for Gaiva." The glow brightened, the Shaper's magic flowing from her fingertips. The cave vibrated underfoot, and she directed the power at the ice blocking her path.

The icy barrier cracked down the middle, crumbling to the cave floor. Several gasps came from behind her, but this time, when Zelle left the cave, nobody tried to stop her.

31

R ien startled when Zelle came running out of the cave, sending a shower of rock fragments in her wake as though she'd used the staff to hammer her way through the wall.

"Zelle, what's going on?"

"We have to run," she answered, breathless. "The Blessed… they aren't what they seem."

"They turned on you?" he guessed. "Like the defectors?"

"Not exactly," she said. "They want to protect Gaiva's rock by any means necessary, and since they can't leave the cave, they decided I shouldn't be allowed to, either."

"Come on." He beckoned her downhill towards the boat. "Better leave while we can."

As they ran down the beach, however, the island lurched beneath their feet. Sharp spears of rock rose from the ground in front of Zelle, as though the island itself was trying to keep her imprisoned. She leapt around the rocky protrusions, but they rose like a circle of sharp teeth, surrounding her. Rien brandished the staff, but his thorns would have little effect on solid rock.

Zelle, however, turned towards the towering shape of Gaiva's rock and raised her hands. "I did warn them."

He glimpsed swirling lights on her hands, disappearing below her sleeves, before the rocks receded back into the earth. With the pale light outlining her entire body, she almost didn't look like Zelle at all, but he couldn't stop to think about what that might mean. He let Zelle climb inside the boat before joining her, and the current swept them away almost instantly.

Rien and Zelle held on to the sides of the boat as they were tossed among the islands, hardly needing to lift an oar to steer. With no map, it was impossible to tell where they were going, but when the Isle of the Blessed slipped out of sight, the seas calmed enough for them to slow to a regular pace.

Zelle let out a breath. "That was a close one."

She was herself again, Rien noticed. He wondered if she'd been aware of the change at all. "Yes, it was. Where do you want to go now? Back to the village? Evita and Aurel should already be there."

There seemed little choice, especially as there was no telling what the Blessed might resort to doing next to convince Zelle to abandon her allies.

"I don't know, but—" Zelle grabbed his arm in warning, and he glanced up. Two eagles flew overhead, shrieking. Both he and Zelle reached for their staffs, but the eagles paid them no attention. Instead, they flew to the north. "You aren't going to like this idea, Rien, but Gaiva's Blades might be the only people with magic in the Isles, aside from us, with the ability and the will to fight against Igon."

"You're right," he acknowledged. "I don't like that idea. Not in the slightest."

The defectors might have powerful magic at their fingertips, but they were as likely to turn it against Zelle and Rien as not. The glow had faded a little from Zelle's skin, but he glimpsed the swirling lines on the back of her hands while she gripped the oars. "I wish the Blessed had been open to talking with them, but they've stayed in that cave so long they've stagnated."

"Speaking of whom, whose side is *Gaiva* on?" asked Rien. "The Blessed? Or anyone who wields one of Her Relics, including the defectors?"

"The latter," replied Zelle. "I don't get the sense that She has any influence over what people *do* with her power. Gaiva has been refusing to talk to any of the Blessed since this morning, but it doesn't seem to have affected their ability to use magic."

Rien's hands tightened on the oars. Putting Zelle's narrow escape to the back of his mind—with difficulty— he had to wonder how the Blessed had been able to impose their will over Gaiva's to the extent that they'd silenced Her voice entirely. It stood at odds with the way Zierne had been able to cut off Rien's magic whenever he felt like it until they'd come to a mutual understanding, as well as the way the staff only seemed to obey Zelle when it felt like it. That, though, had been before the nameless Shaper had put Her mark directly onto Zelle's skin.

Shrieking cries rose, more eagles flying overhead. No doubt they were all heading to the island where the defectors were trapped. Zelle lifted her head to watch them. "If they try to fight me again, I can fend them off, but it's worth trying to get through to them. The defectors aren't on our side, but they want to protect the villagers, don't they?"

Zelle might have a point. How many more allies did they have with magic at their disposal? The Blessed had let them down, while someone among the villagers might even have summoned Igon to begin with. And if Igon *did* target Gaiva's cave, then even the defectors wouldn't allow him to claim Her power.

"All right," he said. "Tell them the Blessed tried to keep you imprisoned and that Igon might be preparing to attack their cave. I doubt even they could ignore that."

"We need to turn around." Zelle gripped the oar, and Rien helped her steer the boat in a vaguely north-eastern direction, following the shrieking eagles that occasionally rose from the fog and circled the Isles.

Rien kept an eye on the birds, hoping that they were making the right choice. If the Blessed had no intention of helping them, then freeing their adversaries might be their only option. At the same time, if Zelle set the defectors free, their anger at her might outweigh their desire to defend their fellow islanders. It was a gamble, no matter how he looked at the situation.

When they rounded a corner, the currents shifted, pushing their boat along until they came within sight of a wide beach littered with debris. Large cliffs overhung the beach, and the eagles circled above, screeching loudly.

"Are they in there?" He peered at the cliffs, under which a sizeable heap of rocks blocked the entrance to the cave. Had Zelle moved all those rocks by herself? Yes— and no. The nameless Shaper had done most of the work, but it was Zelle's hands that glowed as she brought the boat to a stop, bumping against the shore.

As they did so, several of the eagles spotted them and veered towards them, their vast feathery wings outstretched.

"Wait." Zelle climbed out of the boat, holding up the staff. "I'm going to help your friends, though they probably won't be grateful for it in the slightest."

The eagles circled lower and lower. Rien found himself gripping his Relic tightly, but he waited to see what Zelle did first. Lifting the staff, she faced the wall of rocks blocking the caves.

"Come on, Shaper," she murmured. "Yes, I know you think I'm a fool. We can argue later."

The swirling marks on her arms ignited with vibrant white light, and when she raised the staff, the instrument moved as if it were an extension of her arm. A stream of light poured from the staff and covered the rock wall, which began to shake.

The boulders forming the wall tumbled onto the sand, rolling harmlessly to a halt without touching Zelle at all. As the entrance to the cave cleared, Zelle took a step back to stand beside Rien.

Then she lowered her hand, and the light faded from the staff. "Give it a moment or two, and they'll figure it out."

Shouts rang out from the cave, and the defectors began to emerge onto the beach. Several sported the sort of injuries which made Rien suspect that they'd tried to break the wall of rocks down with their bare hands.

A heavyset man spotted them first, approaching them

with an expression of fury etched on his dust-streaked face. "Have you come to declare war on us again?"

"No, we came to set you free," Zelle told him. "I managed to persuade the nameless Shaper to let you out in order to defend the villagers and the Blessed from Igon. I believe the deity is making a move against Itzar."

"You expect us to forget what you did to us?" The female defector with the anchor tattoo on her face walked into view. "You dare to come back here and beg for our help?"

"I'm not begging for anything. I'm asking you to fulfil the promise you made when you turned your backs on the Blessed." Zelle's grip tightened on the staff when they moved closer. "If you hadn't taken my staff and threatened my life, then maybe we could have come to an agreement. As it is, Igon is on the brink of attacking, and the Blessed have no intention of helping anyone besides themselves."

"Of course not," the woman scoffed. "That is why we left their ranks. *You*, though… what manner of magic do you possess?"

Zelle gave them a considering look then her gaze dropped to the staff. The impulse hit Rien to stop her before she gave the truth away, but he knew that she'd made her mind up.

"I am allied with the nameless Shaper."

Shock reverberated through the gathering defectors on the beach.

"You lie." The woman spoke in a hushed voice.

"No." Zelle held up her arms, revealing the swirling marks on her wrists and hands. "What other magic could have moved the seas and the ground beneath your feet?

The nameless Shaper is the Sentinels' ally, and I have allied with Her to defeat Igon."

"Interesting," said a familiar voice. "Very interesting."

Rien's shoulders stiffened. Igon—or one of his five copies—walked out of a doorway farther down the beach, silent as a wraith, and approached the scattered islanders. The deity looked from Zelle to the cave entrance with a knowing glint in his eye. "I thought I sensed some strange magic from this direction, but I never would have guessed this was the cause."

A shocked silence gave way to anger as the defectors turned on the deity, shouting at him in their own language.

"You stole our magic!" someone yelled in Zeutenian. "You will pay with your life."

"You must know by now that you cannot harm me," Igon told them. "Besides, I have no desire to claim any of your remaining Relics… save for one."

"What does that mean?" demanded the female defector with the tattoo on her cheek.

"Gaiva." Igon's smile broadened. "I would like you to ask the Blessed to surrender Gaiva's rock to us. If they refuse, then I will slaughter every single person here in Itzar, magical or otherwise. What do you think about that?"

———

Igon hovered above the bridge, preventing both Evita and Aurel from returning to the village. Evita's hands were shaking, but Aurel did her best to keep her expression calm, indifferent. "I thought it was Gaiva you wanted, not us. I also thought you were allied with the villagers, but I guess your liking for honouring bargains doesn't extend to your own."

She was stalling, admittedly, but Igon had her and Evita trapped on the island while his four copies might be running amok around Dacher right this instant. She had no weapon, except her own Book of Reading, which wasn't designed to be used in combat. The piece of Gaiva's Relic she'd picked up would have had more practical use, except that she could claim no other Relic but her own.

"You know nothing of the bargain we made with the villagers," Igon told her. "Besides, the Blessed are responsible for their fates, and they have hidden themselves away in their cave. They may be cowardly, but they will surrender Gaiva's Relic to protect their own."

So it was true. Igon had gone after the Blessed, with the intention of draining the life from Gaiva's Relic. While the others' stories of the cave had given her the impression that Gaiva's rock was the size of a small island and guarded by Itzar's equivalent to the Sentinels, she doubted that would prevent Igon's five parts from trying to break in and steal it. Worse, Zelle and Rien had gone to the Blessed themselves, and for all she knew, some of the other parts of Igon had already tracked them down.

Think, Aurel. Her hands clenched around the Book of Reading, wondering if she might be able to threaten Igon by bluffing about its true capabilities.

Then again, the book contained a fragment of the nameless Shaper, the same as the staff did. Unlike Zelle, Aurel had never spoken directly to the staff, but she'd conversed with the rock in the Sentinels' cave, although she'd had no way of knowing to whom she'd truly been speaking. In any case, surely even Igon wouldn't be able to drain the life from her Book of Reading.

I hope.

Squashing down her unease, she transferred the book to her right hand and moved as if to strike Igon. He caught her arm, so fast that he'd scarcely seemed to move, and a thrill of dread and defiance flooded her in the same instant.

"What is that?" Igon's gaze went to the book. "Your Relic?"

"That's right." Aurel tugged against his grip, but he held her arm tightly. "I wouldn't try taking it from me, though."

Go on. Try to take the power of the nameless Shaper. She hoped it'd backfire horribly on all five of the bastards.

Igon's free hand was already reaching for the book, but it had barely brushed against the edge before he released her as though the book had burned him. "Traitorous human! Who do you serve?"

"The nameless Shaper."

"Liar." Igon didn't look afraid, which Aurel had hoped he would. Instead, anger glittered in his eyes.

"I'm not lying." She'd hoped for a reaction similar to the one that Zelle had received upon shattering his Relic, though her own actions had been admittedly less impressive. "The Sentinels serve the nameless Shaper, and that is whose power defeated Orzen."

"Whether you speak true or not, it's too late." Clouds descended above the village, and a strong breeze kicked up behind him. "I might not have Gaiva's Relic yet, but I have strength enough to do what I must."

Water drenched Aurel's feet as a wave rose high, breaking against the cliffs. Igon smiled briefly at both of them, and then he pushed Evita off the cliff.

"No!" Aurel ran to the edge of the cliff, but Evita rose into the air before she hit the water.

She was *flying*—not with the dragonet, but of her own accord, with her cloak streaming around her like outstretched wings.

Igon watched in apparent genuine surprise, then he sighed. "You humans do have a tendency to make your lives far more difficult than they need to be, don't you?"

Another wave rose, breaking on the cliffs and soaking Aurel to the skin. At this rate, the whole island would be swept underwater. Aurel ran to the bridge, but the strong breeze rattled the wooden slats, and she didn't trust the deity not to knock her into the sea while her back was turned. The village, meanwhile, was awash in dark fog, preventing her from seeing if the sea levels were rising there, too.

A bat-like shape descended onto the other side of the bridge. It took a moment for Aurel to realise it was Evita, landing from her inexplicable flight. She also appeared to be gesturing in Aurel's direction, but if she was trying to communicate, Aurel couldn't see her face through the haze of fog.

That was when the dragonet's claws caught the back of her coat, carrying her off the island a moment before another wave hit the spot where she'd been standing. *Oh. That's what she was trying to tell me.*

The dragonet flew her over the bridge, just as a larger wave swept over the island, submerging it entirely under the water. As the dragonet landed on the high cliff near

Evita and released her, Aurel stared at the former Changer. "Since when could you *fly?*"

"It's new to me, too, believe me." Evita squinted through the fog at the smaller island they'd left behind. "I think Igon disappeared, but I doubt he'll stay away for long."

"He doesn't need to come back." Aurel gestured downwards at the rising sea levels. "How long before the whole place is underwater? Not just here, but all the surrounding islands, too."

Evita paled. "Oh, Gaiva's tits."

Some of the villagers were already running down to the boats that were littered around the island. No doubt they'd dealt with floods in the past, but not one caused by a furious deity who wanted to drown them all. The fog wouldn't make it any easier for them to reach safety—and what if they didn't have enough boats for all the citizens to escape?

"We have to help them," said Aurel. "They might be the ones who summoned Igon in the first place, but I doubt all of them were involved, and there are innocent people here who won't have a clue what's happening."

Evita sucked in a breath. "Agreed."

As for Gaiva's Relic? Its fate lay with the Blessed... and Zelle.

32

I gon stood on the beach, smiling at Zelle as his threat sank in. If the Blessed didn't surrender Gaiva's rock to him, he would kill everyone on the islands. Zelle had no doubt that he intended to force the Blessed to face the choice of whether to sacrifice everyone else in Itzar to keep Gaiva's Relic safe. Perhaps they truly would sooner see the rest of the Isles sink into the ocean than lose their goddess. Zelle didn't know for sure, but the defectors hadn't lost their fighting spirit. They fanned out onto the beach, surrounding Igon. "We will not surrender to you. You will die before you lay a hand on the people of Itzar."

"Agreed." Rien spoke up from beside Zelle. "Your trickery will not work on me again. You have no allies save for yourself."

The confidence in his voice rang clear, but Igon's indifference turned to anger. "I have everything I need."

A strong wind ruffled the beach, and the waves rose higher, sweeping inward. *Not again,* she thought, gripping the staff. Water swirled around their ankles and surged towards the cave, rising higher. The patch of sand where Igon stood, along with Zelle and Rien, remained untouched, but the waves swept into the cave and dragged two of the defectors out to sea.

The two men struggled, but the waves rose over their heads to pull them under. The whirlpool-like motion followed the movements of Igon's hand, and Zelle's heart sank.

"I've seen that before." Rien stood rigid at Zelle's side. "Was it *you* who conjured up whirlpools in the seas between Aestin and Zeuten in order to sink my ship and bring me to the brink of death?"

To trick him into an agreement, she thought. It made perfect sense, given what she'd seen of Igon so far.

The deity laughed, lazily waving a hand. The sea's currents swirled in time with the motion, and she glimpsed the two defectors' struggles growing weaker as they fought to reach the surface. "I'm surprised you didn't realise sooner, Arien."

Rien's jaw tightened. "You're a long way from where I obtained the Relic that I used to bargain with you. Someone brought you here."

"Daimos." Zelle's use of Rien's enemy's name caused his posture to stiffen. "He brought your Relic to the Isles."

"He did." Rien's voice shook with anger. "Let me guess —he intended to trick the villagers into setting you free."

"I was already free, Arien," said Igon. "I was happy to accept a bargain with them, however. And I was even gladder for the chance to see to it that you kept your word. There's nothing more satisfying than laying a trap and a mortal walking into it with open eyes."

Of course. Daimos might not be here in person, but he'd had a hand in this situation from the beginning. Who else would have wanted to target the wielders of Gaiva's magic *and* draw Rien into a trap in the same instant? He'd even lured Zelle in, along with the Relic of the nameless Shaper, to keep them occupied while Daimos concocted his own schemes elsewhere.

"It's too late for you to change the past, Arien Astera." The seas stirred at Igon's command, and the two struggling defectors disappeared beneath the surface.

Another man strode through the shallows and hurled a shard of ice at Igon, but a wave caught him around the ankles, causing his attack to miss. Fragments of ice soared through the air, and yet every single attack missed its target as Igon used doorways to evade them or manipulated the ocean's currents to drag them beneath the waves.

Zelle gripped the staff. "If you can do anything to stop him from sinking the entire island into the ocean, Shaper, it'd be appreciated."

I rather think the defectors brought their fate upon themselves.

A warning gesture from Rien told her that their boat had long since been swept away, but none of them would have a chance of steering amid the thrashing waves the deity held in his grip. The sea and wind were at his command, battering the small island and threatening to pull all of them into their embrace.

A shrieking noise sounded overhead as two of the eagles descended upon Igon. The wind tried to sweep them away, but the distraction gave Rien the chance to lift his staff. Thorny vines shot from the end and wrapped around Igon from behind. The deity's mouth twisted in anger; blood splattered the glittering waves before being washed away. As he struggled, the stark triumph in Rien's gaze confused Zelle until she recalled how the Igon had controlled him beforehand. If he'd reconciled with Zierne, then it seemed to have worked for him, because the two fought more seamlessly than she'd ever seen. Zelle, on the other hand, could barely keep hold of her staff, as the waters had surged up to her waist.

Raising the staff above the water, she concentrated on the swirling lines on her hands, directing the Shaper's magic at the rocks beneath their feet. The ground rose, little by little, but not fast enough to outpace Igon's control over the waves. The deity broke free of Rien's thorns and turned upon the defectors. The sea grabbed one of them, then two, dragging them into its depths.

"Stop!" She gave a frantic wave of the staff, and several rocks rose to the surface of the water and flew at the deity. Igon conjured a doorway, but not fast enough to avoid being struck. Rien's thorns seized him again, spraying crimson into the waves.

Igon's dazed eyes met Zelle's, bright with fury. "You will pay for that... with the deaths of your allies."

With a twisting motion, he freed himself from the vines and disappeared through the doorway, which vanished along with him.

At his departure, the waves lowered, the sea receding from the beach. The remaining defectors waited for the ground to clear before beginning to climb down from the rocks or emerge from the cave, but several of their number lay on the sand, unmoving. Even their Relics hadn't been able to save them from Igon's mastery over the ocean.

"Powers above." Zelle scanned the area in search of a way off the island, but their boat was nowhere to be seen, and each time the waves moved back, more dead defectors washed up on the sands. She regretted their deaths, but her worry for the villagers was paramount. Aurel and Evita, too.

For all they knew, even the Blessed's surrender wouldn't be enough to keep her friends safe from harm, but she had her doubts that they had any intention of letting the deity get close to Gaiva's Relic no matter how many lives had to be sacrificed in the process.

A large eagle landed upon the sand, and an islander climbed onto its back. The defectors, grieving and battered though they might be, had already begun to mobilise. Rage and sorrow were written into their features, but not defeat. They climbed onto the eagles' backs, shouting instructions at one another.

Despite Rien's look of warning, Zelle approached the nearest group. "Are you going to defend the village?"

"Yes." The woman with the anchor tattoo had survived the attack, but she didn't address Zelle with quite the same level of hostility as she had before. "It is what we swore to do when we left the Blessed."

"You truly do wield a Relic of the nameless Shaper?" A young man with salt-white hair spoke to Zelle. "You helped spare us from death, despite how we treated you."

Zelle let her gaze travel over their group. "I regret what happened between us, but I told you before that we have a common enemy. Friends of ours are in the village. I'm still willing to work with you, provided you don't take my staff again."

Some of the defectors began to argue in low mutters, but others were nodding.

"Let her come," one of them said, in Zeutenian. "We'll be dead by the day's end anyway."

"Agreed," said the younger man. "We must not waste our time arguing. We need allies."

"Ah—we've lost our boat," Zelle added, with a glance at Rien. "Do you have one you can spare?"

"Better than a boat." The younger man gestured to his steed. "We have wings."

"What… fly?" Zelle eyed the large eagles with trepidation. "Are you sure they'd willingly carry me?"

"They're well-trained," he responded.

Not all the defectors appeared to be happy with this development, but the young man who'd offered to help her—who turned out to be called Kolt—coaxed two of the birds over to her and Rien and showed them how to mount them. As they did so, the defectors began to take flight.

Zelle held on tight when her own eagle beat its wings and flew, but she found it much more pleasant to be seated on the eagle's back than dangling from its claws. From this angle, it was easy to see the damage Igon had already caused. Half the smaller islands were already underwater, and the sea levels continued to rise throughout Itzar. It was only a matter of time before the threat reached the larger, more inhabited islands at the front of the Isles. Like Dacher.

Igon had been holding back until now, it seemed, but it also made perfect sense for it to have been him who'd almost ended Rien's life during his trip over the ocean from Aestin. She'd always assumed it'd been Orzen's doing, but perhaps Daimos had more deities on his side than any of them had suspected. Hadn't Rien come here in the first place because he'd been chasing Daimos? She was willing to bet he *had* been here, and he'd planted Igon's Relic as a trap to ensnare them.

As they flew, some of the eagles broke away to fly towards the Blessed's cave. Zelle watched them in bafflement for an instant before the truth dawned on her. Despite being estranged from their goddess, the defectors were still willing to defend Gaiva's rock. Zelle had to admire them for that, at least.

They hadn't travelled far before she caught sight of a cluster of dark clouds that hadn't been visible in the sky before, low enough to mingle with the fog above the islands to the south of their position.

"Where's that?" Zelle craned her neck. "It's not Dacher, is it?"

"I think it is," Rien said quietly. "Igon has made a move against the villagers."

———

Evita barged through the door to the inn, where the owner startled at the sight of her. "What in the name of the Powers is going on out there?"

"The Powers are *here*," she answered. "They're going to sink the island into the ocean. Do you have enough boats here for a full evacuation?"

"You can't be serious." He swayed on the spot as if he might faint. "Yes, we do, but are the seas any safer than the land?"

I wouldn't count on it was the honest answer, but if the

villagers didn't try to escape, they were doomed to die where they stood. "I don't know, but we have to warn everyone."

She ran for the door again, hearing him calling to the servants and the inn's other guests in the background. Outside, she and Aurel hurried down the steep path leading down to the rest of the village. Already, the lower levels were ankle-deep in water, while several of the boats docked at the pier had drifted out to sea. At least they were still within reach, but if Igon returned, she wouldn't put it past him to keep the villagers from escaping the island.

Considering he was perfectly capable of attacking on multiple fronts at the same time, avoiding him was nearly impossible, even if one ignored the sea levels rising at his command. As for the Blessed? Either they put up a fight and risk Gaiva's Relic falling into Igon's hands or they let the villagers die. Neither option was ideal.

Evita and Aurel continued down the path, while more and more of the villagers emerged from their houses and cries rang back and forth as the warning was passed on.

"Keep moving!" Evita told a crowd of bewildered children, hoping they understood the gist even if they didn't speak Zeutenian. "There's plenty of boats left."

At least, she hoped there'd be enough. The sea levels continued to rise, while dense fog swirled around them that didn't make it any easier to tell if Igon was actually *on* the island. He didn't need to show up in person in order to drown everyone in the village, of course, but only Zelle had the ability to bind Igon as she'd done to Orzen, and her binding spell wouldn't work without access to all of Igon's Relics. If Evita had to guess, each copy of him carried at least one, and they'd learned the hard way that even shattering a Relic into pieces didn't diminish Igon's power.

Soon, a steady stream of villagers ran down to the lower levels, many drifting in boats or rowing against the waves. While the fog was thick, the number of boats in the water suggested the neighbouring islands were evacuating, too, their smaller settlements also vulnerable to Igon's magic.

It struck Evita that they ought to find a boat of their own unless they wanted the dragonet to carry both of them at once—but when they reached the street above the lowest level, Aurel came to an abrupt halt. "There's the scoundrel. He's the one who did this."

Evita's gaze landed on Gatt. "What do you want to do, push him into the sea?"

"Feed him to the nearest sea monster, maybe." Aurel strode over to him without waiting for a reply, and when Gatt's gaze fell on them, his expression showed no signs of guilt, only alarm.

"What is this?" He gestured at the waves and the villagers clambering into boats on the level below them. "Are your friends responsible for this catastrophe?"

"Excuse me?" Indignation seized Evita despite their dire position. "Weren't you the one who summoned Igon to begin with? Are you going to deny you drilled a hole in the boat you loaned to us?"

Gatt's jaw tightened, but he lowered his head. "I apologise. I never wanted to harm you, but I wish you'd stayed away from Itzar altogether."

"Why *did* you make a deal with Igon?" she blurted, doing her best to ignore the urgent shouts filling the background. If Gatt had brought Igon's wrath on them, then perhaps he might be able to convince the deity to cease his attack. If she convinced him to… and if Igon was here in person at all. He didn't need to be, not when he had the oceans themselves at his command.

"Why else?" Gatt's expression turned bleak. "Desperation. Over the years, Gaiva has grown more distant, and so have the Blessed. They've retreated into their caves, neglecting to share Gaiva's blessing with the rest of us, and we had no choice but to find help elsewhere."

The waves broke against the cliffs behind them, causing him to flinch. Evita did, too, but she held Gatt's gaze. "Shouldn't you know better than to summon unknown deities?"

"We had no way of knowing the nature of the god who lived within the Relic we found," he said quietly. "It washed up on the beach one day some weeks ago, and I assumed it was similar to the other shards we sometimes find. However, this one *spoke* to us, which is more than Gaiva has ever done, and offered us protection."

He couldn't be telling the truth, could he? His claims about the Blessed's reticence to leave their cave sounded accurate, but there was a world of difference between begging the Powers for help and letting one wreak havoc all over the Isles. On the other hand, she ought to know how easy it was for humans to be swindled by the deities. Rien had been tricked in the same manner, and he'd been far more experienced with the Powers than the rest of them. She couldn't fault Gatt for desiring to protect his home and his fellow villagers.

Aurel advanced on him, driving him backwards towards the cliff's edge. "That doesn't change the fact that everyone on this island is in danger of drowning as a direct result of what you did."

He squeezed his eyes shut. "I know. Powers forgive me. We've all made mistakes, but if I can save my fellow villagers, I will do everything in my power to help you."

"Igon is threatening to drown the Isles unless the Blessed give in to his demands." Evita's gaze dropped to the rising sea and the villagers climbing into boats as they spoke. "Zelle can bind him, but she needs his Relics. All five of them."

"That's right." Aurel's hands fisted at her sides. "If you have any suggestions as to how to pry five Relics from the hands of their deity without being killed, now would be a fantastic time to tell us."

Gatt briefly glanced down at the villagers who sat hunched in their boats, entirely at the mercy of the waves battering them from side to side. Then he drew in a breath. "I do have something that might be of use to you."

33

R
ien decided quickly that while riding an eagle wasn't a particularly pleasant experience, it was infinitely preferable to drowning in the churning seas below. Igon's magically conjured whirlpool had dredged up a flood of unpleasant memories, especially with his revelation of Daimos's involvement in his arrival in the Isles.

Rien should have guessed Daimos's hand had been directing the events which had led to him encountering the deity he'd bargained with in Itzar of all places, and he felt like a fool for not realising sooner. Daimos must have found another of Igon's Relics back at home in Aestin and been unable to resist using it against Rien after learning of its connection to his family. Had the medallion been waiting all those years to ensnare his brother, or had Torben not known the malevolence of the deity to whom it belonged? He'd never be able to ask Torben himself for the story of how he'd obtained it, of course, but it was clear that Daimos had left it behind on purpose. As a trap, in case Rien survived.

Daimos had played a long game. Rien ought to have known from Orzen that his foe was using the deities to act in his place, and he'd probably spread stories around both Tauvice *and* Saudenne to make Rien believe that Daimos was in Itzar. He'd fallen for the ruse as easily as he'd walked into another bargain with Igon.

He shook off the brief flicker of shame. Zelle and Evita would have come to Itzar to save Aurel whether he'd accompanied them or not, and as long as he didn't get manipulated into fighting on the wrong side again, he'd be able to salvage this situation.

Assuming they didn't all drown first.

"Powers above," Zelle remarked from the eagle beside his, looking ahead into the fog. "Is Igon already in the village?"

"I can't tell." He grimaced when his own eagle picked up speed bumpily. A glance behind him confirmed that the fog had spread to the northern islands, too, including the Isle of the Blessed, which had all but vanished beneath the grey haze.

Zelle noticed, too. "Do they need our help over there?"

"We can't be in two places at once." If Igon reached Gaiva's rock, though, there was no saving the Isles. Every one of them would sink into the ocean. "Evita and Aurel might be helping the villagers escape as we speak."

"I'm sure they are." Zelle took in a deep breath. "We'll have to trust the defectors to help them."

Some of the eagles peeled away from their group, heading north. Zelle nudged her eagle's side, commanding it to join them, and Rien did likewise. Side by side, they flew north and back towards the Isle of the Blessed.

A blinding flash of light briefly allowed them to see through the fog, and Rien's heart sank in his chest. All five copies of Igon surrounded the giant statue of Gaiva's head and shoulders, their hands aglow with vibrant blue light.

————

Zelle's mouth went dry as the five copies of Igon closed in around Gaiva's rock, cutting off all possible escape routes. Eagles circled from above, but the wind buffeted their wings, preventing them from landing. Waves had engulfed the island's beach, smacking against the cliffs.

Another gust of wind threatened to blow their own eagles off course. Zelle struggled to keep hold of the eagle's back and grasp the staff at the same time, and nearby, Rien appeared to be having the same difficulty. Below, the seas churned, and the waves rose higher, half submerging the island.

"Can the Blessed breathe underwater?" Rien shouted to Zelle. "Or is Gaiva protecting them?"

"I have no idea," she returned. "I wouldn't count on their help, though."

Even the creator goddess's power was limited in these circumstances, but only one part of Her was in the cave, and the defectors' own Relics gave them the chance to fight back. Their position put them at a disadvantage, however, and so did Igon's control over the elements. Each blast of wind blew the birds into a frenzy and swept the waters higher over the island.

Rien clung to his eagle's back and leaned over to speak to Zelle. "We need Igon's Relics."

"Nobody can touch them but me," she reminded him. "Not without being drained of their own magic."

"I stole one myself."

True, but that was because Igon had handed it over willingly. A dazzling flash of light drew Zelle's gaze before she could think of a reply, and it didn't come from the defectors *or* Igon. The island itself was aglow, the dents in the cliffs that formed Gaiva's eyes blazing as if lit from within. As she watched, stunned, a piercing bolt of energy shot outwards at the nearest copy of Igon.

The deity flew backwards as if struck by a heavy blow, while another attack followed. It was as though the island itself was striking back against its adversaries. Rien hovered at her side, equally awed. "So they do have defences after all."

Good ones, too. Gaiva's unexpected display of magic had put Igon on the defensive, allowing the eagles to regain lost ground. When the bolts of energy ceased, Zelle looked down at the island, fearing the worst—before she realised that all five copies of Igon had disappeared at once. "Where have they gone?"

"They're cowards." The defector who'd spoken in their favour called to them from the back of his own eagle. "If I had to guess, they've gone to threaten the villagers instead."

"Damn." Zelle shifted position on her eagle's back and saw that the smaller islands around the Isle of the Blessed had already vanished beneath the waves. Addressing the defectors, she asked, "Aren't you going to help them?"

"That's what Igon wants," Kolt insisted. "As soon as we leave, he'll come for Gaiva again."

"He wants us to choose between defending the villagers and saving Gaiva's Relic," Zelle surmised. "But—not all of us have to go."

What are you thinking? she asked herself. Choosing between saving the villagers—saving *Aurel*—and staying here was no choice at all, but Rien nodded in agreement. "If Igon is in the village, so are his Relics. They're the only way you can bind him, right?"

Zelle dipped her head, eyes stinging with tears. "I came here to save Aurel. If she drowns on top of everything else, then I've failed... but look at how much power the Blessed have. They *can* help us. I need to convince them to come out of their cave, or else we're done for."

Even if it meant leaving her sister behind. No... she wasn't abandoning Aurel, but sending Rien instead, entrusting him with her sister's life as well as her own. Rien's own expression was equally torn, but he must know that Zelle alone might stand a chance of getting through to the Blessed.

"Do what you have to, Zelle," he finally said. "I'll go after Igon and make sure he doesn't touch Aurel or Evita. If I can grab a Relic or two from him in the process, then so much the better."

"Good luck," she said, her voice catching on the words. There was so much more she wanted to say, but she didn't have time to put words into thoughts—and every moment they wasted lowered the chances of their survival.

"And you." His voice held a rough note, too, but determination simmered in his eyes when their gazes met, briefly, before Rien turned his eagle around and flew towards the rising waves.

———

Gatt led Aurel and Evita to his house. While the stone building sat on a higher level than the flooded part of the island, that didn't make Aurel any less suspicious that he'd turn on them and push them off a cliff, given the chance.

After unlocking the door, Gatt walked through the main room of his house to a sealed door at the back. He undid several locks, prompting raised eyebrows from Aurel. "If what you have in here is valuable, why leave it to sink into the sea?"

"It won't." Gatt opened the door to reveal a narrow room, cloaked in near darkness. Despite the lack of lighting, a faint gleam snagged Aurel's attention.

She stifled a gasp. On a table inside the room lay four identical smooth, round stones.

"Relics." Evita spoke in a hushed voice. "Whose Relics?"

Aurel already knew. "Igon's."

"He told me to look after them," explained Gatt. "They have no effect on me, since I have no magic of my own, so I was able to keep them hidden. When he learns I've betrayed him... but I trust Zelle knows what she's doing."

"You're offering these to us?" asked Aurel.

"If it is truly the only way to save the Isles, then yes." He flinched a little when Evita picked up one of the Relics, but he made no move to prevent her from taking two of them.

Aurel took the other two, and when they returned to

the main room, water rushed underneath the front door, swirling around their ankles. The waves had already reached their level, which meant they had less time than Aurel had thought before the entire island was submerged.

Gatt uttered a curse in his own language, while Aurel ran for the front door and pushed it open. The waves lapped at the edges of the street, while no more boats were within sight. They might have the Relics, but they were stuck here with fog above and water below and no way off the island. *Where did the dragonet go?*

"Powers." Gatt ran out of the house behind them, a horrified expression on his face. "I have a boat, but it won't hold all of us."

A wave shattered against the cliff face, and Evita sprang back with a yelp. A second wave swept across the street, this one rising above their ankles and dragging Evita off her feet.

"Evita!" Aurel's cry cut off when a third wave caught her and swept her over the cliff's edge.

The icy shock of the water took Aurel's breath away, and she surfaced, seeing Evita struggling nearby—her cloak might be able to make her fly, but it wasn't water-proof, and the weight of their clothing made it hard, if not impossible, to fight the powerful currents, because the ocean moved at the commands of a furious deity.

Aurel kicked out, spluttering when the sea rose over her head, and when she surfaced again, one of the Relics floated loose in the water.

"Crap." She seized it in her hand an instant before the waves dragged her downwards again.

Water filled her mouth. Aurel's lungs screamed for air,

while she'd lost all sense of direction. Kicking desperately, she aimed for what she thought was the surface, but it grew farther and farther away. Her vision blurred, fading at the edges.

Cold air rushed in. She coughed and spluttered, while a blurry face appeared before her, its owner pulling her out of the water and onto an... eagle?

Rien?

She coughed again, her body spasming, and accidentally grabbed a handful of feathers. It *was* an eagle, and from the disgruntled noise it made, it did not appreciate a soaking human climbing onto its back.

"Evita?" she gasped out.

"She's out." He pointed to the reptilian form of the dragonet, whose claw had lifted a struggling Evita out of the water.

Once the dragonet had placed Evita onto his back, she straightened upright, relief and confusion mingling on her face at the sight of Aurel on the eagle's back. "Rien? What are you doing here?"

"I thought you were helping Zelle." Aurel swung into a sitting position on the eagle, behind Rien.

"Zelle is trying a last-ditch attempt to convince the Blessed to fight back," Rien explained. "I came to look for Igon's Relics."

"Then I have good news and bad news," said Evita. "The good news is that we know where they are."

"With Igon," said Rien. "Or his five human forms."

"Not quite." Aurel grimaced. "Gatt had them. But he..."

Rien's gaze followed hers to the spot where Gatt's house had once been. The entire street was submerged, and even if Gatt had made it to his boat, it would have been swept away. Worse, her pockets felt distinctly empty despite the heaviness of her soaking-wet coat.

"He had the Relics?" Rien's voice tightened with anger. "He *did* summon Igon."

"Out of desperation," Evita clarified. "Gatt believed our story and gave us the Relics to help us stop Igon, but the house flooded, and—I think the Relics ended up underwater."

"We were carrying them." Aurel reached into her pockets and found them empty, as she'd feared. "They must have fallen out."

"Powers above," said Rien. "We need all five to bind him, but most people can't touch them without being drained of their magic. Gatt has none, but I can't ask the villagers to put their lives at risk."

"I touched them," Aurel said. "Without any effects."

"Wait, you did?" Rien paused for a moment. "Your Relic contains part of the nameless Shaper, like Zelle's."

"And I don't have a Relic to drain," added Evita. "Four of them are somewhere in the water, but he must still be carrying the piece of the Relic Zelle destroyed."

"We'll worry about that one later." Aurel looked down at the high waves, sweeping across what was left of the island. "We need to find the others."

Rien's gaze lingered on the water. "Are you volunteering to dive in?"

A flash of light came from above. A doorway opened in the air, and Igon smiled down at them, the glint of one of his own Relics in his hand.

34

Zelle didn't want to stay behind with Gaiva's Blades *or* the Blessed, nor did she have any desire to leave her sister and the others to face off against Igon alone. But now that Igon had returned to the village, she had one last chance to convince the Blessed to come out and fight for their fellow islanders. With Igon's departure, the sea levels had dropped, exposing the rest of Gaiva's statue. She urged her eagle to fly lower, closer to the side of the rock where the cave entrance was supposed to be.

As she'd predicted, the entrance was completely sealed off. The Blessed must still be alive on the other side, protected from drowning by Gaiva's magic, but she didn't know if they'd be able to hear from outside. Still, she flew closer and rapped the end of the staff against the cliff.

"Hey!" she shouted. "Tamacha!"

"You're wasting your time," said Kolt from the eagle behind Zelle. "They won't come out."

Damn. "It's worth one last try. Tamacha?"

A doorway flashed open at her back, and Igon grabbed her from behind. Zelle tumbled off the eagle's back, gripping the staff in both hands before landing on the beach. Her knees buckled beneath her when her feet hit the ground, but the waves were already rising again.

Zelle looked up at the cliff face, water swirling around her ankles. Unless the Blessed let her into the cave, her only mode of escape was to climb the cliff itself. If they opened the cave, they'd risk the water flooding in, so she crossed to the side of Gaiva's face and began to climb.

The first part was easier than she'd expected, with plenty of jagged rocks to use as footholds, but the cliffs were slippery and having to hold the staff in one hand didn't help her balance. She might have tried to use the Shaper's magic to adjust the cliffs and make the climb easier, but if Gaiva's magic held the island together, she didn't dare risk causing any more damage.

Igon's laugh echoed as Zelle struggled to climb to a higher section of the cliff to avoid being caught in the turbulent waves. Once she'd reached Gaiva's shoulder, she spared him a glance, seeing that the eagles had him surrounded, and she tried not to let the sounds of their fighting distract her as she made her way up to Gaiva's neck. The cliffs were slick beneath her feet, and one slip would send her plummeting into the waves.

Then she heard Gaiva's voice in her mind, as clear as if she stood right in front of the rock. *I cannot strike them again. Not without breaking.*

She startled, her heart in her throat, narrowly avoiding slipping over the edge. When Gaiva didn't speak again, she resumed her climb, hearing the ongoing sounds of

Igon fighting against the ice-wielding defectors in the background.

"What can I do?" she whispered to Gaiva. "How can I help you?"

It's taking everything I have to keep my followers alive. If I relinquish my grip on them, the waters will flood the cave and they will drown.

"What if they left the cave?" Zelle asked. "And came to the surface?"

It would make no difference. One more strike from Igon might be enough to end me.

A splash sounded as one of the defectors was knocked off his eagle and into the sweeping waves. "More people might survive if they leave. Like the villagers. I thought you were supposed to protect everyone in the Isles, not just the Blessed."

Not from here. Not as I am now.

"What does that mean?"

You can't be serious, the staff said in derisive tones.

"What?" Zelle tightened her grip on the cliff as a gust of wind swept overhead, blowing the eagles away from the island. "Who were you talking to? Gaiva or me?"

That will break you for good, the staff said. Zelle *hoped* the Shaper had addressed Gaiva, not her, but Igon's laughter drew closer, and the eagles struggled to regain ground. A glance told her there were only five defectors remaining, all looking decidedly worse for wear.

"Which of you wants to volunteer to be the conduit to help me drain what is left of Gaiva's power?" Igon asked the defectors. "Or will one of the so-called Blessed make the offer in your place?"

So he *did* require another person's help to drain a

Relic, and since Gaiva was bound to all of them, any of them would do. Stalling him wouldn't work either, with Gaiva's rock one hit from shattering into pieces.

A tremor ran through the cliff, while Zelle tightened her grip until it passed. The waves rose, and a spasm of fear shook her. She couldn't climb much higher, not without risking a fatal fall, but the glittering sheen of the water suggested that the deity had already succeeded at chipping away at the rock.

Then a crack travelled up the cliff next to where Zelle hung, clinging to the cliffside for dear life.

"No," she whispered. "Gaiva, no…"

The crack spread, spiderwebbing across the cliff face, and Igon's laughter grew in volume as the statue began to crack, exposing the glowing layer beneath its exterior.

"No volunteers?" Igon shook his head at the defectors. "What would happen if I did this?"

The tip of Gaiva's head cracked open, and Zelle found herself sliding backwards, down the side of the colossal statue. Only the staff kept her upright as she came to a bumpy halt on a rocky outcropping. Above, the entire upper layer of Gaiva's statue had split, exposing the gleaming Relic beneath. Several of the defectors let out furious cries and closed in on Igon, restarting their aerial battle, but Kolt's eagle moved to hover beside Zelle. His expression was despondent.

"Are the Blessed alive in there?" she asked him. "Gaiva said it was taking everything She had to keep them alive."

"You spoke to Her?" His eyes went wide. "This is our fault. We're the ones who chipped away at Her Relic and weakened Her power. We did this."

"Igon did this." Zelle watched one of the eagles attempt

to knock him out of the air, only for him to vanish into another doorway. "Gaiva said She couldn't do anything to help the way she is now, but I have no idea what that means—"

Igon reappeared, hovering in front of Gaiva's statue with a vicious smirk on his face. "What have we here? A volunteer?"

Kolt spat a curse at him in the Itzar language, but Igon wasn't looking at him. Instead, he reached into one of Gaiva's eyes and pulled out the struggling form of Lenza. The apprentice looked at Zelle beseechingly, her eyes round with terror.

"No." Zelle shook her head fiercely. "Leave her out of this. She's a child."

"She has a link to Gaiva, the same as the others," said Igon. "Go on, child. Take my Relic and drain Her dry."

Lenza stumbled back when he placed her on a flatter part of the statue before removing his own Relic from his pocket. Kolt took flight again, but when the eagle flew up to her level, Igon grabbed the girl by the wrist and dangled her over the waves. "If you come near me, she dies. I have plenty of others I can use instead."

"Don't you dare." Zelle, though, stood several feet below them, unable to reach the top. She might have used the Shaper's magic to move the rocks as she'd done to the defectors' caves, but all that was left of the island was Gaiva's Relic, which couldn't be affected by the Shaper's magic.

Or could it? She'd never tried.

I cannot strike them again, Gaiva had said. *Not without breaking.*

385

EMMA L. ADAMS

Yet parts of the rock had been broken before, and Gaiva's magic had survived. So had its wielders.

Igon put Lenza down upon Gaiva's peaked forehead. The girl was sobbing, but Kolt could do nothing but hover on his eagle, unable to reach her without putting her in greater danger. Since Igon was paying her no attention, Zelle waved at Kolt, beckoning him down to her.

When Kolt's eagle flew low enough for him to hear her, she whispered, "Will the Blessed die if they leave the cave? Or will they just lose their link to Gaiva?"

"The latter, but why do you want to know?" His eyes glittered with fury. "They would rather leave their own apprentice to die."

"Not if I have anything to do with it." The swirling marks on her wrists and hands began to glow. "I'm about to do something that will really anger the Blessed, but I wanted to make sure it wouldn't kill them in the process."

"What is it?"

Instead of answering, she one-handedly raised the staff, the light brightening. Even Igon dropped his gaze from the trembling form of Lenza. "What are you doing? Your magic is no use to you here."

In answer, Zelle swung the staff and drove it into the crack spreading across the side of Gaiva's head, revealing the blue crystal beneath. Splintering lines spread where the staff touched the already fragile rock, and Zelle released the Shaper's magic with everything she had.

Igon stared, uncomprehending. Then he let go of the girl's arm. Kolt flew up to grab her, but Igon hardly seemed to notice. He looked down at the statue instead, and at the cracks spreading from the impact of Zelle's staff.

With a deafening noise, the cliffs fractured. Sea water rushed in, sweeping away the breaking shards of rock, and Zelle heard the screams of the Blessed within their caves. Before she had a moment to panic that she'd drowned them all, the rest of the cliff crumbled, carrying her along with it.

She tumbled for several moments before the rock steadied beneath her feet, affording her a view of Gaiva's Relic breaking apart before her eyes. Shards of blue crystal flooded the water, mingling with the remains of the statue itself. Kolt and Lenza's eagle flew high, joining the others, but all Zelle could do was hold onto the staff for balance as the ground underfoot shook with tremors and an endless shower of rocks rained down into the water.

The caves within Gaiva's rock lay wide open, and a bolt of relief struck her when Tamacha surfaced first, pulling herself onto a shelf of rock. Upon catching Zelle's eye, she gasped. "What did you do?"

"I complied with Gaiva's intentions... and the nameless Shaper, too." She stifled an inexplicable grin. "Igon can't drain all of the pieces of Gaiva's Relic at once, can he?"

Igon himself had gone quiet, but the remaining Blessed climbed and swam out of their caves, robes billowing in the water. They gathered on what was left of the island, staring around them at the shattered remains of their deity's Relic.

"You have doomed us all," Tamacha told Zelle.

"No, she hasn't." Kolt flew down, with Lenza sitting in front of him on the eagle's back. "Pick up any one of those shards, and you'll see for yourself what you're truly capable of if you open your mind a little."

Zelle didn't hear her reply. The sea's waters had lowered, leaving her part of the island exposed. Where had Igon disappeared to?

The village, she thought.

She might have bested him, but without Gaiva's Relic, Igon no longer had any reason to leave the rest of the islanders alive.

————

A resounding torrent of noise echoed throughout the Isles, causing land and sea alike to tremble. Rien leaned forwards on the eagle's back, while Igon let out a horrible scream.

The sound was pure anger, raw and unfiltered, and with it came a gale that caught them all in its path. He and Aurel clung to the back of their eagle, while Evita and the dragonet flew past, the beast's wings helpless to keep them from being swept up in the current. Below, the villagers clung to their boats grimly as the waves and wind assailed them.

Rien kept one eye on Igon, who held his remaining Relic. The others might be lost at the bottom of the ocean, but Zelle needed all five in order to perform the binding. Yet the sea was far too turbulent to even consider diving in, and the eagle's wings weren't strong enough to prevent them from being dragged in the wind's path.

Aurel grabbed his arm and pointed downward. He squinted at the village, or the part still visible above the waters, and spotted Gatt, their former guide. The man lay on a floating piece of wood, tossed upon the waves, but when he reached into the water, he withdrew a shimmering piece of rock. A Relic.

As Rien watched, more crystalline fragments rose to the surface of the water. Far too many to belong to Igon. *What are they?*

"No!" Igon shrieked. "How dare they?"

"What is he yelling about?" Aurel shouted in Rien's ear. "What's going on?"

"Those pieces of rock... they're Relics."

Hundreds of them. No, thousands. All were the same shade of shimmering blue, like the piece that had washed up on the beach and that he'd been forced to give to Igon. Did that mean they came from the same deity? Which—

Impossible.

Aurel twisted in her seat to face him. "Tell me they didn't break Gaiva's rock."

"Does it sound like Igon is happy about it?" The resounding scream had faded, but the storm continued to ravage the sea. "He can't drain the Relic if it's broken into pieces."

"By the *Powers*," he heard Evita say. "Look at the villagers."

Rien glanced down at Gatt, who gripped the piece of rock in his hand. He wasn't the only one either. More of the villagers held similar fragments, which glowed vibrantly with white-blue light.

"They're claiming the Relics," he realised. "They're joining with Gaiva."

Whether Gaiva had intended it or not, Her power had spread throughout the ocean, allowing anyone to access a Relic of their own. Directly below his eagle, a bedraggled

389

woman had lifted a piece of the glowing rock out of the sea, her hands alighting. The man behind her stood up in their boat, his face aglow with a new confidence.

Rien understood. He remembered vividly how it felt to be chosen as worthy by a deity for the first time, and it couldn't be plainer that Gaiva intended to give them a fighting chance even if it meant shattering Her rock into countless pieces. At the same time, he'd never seen anything on this scale before, with so many chosen to wield Relics in the same instant. The display humbled him and invigorated him at the same time, and Zierne's power stirred beneath his skin as though in solidarity while villager after villager took in the power of Gaiva.

Igon certainly hadn't planned for this, but Rien had a sneaking suspicion Zelle was involved… or rather, the nameless Shaper was. When he looked for the deity, his gaze fell on a doorway opening in the air. Then a second one. Both Igons glared down at him, and at the villagers below.

"You're outnumbered," Rien told the deities. "You brought this on yourself, you know. Gaiva decided to destroy Her own Relic rather than submit to you."

"They are still weaker than us," said one Igon. "We will destroy them."

"No." Gatt staggered upright, balancing atop the floating piece of wood with his new Relic glowing in his hand. "We will not submit to you any longer."

An icy shard flew from his palms, spearing one of the deities through the chest. Igon staggered, bleeding, and more attacks joined Gatt's. As the two Igons dodged the storm of ice shards, Rien watched the Relic Igon still clutched in his fist. He needed to get it away from him.

He raised the staff, and vines shot from the end, wrapping around his target from behind. Igon twisted out of the way, however, vanishing through a doorway and reappearing next to their eagle.

Aurel yelped as the eagle tipped over sideways, while Igon's hand latched onto Rien's wrist. He gripped the eagle's back with his knees, panic momentarily rising at the sight of the churning waters below. Beneath the fear, though, Zierne's presence remained, undaunted.

Rien let go, throwing himself at Igon and snatching the Relic from his hand. Too shocked to fight him off, Igon shouted aloud, but Rien was already gripping the Relic tight as he tumbled into the waves below.

35

Evita leaned forwards on the dragonet's back, bracing herself against the unpredictable wind currents. For once, she entirely forgot her fear of the drop, because bright lights glittered all over the water—and in the villagers' hands as, one by one, they claimed Gaiva's Relics for their own.

"Rien!" yelled Aurel's voice.

Evita's head snapped up in time to see Rien toppling towards the sea from the eagle's back. At her command, Chirp flew in and caught him before he hit the water, his claws snagging the back of Rien's coat.

"What are you doing?" Evita asked him.

"I have Igon's Relic," he said breathlessly. "One of them. The others—"

"They're in the sea. I know." She scanned the sky for the copies of Igon, but they were too busy dodging shards of ice flung by the villagers to pay her any attention.

Trusting them to keep Igon occupied, Evita told the dragonet to fly over the water, looking out for rocks that didn't look quite the same as the broken shards of Gaiva. The sheer number of Relics floating in the water made the task more difficult, and it didn't help that Igon's magic kept conjuring up sweeping waves and gusts of wind.

None of that deterred the villagers in the slightest. They kept fighting back, hurling attacks at the deity from all angles. Not just them either. The inhabitants of the other villages on the surrounding islands also sat in boats or stood on roofs, holding shards of Gaiva's rock.

"There!" Rien pointed the staff towards a round stone lying on a piece of debris below. They flew lower, and Rien reached out for the stone with his free hand. Once he'd picked it up, Evita flew them higher above the water, while Aurel waved at them from the back of the eagle.

"I can swim," she told them. "If the others have sunk to the bottom, I'll find them."

"Wait!" Evita protested. "You can't—"

Aurel leapt over the eagle's side, crashing into the surging waters. Evita leaned over, alarmed, but Aurel surfaced and waved at her before diving under again.

"I'll make sure she doesn't drown," Rien told Evita. "Put me back on the eagle."

A doorway opened in front of them, and one of Igon's many copies emerged. "I knew I should have killed you the instant you broke your word."

Rien's staff shot a torrent of thorny vines at him, but a gust of wind slammed into the dragonet, flipping them upside-down. Evita gripped Chirp's back with all her strength, but the wind dragged her loose, and she tumbled head over heels into the air. *Not again,* she thought, before the cloak billowed around her, slowing her fall.

Fly, she thought. It was the third time she'd felt the

cloak stir around her as if it held a will of its own, and while she had yet to figure out how to use its power outside of life-or-death scenarios, she was more prepared than before. Spreading her arms out like wings, she shifted her body towards the nearest solid ground, and the cloak carried her above the water to a raised piece of exposed rock that might be the roof of a buried house. She landed in a crouch, the cloak dropping harmlessly to her sides.

"That was a close one." Below her feet lay a fragment of Gaiva's rock. Evita reached down and picked it up, turning the shard over in her hands, but the shard didn't brighten in the same way as the ones the other villagers had picked up. "I guess the cloak is enough of a Relic for me."

She dropped the piece of rock, scanning the sky for the dragonet. Chirp had caught his balance, Rien dangling from his claws, but she didn't see any signs of Aurel in the water. The waves were still turbulent, and despite the villagers' newfound confidence, the forces of nature continued to act against them.

"Aurel!" Evita squinted at the area where she'd vanished under the water, but there was no sign of her, and thanks to Igon, the dragonet had been blown off course.

Evita stretched the cloak out to either side of her, feeling like a fool but out of any better options. The cloak had saved her life more than once, so she ought to be able to exert some control over its abilities by this point. She leaned forwards, seeking the feeling of weightlessness that had seized her when the cloak had helped steer her to safety.

Fly, she thought. *Our lives are still in peril. Please, fly!*

The wind caught the cloak, driving her forward, and she glided above the water towards the spot where Aurel had dived in. Yet no sign of the Reader's bright hair appeared above the surface.

"I can't see her!" she shouted in Rien's direction.

Rien, dangling from Chirp's claws, could do nothing but gape at her. "How are you flying?"

"I'll explain later." A flash brightness caught her eye under the water. "Aurel."

Reaching out, her hands skimmed the surface and then plunged beneath the surging waves. She flew lower, the waves rising to meet her, and salt water washed over her head. *Oh, no.*

She grabbed at the spot where she was certain she'd seen Aurel but found nothing but water. The cloak, so buoyant moments before, now weighed her down.

Then air filled her lungs, sharp and sudden. She coughed, fighting the person who'd grabbed her. "Get Aurel out. She's—"

"She's fine." That was Rien's voice. He held onto her, swaying beneath the dragonet's claws.

Evita stopped fighting him and shoved a handful of sopping-wet hair out of her face, scanning the water's surface. "Where is she?"

"Over there."

Evita's gaze snapped up, seeing Aurel balanced on top of another rocky protrusion in the water. In her hands, two of Igon's Relics glowed.

"I thought you drowned!" Evita yelled at her.

Aurel gave her a bewildered stare. "Sorry to disappoint you? I got the Relics. We have four."

"One more," Rien said from above her. "I'll need to put you down before I can look for anything."

"Igon has it," Evita told him. "It's the one Zelle broke. Chirp, can you fly to Aurel?"

When they neared her perch, Rien released Evita and then freed himself from the dragonet's claws himself. He then waved to the eagle, urging it to come and help them. "Is it just me, or are the water levels dropping?"

He was right. Their island had already grown to encompass an entire roof, the water receding below them and exposing more of the village's buildings.

Aurel swore. "They're heading north."

Evita lifted her head. The clouds were moving, too, dragging the fog along with them. Towards the Blessed... and Zelle.

———

Zelle steered the eagle around, directing it towards the village. Crystalline shards of Gaiva's rock filled the water like jewels, the waves sweeping them between the islands and throughout the region. The land above the water level glittered with shards of rock, and brand-new Relics lay scattered throughout the whole of Itzar, including the area that had once been covered by fog.

Lights pierced the fog, not just from the water but from the hands of the villagers themselves. Her heart lifted at the sight. Itzar's other inhabitants had begun to claim the pieces of Gaiva's magic, and they were fighting Igon with all that they had.

Shards of ice collided with Igon's copies, who hopped in and out of their doorways to dodge the relentless attacks. Despite the strong gusts of wind and the rising waves Igon threw at them, the villagers fought on with determination born of their newfound strength. She glimpsed Aurel sitting on the back of a giant eagle, while Rien rode on the dragonet and Evita was... flying?

"They're heading north!" Rien shouted.

Zelle brought her eagle to a halt alongside him, wheeling around to face the direction she'd just flown from. He was right. The waves had begun to move away from the village and towards the place where the Blessed were still pulling themselves free from the ruins of their home. Had Igon decided to simply drown the Blessed instead of continuing to fight?

"I have to bind him." She addressed the staff. "But first I need his other Relics."

Ask your sister, the staff replied.

"Aurel?" She twisted in her seat, catching her sister's eye. Aurel flew her eagle over to Zelle's other side, and in each hand, she held up a round stone.

"Where did you get those?" Zelle asked.

"Gatt," she replied. "He had the other four Relics inside his house."

"Igon gave them to him as part of their bargain," Rien put in. "The deity broke their agreement, so Gatt returned the favour."

"We have four of them." That left one... *Oh, Powers.* "I know where the other is. It's with the Blessed."

Lenza had been holding it when Igon had tried to force her to drain Gaiva's Relic on his behalf, and if Igon reached her and the other Blessed again before Zelle did... *no, it can't be too late.*

She flew on, against the wind, until they reached the

glittering rock that had once contained the caves of the Blessed. The white-robed servants of Gaiva had climbed onto the rocky mass of their home, and despite the waves whipping around them, they displayed no obvious fear. Had they joined forces with Gaiva again?

"Tamacha," she called out, half expecting another furious rebuke.

The leader of the Blessed turned towards her, her eyes aglow with the same blaze as the shard of rock in her hand. "Zelle... you were right. We didn't know Gaiva's will, not before. We have never been able to sense her like this."

A smile tugged at her mouth despite the urgency of the rising waves. "You worked it out? You can fight now?"

"Yes." Another of the Blessed raised an identical shard, and a similar glow surrounded his figure. Kolt had been right. The Blessed had stagnated after so many years in their cave and had never stopped to consider that Gaiva's magic *could* be wielded in defence of the Isles, not simply locked away for its own protection.

The waves lashed higher, and Rien shouted a warning from behind. When Zelle glanced over her shoulder, she saw a large wave rising from the surrounding waters and heading straight for the Isle of the Blessed. It continued to surge forward, gaining speed and volume as it did so, and Zelle glimpsed what appeared to be a *face* inside the water. *Igon.* He'd thrown everything he had into his last attack, in a literal sense, and if the wave struck the Blessed, they'd be pulverised on the spot.

Some of the Blessed retreated, but others stayed at the front, Tamacha among them. Each held up a shard of rock, the glow spreading from their palms and forming a shimmering barrier around the Blessed's figures. Were they protecting themselves somehow? They stood at the heart of Gaiva's power, after all, and when Zelle's gaze fell on the seas around the island, she saw that the waters had begun to freeze. Ice spread across the surface of the water, solidifying and sweeping forwards to meet the wave.

The solid wall of water began to freeze at its base, but Igon fought back. The seas lowered as Igon drew their waters in, yet the Blessed's power didn't diminish. Every time the wave tried to gain traction, Gaiva's magic turned it to ice, which spread, creeping up to Igon's face.

The deity screamed in fury. A blast of wind struck the Blessed from behind, knocking some of them to the ground—but they had Igon outnumbered, and the surging power of the ocean wasn't enough to resist the force of a Great Power.

With a final surge, the entire colossal wall of water turned into an ice sculpture, while Igon's face glared from within, frozen into a mask of hate.

Zelle tried not to grin as she turned back to the Blessed. "Do you have the last of Igon's Relics?"

"I do," Lenza called from the back of Kolt's eagle. She sat in front of the large man, who looked upon the water with a stunned expression on his face.

Zelle flew to meet them and reached out a hand to take the Relic from Lenza. More eagles descended around the Isle of the Blessed, while Aurel caught up to Zelle with Igon's Relics in her hands. "Where should I put these?"

"Good question." Zelle scanned the remains of the Blessed's island and found a flattened area that might have once been the interior of Gaiva's caves. "There will do."

The eagles landed near the Blessed, crowding around the ruins of the island. Aurel handed Zelle the other four Relics, and while Rien and Evita flew in to join them, Zelle addressed the staff. "Please tell me these are all you need to perform the binding."

Place them in a circle, the staff told her. *The binding spell will take care of the rest.*

Zelle crouched and placed each of the five Relics on the rocky surface as the staff instructed. "I don't have the book with me, so I hope the spell works if I improvise."

The moment she pointed the staff at the circle of Relics, the swirling lights came to life on her hands and arms again. She'd barely spoken the words—"I bind you, Igon"—when the five rocks began to shimmer, lifting off the ground and spinning in circles until they merged into one. A cracking noise sounded in the background, followed by a roar of fury as a spray of water hit her in the back. Coughing, she glanced over her shoulder and saw Igon break free of the ice sculpture and launch himself forward.

The wave caught him, freezing around him. A glow spread, both from the Blessed's Relics and from those below the surface of the water, as the ice seized Igon's body in its grip. There was only one copy of him left, and the raw panic in his expression told her that they'd won.

Zelle turned back to her task. "I bind you to this Relic. In the name of Gaiva, and of every one of her people who gave their lives in defence of the Isles. I bind you with the power of the nameless Shaper."

Igon's scream reverberated in her ears as she spoke, but he couldn't resist the Shaper's magic. Brightness enfolded the one remaining Relic, and the deity's screams faded to silence. The humanlike form of Igon was no more, though the ice remained until it began to crack, thawing harmlessly and turning to water once again.

Picking up the Relic, Zelle faced the Blessed. "Is there a safe place I can put this?"

"This way." Tamacha beckoned. While she still wore a stern expression, her open hostility had vanished almost entirely. "Gaiva will keep the Relic from being found."

Zelle trod carefully across the rocky island, seeing that the interior of what had once been their cave had formed a kind of crater. Already knowing what to do, she threw the Relic into the gap in the centre of the island. In her hand, the staff glowed, the Shaper's magic pushing the rocks inwards and concealing what was left of Igon from sight.

All around, the seas lay calm, as if they'd never been disturbed.

36

Evita and the others left Itzar three days later. They might have stayed longer, and some of the villagers wanted them to, but Zelle and Aurel needed to return to Zeuten before their grandmother got it into her head to come to Itzar herself. Evita was sceptical that she would, but Zelle insisted that nothing was beyond the old Sentinel. Admittedly, Evita had the distinct impression that certain locals would rather not lose any more money to her newfound gambling skills, so perhaps it was for the best that they left before they wore out their welcome.

A large number of people came to see them off, led by Gatt. The former defectors had agreed to loan them a few eagles to fly home, and Zelle and Rien flew side by side, followed by Aurel and Evita. The latter two had taken the dragonet instead of an eagle, but either way, she didn't mind flying home. As long as she didn't look down, anyway, but her recent experiences had put her off boats somewhat, too. The considerable upside to her recent experiences was that her ordinary fears seemed easily managed when compared with rampaging deities.

When they left the Isles behind and flew out over the open sea, however, she found herself clinging tightly onto what turned out to be Aurel's arm.

"Powers above," she grumbled. "I can't feel my fingers. Let go of me."

"Sorry," said Evita. "I'm trying not to look down."

"You don't like heights," said Aurel. "And you still came here."

"Yes, I did."

Aurel gave her a considering look. "I don't think I want you as my servant."

"What?" Evita nearly fell off the dragonet. "You're... you're letting me go?"

"No, you're far more useful than a mere drudge," Aurel commented. "I heard you tricked the people of Itzar out of half their money in a game of cards on your first day."

She grimaced. "I lost most of the money in the floods. And I spent half the rest on paying for the damages."

"Doesn't matter," said Aurel. "You should go to the tavern when we're back in Tavine and see if you can trick a few tourists into parting with their coin. I want to see how you do it."

Evita's mouth dropped open. "I don't know *how* I did it. It was pure luck."

"Like flying with that cloak of yours?" Aurel sat back and grinned. "If you ask me, you have the blessing of the deities."

"And that's supposed to be a *good* thing?" She raised a brow. "After all this?"

"I'd say we might need it, don't you?"

Once they were back in Saudenne, their group disembarked to stock up on supplies for the rest of their journey to Tavine. Rien couldn't deny that he wouldn't mind keeping the eagle close by as an easy mode of transport should he want to cross the ocean again. While Aurel offered to buy the supplies, he turned to Zelle.

"Are you going to stay here?" he found himself asking her. "After we return Aurel to your grandmother, that is?"

"I have no idea," she admitted. "We'd better see what kind of trouble has hit the village in our absence first."

"Like the Changers," Evita put in. "The Senior Changers asked me to join them before I left. I didn't find any connection between their mission in Itzar and Igon's arrival, but I still don't know what they meant to achieve by recruiting me."

Strange, to be sure, but the Changers were the least of their concerns. Rien might have thwarted Igon's attempts to ensnare him, but Daimos *had* been in or near Itzar at one point, and his current location remained as much a mystery as ever. If Daimos learned that the creator goddess was as active in this realm as the nameless Shaper, and with Her Relics in far more people's hands than ever before... their inevitable confrontation would come soon. Zelle knew it as well as anyone, but he'd give her a proper warning before leaving next time. He owed her that much, and he'd see Zelle and Aurel reunited with their grandmother before returning home.

As for Rien? He had a promise to keep to his own deity, to find out as much as he could about Zierne's Relic and how it had come to be taken to Zeuten. The answers were more likely to lie in Aestin than anywhere else, and as soon as his business was done here, he'd seek them out.

This time, he'd keep his word.

———

After stocking up on supplies, their group took to the sky once more. Flying on an eagle was certainly more convenient than a carriage, though Zelle had the sense that Evita much preferred to travel on the ground. Not that she blamed her, given their recent experiences.

Despite her new bond with the nameless Shaper, Zelle didn't *feel* different, despite the marks on her hands and wrists that remained as stark as the day they'd appeared. There'd certainly been a few moments back in the Isles when the Shaper had been in command of the magic she'd used, but with Igon's defeat, she hoped that she would no longer have occasion to let the Shaper take command of her actions. The staff was as much of an enigma as ever, and part of her was glad of it.

With the help of their steeds, Zelle and the others reached Tavine long before nightfall and landed outside the village.

"I hope Grandma's all right." Aurel climbed off her eagle. "I know she's the one who pushed you into coming to rescue me, but she wasn't in great shape at the time."

"I told Marita to check up on her," Zelle reassured her. "She didn't want anyone fussing over her, but I made sure someone trustworthy was ready to step in if her health got any worse."

"Good." Aurel took the lead, and they walked along the dirt track towards the village.

Zelle didn't think she'd ever been so glad to see the tall pines standing under the shadow of the mountains, nor the simple stone buildings visible between the trees. It felt much longer than a mere few days since they'd left.

"I never thanked you, you know," Aurel said conversationally. "For coming to rescue me."

"Didn't you?" Zelle hadn't thought on the matter, truth be told, given the upheaval of the past few days. "I'd like to think you'd do the same for me."

"Of course…" Aurel trailed off. "What in the name of the Powers is that?"

Zelle stopped walking, and so did the others. A high fence surrounded the village that definitely hadn't been there before, while two people stood outside the gates set into the front. *Changers.* They couldn't be anything else, given their shimmering silvery cloaks.

Noticing Zelle and the others, a male Changer with thinning hair called out, "What is your business here?"

"We live here." Aurel stalked over to him. "Who are you?"

"They're Senior Changers." Evita joined her. "Verne and… Briony, was it? What are you doing here?"

"Tavine belongs to the Changers now," said the female Changer, presumably Briony. "On the orders of our goddess, Gaiva."

That's not possible. The remains of the creator goddess were too far away to give commands, and She would never have ordered the Changers to take over the Sentinels' home.

"Why would Gaiva want you to own this village?" Zelle asked of them.

"We do not question Her command."

No. It couldn't be Gaiva. Who, then, did they serve?

"Then can we go home?" Aurel motioned towards the gate. "I need to see my grandmother. The Sentinel."

Verne's thick brows drew together. "The Sentinel is no longer here."

"What does that mean?" Zelle lifted the staff, her instincts warning her something was deeply wrong. "What did you do to her?"

"Nothing whatsoever," Briony said in flat tones. "You are not welcome here."

"I own that house." Aurel pointed through the gates, though the Reader's house was too far back to be visible from here. "I'll go wherever I damn well please."

Rien caught Zelle's arm. "Look over there."

Zelle scanned the bushes and saw Grandma peering out at them from amid the trees. Leaving her sister arguing with the Changers, she veered off the path. "What are you doing in here, Grandma?" she whispered.

"There are only a few of us left who aren't trapped," replied the old Sentinel. "I've been coming down here to look for you every day. I knew you'd be back, and I also knew you'd try to storm straight through the gates."

"What do you mean by trapped?" Zelle's heart lurched. "You live there. Where are you staying if not in the Reader's house?"

"You can guess, can't you? We need to leave."

"What in the name of the Powers?" Aurel marched over to her grandmother. "What are you doing?"

"She claims she escaped being trapped in the village," Zelle told her. "She was going to tell us how the situation came about."

"I don't think any of you understand the severity of the

situation you're in," growled the old Sentinel. "I saw this coming, and even *I* didn't know it'd be this bad."

The breath punched out of Zelle's lungs. "Why didn't you tell us?"

"It wouldn't have done any good if I'd told you before-hand," she said. "You wouldn't have been able to stop him."

"Who's 'him'?" she asked, at the same time as Rien murmured, "Daimos."

She little expected her grandmother to dip her head, acknowledging he was right.

"*Daimos*?" she echoed. "He can't be here. We haven't been gone *that* long."

More to the point, hadn't he been in Aestin? Even if he'd detoured near the Isles to set up his trap, that had been ages ago, and it didn't explain why Daimos decided to take control of Tavine... and the Changers.

"I told you to leave." Briony halted when she saw Zelle's grandmother. "You're wanted for questioning, Sentinel. Come with us."

"I don't think so." Aurel stepped out to bar her path.

"You, too," said her companion, eyeing Rien. "You're Arien Astera, aren't you?"

Zelle raised the staff, but before anyone else could move, the dragonet leapt out of the bushes. Both Changers recoiled at the appearance of the fearsome beast, while Rien whistled, calling the eagles out of the bushes to join them. The dragonet's claws swiped, forcing the two Senior Changers to back away.

"New steeds?" Grandma eyed the eagles. "Good, that'll make it easier to reach the outpost."

"The outpost." It made sense that Grandma had taken

refuge in there, but she had some serious explaining to do when they arrived. "Let's move."

Zelle kept one eye on the Changers as she helped her grandmother mount the nearest eagle before climbing on behind her. Rien and Aurel did likewise, while the dragonet continued to bat at the two Changers with his claws. Once the eagles had taken flight, Evita called Chirp back to her and leapt onto his back, swiftly joining them in the air.

"The base," Grandma said impatiently to Zelle. "Quickly."

"You'd better explain yourself when we get there." She directed the eagle to fly north, towards the snow-capped mountains. The Sanctum was still protected. They'd be safe up there... or so she hoped, anyway.

Unlike Tavine, the Range hadn't changed a bit. Daimos would have a hard job imposing his will over ground directly inhabited by the Shaper, but the village was another matter entirely. Why would he even *want* to take over Tavine? To get at her family as payback for what they'd done to Orzen? He couldn't have expected to find Rien there, surely, not after the trap he'd laid in Itzar. He'd wanted them distracted for a reason, though.

The eagles and dragonet flew towards the tower-like shape of the outpost on the other side of the mountains. Zelle landed first and helped Grandma climb down from the eagle's back while the others landed on either side of her. Of their group, only Evita had never been inside the base before, and she looked up at the jagged tower with wide eyes.

Grandma unlocked the door, beckoning the others into the tower. As they crowded into the dusty room,

Zelle exhaled in a sigh that was half relief, half exhaustion. "They won't follow us?"

Grandma coughed a laugh. "They wouldn't dare try angering the Shaper."

"They didn't have a problem taking the village, though," Aurel growled. "Almost everything I own is in that house. Scumbags."

"I'm sure the gods have no use for your priceless junk collection." Zelle's hands shook with adrenaline, her shock belatedly catching up to her. "Who did this? How?"

"Daimos," Rien spat. "As for how he did it, I don't think he's here in person. It's not the first time he's sent a deity across the ocean to do his bidding."

"This isn't Orzen's work, though, is it?" Zelle faced her grandmother and the others. "Orzen murdered anyone who stood in his way. Those Changers supposedly wanted to question you… and you, too, Rien."

"And they said *Gaiva* told them to take over the village," added Evita. "Which we know isn't true."

"Evidently not," said Rien. "That doesn't change the fact that a deity has them in its grip."

The staff stirred in Zelle's hands. *It is true,* the Shaper's voice whispered. *The third has awoken.*

"Zelle… what is that?" Grandma's eyes bulged at the sight of Zelle's glowing hands and the marks spiralling up her arms.

"Ah… it's a long story." Not that they had anything but time on their hands as long as they were trapped in the outpost. "The staff—the Shaper—said 'the third has awoken'. Any idea what that means?"

Rien's eyes widened. "The third… not the third Great Power?"

"That can't be," said Aurel. "The Shaper is *here*, in the mountain. Gaiva is in Itzar…"

Zelle glanced at the staff. "The third is… Invicten?"

"Gaiva, Invicten, and the nameless Shaper," said Grandma. "The first of those, you claim to have encountered recently, and I'm inclined to believe you. The second is inside that staff of yours."

"And the third?" Zelle's hand clenched on the staff. "You can't mean Daimos is working with Invicten? I thought He vanished around the same time as the other Great Powers."

"That was my understanding, too," added Rien. "Gaiva surfaced recently. So did the Shaper. It's not impossible that Invicten did the same."

"I wouldn't put anything past Daimos," said Aurel. "We still don't know where he got hold of Orzen's Relic. Or Igon's."

"No… and I don't know much about Invicten," Zelle admitted. "Except that He is known as the deity of illusions."

"I know even less than that," Evita put in, her face flushing when everyone looked in her direction. "He's a Great Power, though, and Daimos is willing to bargain with any deity to achieve his goals. We know that much."

"It's certainly fitting." Rien's gaze darkened. "I don't know what stories you have about Invicten in Zeuten, but in Aestin, He is known as a trickster deity for a reason. They say His magic can weave an illusion realistic enough to fool anyone into believing it to be the truth."

A chill raced down Zelle's spine, and she addressed the staff. "The Changers believe they're serving Gaiva's will. Is it possible for Invicten's magic to fool them into believing that to be the truth?"

Yes, regrettably.

"Powers above," she murmured.

Somehow, the enemy had got hold of the Relic of the third Great Power and used it to fool the Changers into capturing an entire village in the belief that they served another deity entirely. With the power of illusion at his command, she could only imagine what else Daimos might do with that magic.

"What's the point of this?" Aurel asked of nobody in particular. "What *is* Daimos planning?"

"He's planning a war," Zelle said, with certainty. "With all three Great Powers on the battlefield."

ABOUT THE AUTHOR

Emma spent her childhood creating imaginary worlds to compensate for a disappointingly average reality, so it was probably inevitable that she ended up writing fantasy novels. She has a BA in English Literature with Creative Writing from Lancaster University, where she spent three years exploring the Lake District and penning strange fantastical adventures.

Now, Emma lives in the middle of England and is the international bestselling author of over 30 novels including the Changeling Chronicles and the Order of the Elements series. When she's not immersed in her own fictional universes, Emma can be found with her head in a book or wandering around the world in search of adventure.

Find out more about Emma's books at
www.emmaladams.com.